The Clearing

JEANNIE MORGAN

NATIONAL
LIBRARY
OF AUSTRALIA

A catalogue record for this
book is available from the
National Library of Australia

Publisher:
ASPG (Australian Self Publishing Group)
P.O. Box 159, Calwell, ACT Australia 2905
Email: publishaspg@gmail.com
http://www.inspiringpublishers.com

National Library of Australia Cataloguing-in-Publication entry

Author: Morgan, Jeannie

Title: **THE CLEARING**/*Jeannie Morgan*

ISBN: 978-0-6482934-2-2

Chapter 1
N.S.W 1845

Andrew bent close to the horse's mane, coaxing, soothing, cajoling her against the bitter suffocating wind, although, for once, he knew *that* wind was his ally. Over his shoulder the dark smudge hung in the air. Had it grown? Had it moved? The ugly orange light spread across the sky, threatening its danger. If only this wind holds… It had been such a long dry summer. What else could we expect… but why here? How had it started?

The shelter of the trees welcomed them as they followed the path by the river, but even the river seemed sluggish in that heat. Then suddenly, the view he loved. The valley, stretched before them, serene, unaware. There was no time to savour it! He spurred the tired horse into a gallop.

The workers in the fields stopped and stared, then catching his anxiety began to gather and follow in his wake. He threw his reins at the stableboy and stepped quickly into the flagstone veranda, pausing for only a moment to knock the worst of the dust from his clothes before invading his sister's elegant sitting room.

In the sudden darkness he tried to focus.

"Andrew! How marvellous!" Emily struggled out of the settee. "But look at you! Have you…" She saw his expression under the dust. "What's wrong?"

As he stepped forward another figure moved quickly to Emily's side, and Andrew became even more aware of the state of his clothes and, more importantly, the danger they may face. The girl seemed to glow, her skin, her dark hair, her figure in its filmy dress. He struggled to keep his voice calm.

"Where's Nicholas? I need to talk to him."

"He's gone to fetch Mama." Emily gestured at her swollen belly. "The baby's due within the month." She smiled at her brother. "Naturally Mama cannot believe... but My Dear, forgive me. Miss Burnett," she slipped an arm through the girl's elbow. "may I present this ramshackle guest... my brother, Andrew Walters. I assure you he doesn't always look so dishevelled!"

Andrew bowed, the girl sketched the suggestion of a curtsy in response, but his mind was elsewhere.

"How do you do Miss Burnett," and returned immediately to his sister. "Who is here? Denny, Bert?"

"Denny went with Nicholas of course, but I'll ring..."

Andrew, however, was already out the door,

"No need! I'll see to it..." and the women heard the "Cooee" echoing along the stones, above his hurried footsteps.

"What do you think it is?" They exchanged anxious glances as Amy settled her friend back against her pillows.

"Well he wasn't exactly forthcoming was he?" Emily smiled apologetically. "I am sorry Dear Amy, he is not always *that* abrupt".

Amy tried not to sound irritated, though she had rarely been treated with such behaviour.

"Not at all! I'm convinced he has his reasons and no doubt we'll learn them in due course." She rang the bell. "We need something cool to drink, and another damp cloth for your neck. It is stifling." She fussed around her friend, trying to ignore the anxiety and tension in the room. Andrew Walters' punishment could wait.

Andrew was headed for the stables when he saw the square figure of Bert approaching like a tugboat at full steam.

"Well, well, and blow me if it isn't Young Bluey! What's all the fuss? The men said yer roared up the valley like the law was after yer!"

Andrew chuckled, despite himself.

"No. Not the law. Not this time! But we have a problem. A fire. A big 'un! She's a few miles back and if the wind holds... but we need to get organized in case. You know the place is tinderbox dry!"

"Yeah. Right." But Bert was not the man to handle this crisis and he knew it. The Squire had left him in charge but everyone, including Bert, knew it was nominal!

"Yeah. Well... Yeah. Right!"

Andrew waited but only for a moment. Bert's feelings were not his only concern.

"We need to ring the bell, Bert! We need to know where everyone is. The water cart must be filled and anything else we can find."

Bert stared into the distance. Andrew gritted his teeth.

"Right. Ring the bell. Right. Collect all the hands. Right."

He hurried away leaving Andrew to spring into action. A very tall, dark-haired young man appeared at his side. He looked vaguely familiar and more importantly to Andrew, competent.

"I'm Kieran Malone, Paddy's son. What do I do? Should I get all the horses up here?"

Andrew nodded with relief.

"Exactly! Up here in the stables and smaller yards. How many men do you need...?" He was interrupted by the sound of a very urgent bell. At least Bert had that right. " If we can bring the cattle into the river paddocks...." He turned to find willing hands already waiting. His instructions came quickly without preamble, " I want everything off the verandas. You, collect the master's polo balls and block all the gutters... and you," pointing to another, "can then fill them with water. I want any rubbish from around the huts and stables gone. The storeroom gutters will need to be filled as well as the stables. I need four men to cut as many green boughs, and mind they are *green* as you can find, and bring them back here. All of you need to cover your heads and your faces-whatever you can find-especially your mouths!"

He turned sharply toward the hills. With dread he realized the wind had turned. He saw his sister's anxious face in the doorway.

"How far away is it?" Her voice was calm though she frowned.

"Well it's behind the range still, but I hate to say it, but I think the winds changed. Get all the windows closed tight-can you close your chimneys? I'll get the blokes up on the roof to cover them. Sorry to be bossy, Sis, but no time for niceties."

Emily smiled and hugged his arm.

"Thank God you are here to take charge, though *why* are you here by the way?"

"Had to organize stock for the Governor at that Church School in Bathurst. Perfect opportunity to visit you. Now don't worry. We're getting organized. We'll be fine Ladies." He bowed his head and was gone again.

Amy watched the door close.

"Is he always a whirlwind?"

Emily smiled.

"Well he's never been able to sit quietly. He started overlanding before he was fifteen and was the boss before his seventeenth birthday! He has no need to do all that travelling himself now, but I think it is in his blood... sleeping under the stars... travelling hundreds of miles."

"How strange." Amy shrugged. "Doesn't he intend having a property of his own? Why would anyone like such a hard life?"

"Freedom! My brother likes his own company I'm afraid." She smiled archly at her young friend. "But by the look in his eyes when he saw you Amy, he may be inclined to stay put for a wee while at least!" She glanced anxiously around. "Oh I *wish* Nicholas was not away! And to have you here at such a time..." She clutched her back... "And I am so useless..."

Amy hurried to her side.

"Nonsense! I'm very glad I *am* here with you." She wrung out a fresh cloth and settled her friend. "Here put this across your forehead. I'll go and check the windows and doors. Will you be comfortable? After all we must all do our part. I for one would not dare to disobey Mr. Walters!"

Emily sat uneasily on the settee. She let her eyes wander around the room. She loved it all so much. Nicholas had been apologetic and had great plans for the house, but for her, this first home, was so dear. Please God. Keep us safe. The baby moved in her belly. No, not yet. Please don't come now.

Amy came rushing into the room carrying a dish of water, which she slopped, all over the hearth.

"*Whatever are you doing*? Surely the girls can do that?"

"They are upstairs. I've done down here. We've dampened the curtains and stuffed every nook and cranny with wet towels and cloths!" Amy was suddenly full of enthusiasm and bustle and Emily was quick to acknowledge her efforts, though privately she doubted how effective they could be.

"How clever of you! But please, be careful, you didn't come to stay to be a scullery maid!"

Amy laughed.

"Well this *is* rather fun. I've told Cook to douse the fire in the kitchen. Just hope your brother approves!"

Emily's reply was to thin air. Amy was a woman on a mission. There was no time for idle chatter, though she heard voices, including her brother's and moved as quickly as she could to find them.

"Not good news." Andrew stood in the doorway, a silhouette against the reddening sky. "The wind has changed with a vengeance. We can see the flames off in the east. Stay here. We're as ready as we can be. Hope we have enough water. The men are working well, even the convicts. All hands on deck. Which reminds me, if you hear noises on the roof, don't fret. I've spoken to Miss Burnett. She seems to be going well."

Emily had questions but she simply squeezed his hand and smiled, as he rushed away. Amy reappeared, splashed water all over the curtains and was gone.

Chapter 2

The smoke was impenetrable. The roar of the wind and crackling flames made it impossible to hear or be heard. Andrew wound the cloth tight around his head and covered his mouth as he ran to check the horses. With few words and many gestures he managed to get his message across.

"Damp bags... over their eyes and noses... especially the stallions. Smoke could panic them. Well done Kieran!" And he was off again to check his ragtag army. He threw the green saplings at half a dozen men, gesturing at them to cover their faces, and sent them to watch for spot fires and burning debris. He peered anxiously into the gloom. It was the fireballs he feared... they could travel miles ahead of the main blaze. How close was it? Then he swore vehemently, as he saw the tops of the trees to his right catch alight.

"Hell and damnation! It's *crowning*! Watch out!" They were all running. Buckets passed furiously back and forth behind the chain of men with their puny branches. Spot fires flared and were doused. Everywhere was smoke and noise. Then he heard crackling and burning nearby. The veranda posts. He slashed at the flames.

"Water! Over here!"

Then he was back in the stables. Horses pushed and jostled, a wide-eyed stable boy ran back and forth with hessian bags. Andrew patted him on the back as he dashed past.

"Well done! Good lad! Keep it up." He waved at Kieran who stood solid amongst it all, his bulk an island of calm as he directed his troops.

Bert's stolid figure emerged in front of Andrew.

"The bastard's all around us."

Through streaming eyes, Andrew tried to assess the danger.

"Over here!"

"At the back of you! Watch out!"

"Take that you bugger!"

Men shouted and swore as they beat at the beast's offspring.

If the worst of it stayed in the trees, thick in the hills, the cleared paddocks gave some respite, but the wind brought sparks and embers and Andrew's dread... the fireballs. Andrew tried to see where the main danger was coming from. With a stab of fear he saw a sheet of flames coming across the uncut wheat fields, straight toward the house.

He gathered five men, thrusting a flaming torch into each hand. It *was only* a slope, but....It was worth a try.

"When I say the word. Not a second before, we'll light a line of fire. Understand. We need to spread out, but all go at the same time!" He waited gasping, peering into the murk as the flames roared toward them. "Now!" He stopped and ran, lighting the unburnt edge, praying his helpers were with him. In seconds a roaring curtain surged toward the leaping flames. The two lines collided, exploded and died. Coughing and gasping they tried to celebrate. Their gamble had paid off for the moment. Then another shout.

"The roof! The kitchen roof!"

Andrew clambered up the overhang, shouting for water. In the gloom he saw the culprit, dry wooden shingles. He kicked and stamped. The water slid into the gaps. Smoke fizzed and belched. Another bucket, then another. Perhaps he was winning. He kicked at the smouldering wood, forgetting he was now on a slippery wet roof. He slid sideways, the bucket clattered over the edge. With a desperate lunge he grabbed at the skillion. His shoulder screamed with pain, but he hung on long enough to gain some purchase before he let go. As he hit the ground, he rolled, trying to soften the impact. He was winded and bruised but before he could draw breath the bulk of Bert was on him. Struggling for air he was rolled over and over.

"What the hell! Get off...!" He pushed feebly at his tormentor.

"'Ad ter stifle the flames! Yer blew up! Proper fireball yerself! Yer might have fixed the roof but youse was the main event!"

Andrew shook his head trying to focus. He realized his shirt was almost gone and more painfully his chest felt raw. It would wait. He leant for a moment on his saviour's shoulder.

"But how are we doing? How bad is the fire?"

"Well the bastard's still going but so far only some of the huts have gone I reckon. And I reckon the wind might be easing now!"

Andrew held up his hand.

"Could be, but we have to keep at it."

A loud crack! Was it a tree?

"What's that, for God's sake?"

"Thunder." Bert stared impassively at the sky.

"You're joking! It *can't* be! All we need is lightning to start more blazes!" Andrew's spirits were almost as weary as his body.

Bert turned away and shouted to the sky,

"Come on Hughie! Send it down! Do yer bit!"

Andrew wanted to laugh at his friend's unique prayer but he hadn't the energy.

"Come on up there! We need yer Hughie!"

And the drops began to fall, circles of mud, of hope.

Bert shrugged.

"Yer can do better!" And the drops came more freely. Suddenly they were standing in rain. Andrew glanced around. Weary faces were turned to the sky, smoke, ash, exhaustion, all were being washed away.

Andrew found himself caught up in a wild polka, the hairy wheezing Cook on one arm, Emily's beautiful friend on the other. Weary bodies forgot their pain. Men laughed and shouted.

Emily watching from the veranda smiled at her friend's bedraggled hair and sodden dress-where was the elegant Miss Burnett now? Then she saw Andrew's chest. It was time to act.

"Cook-hot tea. Whatever you can find, they all need food. Miriam fetch the old sheets and the honey tin."

Andrew interrupted.

"We'll do that, you rest!"

"No! Well if you insist bring me a chair, but you need treatment and I'm sure there are others." The worst burns were treated with honey-soaked rags, weary blood shot eyes were bathed. Bodies slumped where they could.

As she struggled to lift the shreds of blackened cloth from her brother's shoulders and back, without taking the skin as well, Bert pouring water as slowly and carefully as he could, Emily was trying to ignore the ache in her back, and the pain that had moved to her stomach.

"Amy please..." She bent forward leaning on her patient. It was now Amy's turn to continue the treatment, under Emily's anxious instruction. Eventually the shreds were removed and heavily honeyed strips spread gently across the wounds, then bound into place.

"Are you in much pain?" Emily's worried inquiry was met with a wink. Out of the corner of his eye Andrew could see how Amy's hands trembled.

"Almost worth the trouble eh fellas? Not often we have these nurses to tend to our wounds." It was a feeble joke but it broke the tension and met with whole-hearted guffaws. Amy flashed a look from under her lashes and pursed her lips, but then she smiled despite herself.

"Really Sir!" She reproached her patient but her ministrations continued gently and for longer than was really necessary.

Chapter 3

In her lonely bed, Emily struggled to sleep. The day's dramas swirled in her head. How close it had come! What if Drew hadn't come? Oh Nicholas where are you? It has been two weeks already. Surely a few more days. And Mama. Her hand moved fretfully across her belly. I know you'll make all the difference. And Nicholas will bring some more help... even a housekeeper. The thought of her husband brought tears. She wept. Was it tiredness? Relief? Loneliness? Don't be silly you can't be lonely with Amy and Drew. Perhaps some hot milk.

She lumbered out of bed. As she stood a sharp pain snatched at her. She leant on the bed, rocking, trying to breathe. She straightened gingerly... for the moment it was gone. She padded as quietly as possible across the veranda but sharp ears caught the sound.

"Missus." It was Miriam, anxious, wide-eyed, a black figure against the moonlight.

"Yes... you sleep. I'm..." But the dark form was already gone and by the time Emily reached the kitchen, the milk was warming on the rekindled fire. Another cramp caught her as she went to sit, but it too passed. She tried to calm her worried companion.

"No Miriam. It isn't time. You sleep. Today was too much. We all must sleep."

Back in her own bed, sleep eventually came.

◆ ◆ ◆

"Emily! Wake up! There's a corroboree going on just outside *your* window!" Amy burst into the bedroom and flung back the curtains as her hostess struggled to focus. She could see nothing but she could hear the gentle hum of chanting voices. "Perhaps it's the fire. They are celebrating." Amy peered out. "But why outside *your* window? And why *only* women?"

Emily smiled.

"I suspect it is Miriam. I was awake in the night. She's decided it is time to bring her 'Aunties'... to help with the baby..."

Amy's eyes almost popped out.

"The baby!! My Dear you can't mean it? How *dare* they think to be part of it... It's Unconscionable! Unthinkable!"

Emily shrugged,

"Not so unthinkable My Dear. If Mama doesn't come in time..." She smiled at her indignant guest. "I *do* believe they would have had more experience than either you or Andrew..."

"You *cannot* be serious!" Amy remained horrified.

"Well I did have some pains in the night..."

Indignation turned to panic.

"When? How many? Oh Emily!" She seized her friend's hand. *"Don't move. You must stay in bed!"*

Emily patted the hand.

"They've gone, But Miriam was with me and I assume she has taken precautions in her own way." She chuckled. "Admit it Amy Dear, you would really prefer help."

Amy remained unconvinced.

"Well you stay there. I'll organize breakfast be brought to you. As soon as I'm dressed I'll assess the situation." Emily lay back, succumbing, too tired to argue.

Amy stepped purposefully onto the veranda and was hit by the stench of the fire, and the sight of its legacy. A wave of nausea hit her. She reached for the veranda post. Her hand slipped and she stood staring at her greasy black palm through her tears.

"Miss Burnett! Are you alright?" She struggled to focus. A strong hand grasped her elbow as her knees began to buckle.

"Oh... I." she began to sob. Andrew half carried her back inside and settled her onto the nearest chair.

"It's shock! Very natural. I'll fetch you a drink." He went to move away, but she had his hand so he knelt beside her. Her forehead slumped onto his shoulder. He could feel the soft curls against his cheek. He waited, how long he had no idea and eventually her tears stopped. She lifted her head and stared past him.

"It's horrible! It's *such* a harsh land! Look at the poor trees! Even the *rocks* are black! It breaks my heart!"

Andrew tried to sound calm and reassuring.

"It isn't dead. It'll come back. Not the roses. Emily will need to start again with them, but the native plants will. I grant you they are ugly now, but a few months, a year... it'll be green again."

"How can it? How can it *possibly* recover?"

He shook his head.

"Mark my words. Our bush needs the fires - not as bad as this perhaps... but... It has been a bad Season, Seasons, but Nick loves his valley and he'll set it to rights. Granted we lost some stock, but the house, and the horses are safe! Surely we can be glad we saved those?"

She interrupted,

"*You* saved them! *You* saved us all!"

He reddened;

"Nonsense! We all played our part."

"No, Mr. Walters, *you* made all the difference. And now you have the most damage-to yourself!"

Andrew was embarrassed and very aware she still held his hand, as he knelt close.

"Well maybe a wee bit but ..." He stood slowly and placed her hand gently on the chair arm. He laughed ruefully. "The trees look black but a little rain and they'll shoot green shoots all over:

'Feel by turns the bitter change

Of fierce extremes, extremes by change more fierce

Dark with excessive light.'

You'll see, like the Phoenix, the bush will emerge from the ashes." Andrew saw her puzzled frown. "Have you not heard of the Phoenix? I always think of it when we have a bushfire!"

It was Amy's turn to look embarrassed.

"Certainly I've heard of it!" She paused. "It was just I was surprised... I mean... I..."

"You mean you are surprised *I'd* ever heard of it, or 'Paradise Lost'?" He raised a quizzical brow. "I'm not Emily's brother for nothing... and... well Emily may have been your governess but our grandmother!" He smiled. "She had us reading before we could walk, I swear."

It was Amy's blush that betrayed her, despite her denials.

"I did not mean... how could you think..." her voice trailed away.

Andrew was enjoying himself. For the first time he held the upper hand in their exchanges.

"Judge not a book by its cover Miss Burnett. Especially out here." But not wanting to add to her discomfort, he offered his arm, changing the subject.

"Have you recovered? Can I offer you any assistance?"

Amy stood abruptly. She did not intend to be on the defensive any longer.

"Thank you Sir. I am *quite* recovered. I am sorry I have troubled you."

Andrew's eyes twinkled.

"It was no trouble Miss Burnett. In fact I am full of admiration for your sterling efforts. I doubt we could have managed nearly as well without you."

Emily smiled,

"To be perfectly frank, Sir, though I was frightened, especially for Emily... I quite enjoyed... no not enjoyed, but I *am* rather glad I could contribute."

"Miss Burnett, you made a marvellous contribution. In fact, I think we all made a splendid team effort!" He bowed and strode away, trying to empty his mind of the allure of dark curls and soft white skin. She was not for him. As soon as Nick returned he would leave!

It was several days before Nick would return. Amy was left to her own devices. Emily tried to rest as much as possible, although she would rather have been up and about restoring her domain. Her young guest found more and more excuses to spend time with her brother. Andrew was busy, checking stock, fences, and the horses. He needed to ride and Amy begged prettily if she could come too, "sometimes". The "sometimes" became many times. Andrew felt he should decline but Emily was glad to see her friend occupied, and he certainly enjoyed his days when she came.

There was a need to travel to go to check the outer fences. He intended to take Kieran, but Amy begged to come. Although she was a good rider, Andrew was concerned. Emily had the answer.

"I'll pack a picnic lunch so you need not hurry back. And with you and young Mr. Malone I'm sure she'll be safe. Though it *will* be a long day."

"Nonsense, Mr. Walters knows I am a capable rider, don't you Sir?"

Andrew tried to sound reassuring.

"Miss Burnett is a fine rider Emily, if she will not be too bored... she is welcome... and we will certainly do only as much as is necessary."

They set out in the cool of the morning. Andrew was preoccupied, Amy increasingly bored and she began to fan herself ostentatiously, and sigh, just a little.

"Oh Miss Burnett. Forgive us. It is already quite hot, I do apologize. Perhaps we should return now?"

"Oh Emily packed us such a lovely basket. She went to so much trouble. I do think we should find a shady spot and at least enjoy it *before* we return."

Kieran came forward.

"I can go along here at least until the Pass, and check whilst you take Miss Burnett back. It would be no trouble, and it *is* really getting pretty hot, Drew." Andrew hesitated but Kieran was keen to prove himself. "I reckon I could go back then and organize a gang and get them started on the worst. We can't afford to let the stock wander about the hills."

Andrew could see the logic,

"You're probably right."

"Goodo! I'll be off. You bring the lady back in your own time and I'll get those fellas crackin!" He rode away, leaving Andrew suddenly conscious of how alone he and his companion were.

"Perhaps we should go home now... it is quite a distance."

"Oh Nonsense!" Amy pouted prettily at her escort. "What harm is there in sitting here near the river and enjoying it for a few minutes and the picnic Emily so kindly packed?"

Andrew reluctantly agreed. She was probably right and it would be rather pleasant, so he dismounted and held his hand to help her down. Amy slid from her horse and managed to land very close to Andrew so that his hand ended up around her waist. She smiled up into his eyes and lingered before she made a show of selecting the perfect spot for their picnic, whilst Andrew unloaded the basket. Straightening the cloth required Amy to move very close to Andrew again. Eventually, sitting opposite, they enjoyed the contents. As soon as they had eaten Andrew made to pack up, but a soft hand held his from continuing.

"Oh, there is no need to hurry surely. I really am *not* certain I can manage the heat. It is so *cool* here." Andrew hesitated. It was really not quite the thing to be alone like this. He began to argue but a soft finger pressed his lips closed. "Sssh! Don't fuss, just for a few minutes." As she spoke she moved her position and Andrew suddenly found her head resting in his lap. She pretended indifference as she fanned herself with a napkin. Andrew had no idea how to handle the situation. She glanced up at him from under her lashes. "You are *such* a worrier. Do enjoy yourself for once. We don't need to save the world all the time." As she spoke she took his hand, traced its edges then placed it on her waist." I have enjoyed my visit so much more since you came Mr. Walters."

Andrew could barely speak.

"Well... well surely the first days... rather difficult... dangerous..."

She smiled,

"Of course, but so much nicer since," and slowly sat up so that her face was very close, "surely you agree Sir?"

Andrew took a deep breath. It would be so easy to lean forward those few inches and kiss those full lips. Instead he moved away and stood up.

"I'm certain we need to start back." His companion pouted.

"You *are* mean." But she wasn't finished. She held out her hand imperiously, and as he helped her to her feet, she managed to move very close once again.

Their bodies brushed against each other. Andrew closed his eyes as he tried to take control of himself and his situation, but instead he found himself being kissed. For the briefest moment he hesitated before stepping away. Without a word he packed the basket and collected the horses. He cupped his hand. She mounted her horse and from her superior height, snapped.

"I think you are *mean and positively heartless.*"

Andrew stood back,

"I am neither Miss Burnett, but you are in my care and it is my duty to return you safely to my sister." His words were barely out before she dug in her heels and took off across the blackened fields, leaving him to scramble after her.

Chapter 4

When Nicholas returned his immediate concern was for his wife. Then he turned his attention to his acres and his horses.

"Thank God *you* happened along Drew!" He shook his brother-in-law's hand not for the first time. "We heard there'd been fires near Bathurst but not out here. Do you have any idea how it started?"

"No...but whether it was deliberate or not I don't think it was ever meant to come your way... the wind changed just at the wrong time." Andrew was being circumspect but his mother was not inclined to follow suit.

"Deliberate! What on *earth* can you mean? *Who* would light a fire in this weather, in the middle of a drought?!"

"Well I'm afraid there are several new squatters going west who are ignorant. One of them may have started something... or even maybe offended the blacks..."

"What are you saying Andrew? Blacks starting a bad fire... They burn off regularly but I've never known them to deliberately destroy." Nicholas frowned at the younger man, "Or do you know more than you are saying?"

"No I don't, but I certainly intend asking around, I can tell you. I've heard there has been bad blood between some of the newcomers and the tribes. There was apparently *real* trouble in the early days, but I thought it long gone. You and I have never encountered it, but it takes only a modicum of sense to realize there is no need to make enemies with people who know the land and all it can do."

"Well if anyone can find out I know you can Andrew Walters with your fine red hair!" He turned to the ladies, "Always been a favourite with the native warriors haven't you?"

Andrew's face matched his hair, though he knew Nicholas remarks were possibly true. Although there were few black people in his village, he had spent the last five years working in the bush, far and wide, and he had to admit, had always been greeted with courtesy and kindness. Perhaps his auburn curls helped. Maybe they knew how much he loved the bush. He shrugged.

"Enough of that. Kieran was a tower of strength-you've done well there, and the ladies," he gestured toward Emily and her friend, "were wonderfully helpful." His mother noted with misgiving the tender look which he exchanged with the said Miss Burnett as Andrew continued, "We've checked most of the fences and we've gangs working on the worst. I shouldn't stay much longer but whatever you need..."

"Well I'd rather *not* impose but Emily says you were burnt. How is your shoulder?"

Janet Walters forgot everything in her anxiety.

"Andrew, you didn't say! Come! Into the bedroom. Let me check..."

A very embarrassed young man tried to remonstrate, but his mother had instantly made him feel like a small boy rather than the hero of the hour. He followed her docilely out of the room. Nicholas was left to hear the details of their dramatic day from his wife and her guest.

It wasn't until after dinner that Janet's attention centred on her daughter and the real reason for her visit. The men had gone, Janet was in control.

"Stand up girl. Let me see if the baby has dropped yet." She turned to Emily's guest. "Will you excuse us Miss Burnett? I *need* to have time with my daughter... come Emily." and she led Emily purposefully from the room. The door to the bedroom was barely closed before she launched into her main concern. "Well the sooner Andrew leaves the better. You've done a good job on his shoulder, but he will need to wait a few days longer, *unfortunately!*"

"I thought you would want him to stay?"

"Not with *that* little minx here. Like mother like daughter or should I say like grandmother as well."

"Really Mama! What are you saying?" Emily sank onto the bed, could she never please her mother. "I know her grandmother's past... but you have always taught us to treat everyone as equal... How many times have I heard you say it?"

"I was not referring to that. Her own mother is the first to pretend she *is Exclusive* and looks down on the world, and those who did *not* come of their own accord. Perhaps she has convinced herself. No Emily, I was *not* referring to convicts or otherwise. I was referring to both of those 'ladies'," Her voice was heavy with sarcasm. "and their undoubted ability to use their charms to seduce any man who will better their position! You, yourself, knew that the girl's father was befuddled with grief and inveigled into marriage before he could gather his senses. How *much* time have they spent together?"

"Oh! Well he only came the day of the fire... and well... well he has taken her for rides... well she kept asking to go and offering..."

"No *doubt* she offered! She has your brother thoroughly under her spell. *You* should have put a stop to it. And you know she is just playing with him... honing her skills on my naïve son! *He* is the only one who will be hurt!"

Emily tried ineffectually to excuse her guest, though she had to acknowledge her mother was doubtlessly right.

"She *was* a great help Mama, perhaps you are being harsh. Andrew is a handsome…"

"Harsh! Her mother interrupted. "You *know* she has every intention of going to London and snaring herself a fancy husband. No doubt she'll be after a *title* at the very least, and with her flashy looks, and the Major's fortune, she'll doubtless do very well for herself."

"Flashy looks… Mama… you *are* severe."

"Nonsense Girl! Face reality. No I'll *not* sit by and watch my innocent son break his heart over that piece. Now lay on the bed 'till I see where we are up to." She gently felt her daughter's body. "I think we have a few days more. It is never easy with the first…"

Emily did as she was bid, as usual. Then in the evening she watched in reluctant admiration as her mother set out to handle the other situation involving her children.

"And Emily tells me, Miss Burnett, that you are to go to London presently, for the Season? I imagine you are looking forward to it." She smiled at the younger woman. "Or perhaps you will miss your home?"

The reply came at once, Amy's voice bursting with excitement.

"Oh Yes! I am going to London next month! I simply *can't* wait. I have an aunt, my father's sister and she has arranged everything!"

"How kind. And you are to be presented at Court?"

Amy flashed another brilliant smile.

"Oh Yes! I am *so* excited!"

Janet nodded in sympathetic agreement.

"Of course you are. It is *very* important. And do you have your dress and the feathers." She smiled conspiratorially at the girl. "The feathers are de rigueur!"

For the next half hour, Emily watched fascinated as her mother, and, she had to admit, her own husband, led Amy through a detailed description of the delights ahead of her. Amy's face continued to light up. Andrew's increasingly closed down. Emily felt for him, but deep down she knew her mother was right. Amy had been merely flirting with her brother. Andrew had been too trusting and naïve to realize she was playing a game. Better be disappointed now, thought his sister. He'll get over it... but she felt sad and even rather guilty about it all.

Whether Andrew was upset it was hard to tell, but the very next morning he was packed and ready to leave before the ladies had had breakfast. He kissed his mother and sister then from a safe distance wished Miss Burnett a successful journey. She proffered her hand but it was ignored. With a final handshake from Nicholas he was gone before Nicholas had finished thanking him once more.

Lethargy settled on the ladies. Emily was heavy with child and increasingly preoccupied. Her mother maintained a chilly politeness to their guest. Amy suddenly felt the need to travel to Sydney to finalize her preparations. A letter was sent. Her father's coach duly arrived and she left.

"Do write Amy." Emily hugged the girl, but Amy was already far away in her imagination.

"Of course when I have time but you *must* realize I shall be *very* busy." She kissed Nicholas' cheek and nodded to Janet Walters. She couldn't really decide why or how her visit had suddenly become tedious. Andrew had left so abruptly. Well she had so much to look forward to. After all she had only visited Emily out of duty... The people in London would be much more to her liking certainly, and so much more interesting!

Chapter 5
Richmond

New South Wales
1804

To My Daughter,

Do the long bleak nights stir black thoughts in men's minds? In this land where the sun shines high in the great sky and the rivers flow slowly, perhaps there is not the time for men to forge their black desires.

On this day I have a daughter! It is a joy I never thought to experience again. Can you replace the lost bairns? No. But already you have eased the pain. Bonny wee Janet, "Grace of the Lord." Aye that is true. But where was that Grace these long years?

It is time. Time for the truth my wee child. My name and, therefore yours, is not Mc Lean. That is the name of my friend the mighty Cameron, who saved this broken creature. In truth you are descended from a long line of chieftains, from generation to generation. My, our name, was taken from us. My wife was taken, and all that I hold dear. I survived... barely! It was long months before I could have fought to retrieve it. Should I have? I never thought that one day it could matter. That one day I would have another heir. My past life was dead with my beloved wife and bairns. My angel Margaret healed my wounds, and we felt it was better to come away from the past.

Now doubts enter my heart. If in time to come, you, or yours, feel the need to go back, I leave these few articles. The mighty Cameron saved them when he saved my body. They are proof that you have a rightful claim... a claim to your ancient name and inheritance. The lawyers at McPherson and Sons in Edinburgh, know my story. It is in your hands dear child. For your father it is too late, and, too hard.

Go into the world with my blessing whatever you decide.

Your Father.

Andrew stared at the thick yellowed sheets.

"Crikey! Whatever does it mean? Where did it come from? And what's it to do with me anyway?"

Emily began to explain.

"We finally emptied that trunk of our Grandmother..."

Nicholas interrupted impatiently.

"It is *not* where we found it that is the crux of the matter. I daresay it is quite obvious already Andrew, your Grandfather came to this country after something quite dreadful happened! The important matter is rather, you *all* need to decide *what* to do!"

Before Andrew could respond to Nicholas' stern words, he felt his leg being grasped. He looked down into the shining eyes of his nephew.

"Unc Drew! Unc Drew!"

Laughing he lifted the interruption high over his head.

"Hello James. How big you are!" There were squeals of delight from the small boy as he was tossed and tickled. It was several minutes before Nicholas could restore order and draw attention to the matter in hand.

"That's quite enough James! Now as I was saying... you, and your sisters need to decide whether you are interested in this letter and *all* that it implies!"

Andrew tried to concentrate though two chubby arms around his neck made it difficult to breathe.

"Does our Mother know?" He was still not entirely sure what the letter meant.

Emily nodded as she tried to disengage her son's firm grip.

"She was here when we found it. She was just as surprised as we were. She thinks perhaps her father hid it, but I think it more likely that our grandmother tucked it away. It was underneath every layer including the paper lining."

Nicholas was quick to agree.

"Doubtless she felt it had nought to do with her and she was happy to leave it all behind. I'd suggest that's the most likely. The fact *remains*, however, that your grandfather was *clearly* done a great wrong. How *much* do any of you care? Do you feel *any* obligation to right the wrong or would you rather just leave it all in the past?"

His tone was serious, even impatient. Clearly he believed the former. Andrew was confused...

"But how would we begin to prove it?"

Nicholas held out a small package wrapped in soft chamois leather. He unfolded it carefully onto the table. He lifted a large metal circle in the palm of his hand.

"This is a chieftain's brooch, to fasten his plaid. See the feathers at the top. They mean *something significant*. I know that, but what exactly, I'm not sure. Only a leader could wear them." He placed it carefully back on the leather. "And this ring." He held it to the light so Andrew could see. "It is a seal." He pointed to the image traced into the metal. "They are both silver as is the lid on this horn."

Andrew looked even more uncertain.

"But what is that?"

"It is a powder horn, and its decoration matches the others."

Andrew frowned.

"Well even if it is, and the letter is real.... authentic... why all this rush. Your letter said to come immediately. I don't understand... How many years has it been in the trunk?"

Nicholas smiled at his young relative.

"Well we do have something else to tell you. Emily and I are about to travel to England. I promised my mother that I would return, within five years, and that is fast approaching. She assures me she is 'pining away'." He raised an eyebrow. "Whatever! I do need to keep my promise". He looked squarely at Andrew. "And I suggest, propose, you come with us. It will be a grand experience for you and so much more pleasant for your sister who is very anxious about meeting my family." Emily tried to deny it but her words were lost as Andrew replied.

"Me. I!" He stared in astonishment at Nicholas. "Me! You know how to... Doubtless you know all the right people... I mean you two could do it... make enquiries..."

Emily, her son on her hip, slipped her free hand through her brother's arm and pressed her head against his shoulder.

"Oh Andrew, please consider it. It would be so delightful to have your company. And James would like it... wouldn't you James?" James nodded his head but Andrew remained singularly unimpressed.

"Holy cow! I can't think of anything worse than locking yourself in a wooden box for three months! A bloke would go mad!"

Nicholas laughed somewhat ironically,

"No-one would *lock* you in, and it should take no more than two months, more probably six weeks! That was all it took when I came back... out. And it is not entirely unpleasant... You would have your own cabin. There is much to see on the ocean, and in this wide world. You are young. I'd say the perfect age to see the world!"

Andrew continued to look unconvinced. It was only later that he remembered Nicholas' slip and Emily's sudden blush.

"And it's dangerous! Remember the 'Cataraque'... Four hundred dead, drowned after months of travelling!"

Emily's voice was hushed.

"Yes it *was* dreadfully sad... but you must concede, Andrew, thousands have arrived safely. There is no reason to think the worst! Of course I am anxious myself especially with James so young, but I have confidence in Nicholas." She smiled mischievously at her husband. "Besides needs must. Nicholas must return and I have no desire to remain here without him. I cannot afford to. He may well forget us."

She placed her son firmly on the floor and handed him a toy, pretending not to see her husband's severe look, though he squeezed her hand as it lay on the table next to her grandfather's relics.

"Nonsense Madam! You *know* I would not." Andrew watching, felt suddenly uncomfortable as he caught the intense look his sister and her husband exchanged. The moment passed and Nicholas returned to cajoling his brother-in-law.

"I would think it is high time you saw some more of the world. There are more interesting entertainments than are to be found at the "Blackboy Hotel", and rather more skilled entertainers than Jim Brown and Mickey Drew."

Andrew was indignant.

"Of course I know *that* and I'll have you know I have seen others! Besides how do *you* know about 'The Blackboy'?"

Emily ignoring this exchange tried in her own way to persuade her wary brother.

"Please Drew. Please consider it. We really do rely on you to come." She hugged his arm again. "And Nicholas is right. We should both take this opportunity. All the stories we've heard. It will be wonderful to see the real thing... Castles... great buildings... the art galleries. And ... if you do go to Scotland you will see places Grandma told us about. Please?"

Andrew hunched his shoulders and said gruffly,

"And where do you think a bloke could find the funds? I mean enough to travel and then live..."

He was cut short by Nicholas.

"Well Mate, that's no problem. You will be *my* guest and if you don't want to accept that, you'll doubtless become a great landowner and you can pay me back! I can see you in your kilt with the rest of us tugging the forelock in deference." He chuckled at his own joke but Andrew remained unimpressed.

"That's ridiculous. I can't bludge off you. Anyway how long do you intend being away? Surely you'll need me to keep an eye on the place. Not to mention my own gang... Can't see them organizing themselves at all."

Nicholas tone was quiet, even apologetic as he replied.

"As I said you would be *my* guest and *my* family's. Not something I like to dwell on... but... well no need for any qualms about any of it... funds I mean. My family would be deeply offended if you refused their hospitality. After all Old Chap you *are* family whether you like it or not." But Andrew remained unsmiling, unyielding, and silent as Nicholas continued. "Besides young Andrew, I *need* you! I need to find a stallion or two and certainly some good mares. We have plenty of stock but I'm after quality. Can't have John Tait winning every race!"

Suddenly Andrew looked interested.

"Right on Nick.' Old Whaleboat' has set him up good and proper! Got himself a fancy hotel in Bathurst I hear." Andrew smiled wistfully, "Wouldn't mind winning one of the saddles he's been donating to the winning jockey!"

Nicholas looked sceptical.

"Hate to say it Mate but a jockey *you'll* never be!" They all laughed at the idea as Nicholas, seizing his chance, returned to the main topic. "Well good luck to Tait but I'm keen to offer real competition. I hear the younger Dawson is looking at setting up a stud in the Hunter region. Thoroughbred breeding is becoming "the go" and I'm after the best. No-one has a better eye than you Drew. If you won't come as my guest. I'll pay you to be my scout. How about it?"

Despite himself Andrew was very interested.

"No need to pay me... But ... well wouldn't mind looking around with you... England still has the best breeding stock. Or so I hear. We could give those chaps here a run for their money... yeah could be very interesting."

Emily and her husband exchanged glances but left their guest to his thoughts. The seed was sown. There was one problem, however, and later in the privacy of their bedroom Nicholas broached it.

"Almost said the wrong thing By Jove! Do you think Andrew noticed?"

Emily sighed.

"Well whether he did or not, the fact remains *when* we arrive in England, sooner or later someone is bound to let the cat out of the bag."

Nicholas pulled a rueful face.

"You're right on the mark there My Love! Family's bound to tell him. They love to remind me of my foolish past. I suspect we'll need to tell him..."

"Oh no! Oh *please* Nicholas!" Emily was aghast.

Her husband smiled reassuringly.

"Please don't worry your pretty head, Dear Wife. No-one and I mean *no-one*, knows of your efforts on my behalf... well perhaps Kieran's mother has an inkling but she would never say. Don't concern yourself. I'll simply divulge enough to Andrew if and when he decides to come with us."

Emily's concerns were lessened, and there was relief in her voice.

"Oh I am almost certain he'll come now. Thoroughbred horses!" She pouted her lips. "I'll doubtless be ignored completely whilst you both traipse around discussing conformation and pedigree."

As she spoke Emily brushed her hair and began to plait it. Her husband took the brush, laid it on the dressing table and then took the thick strands in his hands.

"Leave it! It was the memory of your hair floating in the water like seaweed..." He pressed it to his face. "And then spread in the semi-darkness, that first time..."

Emily blushed and bent her head.

"I was so shameless. I..."

Without a word, her husband lifted her onto the bed and slowly began to untie the ribbons of her negligee.

"*You* were far from shameless... It was *I* who was shameless, taking advantage of your innocence... I felt such guilt... but if we hadn't... if you hadn't... you slid into my veins... and the *more* I tried to forget you the stronger was my affliction."

"An affliction!" Emily protested, smiling nonetheless. "But Dear Nicholas, when we go to England... Oh I am so very nervous. How can you expect your family to welcome me... I am so ignorant of Society and how it all works."

"There is no need to concern yourself about any of that."

"And naturally they will all want you, and your attention..." Emily was unconvinced.

Her doubts were stifled by a long passionate kiss and his love making.

Afterwards they lay quietly in each other's arms, as Nicholas gently drew circles with his finger on her stomach.

"Long ago I made love to an innocent girl. Now I make love to a woman and each time is more precious than the last. I want you to come to England because I want my family to know how lucky I am." He pressed her hand to his lips. "Of course I confess, when I went back I threw myself into everything... parties, balls, races... scrapes. It was mad, frantic but pointless because ever so slowly I realized there was something else. I needed... I needed someone else." He kissed her again.

As Emily lay in his arms, she knew, at that moment, she was perfectly happy. She tried to hold it in her heart. Whatever lay ahead she would keep this moment. Whatever was to come in that exotic world, she knew, here and now, her husband loved her. But she also knew that it would not be easy. This was her life, her country. She knew her place, where would she fit in her future?

Chapter 6

The blue mirror of the loch stretched before her as Caitlyn waited for the flickering water that lapped around her feet, to settle. She could feel it wrapping around her toes and splashing her ankles. She was *sure* she had seen the perfect pebble if the water would just be still.

All morning the children had been making their own village out of stones and sticks. She just needed one tall thin stone for the spire of her kirk, and she was sure it lay under that flickering water. The children's village, so painstakingly constructed was neat and symmetrical with the kirk right in the middle of the square. It was quite unlike the random scattering of cottages that stretched back up the glen behind her. If the water would just be still. She held her skirts high and stepped further into the loch. It was just as she slid that perfect pebble into her hand, that she heard the first scream.

She turned to see smoke in the distance. The farthest cottage was burning, and as she watched another smouldered then flamed. Then another, then another. It was then that she saw them. The men of fire! They were carrying flames, on poles, and running from one cottage to the next, lighting the roof until it blazed. Men in heavy boots, laughing and shouting above the crackling and the cries. As she watched, the men of fire came closer, closer and closer. She could hear their laughter mixed with the wailing and screaming of her friends, and the barking dogs.

The men in their black boots laughed even louder, when Widow Mary's cat came screeching out of her burning cottage and one of them threw it right back into the flames. And all the while the red-faced man on his horse was shouting and pointing, telling them which house to burn next. It was a line of fire coming closer and closer to the children's little village.

She grabbed her brothers' hands. Where could she run? The laughing men of fire were very close. Oh where was Dadaidh? All the men had gone to sell the cattle. She couldn't understand why. Her father loved his cattle, with their heavy shaggy black and ginger coats and their cream horns. Why was he selling them? And why had these evil men come now? Did they know Dadaidh was away? And why were they burning all the houses? And Widow Mary's cat? Maybe that was why her mother and grandmother had taken everything out of their cottage. All day yesterday they had dragged and carried the beds and the stools and the pots and the pans. Everything! She could see her grandmother sitting on her own chair, next to the pile that yesterday had filled their cottage. She was looking angry. Neanaidh never looked angry.

As Caitlyn ran with her brothers toward the shelter of her grandmother's skirts, the laughing and screaming was becoming louder and louder. She wanted to cover her ears. She wanted to close her eyes. Surely it would stop. Perhaps it was a bad dream.

Then the laughing did stop. There was a terrible scream. Louder, closer. It was her mother. She had been beating out the flames on her cottage, defying the men of fire. She had clambered up the stone wall trying to reach those flames. The roof began to crumble. She was gone!

Other women ran forward pushing past the men of fire. Two of them disappeared into the smoke. They came out dragging

Mama aidh. They were crying and coughing but Mama aidh was quiet. She wasn't crying. She was very still. Caitlyn could see her mother's skirt stretched tight over her swollen belly. It was black and smoking. She could see her mother's feet. One was curled up, the other flopped in a funny way. Neanaidh was leaning over her. Caitlyn pushed forward into the crowd. Mama aidh's eyes were closed. Perhaps she was asleep? She had blood on her forehead. Caitlyn tried to wipe it away with her apron but someone lifted her up and held her back.

Then the noise changed. The screaming stopped. Instead there was a low murmur, then a growl like an angry wolf. Some of the women and children had grabbed stones. They began throwing them at the men of fire, shouting their defiance. The men turned and began to run back. The stones came faster and faster. The women were shouting now. Screaming. Cursing. A stone hit the horse. Then another hit the man on the horse. He turned away. The other men followed. The women ran after them shouting, throwing anything they could find. The bravest one ran forward and hit the horse with a blackened stick. Then others began to hit the stragglers. The men were running now. Running from all they had done. For a brief moment there was triumph, glee, excitement, but then the women looked around the glen that had sheltered their houses. It was replaced by despair.

Caitlyn sat next to her mother, while her grandmother held her daughter's hands, rubbing them, talking to her, calling her name. Fergus and Finlay had begun to cry. She tried to soothe her brothers, hugging them tight as she rocked back and forth. Please Mama aidh wake up. Around her, she could hear voices. Some were angry but already others were upset and worried.

"When will *our* men come back?"

"What *can* we do?"

"What if those villains return?"

"They never left us *one* sheiling to live in! Not one!"

"Why did they come *now*? The notices said next week! We have all paid our rents!"

"They've done this evil work, they've no need to return!"

"Can we move her?"

"Oh *where* shall we sleep? Where can we sleep?"

"The children! It is too cold! They need shelter! We *all* need shelter!"

"Do we have any food? Did *anyone* save their food?"

"How could they do this?!! How could *anyone* do it?!!"

"It's been done before. We all know that. *And no-one* can help us lest they suffer our fate!"

"Aye, they prefer sheep to their kin." The gravelly voice of Blind Willie spoke about the others. "It is as the Great Seer Kenneth, foretold. 'The Clans will become so effeminate so as to allow themselves to be driven from their native land by an army of sheep'!"

"The devil curse them, the drunken scum!"

"How could grown men do this to women and children, drunk or sober!?"

Caitlyn wanted her mother more than ever. Please Mama aidh wake up. Mama aidh will know what to do. Please Mama aidh. She pushed her way through the crowd and lay on the ground, her head on her mother's shoulder. Perhaps that would help to keep Mama aidh warm. Fergus snuggled next to her but Finlay was crying and crying.

Then Caitlyn saw another pair of boots, but these were shiny black and clean. She looked up. It was the Reverend Father. She could see the folds of his cassock and his hand as it touched her mother's forehead. Then she heard his voice, the voice she knew, the voice that had taught her to read and write and count and tell her about the Great World.

"You must come to the kirk. Bring whatever you can to keep out the weather. My mother is preparing the broth." He turned to the strongest looking women. "Can you bring her and the bairns? We must keep her warm. Put her inside the kirk and the bairns as well. Come Mother." He held out his arm to her grandmother. "We need you all to come. Can you walk the distance?" He turned to Duncan MacDougal, the oldest boy. "You Lad, help Blind Willie and you Lass take the Widow's arm."

He started to walk toward the kirk and the people began to follow, wailing and keening as they did in the funeral processions. At the rear of the sorry cavalcade came her mother. The girls had managed to fasten a blanket between two blackened beams, and on this stretcher her mother was taken. She never opened her eyes or moved. Nor during the long night did she move, though her children lay close trying to warm her and their own frightened selves.

Just as the first light came, Caitlyn felt urgent hands lifting her and her brothers. They were hurried outside. She heard noises, cries, groans and a terrible tearing cry. She could hear the Reverend talking, softly, gently. Then she saw her father. He was holding his head in his hands, crouched low, he was rocking back and forth, groaning. The Reverend had his hand on her father's shoulder. She felt very cold and the cold was inside her body as well as outside. She knew her mother's eyes would never open again.

◆ ◆ ◆

"I'll be going to Leith. I have a brother in Leith." Caitlyn heard her father's voice. It was hard and cold. She had never seen him like this – angry and fierce. How many days had passed since the men of fire? She struggled to remember. Now her grandmother, Fergus and Finlay were already sitting on the cart. The pony was already harnessed. Everything that they could fit from their cottage was packed tight, the creepies to sit on and the wooden kirsts filled with father's tools, their clothes, the linen and the pots and pans and spoons and ladles. Neanaidh pointed to the cradle with the horseshoe on its end, nailed upside down to stop the luck from flying away.

"Please Malcolm. All the generations have lain safe in it."

But her son-in-law turned away, white with pain.

"And the bairn that is buried with, and within his mother, will never sleep in it."

Then her grandmother herself turned away to hide her own tears.

For Caitlyn there was another pressing concern. There was no room left on the cart for her. She glanced sideways at the man who was her father but not the man she had always known. Would he forget her and go without her? She tapped his arm.

"Please Dadaidh. Is there no place for me?"

For a fleeting moment his face softened and she saw her old father.

"Whist child. It is for you to walk with me. It is much to ask but we canna fit more on that vehicle and that wee beast of burden. Are you my strong lass?" She smiled and nodded with pride and relief as he continued. "It is not to Leith that we needst walk. Just to Inverness. From there we will catch the Packet – the wee boat to Leith. It is to your uncle we journey. He will help us I'm sure until we find another cottage."

It was a very long way to Inverness. At night she could snuggle with the others in the cart. It was a tight fit but warm. Her father rolled himself in his plaid and slept beneath the cart. On the second day he took one of his old cromacks and cut it short so that she had her own shepherd's crook. It seemed easier to walk beside him and her heart felt lighter to know he cared.

She had tried to keep a count of the days. When the path was good and not too steep they could walk all day. If the road was bad they rested early. Then the precious bag of oats would come down from the cart. Her father would light a fire and her grandmother would take out the spirtle and stir the porridge. Then they would sit close to the little flames with the hot porridge warming their stomachs, but when there was nothing to make a fire, the porridge was cold and lumpy and horrible.

One day as they trudged on she saw an eagle soaring above. So free and so strong. Then as she watched, it swooped low and took a new-born fawn from its mother's feet. That night she cried herself silently to sleep, sharing her own grief with the mother deer.

Chapter 7

Andrew woke slowly, through the haze of sleep he tried to decide where he was. The bed was soft, large. He stretched. Very large. He sat up with his legs over the side. The room was dark but as he sat collecting his wits, a slim figure pulled back the heavy curtains. The figured turned and spoke. Andrew's eyes, blurred by sleep and now sudden light could just discern the figure was male.

"Good morning Sir." He said.

"Morning." Andrew's reply was as much a question as a greeting.

"Yes Sir. It *is* morning. It has gone past nine Sir. Is Sir desirous of breakfast here, or would Sir prefer to retire to the breakfast parlour?"

It was a question. Andrew struggled. He eventually decided he would venture to the breakfast parlour-whatever that was.

"Very well Sir. I have the hot water ready through here, and I have managed to wash some of your shirts and press Sir's outer garments. They are all laid out." He gestured toward a side door. Andrew shook his head.

"By Jove you're a busy bloke! But who are you?"

"I am Forbes Sir. At your service. Mr Manners thought I should act as your valet, for the present. It is, of course, up to you Sir. If you find my service satisfactory and agreeable to yourself." He bowed his head.

"Well you've clearly done a splendid job already! Although, I should warn you Forbes, I'm not accustomed to having a valet. What exactly do we have in mind here? I mean what service do you intend, er... expect to render?" Andrew tried to sound neither rude nor stupid but he was not entirely sure he wanted some cove fussing around while he dressed, or bathed. Not sure about that at all!

Forbes allowed himself a narrow smile, which he hoped was reassuring.

"Mr Manners has already suggested that you may find my presence a little, shall we say, unusual, but I am at your disposal Sir."

A sudden impulse to bundle this individual out the door was repressed. He was clearly inoffensive and eager to please. Andrew replied as pleasantly as he could.

"Well we shall just jog along and see how it goes. Eh?"

Forbes nodded but his smile vanished as he dared to mention his one serious failure,

"I am afraid Sir, your boots. They are not as one would wish just yet... I will keep trying Sir, I assure you."

Andrew laughed.

"I *bet* you couldn't fix them!" As he spoke he stood and stretched, oblivious to Forbes' look of amazement. Mr. Manners was of course, very tall and elegant, but Forbes tried not to stare at his even taller prospective employer. He felt a tinge of excitement. If this young giant, with his perfect physique, really became his charge, he would be the envy of every valet in London.

Within what seemed to Forbes, a veritable rush, and to Andrew, rather longer than necessary, he was dressed and ready to face the world.

"Well. Well. Finally!" Nicholas smiled a welcome at his young relative. "I thought you might sleep the day away and we do have much more to do." As he spoke he stood and turned to his companion who had remained at his breakfast. He was a grey-haired, distinguished man.

"Peter may I present to you my brother-in-law Andrew Walters. Andrew this is my brother-in-law Sir Peter Spencer." Sir Peter rose slightly from his chair and offered his hand.

"How do you do? Must apologize for not being here when you arrived last evening. Trust you found everything satisfactory and to your liking?"

Andrew glanced sideways at Nicholas whose dark eyes were brimming with mirth, but he replied formally to his host.

"Entirely Sir Peter. It is most generous of you to offer hospitality to all of Nicholas' new relatives."

Sir Peter was enthusiastic in his quiet way.

"Not at all! Not at all! We have been very anxious to meet Nicholas's bride and certainly regard it as a bonus to meet her brother as well." He returned to his breakfast as Andrew puzzled over the substantial array of dishes on offer. Decisions were still difficult. He felt his brain was still seemingly back in the ship at the very least. It was not until he was seated that Sir Peter continued. " I understand from Nicholas you have some business to attend to? Please accept anything I can do to offer assistance." He raised an eyebrow at Nicholas as he continued, "It doesn't appear that I need save young Nicholas from his adventures this time, so I shall be happy to be of service to you young man."

Andrew thanked his host and turned to his breakfast. It was Nicholas who continued the conversation.

"Well Andrew, you've survived being locked in a box on the ocean. Despite it all we have arrived safe." Andrew reddened, but it was Nicholas who suffered the most embarrassment as Sir Peter interjected.

"Well not quite locked in a box like you were Nicholas." With this cryptic remark he stood, excused himself and left the room. Andrew stared at his brother-in-law.

"What was that all about? What adventures have you had... 'locked in a box'?"

There was a silence. Andrew sensing Nicholas' discomfiture tucked into his bacon. He was about to change the subject to his valet when Nicholas began quietly to explain.

"Something I should have told you..." There was a pause. Nicholas cleared his throat. "Actually I did travel, 'locked in a box' in a manner of speaking. I travelled to New South Wales more than once. The first time I travelled in chains."

Andrew stared, his mouth open, the fork caught half way between plate and mouth.

"Humdudgeon! I *don't* believe it! You! You! You're *gammoning* me!"

Nicholas shrugged resignedly, took a deep breath and began.

"Well believe it or not I did. I was duped here in London, supposedly killed a fellow in a duel, was arrested, charged and bundled off to New South Wales. No-one knew where I was, so once I arrived there I naturally set about escaping. Managed it eventually. Worked my way back by rather a circuitous route and, once I returned, Peter was able to help me clear my name and apprehend the villains."

Andrew wondered if he were still in his bed dreaming.

"I don't believe it! *How* could you escape? *How* could you get away? They always get lost in the bush. Who knows?" A thousand questions jostled in his brain. "But you... I mean you were... you are..." He shook his head. Nicholas smiled ruefully as he continued,

"Well I'm relieved to know you think I am not *really* convict material. My escape was sheer good luck. Maybe too, it was due to Providence and some very good people. It took several months to arrange. Have you never wondered why Bert and Denny were so happy to come and work for me? I wanted to repay them, and we'd had such adventures they were happy to come and continue to look after me.... They never thought I could manage myself. There were others of course but... Well your family are so respectable, *entirely* respectable... Probably better you know as little as possible... Could put you in a difficult position... Your sister knows the whole story and the wonder is she still married me." He smiled at Andrew apologetically. "I'm afraid the family here like to tease me and that's why you need to know. *Your* family are very careful of their reputation and I honour that, they see things differently to my family, simply because they have *no* idea what being a convict *is*. I just hope you won't cast me adrift. Do you think you can still have me as your brother-in-law?"

Andrew sat stunned. He kept glancing at his companion, his urbane, handsome hero, his elegant wealthy friend... not *just* brother-in-law. He could not begin to picture him locked in a cell with chains around his wrists and ankles.

Nicholas drank his coffee and waited for a response but Andrew had no words. Eventually Nicholas broke the silence.

"It is not an episode I really like to discuss or remember... Well most of it... But you know, despite everything, that wide, wild country got under my skin. I missed that great blue sky and the endless horizons." He grimaced. "Sounds ridiculous I know. I also felt I owed a debt to those who helped me-at great risk clearly. So I returned and the miracle is I met your family and found your sister... so of course I cannot regret... well not all of it." He paused and leant his head on his cupped hands then ran his fingers through his black hair. "But if you don't mind Old Chap, I'd rather let it be if you can too?"

"Of course! It was generous of you to even confide this much." Andrew stumbled over his words. "All fine with me... Especially if Emily... Well no need to tell our parents... Crikey Nick... Take a bloke how you find him... That's my motto. Plenty decent chaps have a past... Well not that I'm saying... I mean obviously in your case rather a nasty mistake... But By Jove... I'm very glad you came back... all in the past... I mean... Hell's Bells Nick, I can't get my mind around it all so I think I'll just forget it!"

Nicholas clapped his shoulder.

"Thank you Mate. I really hoped you'd understand."

Andrew shrugged,

"Well to be honest, lots I don't understand and 'struth! What a story! But let sleeping dogs lie," and he returned to his breakfast.

Nicholas was happy to change the subject. He had plans for the day which apart from anything else would divert Andrew's attention from his far too colourful past.

"Finish your breakfast! We have much to do. I intend to make you the most fashionable chap in London. We are off to furnish you a wardrobe!"

Andrew stared in astonishment at his brother-in-law.

"What do you mean I need a wardrobe! Don't you remember you dragged me into David Jones' Emporium and forced me to buy all that clobber for our trip?"

Nicholas laughed as he replied.

"And as well that I did, you certainly cut quite a dash on our journey. But one must look the part young Drew. When in Rome etcetera."

Andrew continued to grumble.

"When in Rome... You want *me* to ape the gentry?"

"My Dear Chap, you *are* the gentry! I hardly need remind you why we brought you, and rather have to admit... in this regard, *you* may "outgentry" all of us!" He clapped his unwilling companion on the shoulder. "Come on Old Chap! Enjoy! I am about to take you to my tailor and I can't *wait* to hear his response!" He glanced slyly at Andrew, "Or yours! And think of Forbes..."

"Whatever do you mean?" Andrew's question was ignored as he was bundled out of Grosvenor Square and marched into Regent St.

And Nicholas was not to be disappointed. Watching his young brother-in-law being fussed over, hustled in and out of various frock coats, being made to stand perfectly still whilst his neck and shoulders were measured and most amusingly for Nicholas, his inner leg, was all that Nicholas had expected. Meanwhile the tailor and his assistants continued to exclaim over the magnificence of Andrew's shoulders and the narrowness of his waist. Nicholas was forced to walk away more than once to hide his stifled laughter. There were times when he thought Andrew would explode, but once the measuring was done, to Nicholas' surprise, Andrew began to enjoy himself.

Fabric after fabric was spread before him, and Andrew who had handled endless numbers of sheep was fascinated to see the end product. The tailor responded to his interest,

"One cannot surpass John Crombie's products Sir! The wool is of the finest... and he also has exceptional cashmere, perfect for a waistcoat... Perhaps matching Sir's frock coat... One would always wear the coat open... though perhaps Sir would prefer a contrasting waistcoat? A stripe perhaps?"

Nicholas interrupted

"Well in this weather... I rather think a *silk* waistcoat would be more the thing".

Mr Beaumont, anxious as ever to please his long-lost customer, agreed.

"It has certainly been *excessively* hot Sir, but *June* was worse! Everyday up to ninety degrees and *not even* cooling in the evening... No respite... It was quite a disaster for business."

Andrew was surprised.

"Does it really get that hot... I am amazed..."

Mr Beaumont continued.

"It was the *most* unpleasantly hot weather *anyone* could remember... And it continues... We are into July."

Nicholas interrupted.

"Well we *are* in "The Season." The tailor laughed rather more than necessary at the little joke, as Nicholas added. "Yes. Well my young friend will need some suitable clothes but he is also destined for Scotland."

Mr Beaumont was ready with more advice.

"How fortunate Sir! Tartan and plaid are *quite* the rage! You must know His Royal Highness has designed a Royal Tartan. Do *you*, yourself have a family connection in the north? It is very desirable to have one's own clan tartan."

Andrew's eyes met Nicholas' with some alarm but his voice was expressionless as he replied.

"No unfortunately... Rather..."

Nicholas intervened.

"Checks are quite the thing are they not? And he will need a warm cloak and... well an elegant one for evening?"

"Fair Go Nick, I'll make a cake of myself."

Mr Beaumont disagreed.

"Sir could wear one with great flair. In fact Sir could wear *anything* with Sir's proportions." Andrew retreated. The order was finalized and he was left to wonder how he would ever repay Nicholas. It was beyond his reckoning.

Andrew's physique may have met with unqualified approval from the enthusiastic Mr Beaumont and his minions. It was another matter entirely when Nicholas escorted him into his favourite barbershop... the immensely fashionable "Truefitt and Hill" frequented by the 'haut ton' and Royalty.

"To achieve a *fashionable* side parting will be *rather* difficult Mr Manners. We can do our best but the young gentleman's hair... well... one hesitates to say..." The barber was downcast. Nicholas came to his rescue.

"Unruly! Precisely! But I have every confidence in your skill. We know you will devise a solution."

Andrew sat mute while he was shaved, shampooed, trimmed and generally attacked. He emerged eventually from the snow-storm of foam, clean-shaven with substantial sideburns and the semblance of the desirable side part.

"I daresay you enjoyed that as much as the infernal measuring." Andrew grumbled, but Nicholas was unrepentant.

"You cut a dash Drew so stop complaining. I'm not introducing you into Society looking like 'the wild colonial boy'!"

"Are you meant to breathe in those jackets? People 'll think I'm trying to ape those dandies you hear about."

Nicholas guffawed.

"Never! Though I don't doubt they'll try to *ape* you. Just you watch. There'll be padding right, left and centre!" He tried to divert his companion but they were almost out of Regent St before Andrew noticed the awnings and changed the subject himself.

"By Jove... I just realized we are walking under that glass roof. Very smart. Nice change from the metal ones we have at home..." His good humour was restored and Nicholas forgiven. They arrived back in Grosvenor St on their usual good terms, though when he removed his smart new top hat, Andrew's hair had reverted to nature, and the humidity had destroyed the desirable side part already.

Nevertheless their hostess was pleased to see improvements.

"My word Nicholas you *have* been busy... Mr Walters looks *very* fashionable." Lady Spencer smiled benevolently on her visitor.

Andrew blushingly tried to thank her.

"Thank you Lady... Helen, I mean Lady... Spencer... I mean Lady... Madam..."

"Just as I thought. You may call me Lady Helen, which I confess is *not* strictly as it should be but you *are* family now, but in general you would call me Lady Spencer. Your sister's mother-in-law will always be Lady Manners, however, and though Sister Jane is the wife of an earl she will probably tell you to call her Jane, *but* I should begin with Lady Manners also."

Andrew had, during the conversation moved with his hostess into the Drawing Room but he stood, waiting to be instructed, unsure even if it were polite to take a seat as his instructress had already done. Nicholas had disappeared. What should he do?

"You may take a seat." The decision was made for him. "Would you care to sit here?" invited Lady Helen. She patted the chair next to her own, clearly so that he could continue his schooling under her sharp eye. "Now we will begin with the Royals, "Your Majesty", "Your Royal Highness", " Your Highness" are *essential* on introduction after which "Ma'am" and "Sir" will suffice. Likewise Duke or Duchess for example, of Bedford, on first introduction, you should use "Your Grace" as you would to an Archbishop." She paused for breath briefly, while Andrew tried to absorb it all. "Most of the rest you can call "Lord" though a peer who is not a duke you should call "My Lord". There are *far* too many people who liked to be called Lord for *no* real reason." She shrugged resignedly. "So many Pumpkins appearing out of nowhere... money speaks volumes I'm afraid." As she spoke Nicholas and Emily joined them and her eldest son wondered into the room.

"Hello All. And what is my venerable mother complaining about now?" but his words were softened by the affectionate kiss he gave her.

"Now that's enough Simon. I am *simply* trying to help Emily's brother understand the intricacies of society."

Simon pulled a face,

"Good luck Old Fellow. It's *crazy*, especially these days. Can't make head nor tail, especially now we have the coal barons and the railway chaps. Used to only be the Nabobs out of India we had to look out for." He slumped into his chair. "Devilish propriety!"

His mother smiled indulgently but she had not finished.

"Exactly. We now have an *excess* of respectability. I have a great deal of nostalgia for George and his execrable brothers. Instead we have Victoria, and her German spouse, so *engrossed* in matrimony and breeding, we are *all* being confined to *total* boredom. It is all the fault of these middle classes. They ape their betters, or so they think. What do we have as a result... toffee nosed upstarts pressing their Methodist Morality on us all!" Nicholas had arrived in time to enjoy this diatribe. There was general laughter but Lady Helen was not silenced. "You *may* laugh! The fact remains we *all* need to conform, at least when we go to Buckingham Palace!" Nicholas began to remonstrate but he was cut short. Lady Spencer intended the last word. " There is a State Ball at Buckingham Palace to which, quite naturally we are *all invited*. It is very regrettable that you have arrived well into the Season, so *many* opportunities lost." She sighed resignedly. "But we make do with what remains and *this* will suffice nicely to introduce you. The Queen is *very* partial to Balls-she even has children's balls, which my children, Harriet and Jane, say are *very* jolly!" She returned to her main subject. "And you Mr Walters may *look* beautiful but you are *still* a barbarian! Goodness gracious did you not meet *any* titled people in that wild place?"

Andrew began to excuse himself,

"Well Lady Helen, we have The Governor... 'His Excellency' but for the rest they are generally soldiers..."

Nicholas interrupted.

"Of course Dear Nell, there *are* more titled people than we know... because they are generally 'the black sheep' of their families who are paid by said families to stay far away, and be as *anonymous* as possible! There are a few, shall we say, people with pretensions of grandeur who would like to invent a new aristocracy, but generally speaking it is all... well Dear Nell, I think you would find it very confusing."

Lady Spencer frowned.

"Do you mean to say people *don't know their* place?" Nicholas shrugged as he replied more gently.

"It is a new society Nell, and people are generally *finding* their place. For example, there are those who try to ignore ex-convicts, but since many of those chaps, and indeed females, have become *very* wealthy it makes it difficult in business. And in the bush, the countryside I mean, well that is another matter. It can be hard and dangerous, so you really have to take people as you find them... especially if you need their help!"

Lady Spencer sighed.

"I *cannot* begin to understand..." She looked momentarily lost for words but it was only for the moment. She had a project and it was her Beautiful Barbarian. Clearly Nicholas' lovely wife was at home in Society, but her brother... *that* was another matter. She returned to her tutelage with renewed enthusiasm. "Now Andrew, when you go to dinner you must wait for your hostess to tell you *which* lady will take your arm, and *where* you will sit. After, of course, you have assisted your lady. In general, in Society, the gentlemen will remain at the table for port and the ladies will retire to..."

Andrew's muttered "God Almighty" was clearly not quite quiet enough. He was sharply rebuked.

"Don't *blaspheme* young Man!"

"Dear Madam", he bowed his head in apology. "I was simply asking Hughie's help."

She laughed gently and patted his hand.

"Now, Now. It is not that bad and you will always have help at hand... Though *who* on earth is Hughie?" Just at that moment the clocks struck. "Goodness me is *that* the time? I will be late for dinner." Andrew's instructions were abandoned as the lady hurried away to change.

Chapter 8

Caitlyn stared at the little flame. It was the only light. Blackness surrounded her. She was dry and warm but so, so hungry. She fondled the little pebble in her apron pocket. How long ago had she had found it? How long ago had she laughed and played beside the loch? The world of light and colour, the clear cold water, the familiar smell of heather, now all was black here in this strange place, and even when she ventured out it was all grey and dreary.

The flickering light played across her grandmother's bent and crippled hands. The sturdy centre of their lives was broken and weak. Her beloved Neanaidh could no longer go out and find work, earn money, find food. For many months she had toiled, at the time in her life which should have been quiet and comfortable. Caitlyn knew that there was only one person left who could help them all now. She herself would needst find them something to eat. Her tummy rumbled as if in agreement. The once happy little boys lay prone next to their grandmother. The life was seeping out of them all. Their once sparkling blue eyes were dull, their cheeks sunken, their lips cracked.

It had all been so exciting when they reached Inverness. She could not begin to count the bustling people hurrying about, but for all that, they looked familiar, dressed in their plaid. And the voices too, and the words, were familiar. In this dark place she could not understand the words, nothing was familiar. And Dadaidh, there was always Dadaidh, to care for them, get their food, a bed, a place on the boat... 'the packet' he called it. She let herself remember walking over the great bridge... and when they stood on the other side, on the edge of that great river, the bridge's arc and their reflections had made perfect circles in the water.

Then there'd been Leith... more ships, hundreds, big and small. There were many people too, just as in Inverness, but these were different. The sailors who wore trews made of stiff white material. Perhaps that was why they walked in that strange way with their legs apart, stomping along, so unlike her light footed Dadaidh. And then there were the women trudging up the steep hill with the baskets of fresh fish every day.

They had travelled to the cottage of Dadaidh's brother, a rough wooden place, not neat and tidy and white-washed as her home had been. Uncle Bill was much older than Dadaidh but always cheerful and happy... not like his wife "besom" Dadaidh called her. She was *always* complaining and she *never* smiled. But there had been a room in the roof... 'the attic' they called it. Her grandmother had found the narrow winding staircase very hard. Dadaidh had found work somewhere among all those boats. Her only worry had been to stop Fergus and Finlay from falling into the sea, or getting lost among all the boats and strange people.

Where had Dadaidh gone?! Why had he gone without a word! And Uncle Bill too. One day the house was bursting with their talking and laughing and singing. Then nothing! Silence, except for Aunt Agnes scolding and snapping, shouting at the boys, banging her pots. How *could* they go away and leave them? And why both at once? If they had drowned... no the other fishermen would have known... though she heard the strange word 'pressgang' but no-one told her what it meant.

After one of Aunt Agnes' screaming diatribes, Neanaidh had suddenly bundled them all, and as many of their belongings as she could, and brought them up the steep hill, to this place of dark stones and great buildings; to the black cobblestones leading to that great castle. Even the people were dark... so many men in black robes, heads bent, never smiling, never stopping.

The pain in her stomach was sharper than ever. What could she do? Could she leave Neanaidh to care for the boys here, deep under the streets? Surely it would be good to take them into the light... perhaps there would even be sunshine. She could take them, but that left her grandmother alone here in the dark, and *she* could barely move.

When they first came to this place Neanaidh had found work in one of those tall houses. She had washed dishes and pots and pans. She could buy food for them. Sometimes even some special scraps from the tall house, but now her hands were bent and crooked. She could no longer hold things or scrub them. Caitlyn glanced down at her own hands. They were straight and strong.

She roused the boys. They stumbled and whimpered as she held them tight and made her way through all the dark winding spaces; past the old man with no teeth whose snoring kept her awake at night; past the woman who cried all day sitting on her battered chair that had once been covered in silk, its shreds dangling around her torn dress. In one room off the long passage, stood a great bed, with curtains that hung to the floor. Who was behind those curtains? Or was it empty? Beside it, stood a polished wooden table, all carved and shining, and two chairs. It would be so good to have a chair like that for Neanaidh instead of the creepie, which was so low that she could not get down to it anymore! By now the light had started to seep into the passage. Now she could see more and more furniture. Out of the corner of her eye she could see people dressed in warm clothing, and her tummy pangs increased as she smelt food cooking.

At last they stepped through the opening into the narrow alleyway, but the air was still heavy and foetid... nothing like the smell of her silvery loch and wild heather. The boys stumbled and cried, rubbing their eyes, fretting at too much brightness. Nevertheless she dragged them up the slope until they stood at the entrance to their narrow path. In front of her was a great street full of bustle and movement.

She pressed against the stone wall of the nearest building trying to feel the faint warmth from the weak sun. The boys had ceased their crying and were staring wide-eyed at this new world. It was then she realised her mistake. She could not go to any of those houses with two bairns in tow. Across the wide road she could just see what looked like a pool of water. At least she could sponge their faces and tidy herself. She waited, heart thumping for a chance to cross. The road was wide, but because it sloped so much the horses and carriages kept to the centre. Taking her chance she ran as fast as she could while dragging two small boys.

They made it. She leant against a railing to catch her breath. Then she realised there was no pool. It was a large puddle where the rain had been trapped! Undeterred she dipped her grubby apron into the water and gently scrubbed Finlay's face and then Fergus', and finally her own face and hands. The sun was dipping but it still shone where they were, so she tucked the boys beside her as far back as she could from the hurly burly of hurrying feet, scraping wheels, and the clatter of horses hooves on the hard stone.

A flapping black robe paused and a white hand dropped a coin into her lap. Then a lady's head, in an enormous bonnet, came through the window of a big box two men were carrying on poles. The lady called to one of the men and gave him a small pouch, which he promptly dropped into Caitlyn's lap. She jumped up clutching her spoils and dropped a curtsy to her benefactor. Fergus promptly copied her and she realized she would need to teach the boys to bow. They settled back, but no-one else dropped anything into her lap. The sun was disappearing. She gathered the boys and once again risked their lives weaving through the traffic.

With great excitement she placed the pouch and the coin into her Grandmother's twisted hands.

"And *where* did this come from? *Whatever* did you do?" Her grandmother's voice was anxious, frightened, almost angry. Caitlyn did her best to explain.

"Och Lass! I would that we had not come to this but... well this is a gift... you can go and buy some bread at last. I've no way to cook aught, but it is a blessing that, at least for a wee while we will have something in our stomachs."

Despite her grandmother's misgivings Caitlyn began to venture out almost every day, and, almost always she and the boys collected coins. She tried to think of better ways to make money but at least this way was helping.

Two new people moved into their alcove... a man and a woman. Neanaidh soon discovered they were brother and sister, although their matching ginger hair and blue eyes were clues enough. The man, Gordon, had a bushy beard and long hair he tied with a leather thong, while the woman had a heavy plait she wrapped around her head. Much to Fergus' and Finlay's fascination the man had only one leg. In place of the other one he had a wooden stick. He wasn't very good at walking on it, and so he had another, longer one that he put under his arm and leant on. The woman, Annie, came and went most days, but she only occasionally stayed the night. It took a few days before their grandmother discovered that the young woman was a maid in one of the really grand houses. The man was a fisherman who had very recently, lost his leg and come to his sister to recover. The boys became firm friends with their one-legged companion, and even began to learn to talk to him in his own language. He was from Newhaven, which was near Leith, and so was able to keep the boys enthralled with stories of weird fish and terrible storms.

Even for Caitlyn, life suddenly seemed less dark. She tried manfully with the help of Neanaidh and Annie to learn this strange language. Annie was always full of encouragement. Gordon, for his part, soon learned to walk more steadily so that he was able to help her take Neanaidh through the dark winding passage into the light. They would leave her sitting on a creepie stool sometimes even in the sun, but Caitlyn's own stomach was often empty so she continued to brave the busy road and find a place to sit in the sun with her brothers. Most days she was rewarded with a few coins, which helped to keep them alive, but her stomach ached for real food just as her heart ached for her old life.

And then one day a giant came and saved them all.

Chapter 9

It was a pleasant morning, the sun had warmth, the breeze was light and the sounds and smells of a crowded city had not yet crept into Lady Spencer's garden. Andrew, having survived the rigours of his first real dose of Society was feeling quietly pleased with himself. As far as he could tell his tutor had approved of his behaviour. Certainly there had been no complaint as she had smiled benignly and even patted his hand.

"Well Good Morning Sis! I didn't expect to see you out and about so early!" Emily smiled half-heartedly as her brother settled himself beside her on the garden seat." Quite a 'do' last night. Such a squeeze. Apparently the more crowded the more successful! Not entirely comfortable was it, but jolly good fun. All those chaps laden with medals and gold trimmings. Can't imagine how they ever fight in battle!"

Emily raised her eyebrows.

"Surely they wear something less dazzling?"

Andrew frowned thoughtfully as he replied.

"Not sure, to be frank. Anyway so much to see! All those paintings! And the supper was jolly good. Mirrors and candles everywhere! Met so many I can't imagine I'll remember them or who they are in the scheme of things." He chuckled. "Just need to smile and hope... though doubtless her ladyship will set me to rights!"

For the first time he looked directly at his sister.

"What's the matter? Why are you sitting out here instead of breakfasting in, as all the married ladies do... or so I'm told." He frowned "Didn't you enjoy yourself? I thought you looked smashing! As far as I'm concerned... belle of the ball!"

Emily hugged his arm.

"You are kind Dearest! But it was all rather... well Nicholas has so many friends... I... well... there were a few times when I wondered... I had to wonder if he remembered I was there..." She sat twisting her handkerchief into tighter and tighter knots.

"Of course he remembered. Looked jolly proud when the Queen asked for you to be presented... and your curtsy was spot on Old Thing. Didn't slip or wobble like some of them. And the Prince looked very happy to see you." Emily blushed. "Come to think of it you know... I thought Nick was just an ordinary bloke with a bit of money." He chuckled again. "Instead he knows every Lord and Duke in England and even the Queen and her husband!" He shook his head. "Makes you wonder why he... well I mean why he wants to stay in our country... I wonder if they all know..." He felt his sister flinch so tried valiantly to change the subject. "Yes all very exciting for a couple of colonials! Eh?"

"Yes it was exciting... but if Simon Spencer had not been there... he was very kind..."

"Don't be a goose Sis. He was very pleased to have the loveliest lady to look after..." His sister's head was bent and he realised she was trying to hide her tears.

"What's wrong? Come on Sis. What..."

There was no reply as Emily almost ran back through the garden and disappeared, leaving her brother completely nonplussed. It was at luncheon before he saw her again and she seemed her usual self, though suddenly more conscious, he wondered if her smile looked forced. He shrugged to himself... perhaps she was overtired.

The conversation was as usual commanded by Lady Spencer, and centred on the triumphs of her charges and the "bon mots" she had gleaned.

"I must say My Dears, so many people wanted to know who you both were. You looked quite charming Emily and sooo elegant! I'm glad we settled on the cream and that gold lace is quite exquisite. You must agree Nicholas she looked quite delightful." Before her brother could reply she was onto her favourite subject. "And of course since our Beautiful Barbarian stood above the throng he sent many a lady's heart fluttering I can tell you!" She barely paused for breath, oblivious of Andrew's face, the colour of which now, as usual, matched his hair. The family laughingly agreed until Nicholas came to his rescue.

"Come now Dear Sister, you are embarrassing him. Though I daresay when you tower above everyone..."

"I don't tower! Plenty of those chaps in the guards are tall and the footmen, and you Nicholas..." Andrew was indignant but his brother-in-law laughed.

"I can see we will need to set you to work otherwise this will all go to your head! Seriously Old Chap. We've missed the early race meetings, but we've got Newmarket and Goodwood, and of course King George's Day at Ascot! We need to study the form. I've "Bell's Life" and the "Sunday Times" but always better to see them in the flesh."

"Shame you missed the Derby!" Simon was keen to show his knowledge. "Pyrrhus the First was first class." He smiled but his mother only pursed her lips at his attempted pun.

"Really Simon! Well if you young men are going to devote yourself to the Turf, I'm sure Emily and I can find *better* entertainment."

Simon looked ruefully at his mother.

"But it was in all the papers... and someone even wrote a poem,

"Aloft on circling wing, the feathered heralds spring", You are always suggesting I read more..."

"I hardly suggest a poem about a horse race is Literature Simon!"

"Well I thought it rather good..."Simon continued,

'How Mr Gully takes as his own the Derby Stakes
And Pyrrhus is the first in fact as well as name!"

Nicholas laughed despite his sister.

"Hidden talents our Simon. But the breeding... who is the stallion?"

"Epirus, who won twelve races himself and..."

Nicholas interrupted.

"Who was the mare?"

"Fortress... unraced." Simon's tone was dismissive but Nicholas had other ideas.

"The mare is *just* as important you know."

"Well I *certainly* would agree with that." Lady Helen nodded as she gathered herself and Emily and headed for the door. "Come My Dear. We have more to do than listen to all this, though *for once* you are speaking sense Nicholas."

Emily's silence during the meal had not escaped her hostess' notice. As they walked up the stairs she took the younger woman's arm.

"Now Emily you don't appear to be in such high spirits as one would expect after your *wonderful* 'debut'! You looked lovely and seemed to be having a pleasant time... why the long face?"

Emily tried to disagree.

"Of course I had a lovely time. And Simon was so kind... looking after me when he surely would have preferred..."

"Well of course, no doubt he was *very* happy to take care of you, but one would have *thought* my brother should have done that!" By now they were settled in Lady Spencer's own elegant sitting room. Emily managed to sit in the shadow, hoping it would help to hide her feelings. Lady Helen, however, was not so easily fooled.

"Nicholas has so many friends... and naturally after all this time... eager to talk." She tried to keep the catch out of her voice. "Of course people are glad to see him." She paused. "And several of the ladies too..."

"Oh! I expect you mean that rather overdressed blonde woman in that quite *unseemly* red taffeta." A disapproving look passed over her Ladyship's face. "Always rather too inclined to make herself the centre of attention, our dear Lady Shillingworth! But why do you ask My Dear?"

Emily tried very hard to sound nonchalant.

"It was just that I was waiting for Simon to collect some punch... and," She smiled apologetically, "I had sat on a sofa, just for a moment..."

Lady Helen was quite understanding,

"*Such* a squeeze! I *envy* you finding somewhere to rest...but go on."

"Well to be perfectly honest Lady Helen, I was finding it so hard to talk to most of the ladies as they barely came up to my chin and I couldn't hear their conversation. Well there was already someone else on the sofa... a very short lady... in mauve I think... with a peacock feather in her hair... rather prominent..."

Lady Helen's voice was disdainful.

"You mean short and fat and squinty-eyed, looking a *complete* fright with that great decoration sprouting out of her mousey curls. Mary Underwood as I live and breathe... and what pray did *she* have to say?"

"Well Nicholas was quite nearby in a group," Emily began diffidently, "and the blonde-haired lady was leaning on his arm rather... affectionately... of course the lady on the sofa did not quite realise who I was... she remarked... well she said..."

"*Go on!*" It was a command.

"She said it was *such* a shame Manners had been snapped up by some colonial fortune hunter, when Dear Barbara Shillingworth had practically been engaged to him, and didn't they make such a handsome couple." Emily took a deep breath. "She naturally didn't mean to upset me but... I can't help wondering if Nicholas... well..."

Lady Helen was incensed.

"Of course she *knew* who you were... are! *Nasty little piece.* Always has been. *Her* problem is she has three daughters who all look like their mother and are *spotty* to boot!" She laughed derisively, "And she practically threw them under Nicky's feet. What a nasty mean-spirited little toad. *Leave her to me* My Dear." Lady Helen's eyes narrowed. "Yes you just leave her to me!" She patted Emily's hand. "And as for his choice-I admit I was surprised... we all were... when he wrote to say he was married... but well Spencer was remarking only just yesterday what a *godsend* you are. Nicholas is so settled... so mature. He was always so wild and reckless. We all think he is a *very* lucky man." She dropped a kiss on Emily's cheek. "Half of England thought they were practically engaged to my brother, and he cared not a jot for *any* of them for more than *five* minutes let me tell you!" She settled back in her chair. "The pity is, we have only a few more chances to show you off before the Season ends. We will all be at Mannering for Christmas of course but we should arrange..."

Emily interrupted diffidently.

"We, Nicholas, Andrew and I, and Baby James naturally, have been invited to visit an old friend, well in fact I was her Governess. She has an Estate in the North... I think Leicestershire, well her husband has, and she was anxious... she mentioned it last night...

she is very desirous of our visiting for a week or two. Would that be suitable? I mean would it inconvenience you Lady Helen?"

"Do you mean the Countess of Mulray? *Of course* she is a fellow countrywoman! But I did not realise you were acquainted... By all means. It would be very pleasant for you. But do you think your husband and brother will be able to *tear* themselves away from the wretched horses?"

"Well I mentioned it to Nicholas and he seemed agreeable. Apparently some sort of Hunting is on offer."

"Of course, now I think on it, her husband the Earl is reputed to have extensive grounds and a well-known Hunt. *No wonder* he agreed!" She took a deep breath. "Well we shall need to organize some suitable additions to your wardrobe and of course order warm clothes for when we go further north to Mannering. Come on My Dear, I think we should send for the dressmakers." The bell was rung. Her ladyship had a new project.

Chapter 10

"I thought I should go and see your chap about a great-coat-or whatever I need. Though it is so damned hot hard to imagine one could need it." Andrew was enjoying his usual hearty breakfast despite the heaviness of the weather. Through the tall parlour windows a humid haze was blocking the sun, but it was oppressive nonetheless.

"Not a pleasant day to be out unnecessarily Young Fellow," Sir Peter glanced up from his 'Times', " do you need to venture out today?" He smiled thinly. "Though perhaps we should blame you people for bringing the heat with you!"

His son intervened to defend the guests.

"It was unseasonably hot in June, Papa, and they *hadn't* even arrived!"

"Just so. I stand corrected." Sir Peter returned to his paper.

Andrew was unperturbed as he tried to ease the tension between father and son.

"Well whether we brought it or not, it is really no worse than our summer. Are you engaged Nick? Do you think Mr Beaumont will look after me without his favourite client?"

Nicholas laughed.

"He could hardly forget you Old Chap. If you can manage alone, Sister Helen has arranged for me to take Emily and herself to visit some relatives."

Andrew pulled a face.

"Well I think I may need to disappear before she thinks to include Yours Truly!"

Sir Peter interjected with mock severity,

"Now Young Man we must *all* do our duty." But his quizzical eyebrow belied his words.

Nevertheless it was well after one before Andrew left Grosvenor Place. He had barely walked more than a few paces before he began to have misgivings. A cotton shirt and a 'cabbage tree' hat were far more suitable in the heat than his frock coat and top hat. By the time he reached Regent Street, he even began to have doubts about his favourite glass awnings, as they seemed to only increase the glare. He was very glad to enter the darkened oak lined chambers of the tailor. His welcome was just as warm as the heat that followed him into the rooms. He dallied much longer than necessary, enjoying the relief from the heat and the pleasant company, who seemed most interested in New South Wales.

Eventually he stepped into the street. He glanced up. The sun had thoroughly disappeared. For the moment he was relieved until he saw the peculiar green tinge in the cloud. Clearly a storm was coming! He could see that the streets were strangely quiet. There were few carriages and even fewer pedestrians.

The storm, however, was closer than he realised. Thunder, lightning, slashing rain. He turned to find shelter and as he did he heard screams. Two women were huddled together in an open landau. Its two horses were rearing and squealing, tipping it up and down as the women were thrown around inside. The coach-man and footman were in a jumbled mess on the road, trying to scramble to their feet. Andrew ran forward and grabbed the flapping reins, then the bridle of the nearest steed. His weight slowed it momentarily but though he dug in his heels he was dragged along. He threw himself onto its back and managed to settle astride it and reach over and seize the other reins. His arms were wrenching but the horses sensed his firm hand. He leant forward and tried to soothe their terror. They settled enough for the coachman to scramble onto his perch, though they snorted and trembled. Between them Andrew managed to transfer the reins. By now hail was smashing down on all of them. Andrew dismounted and turned back to the carriage. The footman had managed to open the half door and was trying to coax the stricken females to jump. Andrew lifted one clean out of the carriage and her companion followed half carried by the footman. They headed into the nearest doorway just as Andrew heard the glass awnings begin to crack and shatter. The landau and its driver disappeared into the storm.

The owner of the shop hurriedly opened the door and bustled them inside, where his wife began immediately to help the two women. Sodden bonnets were removed and the drenched females were wrapped in dry shawls. Andrew leant against the door trying to get his breath back. The footman huddled beside him frightened and forlorn.

"I'm so sorry M'Lady! It 'appened so quick! We was thrown clear orf! I'm sorry M'Lady!"

The younger woman, almost a girl Andrew realised, smiled through her tears and bedraggled hair.

"Of course it was an accident! *Please* don't fret. No one could have known the storm would come so suddenly." She turned to Andrew. "But you Sir! We must *all* thank you! You saved us all! You were *so* brave! Wasn't he Martha... so brave!"

Andrew returned her smile though he was still trying to wipe his face. He could scrape the water off his shoulders with his hand he was so thoroughly soaked.

"Not at all Miss! Not at all. Poor horses were terrified! What a cataclysm!" He peered through the doorway but could see nothing through the white blanket of rain and hail. He focused on the shopkeeper. "Must thank *you* Sir! We burst in on you and drenched your floor and I'm afraid we may have to impose on you for some time yet."

Two hours passed before there was any sign of a break in the storm. The shopkeeper and his wife did their best to make the unexpected guests comfortable. The ladies settled in for a nice chat with their hostess, while Andrew tried to take the stricken footman's mind off his fate, by discussing with their host, the merits of his stock and the state of the market. It was very heavy going. All parties were clearly relieved when the break came.

"I think Sir I should go myself to the ladies 'ouse, Stafford 'ouse I means." His voice was anxious but determined. "I can tell 'em the ladies be safe an' we can find a conveyance to 'ave them 'ome safe?"

Andrew was quick to agree.

"I think that would be the go Mate! If you think you can manage. If the ladies agree I'll wait here until someone comes. Would that be suitable Ma'am, with you?"

The footman departed and Andrew followed him outside. As he stepped into the street his boots crunched on the hailstones and shattered glass. Whatever conveyance arrived, the ladies would need to be carried to it. He would certainly need to wait.

Mid-winter had descended on London. The hail lay thick on the ground and weighed down trees and rooves. Drains overflowed. The roadway was a fast moving torrent. It was not only the elegant awning that had disappeared. Everywhere he looked windows were shattered. A handful of souls emerged, black figures against their white world. He returned to the shop and tried to make comforting small talk though he felt stunned by it all.

◆ ◆ ◆

At dinner there was only one topic of conversation. Sir Peter, having been in the government office was the main authority.

"It is quite severe *everywhere*! The Houses of Parliament had thousands of panels of the old crown glass smashed... the rough estimate is 6-7,000. And Buckingham Palace hasn't escaped. A skylight in the Picture Gallery broke. Within the hour the water was several feet deep!

"Oh No! *All those paintings!*" Emily was aghast

"Yes... Cuyp, Parmigianino, Steer... not to mention the Van Dykes! But not to worry Emily, My Dear, the staff were magnificent!" He frowned and shook his head. "We've estimated over one hundred thousand pounds worth of glass alone! The Burlington Arcade say they lost almost three thousand windows and skylights!"

The family shook their heads. Andrew added his voice.

"Well I'm afraid those elegant glass awnings in Regent Street are no more! I was walking on what was left of them."

Nicholas interrupted cheerfully.

"Yes. Well fortunately Sister we decided to stay quietly at home," He glanced at his wife. "and it was as well we did, James' nurse had hysterics."

Emily's voice was relieved.

"Well not *quite* hysterics, but we certainly did not want James to be frightened." She glanced affectionately at her husband. "Nicholas was *very* clever. He made it all very exciting." Andrew was pleased to see his sister's usual good humour was restored.

Simon, ever keen to impress his austere father, felt he should have his own contribution.

"Apparently a steamer on the Thames was struck by lightning!" There was general consternation.

"Was anyone injured?" His mother asked anxiously.

"Well not badly apparently but I heard four reapers in a meadow... I'm not sure where... were struck by the lightning and killed. Doubtless their scythes would have attracted it!"

"Oh Dear! We can only hope there are no *other* tragedies," Lady Helen was concerned, although she liked to avoid frowning, wrinkles were so aging!

Sir Peter tried to reassure her,

"Well I feel we seem to be relatively fortunate. I haven't heard of any further fatalities."

Lady Helen's usual equanimity returned.

"Well I am relieved, though no doubt 'The Illustrated London News' will have a picnic! They *love* a disaster!" She turned to Andrew. "I understand *you* were out in it Young Man? I think you should have spared us the anxiety!"

Andrew was very repentant.

"Yes Your Ladyship, I confess I was. I'm very sorry if I caused anyone concern... but I found shelter and felt it safer to stay out of it all."

Sir Peter nodded his approval,

"Naturally, sound common sense Young Man, only reasonable option."

It wasn't until the next day that the real reason for Andrew's prolonged absence came to light. At breakfast Nicholas, Andrew and Simon pored over the "Illustrated News" while Sir Peter, as usual, studied "The Times".

"Hmmm... here's something *rather* interesting!" He paused waiting for an audience before he began to read aloud. "During yesterday's maelstrom, the lives of two ladies belonging to the family of one of our country's esteemed peers, were saved from almost certain death, by the heroic efforts of a stranger. The ladies were caught by the sudden onslaught of the storm. It terrified the horses attached to their open landau. In their frenzy the driver and footman were unseated and the carriage was tossed about like a boat in the wild ocean. Our unknown hero rushed to the rescue. Unable to subdue the horses by securing the reins, in a rare feat of horsemanship he mounted the lead horse and managed to quieten the beasts. Then with the aid of the footman, who had recovered from his fall, they were able to carry the ladies to temporary shelter. Adversity brought out the best in our unknown rescuer, an example to all."

Simon, especially was deeply impressed.

"By Jove! *Fancy* being able to do *that*! A bucking terrified horse! *Who* could do such a thing!?"

Neither Nicholas nor Andrew commented but Nicholas gave his brother-in-law a long measuring look. His suspicions were confirmed, when shortly after, a footman arrived carrying a letter he insisted on delivering to the "red-haired gen'lman hisself".

Simms, the formidable Butler, was unimpressed. The footman was confined to the tradesman's entrance but doggedly maintained his mission. Eventually a message was conveyed to Sir Peter.

"It would appear Andrew that there is a strange individual below stairs who *insists* on speaking to you, and you alone. Can I trouble you to go and sort it out. Apparently even the indomitable Simms is flummoxed!"

Very reluctantly Andrew agreed to collect the letter. He was greeted with great enthusiasm by his companion from the previous day, now restored to his liveried glory.

"Well Guv, and now I *knows* who it was what saved *all* our bacons!" He glanced at the haughty Simms as he continued. "I 'ad to deliver the message so's is Lordship could be sure we 'ad the right cove!" He turned his attention to the gathering throng of staff. " Youse 'ad better know, this 'ere cove is a *right* 'ero! A right proper one!" He bowed low over Andrew's outstretched hand as he delivered the letter. "It is my *great* privilege to 'ave met you Sir!"

Andrew fled with the letter and tried to think how he could avoid returning to the breakfast parlour, but decided eventually there was no escape.

"I *knew* it was you! *You* were in Regent St? I've seen you do that before today, but a stampeding horse! That is something else!" He clapped his embarrassed relative on his broad shoulder. "I just knew it *had* to be you!"

Even Sir Peter was impressed.

"By Jove! How could you manage in *that* storm!"

Simon was awe struck.

"What a *cracking* rider you must be? How long have you... I mean how could... Holy Cow what a feat!"

Andrew tried to reply.

"It was not so hard. Really. I've been astride horses all my life." He appealed to his brother-in-law. "Nick knows. Plenty of stock need... well the poor animals were terrified." He tried to divert attention by passing the letter to his host.

"Are these people you know Sir Peter?"

Sir Peter chuckled.

"My Dear Chap, the *whole world* knows "these people" as you call them. The Duke is one of the richest men in England... in fact his father was reputed to be *the* richest man in Europe."

"And the Duchess is Mistress of Robes to our Queen." Lady Helen breathlessly interrupted. "You say the girl was quite young... she may be a granddaughter perhaps... The Duchess is regarded as the *epitome* of elegance. She has a maid whose sole duty is to set out the duchess' outfits for each day so that it is co-ordinated... matching even to the smallest piece of jewellery." Lady Helen sighed. "And she has *always* looked so beautiful!"

"Well Ma'am, the letter contains an invitation for you, my sister, Nick and Sir Peter, or should I say The Honourable Nicholas Manners Esq, to have dinner at Stafford House on Friday." He raised an eyebrow. "I'd hope Ma'am you won't cry off. I will need to make sure I am behaving as you would approve."

Lady Helen smiled benignly,

"*You* My Beautiful Barbarian are the 'hero of the hour'. We *bask* in your glory. I will be quite unnecessary, but will be by your side notwithstanding!"

Chapter 11

Andrew was angry. Exactly who he was angry with, he hadn't completely decided. He just felt generally annoyed. Of course there was his sister? He tried to remember if Emily had actually *told* him. Or Nick? They had certainly talked about "the Hunt" and the horses and... Perhaps he hadn't listened or perhaps he hadn't connected... but certainly his anger was focussed on one person in particular... the young girl whose beauty had taken his breath away at first sight. She was now a polished gem, glittering at home in her luxurious surroundings. He could remember all too vividly the bedraggled nurse who had tended his burns. The wound on his shoulder was healed but it still burned him. He stared across the immaculate garden. Well she had done well... Very well! The house... did you call it a house? Well, whatever it was, it was enormous by any standards. And she was its queen and very pleased with it all, and herself. But how could she be? Did she not care that her husband was twice... almost three times her own age? He seemed a reasonable bloke, self-opinionated and rather boring but *very* hospitable. He's showered us with entertainments. But after four days Andrew's teeth were on edge. It was fine when he and Nick and The Earl, Torquil Mulray, were out fishing or riding, but there were times when Her Ladyship insisted on coming. And she always managed to goad him... to challenge his horsemanship while pretending to admire it! Well perhaps he was imagining that... but the evenings! They were a nightmare! How she could turn the conversation so adroitly, he had no idea, but a succession of guests were her audience as she teased him, and revealed his ignorance of the world and the "haut ton" as she called it! Whatever the Hell that is?

His eyes wandered around his bedroom. It was enormous. Here in front of the fire was a settee and chairs. He poked at the coals and they blazed along with his fury. The self-satisfied little... He glanced at his slippered feet as he settled back into one of the leather chairs... admit it though..., he smiled ruefully to himself, you are enjoying some parts of this life. His new boots were mirror like. His immaculate clothes appeared like magic... The inimitable Forbes was a marvel. He wondered idly if he could use a valet at home... Poor Forbes! He would probably die of shock.

The sound of a doorknob turning interrupted his thoughts. The rustle of silk. Even in the dim light he recognized her immediately. He stared, the poker still in his hand.

"What the devil!" A slim finger over her lips motioned him to silence.

She floated across the room as she whispered,

"Sssh! I think everyone is asleep. I presume you have dismissed your valet?" She smiled provocatively. "I do find it hard to imagine *you* with a valet."

Andrew gritted his teeth. Another little joke about the country bumpkin! He glared at her as he scrambled to his feet.

"What is this? Why are you here? Surely making fun of me at dinner is sufficient sport Madam?"

By now she was standing very close. He could smell her perfume. He wanted to step back but the chair was in his way. He felt awkward enough... it wouldn't do to stumble.

"Oh Andrew Walters! *Please!* For *four* days and nights I have waited for a pleasant word... one smile... one moment when I thought you... We were such friends... *why* are you so horrible?"

He shook his head as he carefully put the poker in its place and moved away from her.

"Spare me the histrionics! Such good friends!" His voice was heavy with bitter sarcasm. "Good friend! I *wasn't* good enough to be *your* friend. You've got everything you ever wanted Lady Mulray! Leave me alone. I had no idea we were visiting you! I wish to God I had known! I should never have come!"

She sighed plaintively, and her voice quavered.

"Oh *why* are you so angry? We were young... I had to do what my parents wanted..."

"Well you don't appear to be sorry. No one *forced* you into anything. As I remember you couldn't wait to get to London. You are in your element My Lady! Rubies, diamonds, furs, a mansion... all you ever wanted!" His lip curled disdainfully.

"You are so *harsh!*" Her lips trembled and she turned away as if in pain.

"No, just realistic. You have everything you ever wanted. You have no need for my approval."

"Oh. If you *only* knew..." She sighed deeply and her bottom lip trembled anew.

"Spare me the Cheltenham Tragedy! You are the life of the party! The Complete Chatelaine!" He turned away and walked across to the window, his voice becoming hard and bitter. "And of course your amusement is increased now that you have a Colonial to make the butt of your little witticisms."

"Oh Andrew! I was just trying to make you part of the fun."

"Fun! Whose fun!? Your Spidershanks of a husband or his ever-present potbellied friend? Or you endless your "tonnish" friends?" He glared at her as he settled onto the window seat, deliberately rude, sitting while she still stood. She had followed him. Once again he could smell her perfume as he realised his mistake. His face was now on a level with hers. She cupped his face in her hands and kissed him before he had time to react. He stood and pushed her away though he could still taste her lips.

"Have you gone mad? You are married. Where are your wits? Or is this how married women behave in Society?" The last words were heavy with bitterness.

"*Married!*" She flung the word at him. "Do you know what marriage is... for me! *I* am simply the latest *specimen* in my husband's collection! I am displayed to the World... but there is no love... or even affection. Papa's fortune to spend and my face and figure... to make others envy him. That is *all* I am!"

His eyes narrowed. What was she saying? Was it another of her traps, her feminine wiles to arouse his sympathy?

"Well he showers fine clothes and jewellery on you. What more did you want? He is your husband. I don't believe you were dragged to the Altar, Madam. Not for one minute. You made the bargain willingly I've no doubt."

"Oh Andrew. I admit I like the luxuries... and being a Countess. What would those snooty girls back in Sydney say now? But I want more..." She stepped close and threw her arms around his waist and pressed her head against his chest. He could feel her with every fibre of his body. He knew how much he wanted her. Her hair was tickling his chin, the curves of her body fitted against his. For the briefest moment he hesitated. Then he took her hands and broke the embrace.

Now the tears fell. He watched her. How genuine were they? How genuine was anything she said? Suddenly she dashed away her tears, dragged his head down and kissed him again. This time she was successful. He lifted her and held her close as he returned her kiss. How long it lasted he did not know. Then just as suddenly she slipped out of his arms and was gone.

He flung himself back onto his bed, staring at the canopy above. Why had she come? What was she up to? He doubted every word she had said, but even so, she knew how to get under his skin. For sure and certain she had. He changed into his nightshirt and returned to bed but sleep did not come.

He stood in the stables brushing down the fine thoroughbred the Earl had assigned for his personal use. A fast ride in the early dawn had calmed his mind. Or that had been the idea but now as he dragged the comb through the horse's mane he was not so sure. He had discarded his riding jacket and rolled up his shirtsleeves. He was at home here, tending the horse. He wondered who would be tending his horses, and whether they were doing it as well as he hoped... His mind was thousands of miles away when a slim hand slid up his arm under the sleeve. He could feel her body pressed against his back. He stood very still, as much to keep the stallion calm as to collect his wits.

"What in God's name are you doing?" He hissed.

"Don't worry no-one can see. No one knows I am here... I couldn't sleep. I had to see you. I saw you ride out so I slipped down and waited in the tack room. The grooms are out exercising..."

He turned slowly, trying to move away from her embrace without upsetting the horse.

"Have you lost your mind? There are stable hands as well as the grooms?" Her slim finger touched his lips.

"Hush! I am going... but..." And she was gone. He turned back to the horse. What was he to do? He was due to go North... perhaps he could pretend he'd been summoned... well not really... Emily and Nick were involved in his plans...

The day and evening passed as usual. He kept his distance from his hostess, while he tried to gauge how much of what she said had any truth to it. He had to admit the Earl, the very attentive host, did seem to prefer the company of his rotund friend. Her Ladyship appeared for dinner as beautiful as ever, her manner was charming to all, though he found himself wondering if her manner was... He pulled himself up. She was not to be trusted. She had hurt him once. It would *not* happen again. He joined the conversation between Nick and the Earl's dear friend, though he knew very little about the people that Whittaker delighted in discussing, especially their weaknesses and foibles. What a nasty little blatherskite! Mealy-mouthed and nasty. He was glad to retire for a game of billiards with his brother-in-law, and avoid the card game the Earl had arranged.

"I think I'll turn in Nick. Didn't sleep so well... need an early night. After all we have the Hunt tomorrow don't we? Early start. I gather we have all sorts of rules and regulations. I think I'll need a clear head." He turned to put his cue in the rack as Nick quickly agreed.

"Well it is only "cub hunting" not the ' Quorn' after all," Nick chuckled, "but I know my wife will be pleased if I retire early. She is feeling a little under the weather." He smiled ruefully. "To tell truth, I think we are all feeling the pinch with non-stop Society! I for one am out of the habit."

Andrew smiled his agreement and excused himself. The indefatigable Forbes was on hand, but as usual Andrew declined any further services once the precious boots were removed and his dinner jacket safely replaced by a dressing gown. Andrew had come to like his valet but still refused to be undressed by him, and Forbes had come to accept if not approve.

Forbes had left a snifter of brandy on a small tray near the fire. He settled back to enjoy his nightcap, but despite himself he knew he was listening, waiting. The door opened silently and she slipped across the room smiling conspiratorially. He tried to look unmoved. She was no longer wearing her elaborate hooped dinner gown. Her hair hung loose over what looked like froth. Without hesitation she sat on his lap and wrapped her hands behind his head and began to kiss him. Whatever her schemes Andrew gave in and relaxed his guard. She smiled triumphantly as she took his hand and slid it under her gown and, for the first time, he felt her bare skin. He closed his eyes lost in the pleasure. His heart began to pound even more as she guided his hand up her bare breast. Her kisses were more and more passionate and she began to murmur his name over and over. She stood and pulled him across the room onto the bed. By now her busy little hands had undone his shirt and pushed it, and the velvet dressing gown, off his shoulders. He felt he would explode. Even his brain was thumping. He no longer cared whether she was married... all he knew was that she was there naked against his own now naked body. All he knew was that if he died now he would die happy.

They lay quietly exhausted. She curled against him smiling, replete, satisfied with herself and her triumph. Out of the corner of her eye she smiled archly.

"I think, I suspect My Darling... that was your first time."

Despite himself Andrew nodded. She clapped her hands.

"I am so glad. So special My Darling Boy!" She touched him on the nose, then on the lips and began to tease him until he ceased her wandering lips and began to make love to her on his own terms.

"I *must* go but *how* can I bear it?" She clung tight one last time then slipped out of the bed, into her gown and was gone in the blink of an eye. What had he done? What had they done? He knew, for now, he cared very little about his conscience as he stretched back on his bed.

Chapter 12

"Well it *is* only September Drew. We'll be joining the 'Quorn' or such in November, so that means you must make sure you will be returned to Mannering by then." Nick managed to move closer to his brother-in-law as he continued. "This is just a training run for the hounds, and the new riders. Shouldn't be a problem for a 'crack' like you Mate."

Andrew tried to look in control but the horse he was on, continued to fidget. Earl Mulray had organized "just the perfect horse, Old Fellow, for *you*." Drew patted its chestnut neck trying to calm it though it was difficult. All around horses and riders jostled and laughed.

"Well you're certainly mounted above us all Mr Walters." The thin nasal voice of his host made him turn too sharply, and he had to steady the horse anew before he could reply.

"I must thank you Sir! Most generous! A prime specimen. It is a wonder you don't ride him yourself."

The Earl admitted smilingly,

"Oh! It was my wife who *chose* him for you. We knew you would need something over sixteen hands, and as a matter of fact he is a trifle inexperienced, so we agreed it would be a capital idea to have such a fine horseman as yourself, to give him the edge."

Alarm bells rang in Andrew's head. What was she up to now, but he replied politely to his host.

"Well he is a mighty steed. Do you breed hunters yourself Sir?"

The Earl was happy to show him his knowledge.

"Well no. There are a number of English dealers who sell imported and local Hunters. I think yours came from Mr John Darby of Rugby... but I cannot be entirely sure... Whittaker tends to handle these things."

Andrew tried to sound interested, though he doubted the Earl's real expertise,

"And what especially does one look for Sir... in a good hunter, I mean?" The Earl, never one to display ignorance on any subject was slightly disconcerted by such a direct question.

"Well you need a good head and great strong shoulders... well... well one tends to rely on one's experts of course..." Andrew realizing his mistake tried to remedy the situation.

"Of course Sir. You have a great deal to manage I am sure..." He was saved by the arrival of servants with hot rum toddies to fortify the riders. Then they were away, moving at varying speeds to follow the hounds who had headed for a thicket in the distance.

Whether it was the rum, or his night's entertainment Andrew was feeling euphoric, but his mind snapped back to reality as he realised very quickly, that his horse was neither well trained, nor particularly amenable. The Countess might sigh and beg for more in bed, but in the daylight she was clearly very capable of tormenting him. He would need to be on his mettle he realized, as he cantered toward the thicket.

"Well let's hope there are quarry to be found eh?" A passing rider shouted. The cavalcade continued to advance. Suddenly the huntsman shouted. Hounds and riders surged forward. Andrew was surprised how fast the hounds could run. It was all he could manage to keep them in view, but this chase was short-lived. The quarry too was inexperienced. Then a second quarry was spotted. Andrew was in full flight, dashing across the fields and splashing through streams as he tried manfully to keep the hounds in sight.

The ending was rather bloody, and as an unwelcome joke, Andrew found himself being smeared with the warm blood of the dead fox by Whittaker, who gleefully explained,

"Usually do this to the children... but *your* first Hunt Sir so couldn't let it pass!"

Andrew resisted the urge to flatten the rotund funster, and tried to look pleased... Bloody weird people! How is this fun! But his mood improved later when he was able to sit down with some of the more experienced riders as they ate a hearty luncheon, and glean the secrets of choosing a top animal for the Hunt.

"Well if you want a 'made' horse, Horncastle Fair is the place to go in Lincolnshire... and the Irish bred horses are in demand these days." A grizzled old chap, whom Nick had introduced him to as Squire something or other...Uns...something... was very happy to enlighten the newcomer. "Yes they get them as two year olds and put them in the hands of jumping tutors. They are taught to leap by being driven over all sorts of fences for three or four weeks. I've heard they are often fitted with a snaffle and a surcingle... one man leads, the other follows with a whip... they teach them this way so that when they jump they cannot pitch on their heads but learn to drop lightly on their haunches. Then they are turned out until they are four when a boy will remind them of those lessons and get them used to the hounds. A good system I say... though it takes patience!" Andrew was fascinated but the Squire was no fool.

"Come now Lad...it is clear as a bell *you* know how to handle a horse." Squire Unsworth looked sideways at his audience. Andrew smiled but pleaded ignorance of the Hunt and hunters in general so his mentor continued,

"Well the Shropshire breed *were* very dominant, but nowadays... and the Northern men are not keen on a chestnut... claim they don't do well in the cold... sounds nonsense to me."

Andrew nodded as he agreed.

"Well my chestnut today did well, I must say!"

"Aye Lad! And you managed him beautifully. You have fine gentle hands for such a great fellow as yourself." He frowned in concentration. "Well now the head... the head is the most important... a fine head with a good eye... almost standing out." He paused, his brow even more furrowed. "Then a short lean neck, great depth in the shoulders, forelegs well put on and all sinew! You," pointing at Andrew, "would especially need a wide back and broad across the hips... and you always need great length from the hip to the hock for the fences!" The Squire had been joined by another of the riders, also keen to impart his knowledge.

"I always like a good slope in the croup Squire. What say you?" This expert who seemed even older and more weathered than Squire Unsworth, held out his hand to Andrew. "I've rarely seen a rider with a better seat young fellow. Mind I was a trifle concerned when I saw the Earl had given you that chestnut... taken more than one rider on a merry chase *and* at a rare pace..." Andrew joined in the laughter but he was seething. He knew, all too well, whose idea it had been. "And do you not Hunt in that new country of yours lad?" Andrew hesitated and his silence was filled by Nicholas who had joined the little circle.

"Not generally... some of the officers did and the odd squatter... I mean landowner... but nothing as well organized as this."

"But surely the kangaroo... could it not be hunted?" Squire Unsworth wondered.

Nicholas chuckled,

"Well yes, though even your hounds would have trouble keeping up with the kangaroo, Sir. No! Believe me, to hunt a kangaroo successfully like our Natives do, you need patience and guile." The conversation turned then to the strange exotic land with its amazing animals. It was not until much later that horseflesh returned as a topic of conversation.

It was a family dinner. There were no visitors, no extra faces and so for the first time Andrew found himself on the left hand of his hostess at the table. Fortunately, Nicholas was opposite him and so Andrew was spared the necessity of speaking more than was absolutely unavoidable. He could instead concentrate on his meal and make rather laboured conversation with the mouse-like female who appeared to be the Countess' companion. Mary Simpson was either very shy or very stupid. Andrew could not decide which as he struggled on. His concentration, however, became interrupted when he felt a small foot sliding up his leg. He glanced at his hostess but she was apparently engrossed in Nick's words. How could she manage to chat so casually while her foot moved slowly back and forth and higher and higher...? It was a relief when the ladies decided to retire but he was forced to hold his napkin in a strategic position to hide the bulge in his trousers. He could cheerfully throttle the little minx!

The men settled down to enjoy their port and the conversation returned to horseflesh.

"Well Sir, it was a great deal of fun today," Nicholas began, "but it is rather thoroughbreds and general carriage horses we are *most* interested in. I think we would have scant need for Hunters as such."

The Earl, the 'expert' was ever ready with advice.

"And are you looking for progeny or breakers, or a stallion or two?"

"Yes all of the above. We are rather sorry we missed most of the Racing Season. Think I gather last year was most exciting with... 'Sir Tatton Sykes', if that's his name?"

"Well it *was* 'Tilthorpe' but Oates, or Scott thought to curry favour with the Baronet by changing its name to his," Whittaker, the font of all gossip took the floor. "and it would have been an exceptional stroke ...but..."

"What do you mean?" Andrew interjected. "I understood he was the horse of the year?"

"We all thought he'd win 'The Triple Crown'! I can tell you I lost *my* blunt along with a number of friends... I doubt they'll ever forgive me." The Earl interrupted bitterly.

"We were so confident he would beat that devilish 'Pyrrhius'!"

"Well from what we've heard 'Pyrrhius' is a damned good horse!" Nicholas exchanged amused glances with Andrew. "In fact we were entertained by young Simon, my nephew, with an ode to the beast!"

"And I daresay he *is*! But Sir Tatton had won the 2000 guineas at Newmarket. The St Leger at Doncaster, when he fronted up to Epsom..." The Earl's voice faded at the memory of the horse's defeat but more importantly the size of the purse he had wagered on such a 'sure thing'.

Mr. Whittaker ever alert to ingratiate himself with the Earl, joined in,

"Well of course he *would* and *should* have won if it hadn't been for that tallow-faced nincompoop of a jockey!"

Nicholas frowning, interrupted,

"But Bill Scott is a first rate jockey... and trainer... or so I've been told..."

"Yes! My Dear Sir! But he is an incorrigible *soak!* Which is why I've no doubt his father threw him out! The horse *should* have won, and we would have been spared a great deal... of disappointment!

That wretched jockey had been drinking *all* morning. Then when he turned up for the Derby he had a violent altercation with the Racecourse Starter... can you imagine *anything* more foolish!" Whittaker rolled his little eyes and pursed his plump lips. "Well of course he *missed* the *start!*"

"I swear it was two lengths," groaned the Earl.

"Precisely! But the noble beast fought his way through the field and took the lead! Can you believe it!? *What* a horse! All Scott needed to do was ride him out, but by this stage he could *barely* stay in the saddle! Sam Day, who of course was *not* 'drunk as a skunk', managed to lift his mount and win by a nose!" Whittaker shook his head in renewed despair.

The Earl added soulfully.

"Scott was adamant he *did* win you know. He ended up right under the judge's stand and Scott swears the judge didn't see him!!"

Andrew and Nicholas tried to look sympathetic to the tale of woe, though privately they enjoyed the story and shared their mirth later. Nicholas tried to ease his host's pain by changing the subject.

"We're looking forward to 'Trove' though and we've heard Lord Stradbroke's 'Boarding House Miss', is a good chance."

"Yes well I doubt that, but you haven't missed all of the fun including the St Leger," the Earl suddenly realized his duty. "I say, must join the Ladies, Old Chaps, we'll certainly be in the bad books..."

As the stood up Whittaker had an idea.

"We should all go to Doncaster and retrieve our guineas!"

The Earl was all enthusiasm.

"Capital idea! What do you say Manners? I am sure we can go for a few days and be back in time for my birthday. Can't be away for that." He smirked. "The Countess would *never* forgive me! I'm sure Old Boots will put us up..."

It was therefore very late before Andrew could complain to his tormentor.

"You're a wicked, wicked woman!" He held her away from him. "I will never sit near to you again Minx!" The minx giggled and slid through his arms.

"Are you *very* angry... are you going to punish your little Amy?" He tried to reach her but she, laughingly ran around the room. Eventually she allowed him to catch her and succumb to his love making. Afterwards she lay in his arms wistfully stroking the arm that held her.

"Oh Andrew, *how* can I live without you?"

He shrugged,

"Well you've managed very well thus far!"

"Oh but I didn't understand... I didn't know how *wonderful* this could be." She sighed deeply. Andrew said nothing, and ignored the uneasy thought that she seemed an accomplished lover. Instead he said,

"But you are married...I mean the Earl... you said yourself he thinks you are beautiful..."

"Oh Andrew Darling! *If you but knew!* He is not the least interested in this..." She waived her hand vaguely over their entwined bodies. "Of course when we were first married... for the first few weeks he tried to do 'his duty', to produce an heir!" She shook her head. "Neither his heart nor his manhood were in it."

Andrew frowned.

"But surely... I struggle all day to keep my hands off you!"

"Oh My Darling! Really! But you are so curt and distant!" She snuggled her head against his as she began to slide on top of him.

"Hell what else can I do? He is your husband, my host, this is my first experience of 'cuckolding' anyone!"

"And isn't it *delicious* fun!" She kissed him on the lips and then began to shower kisses over his naked body. It was not until much later that she added a footnote which sent a chill down Andrew's spine.

"Of course, *once* a year on his birthday he *remembers* his duty!" She pouted. "His birthdays are *not* something one looks forward to!"

Almost a week had passed-nights of passion and days devoted to Nicholas' pursuit of good horse flesh. Andrew was glad when the expedition to Doncaster interrupted it. His head was fogged with pleasure and guilt! He needed a break, time to take hold of himself, and he had to admit, he was looking forward immensely to seeing some of the best thoroughbreds in the land.

"What do you fancy My Lord?" Andrew felt constrained to be polite and show deference though his mind whirled with Amy's comments.

For once the Earl was unsure.

"Not entirely 'au fait' with the field Old Chap. What's your fancy?"

Andrew replied hesitantly.

"Well I did read something about a 'Von Tromp' owned by the Earl of Eglington..."

Mr Whittaker would have none of it.

"Oh No! Doubt that will stay the distance. No rather rely on the Scott's, Dear Fellow!" Andrew said nothing in the face of Whittaker's endless expertise.

A pleasant time was had by them all. The Earl was able to introduce his exotic visitors to his acquaintance. Nicholas was able to meet more than one old friend. Whittaker was able to catch up on all the latest gossip and Andrew was able to make a handsome profit when, despite the expert advice, he backed 'Von Tromp' and watched with delight as John Marsden rode a brilliant race to win.

The morning after their return he left for Scotland despite the Earl's protestations and his Countess' midnight tears.

Chapter 13

"I would counsel against walking Sir!" Forbes dipped his head deferentially but he was clearly serious. "It is a steep inclination and though the sun is indeed trying to shine, Mr Walters, it could be replaced by that rain they call "mizzle". Do allow me to summon a conveyance." He waited anxiously for Andrew's response, not being used to offering advice, except of course in matters of dress.

"Oh I don't mind a touch of rain, and I feel like some exercise." Andrew replied offhandedly.

"But one has heard that the laneways are... not... salubrious. Indeed one is led to believe they are filthy *and* dangerous. Besides one would not wish to arrive with a... with a dishevelled countenance... if I may be so bold Sir!"

Andrew chuckled,

"You mean my infernal hair!" He shrugged his shoulders. "Well Forbes, if you feel so strongly I'll travel in a conveyance but on one condition. You come too. You should, at the very least, visit that Castle before you leave. What do you say?" He raised an eyebrow. The valet looked far from enthusiastic but it was clearly the lesser of two evils. His employer was young and healthy and... well very large... but who knew what lurked in the wynds and lanes that led from the neat new part of town to that dark place above.

"If it pleases you Sir." The valet sighed resignedly. "But I am in some confusion as to the need for your appointment to be up there," he pointed shuddering, "rather than in this area of the city."

"Oh I've been told the lawyers, advocates, they call themselves here, like to be up in the old historic part." He smiled mischievously at his reluctant companion. "Come now it will be an adventure." The valet only shuddered again.

After a brief and, Andrew felt, a somewhat unnecessary journey up Bridge St into the Old City, he found himself at the address mentioned in his grandfather's letter.

"Och! And then *you* are Jamie's grandson! And a braw laddie indeed you are!"

Andrew peered through the gloom at a small man dressed entirely in black. The only relief was his grey hair and the shine of his silver shoe buckles. Andrew had stepped into the room directly from the street and had had to duck his head in the doorway. He continued to feel that he could not stand up fully. It was not a large room, to his left was a staircase and to his right, two chairs were arranged next to a struggling fire, that barely warmed him, or the rest of the room. His host had been seated at a desk on a platform that filled almost two thirds of the whole space.

Andrew shook the man's hand as he introduced himself.

"Yes Sir. I am James McLean's grandson. My name is Andrew Walters but the family are now beginning to wonder what our grandfather's name was."

"Well now... is that so? My name is McPherson, Cameron McPherson, Advocate". He motioned Andrew to take one of the chairs and sat himself in the other, giving himself a more equal view of his visitor. "And what is it that makes you wonder Laddie? And for that matter what has brought you to these shores?

I received your letter but I remain curious." He settled back watching Andrew closely.

"Well to come to the point Sir, some months ago my sister discovered a letter written by our grandfather... and some objects that had been hidden. To be honest we aren't sure if it was my grandmother or our grandfather himself, who hid them. My mother was as mystified as the rest of us. So we, rather I, have come to you. Would you care to see these Sir?"

The advocate nodded and held out his hand.

"If you are happy to show them to me ... I *am* quite intrigued." Andrew handed over his bundle and waited while the other man carefully unfolded the package and slowly read the letter.

Andrew watched his face anxiously as the Advocate muttered to himself.

"Oh! Very interesting! Well I never! I wonder how they explained the seal... and... well after all this time!" He turned to Andrew. "This is a small treasure trove My Friend." He smiled at his guest. "I have heard the story many times but... well to tell truth... I often wondered were it true." He chuckled again. "What a story. The mighty Cameron! I *should* have known. I think you may find yourself very grateful to him." His face became very serious as he continued. "This will not be easy... many years have passed... No we will need to go about this with care... but ... *what* a discovery." Andrew sat quietly, somewhat baffled. His host suddenly stood and began to usher Andrew outside.

"Och! A wee dram! A wee dram we must have! Yes, and I can tell you what I know Lad, but it is my father who will remember most. Tomorrow we will visit him, but for now let us find a cosy spot." He stopped suddenly and held out the package. "Do you entrust me with these?" Andrew nodded, and watched as the lawyer slipped back to his platform. Andrew heard the sound of a heavy door closing. "There. They will be safe... we canna be too careful Lad. No... No. And you yourself will need to be 'vairy' careful. I wouldna mention any of this... not to a living soul! Dangerous. There is considerable danger especially to you." His voice was sharp. "Who else knows?"

Andrew suddenly felt uneasy, though puzzled.

"Well my family at home... and my sister and her husband... They are here, well in England." He frowned. "But I doubt Nick would have mentioned it... no he seemed to understand. It was *he* who insisted we come to England... Scotland I mean."

"But can he be trusted? When money or inheritance are involved..."

Andrew interrupted.

"Not Nick!" He laughed. "No Nick seems to have more money than he knows what to do with. I would say he is probably just as concerned as you Sir."

The tavern chosen by his guide seemed even gloomier and darker than the office they had left, but they settled into a cosy alcove and Baillie McPherson began the story that he had been told.

"Your grandfather was in the Army, a Highland Regiment of course, and had been away for some time... I think overseas. His own mother had died and his father had remarried. Your own grandfather himself, had a wife and twin bairns. I think, they were sons. He returned unexpectedly. His own father was overjoyed as, no doubt, were his wife and bairns." He paused to sip his whisky. "But within a week there was a dreadful tragedy. The story went that a fire had destroyed the wing of the castle where your grandfather and his family were sleeping. All but one bairn perished. The shock for the old Laird was too much. He suffered a terrible stroke and was paralyzed. The bairn who survived became the Laird though he was only an infant. The new wife was the *real* Laird. A great tragedy. He sat back and slowly swirled the whisky in his glass, "But it was not the real story. Not the true story at all." Andrew sipped at his own whisky, waiting, intrigued and impatient. Around them men laughed and shouted. Finally Cameron McPherson began.

"The *real* story... which to be honest I have not always believed until *this very day*... is this. My father's dear friend Cameron, after whom I was named, was the Batman... do you know what that is?" Andrew nodded. "Well he was more than that, of course... you don't fight side by side in war without becoming close. They were, it seems, great friends," He smiled and continued modestly, "and unlike myself, that Cameron was a big man... just like yourself. He was there in the Castle, sleeping in that same tower. He heard noises and rushed to the family... but he was too late." He paused and shook his head. "There were men... he was never really sure how many... perhaps three or four. They were in the act of setting fire to the entrance to the family's bedchamber, but he was *too* late. The nurse and the bairns were all dead... their throats slashed! He raced to the parents. James' wife was dead. An assassin was bent over his master. He killed that assassin. He could feel James' heart beating. Perhaps he had fought the murderer who had missed his victim in the dark, but James was badly hurt! Cameron gathered him and the articles you have shown me today and escaped, carrying your grandfather. We can presume that when the fire was quenched they found the body of one of the murderers and assumed it was your grandfather.

As I said, his own father was struck down. The wife, who, we can be sure, devised that *dreadful* scheme, passed her own son, whom no-one had known about before, as the rescued bairn. He became the Laird and *his* own son now lauds it over all." He took a long sip of his whisky. "It is a great crime. A *terrible* crime and for these many years it had gone unpunished!" He shook his head in sorrow and frustration. "An imposter and his seed… all these years living off the terrible massacre of those fine people."

He sat in thought, slowly twirling his glass. Andrew tried to imagine it all… but it was so foreign… castles, murder, intrigue… beyond his experience. Especially… well he came from a country where England had dumped all her criminals… and they *weren't* murderers…well rarely. How can this dreadful crime go unpunished for all these years?

McPherson straightened his shoulders, his voice firm.

"But *now* we can have justice." He stared across the table at the silent Andrew. "Well I presume you will *want* justice." Andrew said nothing. The lawyer assumed acquiescence as he continued. " It will not be easy. He is a powerful man, your enemy! I will need to gather other evidence. It may take time. No it will not be easy but we owe it to your grandfather."

Andrew was not so sure… was it really his responsibility?

"But my grandfather. Why didn't he challenge them… the wife… or whoever?"

Baillie McPherson had the answer.

"It took over a year before your grandfather recovered his health, but I doubt he *ever* recovered his broken heart. Your grandmother, Cameron's wee sister, nursed him day and night. It was natural he came to care for her. He wanted to forget. They went away and made a new life. And it would seem a good life, young Andrew, if *you* were the result!"

Andrew reddened at the compliment but he was inclined to agree, though he had only the barest memory of that quiet gentleman.

"From what I know it *was* good. My grandfather was a successful farmer, until he began to suffer arthritis… perhaps it was as a result of… of his past. He died when I was quite young. Then eventually my grandmother came to live with us, until she died.

She was... she was the *heart* of our family." He blinked back the sudden tears, embarrassed. "My mother was, is, the only child... a woman I mean, does that matter?"

The lawyer smiled.

"No Lad. It is neither here nor there in this country. *She* is the heir. It is no matter she is female... and then... there is you."

"Well I'm not the eldest." Andrew interrupted.

"It is *your* inheritance, but let me warn you, whatever are the rights and wrongs we may not succeed." He frowned. "And as I said before, say nought!"

Andrew shrugged.

"Well to be perfectly honest Sir... I'm not sure I would want it."

McPherson was horrified.

"Not *want* it? Come Lad it is not only your birthright, but your *duty*."

Andrew said nothing, his silence once again taken as agreement.

"Now I will let you go, but come back to my chambers on the morrow and I will... we will plan our campaign. The family... my family will be delighted. In fact, I must introduce you. Yes! Come tomorrow and I can take you to meet my father." He rubbed his hands together. "Marvellous. Marvellous. Tomorrow Lad." He stood up. "Wait. How foolish of me. *I* will collect *you* tomorrow. My father lives in the new part of the city. At noon. Give me your address." Satisfied he disappeared out of the tavern.

Andrew made his own way through the dreaded lanes, lost in thought, trying to imagine the pain endured by that quiet, gentle man he had known. The rain had started to fall and he pulled his cloak tighter. October! Already cold! At home Spring would be everywhere. The bush alive with birds and baby animals. Flowers full of nectar. The gums showing their new red tips, their trunks shedding great strips of bark... white and naked in the bright sunlight. What could all this mean? Did he want to be part of it? What sort of country was this? *Who* could cold-bloodedly murder women and children and go unpunished? Of course there had been massacres of blacks, and sometimes whites, but it was a frontier country with problems and he'd seen things that made him sad but .... Even those Myall Creek bastards, who'd slaughtered an innocent tribe, had been tracked down and executed! Thanks to old John Hubert! If Plunkett hadn't kept at it... Well he *had* and at *least some* had met their fate though there *were* others...especially in the north... Was there a different law for the rich here as well? What did the letter say... 'long dark nights'... 'black thoughts'?

It was only when he reached the bustle of Princes St that he took stock of his surroundings. Unlike the dark, cobbled street and teetering houses above, here was a classical formality and neatness. The street itself was perhaps not as wide as its big brother above, but it was flat and expansive, not pitched and badly cambered, and to his left were pleasant gardens. He shook his head, trying to focus on them, rather than the terrible story he had heard.

Forbes was even more aware of the contrast between Old and New.

"But the Castle must have been interesting?" Andrew asked trying to push his own visit, and all it entailed, out of his mind.

"What a dark gloomy place, full of guns and swords and every manner of weapons. There is even some great gun they seem inordinately proud of!" Forbes pursed his lips disapprovingly. "It is far more salubrious in this area. No wonder the city fathers felt the necessity to create a New town."

Andrew was barely listening to his valet's diatribe. His thoughts kept jumping back to all he had heard.

❖ ❖ ❖

Baillie McPherson's father lived in a small but elegant apartment in the tranquil Charlotte Square. The elder McPherson was obviously very frail but from the first moment, Andrew realized, his mind was as sharp as ever.

"And though ye be the grandson of James, you are clearly the nephew of the mighty Cameron. Ye owe your size to him. Aye to him, God rest his brave soul. But I do na ken how a great Scots lad could have such a Sassenach name."

Andrew had barely settled into the proffered seat before the questions began.

"And my son says you have the letter... from Jamie?"

"Yes Sir." Andrew replied quietly.

"And you knew *nought* of it or its history these long years?" The elder McPherson persisted.

"No Sir." Andrew answered.

"Well it is not to be wondered at I suppose... a new life in a new world." The old man shook his head and to Andrew's silent amusement, his wig bounced up and down. He turned to his son.

"Well I ne'er doubted Cameron but now we have the proof, but even so ' twill be a long hard road. A long hard road. Are you prepared My Son?"

Baillie McPherson nodded.

"*I* am keen. Cameron's efforts alone deserve a reward, but I fear Mr Walters is *no* so keen." He turned to Andrew. "Am I no right lad?"

Andrew tried to sound conciliatory

"Well naturally justice should be done... my grandfather's rightful legacy... I mean... Well Sir I belong to a new world... I live there. My heart is there. I... does this mean I would need to stay here?"

McPherson Senior was sympathetic.

"Well the whole process will take time Lad. Months, even years, you can return if necessary, *only* if we succeed."

His son interrupted.

"And I would recommend Mr Walters *does* go away. If of course, you are prepared to trust us with the process. If and when we succeed you would need to come back here. And to be entirely frank... well if word leaked... a great deal is at stake... your life.... Well I feel you would be safer in that faraway place."

His father nodded.

"Very true. We will handle it Lad. You can go home in the meantime."

Andrew, relieved, tried not to offend.

"Well this is a beautiful city... and country Sir, but I have responsibilities..."

"Of course Lad, but it is *your* home that I, for one, want to hear about." He slowly eased himself from his chair and reverently took down a book from his shelves.

"Banks' masterpiece! I have studied this, all of these years. We are intrigued by these exotic animals and the vibrant coloured birds! Have you seen any of these yourself, Lad?"

Andrew stared at the intricate drawings..

"By Jove Sir, these are beautiful." His finger traced the edge of a kangaroo, half expecting to feel the fur. "Of course I've seen a goodly number...I have spent most of my life travelling in the newer areas...the areas I mean that have been opened up to the farmers...we call them squatters."

"And what of the original inhabitants ? Do you see them?"

"Naturally."

"But are they not dangerous?"

"*I've* never found them anything but friendly, but...well they have *not* prospered. In the early days many died...the sicknesses were new to them. And then there were killings, on both sides, black and white, but at least the worst massacre of a defence-less tribe was punished…eventually. The murderers were hanged. Mind you, many have …well you know the old saying 'if you can't beat 'em join 'em. They are great horsemen and I've had several working with me. In fact one of them is my right-hand man."

"And do they have land?"

"No I'm not certain…I mean they are nomadic. They don't want to sit down in one place…There's a minister, Dissenting I think… Barzillai Quaife…I think that's his name…whose keen for them to have land rights. I wish him luck! The British Government is not even keen to grant blokes like me, land. Very generous with the immigrants, *not* your native born!" Andrew shrugged. "I didn't realise you would be so interested in our Southern land Sir. "

McPherson spread his hands,

"My Dear Lad! Your country is the most exciting *new* world to me, and my fellow members of the Linnean Society! So much to study." He frowned. "If only *I* were younger I would go myself. I look at these paintings of waratahs and I long to see them in their surroundings."

"Well *they* are spectacular but there is another…a lily that grows twenty feet into the sky, and *its* head can carry dozens of blooms." He smiled to himself. "You see them in the mountains, the Blue Mountains. Perhaps you have heard of them?"

"Aye, but *why* were they so formidable? I understand it took *many* years before they were crossed…I've read they are no much above two, even three thousand feet at the highest?"

Andrew shrugged,

"Well it is hard to describe them. They are not high as you say, and they generally don't have peaks, but as you travel along the tops of them, and mind, they can be narrow…the paths, I mean, you look down upon dreadful precipices, and great chasms, into ravines which can lead nowhere. The cliffs as you stand there are hundreds of feet deep, massive sandstone walls. They are monumental! The only way through is across the top, and *that* can be dangerous too." He shook his head. "From any distance they do appear blue...even violet, and they *look* serene, just like the rest of my country, but there are always dangers...for example you can *never* camp too close to a river. A raging torrent can come from nowhere, or the snakes come for a drink on dusk...The aborigines have learnt the landscape. They have changed it with their fires, but *they* understand it. Too many of the newcomers don't. I am sorry I am talking too much Sir. I beg your forgiveness."

McPherson smiled and shook his head.

"Never Lad! Believe me I have been fascinated, and it is *such* a pleasure to hear you talk about it all...a place dear to your heart." Andrew nodded ruefully. "And the eucalypts. So many varieties! I would very much like to see and smell them."

"Well I *can* help you there Sir," Andrew said as he reached into his pocket, pulled out a small bottle, opened it, and offered it to his host. "that is eucalyptus oil."

McPherson wafted it under his nose excitedly.

"It is quite pungent but surprisingly fresh." He returned the bottle carefully. "Thank you. *That* is a rare treat, and now, tell me about..." It was very late when Andrew managed to leave.

Chapter 14

The following day, braving the sleety rain, Andrew presented himself at Baillie McPherson's Chambers, ready to sign whatever was required. The search for justice... well, at least justice for our grandfather. The welcome this time was much warmer. Andrew was ushered up the stairs into a pleasant room, sparsely but elegantly furnished. A plump woman with bright red cheeks and a ready smile, relieved him of his damp cloak, settled him in a comfortable chair, and plied him at once with tea and scones. Even the fire blazing in its grate seemed to offer a warmer welcome.

His host came in and made himself comfortable and sipped his tea. He smiled at Andrew.

"And now Laddie, before we sign these documents tell me a little bit about yourself? Have you been in Scotland long? Is this your first time in our 'Auld Reekie'-Edinburgh I mean?"

"Well in Scotland... not long. I have been north, but this my first visit to your city." Andrew tried with some difficulty to negotiate the delicious scones and the lawyer's questions.

"North? How far north then... have ye been all the way to Inverness?" There was a hint of surprise in McPherson's voice.

Andrew managed to swallow his last mouthful.

"Well yes Sir. I have been to Inverness and it is a lovely city, but I also went further... to Sutherland Sir... I was visiting Dunrobbin Castle."

McPherson's surprise was now clear.

"*Dunrobbin*! Och Lad that *is* north, but how come ye to *that* place?" The question was abrupt, making Andrew nervous. Had he offended this man? But how? He continued his explanation hesitantly.

"Well Sir I rendered a small service to the family, and so I was invited to visit."

"What *small* service canna given ye *that* invitation?"

Andrew continued, though he could feel the sudden hostility in the room.

"There was a storm in London and I helped two of the ladies in the family to safety."

The lawyer's tone softened.

"Well 'tis a rare honour Lad, a *rare* honour. And is the Castle grand? And did they make you welcome?"

Andrew relaxed a little. He smiled as he remembered.

"They were most kind Sir, and the Castle is indeed grand. I saw it first from the sea. It climbs high into the sky with many pointed turrets and a tower, all gleaming against the sky. The sun was shining. It was *quite* awe-inspiring. The Marquis took me on his yacht from Inverness, and we arrived at these great iron gates, which open onto the sea. Then we were taken by a carriage through the gardens, that were perfectly symmetrical and manicured, and up around the building to the back, and that was where we entered it." Andrew shook his head in remembered amazement. "To be frank Sir, I have been in some large houses, even the palace, since I came to England but I think Dunrobbin is *the most* dramatic. It seems to rise out of the sea!"

Baillie McPherson smiled at Andrew's enthusiasm, but there was a glint in his eye nonetheless.

"And the estate? Did ye tour the land, Lad?"

Andrew's enthusiasm increased.

"Crikey yes. And I saw all the great improvements the family have made."

"Did ye now, did ye?" The harsh note had crept back into McPherson's voice though Andrew was oblivious.

"Oh yes Sir! Perhaps you know it was the present Duke who modernized the Castle, but it was his father the first Duke, who modernised the estates. He introduced efficiencies and the new ways. He built roads and bridges. Many of the people learnt new skills and he built them cottages and reorganized the old ways. At first he made great sheep runs, though it seems that has changed. Did you know the people were so grateful they have made this statue of him? It overlooks them to this day."

"Did he now? And the people are happy and contented you say?"

"Well everyone I saw, seemed so." Andrew frowned slightly. "Although not that I mentioned to anyone there, but, to be honest, I was surprised that they concentrated on sheep." He hesitated, unsure even now if he should offer criticism of his illustrious hosts to a virtual stranger. "I mean we have much greater areas for sheep and our wool is regarded as very fine... I mean..."

Baillie McPherson was quick to agree.

"Aye Lad. It is clear that is so, even to the Sutherlands and their ilk... their future wealth canna depend on their four-footed friends." His lip curled disdainfully. "Indeed many of those sheep and their covetous owners are gone already!"

Andrew, still enthusiastic continued.

"The Marquis is now intending to have railways built, so that the tourists can travel north... apparently the Queen, and her husband, have made Scotland *very* fashionable. He feels that is the future."

"*The future!*" McPherson snapped. "But what of the past I say? *What* of the past?"

Andrew paused, embarrassed...

"I beg pardon Sir. It is clear I have offended you. But... well I don't quite understand?"

The Advocate took a deep breath and patted his visitor's sleeve.

"No Laddie. Not you. *You* have not offended... but there was... and still is a *great* offence." He glanced at his guest but clearly his thoughts were elsewhere. After a moment's silence he began, his voice flat, no longer bitter but rather resigned.

"*Och*, the Duke, the first Duke of Sutherland was of the ilk... a 'liberal' man full of the new ideas. He was always entirely certain that *he* knew what was best for everyone, whether *they* liked it or not, *and* he had the wherewithal to carry out his improvements, no matter who stood in his way." The lawyer sighed. "It is difficult, perhaps, for an outsider to understand Lad... and that family have gone to great lengths to whitewash history. They even had that American woman who wrote that novel... Harriet someone..."

"Harriet Beecher Stowe." Andrew said helpfully.

"Och yes! That's the one 'Uncle Tom something'. They had her come to visit and she wrote "a paeon of praise" for the American audience. Methinks they try too hard... I suspect even *they* have their moments. I'll admit they did provide houses and employment of a sort... but their followers, the chieftains who copied them have rarely done that!"

Andrew was obviously perplexed. His companion began to explain more clearly.

"For all the centuries, the Highlands had been filled with Clans. Each clan had a chieftain who ruled them, and led them in war... and *they* surely *liked* the war! Believe you me. He was their leader, but the land itself belonged to the *whole* clan. As the great French philosopher, Sismondi said, 'Now the Gaelic tenant has never been conquered; nor did he forfeit on any after occasion, the rights which he originally possessed'. Then the meddling Englishmen decided to *tidy* things... to bring *their* rules and regulations to those people. They decided that the *chieftain*, not the clan, *owned* the land. It was a hard life but the people were healthy and content with their old ways. When their chieftains called them to arms they were *mighty* warriors! You may remember that fiend Napoleon... and the Battle of Waterloo... it was the Highlanders who held firm... who fought to the last man to thwart the Frenchies in that farmhouse!"

Andrew offered a comment.

"I have certainly heard of Waterloo Sir. My own father lost an arm in that battle."

"Well! Well! It was a *dreadful* battle... or so I've been told... and your own father! Well! Well!" He paused to sip his tea, and fortify himself with a mouthful of scone, before continuing.

"Well, the chieftains... not all I'll concede... but many of them, *most* I would say... began to see themselves not as the "father" of their fellows, but as great landowners. Many of them went South and learnt the ways of the English-those *Sassenachs*! They built grand houses and lived grand lives... *Increasingly expensive grand lives*. They put up the rents on their relatives back in the Highlands. Then they put the rents up again, and again, until many of the tacksmen – their managers, left in disgust. Many of those fellows went across to Canada, those who survived the voyage...many did not. So when those chieftains heard about the great Sutherland experiment... the great 'money-making improvements' they joined in. Sheep! Sheep! A fortune to be made!

But there was a wee problem, The Clans were in the way of the sheep, and so they were removed." He stood suddenly and ushered his guest to the window that looked down on the wintry street. "See those bairns…over there by the St. Giles' Church… Do you see them?" Andrew nodded. "That is the result of the chieftains' great improvements. Three wee bairns begging on the street. Where they come from I dona know… at night I mean… but I wager they came from the Highlands originally! We have no so many here, but Glasgow and Liverpool are full of those poor souls. Their houses were burned, their animals confiscated and they were forced to walk off their land… *the land of their ancestors, to make way… to make way for sheep.* Or in other cases, long before they were to be evicted, all their grass was burnt so that their cattle starved, and while the menfolk were trying to look after the cattle, the brave chieftain sent his henchmen to tear the houses down, around the heads of the women and children. There was no place for the Gaels in this '*brave new world*'!" He turned away and faced Andrew, his voice quiet, but full of anger. "In nine years, fifteen thousand souls were cleared from the Sutherland Estates alone. God alone knows the *real* number for the rest. Give him his due the first Duke sent them to the coast and gave many a wee cottage and declared they could be fisherman, and so eventually they became, if we disregard the many who lost their lives learning. Many simply left for the Americas. As the Reverend Donald Sage said, 'It was *the victory of the lord of the soil over the children of the soil.*'" McPherson sighed deeply and almost to himself Andrew heard him say. "O. chan lil ach sgiala bronach! Sgiala bronach. Oh only sad news. It is a sad story."

Andrew stood staring across the street. It was cold. The roadway was busy. Who would send three children to beg? His mind swirled-the luxury of Dunrobbin, the success of its modernized estates-at what cost? Surely the kind hospitable people who had welcomed him... As he watched he saw the eldest child, who was obviously a girl, stand and take the other two children by the hand. A puddle of water collected near the church steps. She dipped her apron into it and scrubbed the faces of her charges and with her fingers tidied their hair. Andrew felt a sharp pain in his throat. She was trying so hard! The children then began to make their hazardous way across the road, through the traffic. Andrew held his breath. Fortunately the only large carriage was labouring slowly, and most of the lighter traffic had thinned out.

The children seemed to be heading for a laneway further up the street. On an impulse he raced down the stairs, followed by a bemused lawyer. He reached the street just as the children reached safety. His long strides brought him to the children as the girl stopped to catch her breath.

"Wait!" The command was breathless but successful. He stared down at the three waifs, suddenly lost for words. Why had he followed them? What was he to do now? The girl stood quietly returning his gaze. Her wide green eyes registering surprise but no fear. Her brothers' eyes were wide with amazement. Fortunately Cameron McPherson had caught up with the strange little group. He glanced up at Andrew.

"Well Laddie? What nooow?"

Andrew shook his head, at a loss.

"I'm not sure... Can you ask them where they go? Ask them... do they have any food? Oh Lord I don't really know...." He squatted on his haunches and held out his hand. The girl stood motionless but one of the other children came toward him and put his tiny hand into Andrew's, and stood staring at it.

McPherson spoke softly, in Gaelic,

"Aye Laddie it is a grand big hand." The child nodded slowly as the lawyer continued. "And what is your name Laddie?" The child looked to the girl who nodded slightly.

"Fergus William Ross, Sir."

"Well. Indeed, and it is a fine name. And is this your wee brother?" The wee brother joined Fergus, moving close to Andrew.

"Finlay. He is Finlay. He is my brother." They stood staring at the strange creature who had sprung into their lives, but Andrew was watching the girl. Clearly, now that her charges had moved out of her reach she was looking anxious. He glanced meaningfully at the lawyer who took the hint. A conversation lasting several minutes between the girl and the lawyer left Andrew none the wiser.

McPherson turned back to Andrew.

"I asked her in the Gaelic, who they are and where they stay."

"And?" Andrew said quietly.

"Well, they are, as we surmised, from the Highlands, and they came here with their grandmother. She seems to be ill, or crippled." He shrugged his shoulders. "They live in one of the Closes, a type of tunnel... they used to be lanes but have been built over."

"Ask her if we can meet the grandmother?" Andrew found himself saying.

"*Whatever for Lad*? What would that achieve?"

Andrew shook his head.

"I'm not sure...but... well can we give them some money... Perhaps we could come back tomorrow and meet the grandmother? Do you think that would be better?"

"Aye Lad. I'll ask the wee Lassie if we can come back tomorrow."

Andrew watched nervously as the lawyer gave the girl some coins and relayed the message. She turned her head and examined the strange creature, squatting in the street, holding the hands of her brothers. Slowly she nodded her head in agreement before gathering her charges and disappearing down the lane.

"Thank you Sir! I don't really know why I did that!" A slightly sheepish Andrew was trying to explain. "Maybe it was the shock of the story... of all that happened..."

"It is no matter Lad. To be honest you have done what too many of us have ignored. We will see what the morrow brings. Eh?"

Chapter 15

Andrew slept badly. He had thoroughly enjoyed Dunrobbin Castle and *everything* he had seen, and, *everyone* he had met. How could he reconcile that splendour with the story McPherson had told? How could he reconcile it all with the starving faces of three children? He was still struggling when he arrived at McPherson's Chambers.

"Good morning Sir. I wondered if you would have decided I was *completely* mad by now," Andrew said quietly.

"Not at all. No. As I said, you acted honourably Lad. We will go, once the bairns arrive, and find their grandmother, and, I am certain you will know what to do." The reassuring words gave Andrew some encouragement but he really wondered what he was getting himself in to, and the third time he cracked his head as he struggled to follow the children, and McPherson, through the ever darkening passage, he was convinced he *was* mad. He was developing a headache in more ways than one! Deeper and deeper they went into the black. Eventually they stopped in what seemed the deepest, darkest space. Faint candlelight showed a dark shape on a narrow cot. The children clustered around it and Andrew watched, as the girl tenderly helped the figure on the cot, sit up. He saw the white hair and fine-boned face of an old woman, but her voice was light and lilting.

"The *giant*! I see my bairns *were* telling the truth!" She smiled and held out her crippled fingers.

"How do you do?" Andrew bowed low. How stupid to say such a thing. He cringed inwardly. Clearly she was *not* doing well. The old woman, however, continued to smile. A conversation in Gaelic between his companion and the woman left him feeling even more uncomfortable, but McPherson was pleased with himself.

"Of course! We were right! She and the children come from Ross... they have had a number of Clearances of late." He shook his head in disgust. "The children's mother died during one of them, and their father has subsequently disappeared. As you can see the old lady is too ill to work anymore. It would seem that she had employment but..." He glanced at Andrew. "What do you want to do now?"

"Well they can't stay here. How can *anyone* live here in this black hole? No wonder she is crippled. Surely we can find some-where... *anywhere* that is better that *this*!" Andrew was feeling embarrassed and frustrated. "We can surely find somewhere. And then I will take them with me... back to my country."

McPherson looked dubious.

"The old lady is vairy frail. We canna be sure she would survive until then... or the journey."

"Hells Bells! I don't know. *All* I know is we can't leave them *here*. She surely won't survive and neither will they." Andrew's voice was harsh. "I will pay for them to stay somewhere ... with decent food and lodgings... even the old lady *must* improve." Andrew's angry voice had made the children cling closer to their grand-mother. He realised his mistake.

"Oh Damn! Please explain to them. I'm sorry I spoke so sharply... and to you. I realise I am being... being difficult but if we could just get them somewhere?"

Cameron McPherson patted his arm.

"It is no problem Lad. I can ken your anger is at whatever has brought them to this pass. I can make arrangements to have them looked after for however long is needed, whilst you make your arrangements, but," he smiled at Andrew. "do you no think we should perhaps... we should discuss it with them? After all they... well we are strangers."

Andrew reddened.

"I am behaving like a fool. Forgive me Sir?" McPherson patted his arm again and then turned to the grandmother and began to explain. Andrew saw the children's eyes light up, but it was the grandmother's face he studied anxiously. McPherson turned to him.

"She wonders who you are and why you would concern yourself about perfect strangers? Do you have an answer?"

Andrew shrugged helplessly.

"How can I? I don't know myself." The conversations continued while Andrew watched. Finally the lawyer stood up and turned to Andrew.

"She thinks it can only be God... 'Dhia' who can have sent you." Andrew looked suitably embarrassed as McPherson went on. "For the children's sake she wants to go with you, if she possibly can. If she cannot, she will allow you to take the children anyway."

Andrew shook his head.

"Tell her she *will* come too. I *know* she will." McPherson relayed the message. The woman held out her hand and Andrew, bending low, took it. The woman leant forward and kissed his hand. Andrew felt a lump in his throat. Suddenly he was responsible for this ragtag family! He shook his head. How had he managed it? At the same time he felt happy even light-hearted! You *are* mad Andrew Walters! Completely mad!

Chapter 16

"It is very generous of your father Sir, to find room, to take in my... my little clan." Andrew said apologetically.

"Och. No. his apartment is roomy and pleasant and since my mother died he has been vairy lonely, and Jenny is thrilled! She loves children and... besides, Andrew Walters, my father and I, both of us, feel shamed that a perfect stranger stepped in and did the Christian thing. It is too easy to look away... to think 'someone should do something.'"

Andrew begged to differ.

"Well *I* am doing *very little* myself. I think your father's house-keeper is working the hardest."

McPherson nodded, then with a sly smile he continued

"To tell the truth My Friend, my father is so happy to see you he would do anything to delay your departure. Cameron McLean was his *dearest* friend and you are so much in his image, the sight of you gives my father great joy."

Andrew shook his head in denial.

"But he barely knows me."

"Och that is of little consequence... you are a feast for his old eyes. You can repay his hospitality tenfold just by visiting with him and telling him more about your exotic land."

Andrew shrugged.

"Well that's easily done, and I'm privileged to do it. At least he seems to understand me... no matter how hard I try the children don't really seem to know what I am saying." He complained. "Are you sure they really do understand English?"

McPherson chuckled.

"Och Aye! They understand *our* English not your strange English. *You* may be speaking English, and it is quite lovely you do speak it, but your accent is foreign to them."

"Accent! What accent?" Andrew snapped.

"Well ye no sound Scottish My Friend."

"So what can I do?" Andrew spread his hands.

"Be patient. These bairns have quick ears. They will soon become accustomed. Give them time... just gi' them taime." He grinned.

There was no such problem with their grandmother. She could understand... even understand Andrew's actions, more than he could himself. The Elder McPherson's apartment opened onto a small enclosed garden. Each day, if it was at all fine, Andrew would help her outside where they could sit comfortably on a bench. It was here that he learnt the details of her life and family. Her name was Moiragh McGregor but very rapidly Andrew found himself calling her Neanaidh, as the children did.

Many of her stories reminded him of his own grandmother's reminiscences, but *not* the last dreadful time. Of the fires. Of the grief for her daughter. The endless travel. The hope when they reached Leith replaced by the absolute despair. Of the slow descent into helplessness and starvation. Most terribly of all watching the children slowly dwindle away.

"Nevertheless, I still wonder why you trusted me? I really wonder..." Andrew mused. The frail hand patted his arm as she replied.

"I knew at once that you were a good man. I am an old woman. I have seen good and evil these long years. It is no hard to judge." She laughed gently, turning her twinkling eyes toward him, she continued…"I have prayed day and night to the Lord and especially to St. Jude." Andrew looked puzzled. "St Jude is the saint of lost causes, of impossible hope, and when I saw you, I knew he had answered my prayers." Andrew scoffed gently,

"I can't imagine I am the answer to anyone's prayers."

"Being kind to the poor is like lending to the Lord. He will reward you for what you have done, as the Good Book says." Moiragh retorted with a smile.

"But it is not for the reward!" Andrew replied gruffly. "It… I… I hated to see you all in that… that black hole! Though I am still amazed you came with me."

The old woman smiled.

"I knew you. I knew you at once." Andrew frowned. "I must have known you… in a previous life. My heart smiled when I saw you."

Andrew raised an eyebrow teasingly he asked.

"A previous life! What does the priest say about that I wonder?"

"Pffft! *I* am a Celt! I can have my own thoughts. I know there is more than just this brief span… you will learn." She changed the conversation. "Enough! Tell me more about this wonderful place you are taking us to."

Each day she seemed to have more energy. Each day life eased back into her frail bones. Andrew began to feel in his heart she would have the strength for the adventure she longed to make.

Forbes had been amazed when Andrew decided to extend his stay. The delights of Mr. Manners' family estate beckoned. Andrew considered making legal issues an excuse, but decided the truth was simpler. Whatever his valet thought, he insisted on sharing his expertise. Andrew, rather gingerly took him to meet his charges. Forbes saw at once what must be done! He trimmed the boys' hair and organized their clothes. Jenny and the girl were taken to buy suitable outfits for a young lady. Andrew's purse continued to suffer but Caitlyn's shining eyes as she paraded shyly in her clothes, were his reward.

Fergus and Finlay had, as McPherson promised, soon become used to Andrew's accent. They spent most of the time climbing all over their new friend. He brought a ball and taught them to kick it around the garden with mixed results. McPherson's elderly gardener complained.

As for the girl, Caitlyn kept her distance. Andrew even wondered if she understood English, although he was sure he had heard her chatting away to Jenny. It annoyed him but he wasn't sure how to approach her. It was the third day. He could hear the voices in the kitchen, then a burst of laughter. He stepped into the cosy room and demanded an explanation.

Caitlyn, caught unaware, laughingly explained.

"Fergus just asked Jenny a very important question."

"And?"

"Fergus wanted to know, if he were hungry, could he ask for something to eat. So Jenny picked him up and *opened* the lid of the biscuit barrel." She turned to the housekeeper. "His face was a picture wasn't it? We could not help but laugh!" For the first time she smiled directly at Andrew. "Fergus thought the biscuit barrel was a miracle. You are too kind to us. I am frightened this is all a dream... but then I see you, and *you* are *too big* to be a dream." In the background he heard Jenny's sigh. He himself found it impossible to talk for the all too familiar lump in his throat. Instead, he laughed and the moment passed. Clearly Caitlyn had understood him from the beginning! Gently, gently he began to befriend her.

The baby, Finlay, by day a happy four year old, woke almost every night screaming,

"Tiene! Tiene!"

"It means fire," a tearful Caitlyn explained, "and we can't stop him crying." Andrew had no suggestions. Then Jenny came to the rescue. She took the child into her own bed and nestled against her soft body, listening to her gentle voice he began to sleep the night through. Andrew could see his charges were safe and happy. He could leave, but there were tears, and a final complication.

"Do you remember Gordon Macrae? The man with one leg who helped us to come here?" Caitlyn's eyes were wide, imploring.

"Yes." Andrew said warily

"Well Gordon Macrae has a sister." Caitlyn's voice was anxious.

"And?" Andrew asked.

"Well they are our *dear* friends. Annie brought us food whenever she could, and Gordon helped me with Neanaidh." Caitlyn bit her lip.

"And?" Andrew raised an eyebrow.

"Well they want to come with us... when we go with you." Caitlyn's eyes filled with tears. Andrew was undone. With his thumb he lifted her chin and tried to sound severe, though his eyes smiled.

"Tell them they can come... I will make the arrangements, *but* I am not made of money Young Lady. Please *try* to refrain from inviting the rest of Edinburgh to come along!"

Caitlyn took his hand and pressed it against her heart .

"I promise Dearest Giant. I promise."

Chapter 17

"It is such a sad story!" Unconsciously Emily put her hand on her belly, where she could feel the first movements of life. "Imagine losing your entire family."

"*And* your name and inheritance," Her more practical husband added. "and, do you *trust* these lawyers to pursue it Drew? Why would they?"

"Well it seems the man who saved our grandfather was the greatest friend of McPherson the Elder. He has long wanted to try to bring justice and acknowledgement for that fellow. And the interesting... well it seals it really... that fellow, was our grandmother's brother. In other words *our Uncle*. It all happened later of course... it seems our grandmother nursed James for over a year before he recovered. He wanted to get away. He saw no joy in fighting for his name so he took our grandmother and left."

Nicholas pulled a face.

'I think he should have tried."

"But why?" Emily could think only of the terrible loss of his wife and children. "He came away and found peace... and a new family. I can understand that."

"Do you remember him?" Nicholas asked gently.

"Oh yes I remember him well. He was always quiet and softly spoken. But he would tease us and play jokes, and he *cheated* dreadfully when we played games so that *we* always won." She smiled to herself. "He was probably quite tall but not broad... not like you, Brother Dear."

"I have some memories but I'm not sure if they are mine or things I heard..." Andrew tried hard to recall.

"And so we wait," Nicholas was sceptical. "and *hope* that justice will be done."

"I'm sure if it is possible the McPhersons will manage as well as anyone. It is not so much a matter of money, but rather persistence." Andrew was keen to give credit to his new friends. "The only instruction I was given was *not* to say a word to *anyone*. They were adamant! According to them if word got out, my life, and yours Emily, could be in serious jeopardy." He shrugged ruefully. "Hard to believe but they were *very* serious."

"Yes I'm inclined to agree," Nicholas said thoughtfully. "Hadn't thought of it, but much at stake... not just the inheritance, but reputations, power and privilege."

"Well shouldn't be a problem." Andrew declared. "I intend going home as soon as I can, with your permission of course Nicholas, and Emily's name is Manners, so shouldn't connect her."

"Go *home*! Oh Andrew I thought you were having a marvellous time. You certainly seem to be enjoying yourself." His sister was dismayed.

"Oh Yes. Capital. Knowing Nick has many advantages." Andrew added.

"Knowing me. Rubbish, *I've* never been invited to Dunrobbin Castle!" Nicholas declared laughingly.

"My goodness, we haven't heard. How was it? Did you enjoy yourself? Were they very kind? Is it very luxurious?" Emily's words tumbled out in her excitement.

"Slow down Sis. Yes it was very grand. Yes they were very hospitable, and yes I had a pleasant time." Andrew replied.

"What did you *really* think Andrew? I detect some reservations." Nicholas remarked quietly.

Andrew reddened and tried to prevaricate.

"Oh No! It is a *great* estate and the castle itself is *very* spectacular, almost rising out of the sea. The family are very proud. They invited others of course... which is one of the reasons I want to go home shortly." He turned to his sister. "One of them was your Captain Mc Millan, the chap whose children you were governess to." Andrew was too engrossed to notice that it was Emily's turn to blush. "He offered me a *great* opportunity. Oh and he sends his regards of course." He paused for breath. "He wants *me* to manage 'Barraburn'-his property near Bathurst. He doesn't want to sell it at present but he wants someone to take charge... the Stock and Station Agent has been overseeing it, but Mc Millan feels it could be neglected somewhat. And of course with the drought... probably could do better... that sort of thing. Well anyway he's rather too busy himself... he is some Earl or something... he is concerned because of Mrs Mc Millan's grave being there. Handsome offer I can tell you! So I am keen to go home... it means I should be able to start buying somewhere for myself... land I mean. The government have never made it easy for natives like me to get land. Very miserly except of course for the chosen few. Generous to new-comers, but very begrudging to coves like us. Even Hamilton Hume took years to get a fair go after all the great exploration he did. Sorry Nick, no reflection on you of course."

Emily smiled at her brother as she enjoyed his excitement.

"That is wonderful news! For you, but *also* Captain Mc Millan, but... did he mention the children?"

"Oh yes. All fine and dandy. But you know that. You still write to them." Emily blushed anew, and avoided her husband's raised eyebrow and she agreed.

"Yes, to the children I do."

"So when do you want to go? We have several horses and sales to visit... can you fit that in?" Nicholas teased.

"Of course! I was hoping March... if that is suitable? I owe you so much Nicholas, not likely to leave you without doing my bit." Andrew was almost indignant at the suggestion, but then his tone changed. " But... well... not sure how to... not sure what you'll think... and I will need some... some extra... some extra funds... just as a loan."

"Damn it Andrew! Don't tell me *you've* been gambling or..." Nicholas teased but pulled himself up as he saw his wife's shocked face.

"Hell's Bells. What do you take me for? We did play cards at Dunrobbin but for pennies... they are not that sort of family... and where else could I have managed?" Andrew was affronted, until it occurred to him that the explanation would probably sound even more outlandish. With a deep breath he began to explain. "When I got to Edinburgh I found out... well I was told about... well I heard things that shocked me." He turned to his brother-in-law. "Have you ever heard about what happened at Sutherland... and other places in the Highlands?"

Nicholas shook his head. "Well I heard a few stories... about how the people in the Highlands had been shipped to the coast but that's all... I think."

"They were shipped certainly." Andrew's voice was bitter. "They were *forced* off the land. They were *made* to go to the coast to be fishermen. Their houses were burnt and their stock taken. They had no more idea about fishing than flying! I can tell you *I* was shocked to the core. They, the Staffords are fine people. They were so very kind to me but... it happened. The clansmen bled, and died, for their chieftains over the centuries, believing that honour and tradition meant their descendants had the right to stay on their land forever! Then the lawmakers in Westminster gave the land to the chieftains and their clansmen nothing. And… well I saw these three small children begging and I just *had* to do something."

Nicholas shook his head wonderingly as he asked quietly,

"So what *did* you do Andrew?"

"Well I collected them and their grandmother." He spread his hands in a gesture of helplessness. "I mean if you'd *seen* where they lived… I can't describe it… so the McPhersons are caring for them for now… but… but… well I've promised to take them all home with me… and I'll need a cabin. The old lady could *not possibly* go steerage. And then, then… well there are a couple of others…"

Nicholas tried to look stern but it was too much. He guffawed shaking his head.

"Others? What others? Why pray cannot the old lady go *steerage*? Andrew… our innocent abroad!"

Andrew had a problem. He resented Nicholas' mockery but he knew it was probably justified. Besides he needed money.

"Well *she* is badly crippled with arthritis… and the children are young, and well I did tell the other two they would need to go steerage, even *if* Gordon finds it tricky."

"And why pray would Gordon find it *tricky*?" Nicholas was still laughing.

"Well he only has one leg." Nicholas looked at his wife who was trying hard not to join in his glee. He stood up and thumped her brother on the shoulder.

"You are something else young Andrew! Instead of flirting with all the ladies of Edinburgh, and Sutherland for that matter, *you* are instead collecting waifs and strays and one-legged chaps to look after. Only you Andrew. *Only you!*" He shook his head in wonder. "Come, tell us how old are these children? And, who else is there?"

Andrew, looking particularly sheepish, tried to explain,

'Well there are two boys, one is four and the other is six, and their sister is eleven. And Gordon has a sister... with *two* legs," he added defiantly, "and she is a maid... she was the only one getting money, except for what the children managed, begging".

Nicholas looked at his wife, his tone resigned.

"Well My Dear. What do you think? Should we help your brother?"

Emily smiled tenderly at him and at her anxious brother.

"Whatever you think Nicholas." But she already knew his answer.

"Good God Andrew I thought the least you would do is fall in love with a Highland lass, or drink too much whisky. Instead you behave like a *missionary*." Nicholas declared roundly. "*Come* we have *much* to do, horses to see, places to go..."

"And lots of balls and parties to enjoy." Added his sister helpfully.

Chapter 18
N.S.W. 1851

The horse immediately dipped his head and began to drink. "Good idea old fellow. Good idea!" Andrew knelt and cupped the bubbling water in his hand and quenched his own thirst. Then he dipped his hat in, and tipped its contents over his sweating head. Late May and still hot. He felt for his watch and remembered, not for the first time, it was back on the side table next to his bed at Barraburn. He shrugged and held his hand out, filling the space between the horizon and the sun. He lifted one finger, then another. The sun shone through the gap he had created, probably an hour until sunset...even a bit less. He could make it before dark at a pinch. No. He should call at the 'Wellington Inn', and check on Mrs Lister and her son John. Such a tragedy! Losing her husband. And...if he *were* honest he had another reason... there'd been so much talk. Only one word on everyone's lips...It had always been ' wool'! Now it was... '*gold!*' A collective madness!

As he approached what had been a lonely outpost, that *collective madness* was before his eyes. A steady stream of men walking, of men pushing wheelbarrows piled high, of men on horseback, even whole families, trudged slowly toward him, laden with picks, shovels, and large pans, all shining and new. There were drays and carts sagging under the weight of tents, tools, and bags of flour, sugar and tea. Most of the travellers wore boots that were already dusty and worn from their hard slog. More ominously, many of the men carried firearms. The majority were dressed like himself, in moleskin trousers tied with a sash at the waist, long boots, a cotton shirt under a flannel blouse, a coloured kerchief at the neck, and a cabbage tree hat furnished with a colourful ribbon. There were others however, dressed for a jaunt in the country, in tailored jacket and top hat. He rolled his eyes at the thought of how unsuitable they looked for what lay ahead.

"Good Afternoon Ma'am." He smiled at the neatly dressed woman standing behind the bar.

"Andrew! Oh what a pleasure to see a *familiar* face!" and she stepped into the lounge as she spoke. "As you can see I have been much more used to strangers...and *all* in a desperate hurry, I can tell you." She held out her arms and was enveloped in a hearty bear-hug. For a brief moment she rested her head against the friendly shoulder and sighed, but then she stepped back.

"I thought to call and see how you were getting ...how things were. Such a tragedy...the Captain...in the prime of life. Are you managing? And John? Haven't had a chance since the ...since the funeral."

"Oh I manage...*we* manage." And...she gestured toward the crowd inside the room and passing by outside. "We haven't had time to grieve...the world has gone crazy!" Andrew smiled.

"So I see! I've been out west. I was sourcing some stock for myself originally, but that's all changed...I *can't* keep up the supply to the yards and *now* I see why." Susan Lister held out her hands,

"Exactly! Exactly! I can barely find enough myself for all these." She shrugged philosophically. "But no need to complain....I could be sitting here with nary a customer in sight." Andrew nodded,

"F'r sure. But are you on your own? Where's John? Isn't he here to help?" She stared past him, at the door, as if her son might suddenly appear.

"Oh he comes home in the evening ...and he works hard when he is here with the heavy work but...well you see he was in at the beginning of this madness...and he wants to find his own 'El Dorado'...especially *now.*" Her mouth twisted with bitterness. "Especially now the lads feel they have been *diddled.*" Andrew frowned.

"What do you mean diddled? Who has betrayed them?"

"Don't tell me you haven't heard how Hargraves the 'great explorer' found gold, and how he has been heaped with praise *and* all the *rewards!*" Andrew nodded.

"Of course. No-one can talk of anything else as they abandon hearth and home. Hargraves is the hero of the hour. I read just this week in the 'Bathurst Free Press', words to the effect that the existence of gold is clearly established, and credit and any reward, should go to him." Susan Lister's eyes filled with tears.

"On top of losing my husband, now *this.*"

By now the barroom was beginning to fill with tired and thirsty men. Andrew found himself behind the bar pouring beers and shots, while Mrs Lister and two young girls scurried back and forth, trying to dish out food. When John arrived he barely had time to acknowledge his mother's new assistant before he was sent to tap another keg. Any thought Andrew had of travelling to Barraburn, quickly disappeared. It was almost midnight before he could settle down with his hostess and John.

"I am confused...I mean you began to tell me...truly I was not meaning to offend when I mentioned the account in the paper..." Andrew said apologetically, as he sat cradling his hot mug of tea.

"*You* are not to know. He has been *too* clever by half...for us." John Lister shook his head. "Give credit where credit is due...

Hargraves was the one who told us how to make a cradle...and he was certainly sure there was gold around here...but *we all knew that* anyway. I mean we all knew there were specks in the river, and Yorkey had found his nugget, though he tried hard to keep it to himself. We *all* knew." he kicked angrily at the hearth. "But *we* did all the work. *We* found the good stuff!"

"What do you mean?" Andrew asked gently.

"It's a long story Andrew...It's strange how things turn out." Susan Lister spoke almost to the fire as she remembered. "Hargraves was a cabin boy on my husband's ship. He can't have been more than fourteen or fifteen. He was very good to John here, who was but a wee boy. Can you imagine my surprise, when he walked in here in February. He's a big man...not quite as tall as you, but much, much heavier...hard to recognise that cabin boy let me tell you." She sighed and paused as John, a bitter note in his voice, chimed in.

"And we *welcomed* him and when we heard it was gold he was after, I *showed* him these specimens I'd gathered, and ...I offered to show him where he might be lucky! I mean *he* was going all the way to Wellington *Town*. He'd never thought of Wellington *Inn*!! He was hell bent on finding *his* gold out west. *We* were the ones who persuaded him to explore here. I offered to show him around...but, to be honest, we've not been here so very long, so I asked Jamie Tom for help." He paused, his mouth grim. "Jamie is a crackerjack bushman and knows the place like the back of his hand." He shook his head in disgust. "So off we go where Hargraves said we'd find a fortune. The *Great Expert*! Eight stinkin' hot bloody days later... bugger all! Sorry Mother. So off the *expert* goes to Wellington *town*." He took a deep breath and shook his head again. "We were that bloody trusting. Sorry Mother, but a fella gets pretty hot under the collar!" Andrew waved his arm toward the sleeping men on the veranda or rolled in their swags on the bare ground.

"And so how did you find gold to start all of this?"

"Well when he got back he told us about a California Gold Cradle. He'd been to the California Rush…he'd done no good but he learnt a bit…about this contraption for starters. So he shows us…well as a matter of fact he showed Jamie's young brother Will. Will's a magician …can build anything. So we get the cradle built, but Hargraves is off to Sydney town…he was talking about going *all the way north* to Moreton Bay…shows how off the mark *he* was. I actually went part of the way with him. Afore he left we all agreed…me, Jamie, Will and Hargraves, himself, that we would split anything we found, equally. Fair and square we would be *equal* partners." He paused to sip the last of his tea. "Whilst he was away we thought to give the cradle a whirl…a practice run. Well the three of us and another of the Toms…Henry, gave it a go at a place *we* liked. Bugger me dead! Sorry Mother…we hit pay dirt! You need water to use the cradle you understand, and there was always good water down at the junction near Yorkey's Corner. It was only me an' Will working at the time." His face lit up. "And *did* we do *well*!! We settled the horses and had a bite to eat. Young Will started poking around and would you believe it he found this real *nugget! Just like that!* So we got the fancy cradle and set to work. In *three days* we got four ounces including another two nuggets! We were a bit further down the creek by then. I, myself, found a lovely little nugget in the shape of a heart. So we send off a letter to Hargraves in Sydney and he comes hot-footing it back." He kicked the grate angrily again. "Unbeknownst to us, *he'd* already claimed he'd found gold and written a letter to Thomson, the bigwig in charge, claiming *his* discovery and asking for his reward. Well we Mugs gave him what we found and, give him his due, he paid us for it, and off he went to Bathurst. He gammoned us good and proper. Here's us thinking we are *equal partners* still! Proper gooses we were.

He'd had this friend who'd written to the Herald in Sydney already, before Hargraves had come rushing back here, telling the world there's gold out here. Now Hargraves gets this friend who's a metallurgist, to make most of our gold into a tidy specimen and then he covers himself in glory as *'The Great Discoverer'*!" The hearth received another savage kick but even that could not assuage John Lister's anger. He banged his mug on the mantel-piece. "So's words out. Hargraves gets himself *all the credit and all the reward!*"

"But surely you can claim *some* credit....It certainly doesn't sound fair...not at all...jolly unfair I'd say!" Exclaimed Andrew.

"Yeah well we are trying...but who are we? A bunch of country bumpkins up against a real flash cove. He's English born...not your native born. A fancy gentleman or so he makes out he is." John slumped back into his chair. "He jumped the gun on us good an' proper!"

"But everyone around here knows you...and they *certainly* know the Toms." Andrew smiled reassuringly. "I mean Old Man Tom is even called ' The Parson'. His word would count more than most surely?"

"Yeah but the problem is, it isn't the folks around here that counts...Hargraves has the ear of all the toffs in Sydney Town." John grumbled.

"I would certainly write a few letters and state your case. If you need a reference, count me in." As he spoke Andrew stood and turned apologetically to his hostess. "But if you don't mind...I am flat strap...been a long day...I think I'll turn in." Susan Lister stood quickly and gestured rather helplessly.

"Please make yourself as comfortable as you can in here Andrew. It is all I can offer...we are full to overflowing, as you can see." She looked anxiously at her guest and in reply Andrew kissed her cheek.

"Not to worry Ma'am. You can make me a good breakfast."

Chapter 19

After the promised breakfast Andrew and John set out to see all the excitement. It was the noise, however, that struck him first. The gentle sounds of the bush had been replaced by a constant hum ...the combined sound of many voices, interrupted regularly by sharp whistles and urgent shouts, and as they reached the hill overlooking what had been a quiet oasis, the noise increased tenfold. Andrew stared down at what had been the deserted junction of two placid creeks. Now it was swarming with men hard at work. Some were carting water, some digging fresh wounds into the already churned earth, while others tended the wooden contraptions which he presumed were the famous cradles.

The two riders carefully picked their way down the steep bridle path through lichen clad granite outcrops, and the never ending procession of new arrivals, clad in excitement. The noise was even louder, but now his senses were invaded as well, by the smell of turned earth and men's sweat. The peaceful little valley was gone. The tall river gums and sheoaks had long been sacrificed. Even the gnarled and twisted trees on the slopes had been replaced by tents, bark huts, gunyahs, canvas-covered drays, gigs and tethered horses. High above, hawks and eagles soared and hovered, seemingly intrigued by the frantic scene below.

Two of the Tom brothers were already hard at it, and the extra hands were immediately put to work. Andrew's first attempts to 'rock the cradle' were greeted with guffaws. He was promptly relegated to water-carrier, which meant he had to repeatedly navigate the squelching, slippery sucking mud. All around him muddied men of all shapes, sizes and colour, toiled furiously in single-minded pursuit of their dream.

Eventually he was allowed a break while John showed him how to pan for gold, upstream, in a large flat dish with an inverted rim. He managed to isolate a number of yellow specks which were carefully retrieved by his tutor. He squatted on the bank, gratefully taking a breather. It was all hard work and *not* work he was used to. He glanced up at John,

"Fair Dinkum Mate this is bloody hard yakka. You sure as Hell need to work together, lot to do. Mind, I have noticed the odd bloke who seems to be on his own though." John nodded.

"The Hatters you mean. Well they rarely last more than a few days. Usually find a mate quick smart. Mind you...there's one bloke I've seen...Deadset *amazing*! His claim was two hundred yards from the river I swear, but he'd dug himself a deep hole... below the level of the river I suppose, 'cos it filled with water. Well the little bugger set up a pump and used that to wash his cradle while he rocked it with his foot...the cradle I mean. Bloody Ingenious! The little bugger never stopped." he tapped Andrew's shoulder. "And neither should we. Come on Mate."

They returned to the cradle and this time Will patiently explained the technique.

"Slowly, slowly Bluey. See it's just a series of sieves. The top one you can see, then under it a couple more." Andrew leant close to the square wooden box as Will continued. "And the rocker at the bottom has a series of riffles to catch the ore. It's much heavier than the mullock...I mean the sand and gravel and mud." And this time Andrew's efforts managed to meet limited approval from the architect. "Not bad...just keep it gentle...not bad...keep it going like that...yeah, that's it." Andrew was finding every aspect of gold mining hard. His boots and trousers were permanently caked in mud. His shoulders ached, and now his leg was complaining as he tried to rock the cradle successfully. In the recent past, his life had been easier...managing Barraburn had clearly made him soft. The sudden flecks and occasional tiny pebbles of gold were rewarding to see, but he felt quite immune to the feverish excitement of his fellow diggers. Even so he spent two pleasant nights in the roomy bark hut, but with alternating brothers, shepherding their claim.

"A while since you camped out I reckon Drew." Harry teased. "Getting soft now you're a manager eh? Used to the cushy life!"

"Too right." Andrew smiled ruefully. "And it *is* bloody hard work though. Do you reckon it's worth it?"

"Bloody Oath!" Will interjected. "We're making a tidy sum, though our father will only allow two of us to be here at any one time. He is working just as hard growing food for this mob." He waved his arm, pointing to the crowded scene. "And he's not happy he mostly only has women to help him." He shook his head. "There's hardly a bloke left in Byng. They're all here, head down, arse up, finding their fortune!" He laughed. "Mind you, I myself, have made a tidy sum just making these new chums their cradles."

They were interrupted by a tall stooped man with a gentle cultured voice.

"Evening Chaps, how did we fare today?" Will half stood as he introduced the newcomer to Andrew.

"Bit of colour Prof. Bit of colour, but had to teach Old Bluey here the ropes. Andrew meet our resident intellectual, Professor Bolding...Prof, Bluey here is a local." Andrew shook hands and settled down somewhat intrigued...should he enquire...could just be a nickname. The professor himself provided the answer.

"Not quite a professor yet, but decided to see the world and ended up here...having a jolly fine time and doing rather well, I have to concede. We are a polyglot mixture, shepherds, er... ex-government fellows, and, well, here he comes as I speak, a classical musician...Good Evening Raoul, I hope you have your instrument at the ready." An olive-skinned, delicate young man arrived, with his instrument in his hand, and, after the necessary introductions began to play. A plaintive classical refrain was quickly replaced by cheery favourites.

Sitting around the campfire brought back pleasant memories, but even with its warmth Andrew could feel the chill.

"Winter's on its way. How will you go out here? And how do you think your mates will handle it? Not many of them have such a decent hut like this one."

"To be revealed." Will chuckled. "It snows up here as you well know. I doubt many of these coves have stopped to work that out. But that reminds me, do you mean to stay? We've been lucky these few days. The Gold Commissioner hasn't been around. You don't have a licence do you? Hardy is a reasonable fellow, but if you stay you'll need one. Though they're bloody expensive!"

Andrew shrugged,

"Well I wouldn't want to break the law. Could embarrass you, and especially my father. A Clerk in the Court House, he'd be mortified. If Hardy comes tomorrow I'll get one but I reckon I'll be off,...though I'll be back soon I hope. I should have been at Barraburn before this I can tell you." The sound of a mouth organ carried through the night. Harry nodded,

"Raoul's got a bit of competition. Sounds like Old Nosey's at it. Next thing Black Bill 'll haul out his didge."

"I didn't think the blacks would be here?" Andrew was surprised.

"Nah not diggin'? Just making a few quid, mainly around the horses." Will grinned. "Quite a combination, a mouth organ and a didgeridoo!" As expected the didgeridoo joined the plaintive sound of the mouth organ and then a fine Irish tenor floated above them.

"Crikey! That sounds bloody good! Do you have this every night?" Andrew was enjoying it.

"Most nights, though depends a bit if Paddy has got on the syrup a bit early. Mind you he's not the only one who can hold a tune, Davy Davies can sing a treat..." Harry said. "and more blokes arriving every day, who knows what they can do."

"It all seems peaceful enough...have you had any ...problems?" Andrew asked.

"Nah...we're pretty well organized. Anyone does the dirty gets short shrift...run off the place quick smart." Will shrugged and shook his head. Harry agreed.

"Yeah, couple of shysters tried last week. Hung around the tents and managed to nick a few ounces here and there. Got a thorough shellacking for their efforts. Nah we're pretty well organized. Which reminds me, you'll find we use that gully yonder for a comfort stop. We call it 'eau de cologne gully'."

Andrew frowned.

"But isn't that the Gold Commissioner's house? It is rather near."

"Yeah it is, isn't it." Will grinned cheekily.

"But did he not know...I mean which came first, his house or the pissing... er... place?"

"Well and that's a matter of conjecture to this day," said Will, with relish.

The next day Hardy came. Andrew bought his licence and made his farewells. He had much more than gold to think about as he rode slowly away.

"Cooee!" The whiplash sound interrupted his thoughts. He turned to see a familiar figure, arm waving, seated under one of the few remaining trees.

"Grasshopper! What are you doing here? Surely not fossicking for gold?" Andrew slipped from his saddle and shook the outstretched hand.

"Na Boss! Na. Them digger fellas need fellas to mind the horses and carry the water. Plenty fellas too busy," He pointed to his own chest. "Plenty fellas pay plenty quid to us." He gestured toward two women who were walking back from the creek carrying the said water. Andrew shook his head in mock disapproval.

"Who's carrying the water? Looks to me like your lubras are doing all the work you Old Black Bastard." Grasshopper laughed gleefully.

"Too right Boss! But the horses...that's my yakka, like when I work with you. Them lubras do the water yakka." Andrew smiled.

"Trust you! Too fly by half you are. Well good luck to you. I think plenty crazy fellas over there." He pointed to the swarming activity. "How many fellas will find treasure do you reckon?"

"Well them fellas plenty bugger up our water Bluey." He frowned and shook his head. "Them ol' fellas," He pointed toward the hill opposite where, for the first time Andrew noticed a black camp. "them ol' fellas plenty mad. No trees, no kookaburras. Who wake up the Sun if no kookaburras!? That's what our people say." Then he grinned. "But me make plenty money." He laughed again, slapped Andrew on the shoulder affectionately, and then waved cheerily as Andrew rode away.

Andrew did not, however, head for home. Temptation prevailed. He headed east until he reached another branch of the river, then followed its twisting course south for several miles. He pulled a map from his pocket and tried to open it on his lap, but space and the breeze made it impossible. He squatted on the ground and spread it carefully, holding the corners tight with rocks. The eastern curve of the river marked on the map looked right...or was it? He clambered up the nearest hill and with trembling fingers pulled his compass from its case... the reading matched the map. He was there! Finally! For as long as he could remember he had *longed* for his own land...his own Run. All the years droving other men's stock to their Runs, he had longed for his own. Now he had it! Four years managing Barraburn had given him the chance...and the funds. It would take time...a hard slog but worth it. He turned his head from side to side. As far as he could see in any direction it was *all* his! He yelled aloud and threw his battered hat high. Those mad bastards could dig their hearts out. *This* was his 'El Dorado'. He clambered down the boulders and sat on his heels studying the map. His finger gently traced the outline of his domain...well two domains. He'd been *very* lucky... two smaller runs had become available on either side of the river at the same time, and a sympathetic agent had given him first opportunity, not to mention an even more understanding bank manager. Guaranteed water! In this country *that* was better than gold! He'd camp the night. A private celebration. There was a homestead of sorts on the southern edge but he was happy to just stay here and enjoy it. He'd be pushed to reach the home-stead anyway. It would be cold but a good fire would help. There was enough loose bark on the trees to make a temporary shel-ter...Grasshopper would be proud of it ...well maybe, and the ever generous Mrs Lister had given him enough food to last for days.

He made a fire and when it settled, shoved his damper in the coals and hung his billy can over it. While his meal cooked he wandered down to the river's edge. A great tree grew close to the water...an ancient gum. Its trunk was massive. How long had it been here? He settled beside it. It was a friend, a great silent presence. He studied its roots. Some had gone over the bank into the water, while others marched back firmly grasping the earth. In its youth it had no doubt been high on the bank, but either the bank had washed away or its girth had crept closer. Either way he felt a sudden twinge of sadness. A decent flood would knock more foundation away. Eventually it could topple into the water. He shrugged, for now he would enjoy its benign spirit. A sudden chill interrupted his pleasure. He glanced up at the sky. Even through the canopy of leaves he could see the speckled, scudding clouds. 'Struth! A storm! Probably snow! Even as he swore to himself the temperature was dropping and the wind screaming. He'd really need shelter. More than a swag under a tree!

He didn't know the area. Probably caves in those rocks but it's a bit late to start looking. His eyes roamed, searching. He stood and walked around the base of his friendly tree and his heart leapt. Part of the trunk at the back was hollow...either it had been two saplings that had grown together, or long ago, something or someone had made a decent gap. He squatted, peering inside. A tight fit. No room to stretch out, but beggars can't be choosers. He hurried back to his horse, who was whinnying and jittery. He clicked his tongue and tried to soothe the horse and his own nerves.

"Now Fred, she'll be right. We're stuck here for the night...I'll give you my groundsheet but I'm taking the blanket. That's fair eh?" As he talked he quickly retrieved his belongings and positioned his saddle close to the gap in the trunk. I'll drag that closer once I'm inside...should block the draft a bit. He unrolled his swag and fashioned a coat for his horse and secured it with rope and then tethered Fred close to the tree, hopefully on the sheltered side. The wind was fierce and getting colder by the minute. He pushed the blanket into the hole and then his saddle bags. Crikey, just hope there are no Joe Blakes in there. He hadn't thought to check...looks a tidy spot for a hibernating snake. With the point of his rifle he poked warily into the crevices. Nothing moved. Here's hoping. He tucked his oilskin tight and wriggled into his shelter. It was surprisingly high. He could sit easily. Well here we go. By now the wind was howling. Dust, leaves even branches hurtled past. It was suddenly very dark. He settled back against the smooth leather of his saddle bags and ate a goodly portion of Mrs. Lister's pork pie. Could do with that cuppa....Instead he took a long swig from the silver flask that had been in his shirt pocket. The flask, its whisky, and the bitter cold reminded him of Scotland. He shrugged, those damn letters keep coming, each more insistent than the last! They tugged at his conscience...but... well bloody weather like this ...who needs this most of the year? Snow and misty rain the rest of the time. How many settlers just around here are glad to have escaped that. Why should *he* go back? And if he did what was waiting for him? Better off here where he belonged ...even on a night like this.

He dozed but never really slept even after the wind had died. At first light he untangled his stiff limbs and climbed into a white world. He stamped his feet trying to warm them while he rubbed his hands together vigorously and blew his warm breath into them. He checked the horse.

"Bloody Cold Old Mate!" He pressed his cheek against Fred's shoulder, enjoying the warmth. "We managed though, eh? Here have a drink. We'll be off soon. Have your own stable tonight, Old Fella. Both of us 'll have our own stable!"

He needed more water. He crunched the few feet through the snow to the river bank. In close, the river was iced over. He knelt and cracked the thin sheet with his billy can. He was close to his tree but from a new angle. He peered through the water at its roots anxiously trying to judge how sturdy its hold on the bank. A sudden glint caught his eye. What was it? He lay stretched out on the snow and managed to reach the roots. He felt something.

It was hard. He dragged his freezing hand and its contents back through the ice. It was ...well it certainly looked like...maybe it was! It was the size of his little finger, smooth, gleaming, yellow! Ignoring the cold he lay full length and began to feel more carefully among the roots. Another hard lump... much smaller... not much bigger than a pea. His heart began to race. For several minutes he scrabbled blindly. More and more glittering pebbles rewarded his fumbling frozen fingers. He sat back nursing his hand and stared at the contents of his billy. It was almost half full! He shook his head. If he were really honest he'd felt rather superior to John and the Tom brothers. He'd been happy to help them but privately he'd felt there were more important things to do than scratch in the dirt. But Now!!!! The sudden rush of exaltation! Joy! Relief from care! Sudden wealth! The sheer beauty of it! *Now* he understood. They were obsessed by a dream. By hope! And he...he had stumbled on it....he felt a pang of guilt... but....he shook his head. He had more to think about. What could or should he do? He had no equipment. Was there more there caught in the roots? It was too cold to stay and try. He was soaked through anyway. He was already overdue at Barraburn. If he staked a claim it would be a signpost to any passer-by. Dig Here! He was a long way from Ophir...almost twenty miles, but even so, someone could wander here. No. Better to leave it. Come back with at least a decent shovel and panning dish...and less snow. Besides he'd done well...very well! Surely this would go a long way towards paying the bank. On the other hand if he suddenly appeared with all this...no....

He stood back and studied the scene. He scattered the ashes from his fire and strew leaves and twigs where it had been, and where he had lain. He carefully wrapped his treasure in his kerchief and stowed in the depths of his saddle bag. Then he saddled Fred and led him away from the tree. He studied the area.

The snow would melt. Only a blackfella would know anyone had been around. He tried hard to be calm and methodical but all the time his heart thumped with excitement. He lay his hand on the venerable trunk. His tree. His mighty tree. Shelter and now, bountiful provider.

Chapter 20

Caitlyn sat quietly on her bed. It was *so* lovely to be home... in this place...with the people she loved. Andrew and Neanaidh had insisted she go to school and ...well it was... it was naturally what one should do. *They* knew what was best. And, of course she had enjoyed it, but at the same time she had counted the days to be here. After the first few weeks she had stopped crying herself to sleep...and she *had* made friends...and being educated was *so very* important! Her hand smoothed the intricate pattern of the bedcover. It looked like a Paisley design but different. Rose said it came from India. Well now she knew where India was...if she hadn't gone to school.... She turned to the small polished cedar table beside her. A lamp, a candle holder and her Bible, Mrs Manners had given it to her...the first book she had *ever* owned! Beside it lay her treasures. She lifted the little stone and pressed it to her cheek. Her eyes stung with unshed tears.... Oh Mama aidh why? Why did you die? The pain in her chest stabbed at her...the familiar tearing ache. It would always be there but she hid it from everyone. She was *so* lucky. She must not upset everyone. She *must* make them proud. And her brothers... if *she* cried *they* always cried, though she wondered how much they really remembered...It was her duty to be their mother as much as she could. The pebble was back in its place...be grateful! She took the smooth shell, shaped like a cone, and held it to her ear...the sound of the sea. The wide, wide sea. So many weeks on that sea. How far away was her old life? How far away were the loch and the cottage and her Mama aidh? And then Dadaidh ... *Stop it*! Be *glad*!

She had found it on the sparkling sand, when Andrew had taken them for a picnic on the beach, when they came to this new world. The boys had run back and forth chasing the waves that slid onto that sand, laughing whenever the waves caught them! Laughter and joy, they could run free in the sunshine after the long weeks on the boat, in a world where they had food and shelter, and Neanaidh herself, had walked again. She listened to the sound of the sea. The wide, wide sea. So many weeks on that sea. How far away was her old life...the loch, the cottage...Mam aidh... and then Dadaidh. *Stop*! You are a lucky girl, Caitlyn. Be grateful! Be glad!

A commotion outside, the boys' excited yells, interrupted her. From her window she saw two small boys running toward a rider, who, as she watched, leant down and lifted them both up. Finlay sat in front, Fergus behind, their faces glowing with pleasure as Andrew turned toward the stables. She longed to join them... but... well fifteen, almost sixteen year old schoolgirls certainly should *not* run helter skelter after them. Instead she brushed her hair and retied the ribbon around it and tidied the sash at her waist. She was only half way down the stairs as Andrew and the boys came through the door. Finlay was balanced on Andrew's broad shoulders while Fergus danced around like an overgrown puppy.

"Nathan took Fred! He said he'd brush him down! So Andrew can have a rest! Did you see us on the horse?! We could *all* fit! Did you see us?" Fergus shouted.

"Andrew's been to the diggings! You know where they are digging for gold!" Finlay tried to sound knowledgeable. "He had a go at digging himself."

Andrew smiled and interrupted gently,

"Not digging exactly. I'll explain how they get gold..." He glanced up. "Well! Well! My word. Who is this?" He held out his hand and helped Caitlyn down the last few steps. Then he held her away from him. "Goodness Boys. We have a pretty young lady come to visit. Aren't we lucky?" Caitlin blushed at the compliment but her heart lifted and her eyes shone with happiness. Andrew was here. Andrew was home. And *home* was wherever Andrew was. "You look very smart, young lady. I hope it is for our benefit?"

"Yeah. She has been getting herself gussied up every day in case you came home." The ever helpful Fergus declared. Caitlin's blushes increased, though she tried to sound nonchalant.

"Nonsense, Fergus. We didn't *know* when Andrew would come home, did we? But we *do* know we are having visitors." She turned to Andrew. "Your sister Mrs Manners, and Mr Manners, are coming to stay. They are going to an important dinner in Bathurst, so they sent word they would be coming to stay for a few days." She gave Fergus what she hoped was a haughty stare but then turned to Andrew and chuckled. "Rose... I mean Mrs Jones has been like a whirlwind. She, Annie and Mary and even Neanaidh and I have been put to work, I can tell you. And Gordon has cleaned *every* window! And I hope you notice how immaculate the stables are? And Will has collected every fallen leaf in the garden. Is Mr Manners such an important guest?"

Andrew shook his head.

"I doubt it is *Mr* Manners who is important. Emily, my sister was the governess here. I'd guess that *she* is the special visitor, and the children. Doubtless Miss Rose will be desperate to see the children. No Emily was here when Mrs McMillan... when she left them all. It was a terrible time and from what I've been told Emily was... My sister took care of them all and helped them all in her own quiet way." He glanced down at his dusty clothes. "Well no time to waste. I will need to scrub up so that *I* don't let Rose down." He laughed, "Fergus could you go and ask Mrs Jones if I could have some hot water?" and he disappeared up the stairs.

Chapter 21

"Well we are *two days* later than we intended!" Nicholas Manners sat back in his chair. "My compliments to you all. This has been a delicious meal. Someone is a marvel! I doubt the food will be near as good at this dinner we are going to." He turned to the figure at the end of the tale. "I presume Mrs MacGregor, I am indebted to you." Neanaidh smiled gently as she replied,

"I'll take the compliment Sir, but on behalf of Mrs Jones, and Annie,... and Caitlyn of course."

"It is a wonder we are *only two* days late." Emily said, shaking her head. "Do you realise we waited *all day,* to cross the Nepean River, there were *so many* people! The ferrymen were *exhausted.* And when we finally reached the family in Hartley, we had to *all* cram into the Court House with Mama and Papa, because there was no room in *any* of the Inns... even Bessie and Richard's."

"Gold! Gold! Gold!" Nicholas interjected. "No one can *think* or *talk* of anything else. We happened to be near the Bank of New South Wales when the first Gold shipment arrived in Sydney. A great crowd gathered within minutes."

"I think I counted *six* armed men escorting it on the carriage, and there were armed outriders as well." Emily said wide-eyed. "The shops and businesses are all struggling. Every Tom, Dick and Harry has left town to go to Ophir. The government is trying to stop it, or at least warn people... there was a poem printed, per-haps in the paper, I forget where:

> "The Bathurst way is steep and long,
> The mountain airs are keen and strong,
> The winter rains are heavy too;
> And food is scarce and dwellings few.
> These things are disagreeable, no doubt,
> But virgin gold is lying all about."

"I doubt *that* will stop people. I've even heard they have started to arrive by ship." Her husband added.

"Well I hear quite a few of the sailors themselves have just *abandoned* ships." Emily said. "Though I heard one story, which may be apocryphal... a cook and two sailors deserted their ship, went to the diggings, and found several nuggets, so they just hur-ried back to their ship before anyone noticed, and have gone home *considerably* richer."

"Those are just the stories that encourage others!" Andrew added. "I was coming home from Wellington and the closer I got to Bathurst the crazier it all became." He shook his head. "The place will *never* be the same again. Even if many of these fellows go home, I'll wager many will stay. Though to be honest the real money is going to go to the suppliers." He chuckled. "Do you remember the inimitable Forbes... the valet you supplied for me Nick? Well Cedric Forbes Esquire, quickly realised that I had no real need of a valet here, of course... I *had* warned him. He has now become the proprietor of "Superior Gentleman Outfitters". He was enjoying modest success until lately. *Now* he is selling everything he can lay his hands on. He'll end up richer than all of us!" His voice changed as he spoke formally, "One can only be impressed by the entrepreneurship of our worthy colleague, who will supply the apparel and regalia befitting a successful explorer of our goldfields, and probably supply said miner with the vocabulary he will need as well." They all laughed affectionately at memories of Forbes' convoluted grammar.

"Does he still talk like that? Even here?" asked Emily.

"Absolutely and the locals are invariably impressed." Andrew chuckled again. "Good old Forbes. He taught me not only how to dress in Society but also how to survive its intricacies!"

"Forbes is not the only beneficiary. The papers are full of advertisements for 'essential supplies for prospective diggers'." Nicholas explained.

"Well I thought *I* would certainly need 'Flake Chocolate' which provides more nourishing and stimulating qualities than any other beverage." Emily interrupted smiling. "Makes a pleasant change from shovels and spades!"

"Well *my* favourite is the cordial that opens the veins and gives the miner great strength." Nick explained. "It will doubtless help them to rush, even faster west, to their El Dorado."

The gentle voice of Moiragh MacGregor floated along the table.

"I fear too many of them are chasing the wind."

"Exactly. How *many* will find their fortune?" Nick mused. "On the other hand *I'm* doing very well supplying horses, and you must be selling as many beasts as you can, Drew."

"Too right! You're spot on there." Andrew agreed, but then he paused and made a show of finishing his dessert. How much should he divulge? He took a deep breath. "As a matter of fact I went to Ophir, and I seriously doubt how many are making real money. It is hard work now. Most of the alluvial gold has gone. And of course the weather has turned. From what I saw, very few are prepared." Andrew shrugged. "Got caught in a bad storm myself." Before anyone could ask questions he turned to his brother-in-law. "Which reminds me. What *is* this important dinner? I realise you were coming home from Sydney and always glad to have your company... you were in England *such* an age... but what else brings you?"

"Oh! I assumed you would know. Assumed you would be going yourself. It's to honour Hargraves. Bathurst and its citizens are *very grateful* to the Great Gold Discoverer. Very grateful indeed! There is to be a dinner, and a gold cup is to be presented to him. It has certainly put Bathurst on the map and *all* due to him as I understand it."

"The Great Discoverer!" Andrew's voice was full of sarcasm. "The Great Hero! I think *not* thank you very much. Count *me* out." Both Emily and her husband stared in surprise.

"What do you mean? Why do you sound so angry?" asked Emily.

"Well I've been to Ophir as I said and heard *quite* a different story that's for sure." Andrew's lips were set in a straight line. "Hargraves never even found the gold he flashed around Sydney. Young John Lister and the Tom boys found *that* gold, *nowhere near* the place Hargraves pronounced as the Great Discovery."

"But surely he found some?" Nicholas remained unconvinced.

"A few specks according to the boys. *Then* he went off back to Sydney and made all the announcements. It was *while* he was gone the boys found the *real* gold. According to them, they *thought* they were *equal* partners with Hargraves, so when they found the real stuff they gave it to him and *he* took all the credit... and the rewards." Andrew shrugged. "The way of the world... newcomers get all the advantages in this country." Emily blushed and tried to mollify her brother. After all most of the people at the table were newcomers of one sort or another.

"I'm sure there is another side to the story Drew. There always is."

"Oh I'll admit Hargraves taught them how to build the cradle that they used, and paid them *some* money for the gold they found, but he had no real part in finding Ophir. He was actually headed further west." Nicholas interrupted quietly,

"Give him his due, he has certainly been *the catalyst* for the excitement. Do you think John Lister, or even 'Parson' Tom would have created this 'Gold Rush'. I rather think they would have gone along quietly collecting gold and keeping it to themselves. This way, *not only* Bathurst, but the *whole* country will benefit... I heard that some of the diggers have already moved further along to the Turon River. The *Rush* is on! Who knows where is will end? You must admit Hargraves is the one who brought it out in the open." Andrew nodded. He had a sudden pang of guilt. Wasn't that precisely what he was doing himself?

"Granted Nick. You have a point but I don't really fancy going to your dinner. Out of practice."

Emily laughed and shook her finger at her brother.

"Nonsense! The toast of London! You've had more practice than most." Andrew shook his head.

"That was *years* ago. Besides too many 'Would be's if they could be's'... jumped up vulgar make-baits, trying to forget who they are." Nicholas laughed.

"Oh come now. You sound like my sister."

"By Jove! There are *always* the Davenports! One cannot forget the Davenports. Do they deign to acknowledge you now, Emily? Too high and mighty in the old days." Andrew said.

Nicholas sensing his wife's discomfort replied for her.

"Naturally they do, and we take great delight in *being especially* charming. Don't we My Dear? It causes them *such* a problem. But one must sympathise with that poor woman-a bovine son and three heifers for daughters. No wonder she resents my *elegant* wife." There was laughter and general uproar at

Nicholas' unexpected remarks. He waited for quiet before he continued, explaining to the others, "When Emily was here as a Governess, the son of the Davenport family condescended to make her an object of his attention, despite his mother's *very* public disapproval. That was until Nathan and Will intervened... with the assistance of a very aggressive billy goat... or so I've heard."

Once again there was general laughter and demands to he told the whole story. Andrew's bad humour disappeared. Nicholas had a point, a rather relevant point if he were completely honest. Besides he may even get the opportunity to meet the Great Man. The Hero of the Hour. Maybe even mention his friendship with the Listers. Despite his pangs of guilt, he wasn't ready to divulge his own gold discovery. Instead, looking around, trying hard to keep his voice matter-of-fact, he said.

"I have something... a bit of news. I bought some land... well two runs actually, not far from here." He grimaced, trying to make a joke. "Maybe the Davenports will acknowledge me if I'm a land-owner and not *just* a manager. What do you reckon?"

General hubbub followed,

"What the Devil !"

"Where?"

"You sly fox!"

"Oh no, will you need to go away?"

Andrew held up his hands for silence.

"No. A day's ride. No more. I was really lucky. One on each side of the river, and they basically line up with each other. Bonzer! Real river frontage. They are both run down... chaps lost inter-est and the bank manager knew I was interested. I pestered him enough poor bloke." He turned to his sister. "How long have I wanted land of my own?" Emily nodded and leant across the table to squeeze his hand.

"Since you could *talk* I think! But how can you manage? You said yourself everyone is having trouble with labour. Nicholas is concerned at what we might find when we get home."

"Yeah! Could be a problem but for now I will just use it to run sheep and cattle... if I can *find* any. As for labour, well we've noticed here, the blacks aren't too interested in gold, so I thought I'd suss them out. The McMillans established a good relationship with the people here... all a question of letting them work it out... who wants to work, who wants to go walkabout. As long as you're flexible, no problems really. I was talking to old Grasshopper, who was one of my gang when I was droving... he's at Ophir making money handling the horses. He's a Dharug man, though he's sure to know some Wiradjuri fellas from around here." Emily glanced around the table.

"Perhaps we could leave you Nicholas. You can discuss all the details. I want to check on the children. I *imagine* they are having a fine time with your brothers, Caitlyn." As she spoke she stood and was joined by Caitlyn. Nicholas hurried to help Moiragh MacGregor to stand, but she smilingly dismissed his proffered arm.

"Thank you my Dear, but *I* am a new woman. Have you not noticed? The sun has warmed my bones... and my heart." She smiled serenely at them all. "There is not a day that passes, that I don't thank the Lord for all this, and all of you." Emily felt the tears in her eyes and she was certain her brother's cough was to hide his feelings. She slipped her arm through Moiragh's as they left the room. Already Emily felt the older woman's gentle presence was, in fact, a gift to them all.

For Emily, however, it was bittersweet to be at Barraburn. So many years ago it had been a place of happiness, but then, great sadness. It was a delight to see old friends, Rose, Mr Jones, Nathan, Will and other familiar faces, but there would always be an ache in her heart... for the children she had mothered, their father who... and especially his wife, her friend and confidante. Tomorrow she would slip up the hill and tend the grave. Tea was waiting for them in the sitting room where the logs blazed cheerily, sending dancing lights around the room... the room she had worked so hard with Rose, to furnish. She had never dreamt that she would have her own rooms to furnish! She excused herself and hurried up the stairs. The nursery was quiet. James was asleep snuggled between Fergus and Finlay. Baby Meg was in the cradle under the careful eye of Annie. She could relax. It had been quite a journey. She envied her sleeping children.

In the dining room Andrew handed the port to his guest.

"Actually have a bit more news Old Chap. I'm not sure what to do to be honest. Feel guilty after your remarks." Nicholas raised an eyebrow.

"Guilty!? What should you feel guilty about? Perfectly reasonable to get yourself a run! Congratulations I say."

Andrew fiddled with his glass;

"Not the land actually..." and he slowly took the first nugget he had found, from the inside pocket of his jacket and set it on the table. The candlelight caught it, and even against the polished wood, it glowed.

"I say," Nicholas held it in the palm of his hand. "I thought you *only* helped out at Ophir. This is a jolly nice little keepsake!"

Andrew shook his head.

"It's *not* from Ophir."

"So? Where is it from? Unless you don't want to tell me."

Andrew frowned, trying to appear unexcited.

"Well it's not just a keepsake. I've several more, some much smaller but not *all* of them. I found them when I camped on my new Run." He explained his good fortune. "And now I'm twixt the devil and the deep blue sea." He sighed. "I can't go back until the weather breaks… I could, but panning in this weather not my idea of fun. Besides if I can't shepherd the find, I don't want to draw attention to the place. Then your comments about Hargraves… well pricked my conscience… aren't I doing exactly what you said John and the boys would do? On the other hand if I arrive in Bathurst with… with my stack, I'll have the horde combing my place. The bush telegraph 'll run hot!"

Nicholas studied the nugget enjoying the feeling of the smooth weight in his hand.

"No! Can't go to Bathurst. No you'll *need* to go to Sydney yourself and sell it there. No-one would know you there." He laughed. "Should keep the bank happy. You'll be able to pay for your land outright if you have half as much as you say!" He continued to cradle the nugget. "How much is this worth do you reckon?"

"Well, they are giving three pounds fifty an ounce, and *that* is probably a few ounces there. When you think an average week's wages 'd be one shilling or a bit more… well it makes you think!"

Nicholas shook his head slowly in wonder.

"Maaaate! This will set you up for *life*. You can pay the bank, buy as much stock as you can and while this madness lasts…Fair Dinkum! Well *you* deserve a stroke of luck and you've had it."

"Don't I know it! If the storm hadn't hit I'd have left, none the wiser." He glanced anxiously at his brother-in-law. "You don't think… well keeping 'mum'… quiet I mean."

Nicholas laughed and clapped him on the shoulder.

"You can do nothing else at this stage. When you get the chance go to Sydney, pay the bank and get whatever stock you can buy. I'll wager you'll have a healthy bank balance notwithstanding. *Relax!* Providence has rewarded you and as I'm sure Mrs MacGregor would say, you *deserve* it." Andrew sat back in his chair, relief written all over his face.

"Hard to believe. *Still* can't believe it really. Just fell into my hands. Makes me sympathize with all those mad buggers rushing to the diggings. I can tell you I sat there staring at it all and I'm not sure I believe it yet." Nicholas went to stand.

"Nonsense. *It's real*, bloody real and I couldn't be more pleased for you, but we need to join the ladies... Your sister will not thank me for monopolizing you."

Andrew held his brother-in-law's arm.

"Wait. Something else I need to talk to you about... Scotland... the letters keep coming. McPherson says our claim has been recognized. It is official! Our grandfather is... was... well *we* are the rightful heirs. They want to proceed..."

Nicholas stood.

"This is between you and your sister Old Fellow. You need to talk it over with her... and your family. Damned complicated business... but hard to ignore it. Come. You can talk to my wife."

Chapter 22

As Emily came back into the sitting room to join Caitlyn and her grandmother, her eyes roamed… so many memories… so much pleasure and… so *much* sadness. Unconsciously she caressed the piano as she went to find her chair. Moiragh smiled at her.

"Were they good memories My Dear?" Emily returned the smile as she replied.

"Is it so obvious? You know it was a time I enjoyed very much. Mrs McMillan was a wonderful woman. I loved her." She sighed. "I certainly loved the children and still do… we keep in touch." She nodded towards the piano with a twinkle in her eye. "I was always expecting a little man to jump out from behind that curtain!" Caitlin clapped her hands.

"That is *exactly* what I thought when I saw it first!" She turned to Emily her eyes shining. "It is *very* exciting to have you visit Mrs Manners. Everyone was so excited. Especially Rose… I mean Mrs Jones… and Nathan too. They must have missed you. Did you leave when the Captain left?"

"Hush Child… you will have Mrs Manners thinking you are rude." Moiragh tapped her granddaughter's hand.

"No of course I don't Mrs MacGregor. I am *very* glad to hear I wasn't forgotten and they were all happy to see me. It all happened so quickly. One day we were all muddling along, settling down after... after we lost Mrs McMillan. The next day it seemed the Captain and the children were leaving." She drew a long sigh and was silent for a moment lost in her memories. Then she straightened her shoulders. "But it is so wonderful to see it come back to life... 'Barraburn' I mean... to have the boys, your brothers, rushing around helping Nathan, or hindering..." She smiled. "Probably both." Caitlyn was still curious,

"Did *you* leave when *they* did?" Moiragh frowned, but Emily simply shrugged her shoulders.

"Well of course! I was the children's governess. When they left I wasn't needed anymore."

"But you could have gone with them... to look after them on the trip... and after..."

"Hush Child!" Moiragh chided the girl, but Emily was not upset.

"It was so *very* hard to say goodbye to them." Her eyes misted over. "They are all well and growing apace, and perhaps, one day they will return."

"Did you not visit them when you were in England?" Caitlyn carefully avoided her grandmother's stern look.

"Well it *was* rather difficult... I had James and then Meg was coming... I did not care to travel."

Emily was very keen to change the subject. She suspected Caitlyn's questions were heading rather further than she herself wanted to divulge. It was a relief when Andrew and Nicholas came into the room. Watching the girl's face light up, and her enormous green eyes follow Andrew's every move, concerned Emily. She tried to placate herself... it was natural... she was a child... he had rescued them all... the boys adored him... in fact even Nick's demanding sister adored Andrew... he was that sort of person. Emily's concerns would have increased if she had heard the conversation between Caitlyn and Rose later that evening.

"Why did Mrs Manners leave?"

"Well it was *entirely* natural child! Her position was as governess to the children, after all." Rose said matter-of-factly.

"But she left *before* them. Nathan told me. She went to visit her family."

Rose shrugged her shoulders.

"We *did* wonder... we all thought... hoped I suppose." Her voice died away as she concentrated on mending the socks in her hand.

"What did you think? That she would go with them to Scotland... even marry the Captain?"

Rose shook her head.

"You are *too* curious child! Though I must admit we did wonder why she left early. It seemed quite natural... the children loved her...."

"But he was so *old*." Caitlyn declared.

"Nay child... not that old. And Emily was always a very sensible girl. We thought it would be a good match for her... and the Captain." Rose folded the socks and reached for another. "Though we are all very happy to see her with a fine husband and babies of her own. Now child go to bed and stop asking such impertinent questions." Caitlyn stood and dropped a kiss on the old woman's head. "Hear! What is *that* for? Go to bed you Baggage! You will be too tired in the morning."

Caitlyn did as she was bid, lost in her own happy thoughts. She floated up the stairs. If Mrs Manners could marry a man as old as the Captain must be, then... well Andrew was nowhere near as old...?

The following evening saw Caitlyn perched on the bed in Emily's bedroom watching with surprised admiration Rose's expert fingers arrange their guest's hair.

"You are so clever Rose! I didn't know you could do hair so beautifully." Caitlyn said, clearly impressed.

Rose nodded though her mouth was full of pins. Eventually she spoke,

"Mrs Manners has such beautiful thick hair it is a pleasure for me to do it."

"Thank you Rose...I *always* felt unlucky, my two sisters have black curls and Andrew has his red ones. Our grand-mother was always disappointed we did not *all* inherit her crowning glory, only Andrew! The only thing we have in common is brown eyes!" Emily smiled at the girl in the mirror, "You would be surprised. Rose has *many* hidden talents. But she was, after all, Mrs McMillan's personal maid before she was anything else!"

"Personal Maid. What is that?" Caitlyn frowned.

"Oh a lady's maid is a *very* important person. In the grand house she is almost as important as the housekeeper. A very superior person... like the gentleman's valet."

Caitlyn chuckled,

"Like Mr Forbes! When we were on the ship and in Edinburgh we called him Forbes, but *now* Andrew says we must all call him *Mr* Forbes... and I *always* curtsy," Her eyes sparkled. "and he bows very grandly to me, I think he *really* likes it."

Rose laughed as she agreed.

"Oh I *know* he likes it. Mr Cedric Forbes is come up in the world. I hear he is on the Chamber of Commerce! He has them bamboozled with his speeches no doubt!"

"But what does a lady's maid do? I know Forbes looked after all of us, not just Andrew." Caitlyn was intrigued. "Do you have a lady's maid Mrs Manners?"

Emily smiled at her in the mirror again.

"Well tonight I have a *very* superior lady's maid do I not? When we were in England, Lady Spencer organised one for me, but I am happy just to have a housekeeper and a nurse for the children.

That is sufficient normally." Rose paused, hair pins in one hand, the brush in the other.

"When we were in India I was *always* busy. Mrs McMillan often changed her dress five times during the day! It was so *hot*, but even in England a lady often changes... well... there is her morning dress... and if she rides, her riding dress and an afternoon dress, and always she would dress for dinner. In India we had 'tiffin' as well and that was *another* frock. Someone has to help her, and look after her clothes and do her hair." She finished her creation and held a mirror so that Emily could admire the back view. "Is that to your satisfaction Madam?" She asked in mock formality.

"Oh Rose of course! You are marvel... I have this pin... what do you think?"

"Just right! Now for your dress." Rose was in her element. She shook out the layers of glossy silk and lowered it over Emily's head very carefully, and fastened it at the waist. It billowed out over the crinoline to Rose's satisfaction.

"Beautiful... now your bodice." As she began to fasten the row of buttons, Emily was watching in the mirror. She could see Rose was struggling with the last few, and saw Rose's eyes glance at her breasts.

"Yes... I *know* what you're thinking Rose. Nothing gets past you. But it is early days. I can't be really sure until next month." Rose nodded.

"It's always wise to wait the three month... then you can be sure."

Caitlyn's eyes travelled from one to the other.

"What do you mean? Are you... do you mean... are you having another baby Mrs Manners?" The words tumbled out.

Emily smiled gently as she replied.

"Well I'm hoping but..."

Caitlyn jumped up, her body rigid, her eyes full of tears.

"Oh Mrs Manners! Oh you *must* be careful! Oh Ma'am." And she began to cry then sob.

Rose rushed to her and held her tight as she tried to soothe her.

"Now now Hinny. Now now. There's nothing to worry."

Emily joined her, holding the girl's hand.

"It is natural Dearest. A gift from God." She tried to talk gently despite the noisy sobbing.

"My Mummy was pregnant. Her big tummy made her fall... she wouldn't have fallen... otherwise." The explanation came slowly between sobs. Rose and Emily exchanged tear-filled glances. Caitlyn rarely mentioned her mother. Rose eased her toward the bed and managed to seat them both.

"Do you want to tell us... mebbe t'would ease your heart Hinny?" As she spoke she wiped the tears from Caitlyn's cheeks, but it was difficult. The girl was doubled up, her head almost on Rose's lap, her body in the agony of grief. Then slowly the tears eased, she looked around blindly, lost in her pain. Then she focussed on Rose.

"I can't! She was so beautiful. She was trying to save our house. The men of fire just laughed. They *laughed*! They would have left her to burn! " She gasped. "Oh Dhia!" Her tears returned but the wrenching sobs were gone. She lay exhausted, buried in Rose's lap. Emily held her hand and stroked it as she spoke.

"It is a terrible story and you will never forget. But you will begin to remember your mother before that terrible day. Was she tall? Did she have beautiful black curls like her daughter? Do tell us. You all three have black hair, don't you?"

Caitlyn's eyes turned to Emily as she took a deep breath.

"She looked like me. I look like her. I *can't* look in the mirror. It hurts. It is *too* hard. Fergus and Finlay look more like our father, but... Oh," and she covered her face and groaned.

Emily took the limp girl by her shoulders and turned her gently to face them.

"Dearest Caitlyn. It is *wonderful* that you look like her. Think of the pleasure it must give Neanaidh, to know her daughter is *not* completely gone. When she looks at you, it must help her pain." She slowly turned the girl so she faced the mirror. "Look at you. You are lovely, black curls, beautiful skin and those eyes! How exciting and exquisite! You will break *many* hearts. And when we find your father I am sure *his* heart will leap with joy to see you. What do you say Rose?"

Rose stood and lifted Caitlyn's hair and twisted it high on her head.

"Just look at you Hinny! I'll have you the belle of the ball first chance. Another year and you'll *cause havoc* with the Bathurst beaux." Caitlyn giggled through her tears.

"You are silly Rose, but I love you." And she threw her arms around the sturdy figure. Emily and Rose exchanged relieved glances. The dressing of Emily resumed. As Rose fastened an emerald and diamond necklace around Emily's neck, Caitlyn sighed with awe.

"You look like an angel Mrs Manners." Emily smiled and reached for the girl's hand as she replied.

"Thank you Dearest Girl. But remember you have your very own angel who is *always* with you, though you can no longer see her, she will always be there!"

Chapter 23

The figure strode purposefully from Princes Street up to the old city, up to his fate. The icy wind whipped at his heavy cloak. He pulled the muffler higher, tighter around his mouth, and jammed his hat lower. Andrew resented every step. The wind matched his mood... "The bloody wind's nasty... could blow the milk out of your tea!" The sudden thought, the dry humour of his countrymen carried him back. He longed to be home. Why me? Why do I need to be the one! Damn Cameron McPherson! Damn the Imposter...whoever he is! All I want is to be home! Everything was going so well! Unimaginably well! A run, stocked with good cattle...a ready market. Money in the bank. A regular income overseeing Barraburn. And most importantly seeing Neanaidh and the children healthy and well.

For so long he had managed to avoid this, and all it entailed, but the letters had come, each more insistent than the last. "You know Walters, the chief is the father of his clan, and you, whether you like it or not, are *that* father. They need you!" and another "I know the dreaded Sassenachs have changed the law. But know this, the Gaels have *never* been conquered in war but they are now to be defeated entirely by their own!" And then the last most urgent of all... "The Usurpers profligacy has reached new heights! Having ignored 'his' ancestral heritage and obligation and used the land as a 'milking cow' for his extravagance, he has decided like many others of his ilk, to decimate it! He has given the tenants until the end of March. Then they must go! To where? To what fate? You, of all people, know what that means. You have a conscience My Friend. You have demonstrated that! I am appealing to that conscience now." Dragged by that conscience from sunshine and warmth to *THIS*. And what am I to do? Well doubtless Baillie McPherson will have it all organized.

First another boat trip... well to be honest it was much improved I must concede that. The "Great Britain" is fast and modern. And to see old friends, Sir Peter, Lady Helen and their family, especially the fun-loving Simon, was not to be sneezed at. Sir Peter had raised an eyebrow and in his quiet way greeted his visitor with.

"Well Dear Chap it is a great pleasure to see you, but *you* must be one of the few people leaving your country. The whole world seems intent on going there to find their fortune!"

Lady Helen's welcome had been much more demonstrative as she clapped her hands excitedly before extending one to her guest.

"My Beautiful Barbarian you are come back to us! How *delightful*! How are you and my brother and Emily and the babies!? Oh we *absolutely* must hear all your news. And all the excitement we are hearing about the gold rushes. Have *you* found any? Oh do tell and why you are here I *must* know." Her husband had managed to interrupt,

"Well perhaps we can allow our guest to accompany us into the Drawing Room, instead of remaining here in the Hall, and offer him some refreshments before he answers all our enquiries."

"Of course. How thoughtless of me. *Thank you* Spencer for reminding me of my duties." Her tone had been rather sharp... clearly her husband had not quite pleased her Ladyship, though she had hurried to welcome her favoured guest into the elegant sitting room. "Now My Dear are you warm enough, it so *dreadfully* nasty out. I declare this is almost as cold as that last Winter you spent with us and *that* is supposed to have been one of the coldest ever!"

"I am very comfortable Ma'am I assure you, and tea would be most welcome thank you...I hope I have not arrived too early, but the coach trip was much faster than I had bargained for."

"*Not at all!* The earlier the better would you not agree Sir Peter? We have been looking forward *immensely* to seeing *you* and hearing your news." Lady Spencer had rung the bell and in an instant a neat maid carrying a laden tray arrived. As ever, Simms had anticipated her Ladyship's needs. The next few minutes were taken up with general conversation while Andrew gratefully consumed his hot tea and several dainty sandwiches. Sir Peter's curiosity was still keen,

"And is all well? We have heard so much about this Gold Rush of yours. Have you been caught up in it yourself?"

"Well to some extent we *all* are. Trying to keep up the supply of food, horses and provisions is,...is almost impossible. Nicholas has been particularly busy. We have a thousand customers where before we were lucky to see a dozen! Of course it happened so quickly the government is scrambling to catch up and keep order. Mind we have not had any of the violence, so far, that we hear about in California, but that may change. In fact many of the original diggers were farm hands and farmers who were leaving to go home for Spring ...sowing that sort of thing.... Although the new arrivals have come from afar so they will doubtless stay. The first flush happened near to us and as a matter of fact I happened to visit Ophir in the first weeks. It was Bedlam! So many people and so ill-prepared. It snows in that area and it *was* Winter." For the next half hour the conversation centred around the collective madness that gold could, and *had* caused, until Lady Spencer grew tired of it and returned to her original question.

"And are you to able to tell us *why* you have returned or is *that* private?"

"Now My Dear Wife, Walters need not divulge his secrets however much we would like to know them."

Andrew, however, shrugged and began to explain,

"You may remember Sir, when we were here before we had a letter that Emily had discovered, about our family?" Sir Peter nodded. "And you kindly offered assistance. The truth is I left it all in the hands of the lawyers my grandfather had mentioned. They were very interested. Very! They, well the elder McPherson, had remembered my grandfather and the story. Until they saw the letter they had never been sure how true it all was. To tell the truth they were far keener...far more inclined to pursue it than either Emily, or I was. Well they *have* pursued it all and matters have rather come to a head. It seems the Lord Provost is convinced, sympathetic at least to our claim...." He paused and smiled ruefully. "It was rather strange...when I was here the lawyer *insisted* I meet the Lord Provost."

"And what did he say that amused you?" Lady Helen demanded.

"Well he simply laughed when he met me and said something like "The Old Dog". I think he was talking about my great grandfather... He and the lawyer both laughed and he said, 'Can't deny the resemblance can we?'"

"How *fascinating*." Lady Spencer had clearly been intrigued. "So what is to be done?"

"It seems I am to go to Edinburgh and meet the Lord Provost formally, and, I presume he will give his verdict. The problem is what am I supposed to do next...what will happen."

"Is there a title...estates...*who* are these people who have *lived* a *lie*?" Her Ladyship said indignantly.

"Well it *is* possible the current...incumbent, does not know. After all it would appear it was his grandmother who orchestrated the fraud, *and* the murders of our grandfather's wife and children. At this stage I, we, don't know his identity. When I go to Edinburgh I will be told. To tell the truth I don't know how I feel. It is strange... more of a burden than anything..." Andrew had hunched his shoulders as if already carrying a heavy load. Sir Peter clearly had disagreed,

"My Dear Boy. You *cannot* deny your heritage which, it would seem, is very distinguished and ancient!"

"I realise that Sir, but I also have responsibilities at home."

"Well you may be assured of our assistance Dear Chap, in whatever shape or form. And I am sure my wife would do *anything* for you. Indeed one could become quite jealous." He had winked at Andrew while his wife had feigned indignation, and then joined in the laughter.

"The one thing you must do before you go North, Andrew, is visit The Great Exhibition. I, for one, was sceptical, very sceptical, that the German Consort could *possibly* arrange *anything*...apart from his wife's pregnancies that is, but *I* have been proved wrong." Lady Helen announced.

"You are rather harsh Dear Wife," Sir Peter remonstrated, but with a smile. "we have all been more than once, so I can vouch for it especially the ...er...revolution in water closets."

"Water closets?" Andrew asked.

"My Dear *you* will be intrigued. I will allow Simon the opportunity to enlighten you. I think that would be preferable...mind there are some amazing sights...from *every* corner of the Globe." Lady Helen said. "One *is* impressed."

"Oh Mama, you are *too* severe." Elizabeth, the Spencers' fashionable eldest daughter, who had arrived in the midst of the discussion, dared to disagree. "The Opening was *quite* delightful. The Queen and Prince Albert arrived leading by the hand their children, the Prince of Wales and the Princess Royal. The Queen was beaming with pride, *especially* of her husband, and the crowd cheered so loudly we could scarce hear the cannon. Then as she sat on a throne, a choir of a thousand voices, or that is what I was told, sang the National Anthem. Then the Prince made a speech and she replied, and you could tell how thrilled she was. Then the Archbishop said a prayer and then the choir sang the Hallelujah! I can tell you I had tears, it was *so* moving." She turned to her husband. "It was, wasn't it?"

"By Jove! It was *capital*. Then the Royal Party toured the entire place and people cheered their heads off wherever she went. Unlike Sir Peter and you, Ma'am we were *not* in the front row but it was a first rate show, and the building itself is *amazing*...entirely glass...Paxton's triumph!" Alastair agreed wholeheartedly with his bride.

"And then when she had toured the whole place she declared it open! " Elizabeth said emphatically. "You must go Andrew. You *must*. There is so much to see."

The great Exhibition had indeed been fascinating.

It had been pleasant to be in London, but then far from pleasant. What had he expected? Had he *really* expected to see her unchanged after almost five years!!! Nevertheless he'd found himself watching for her...even wanting ...what? Ridiculous Walters, you are a fool. And then at the Opera he'd seen her, a glittering beauty, on one side her husband and inevitably Whittaker, on the other, a handsome young man with whom she was clearly on intimate terms. Lady Spencer had seen where he was looking.

"Ah yes! Emily's little friend has become the 'femme fatale' of Society... a succession of 'friends' always young, always handsome, but she seems *not* to notice their marital status." Andrew had tried to keep his voice casual.

"But she is with her husband Ma'am." Lady Spencer had laughed ironically,

"Of course....So much more *respectable* if one has a compliant husband."

"But surely he..." Andrew's doubts were interrupted,

"Oh I doubt it. Since she has delivered him of an heir she can do *no wrong*. I doubt he would deny her *anything*." The Overture had begun. The conversation had ceased.

That, however, was not the only time he had seen her. This time a Private Ball...well how 'Private' was a ball with three hundred people!? Overpowering! He had stepped out onto the terrace. It had been a relief... cold but clear. He had wandered to the edge and gazed at manicured lawns and neatly shaped trees. Such studied elegance. He had longed for rugged beauty, jagged cliffs and the sharp clean smell of the bush. Homesick already! Get a hold of yourself Walters. Who knows what lies ahead and for how long?

The wind had sharpened. Back against the wall was a seat sheltered by two enormous plants shaped into great balls in their elaborate urns, fashioned within an inch of their lives, like the throng inside, but he was glad of their shelter as he settled on the seat. A couple had emerged through the same French doors. In no mood to chat, he leant back further into the shadows and smiled to himself as he realised, neither were they, as they stood locked in a passionate embrace silhouetted against the pale moon. Then the female half of the silhouette had stepped back slightly, her face tilted entreatingly as she spoke.

"Oh My Darling, how *I long for you*. I *cannot* bear it, when can we meet? I... every moment I *long* to be with you."

Andrew sat frozen. The familiar voice. *The Oh so familiar words!* He should cough, but instead he sat fascinated like the helpless prey before a coiled snake. Every word struck his heart... or was it his pride? The uneasy thought he'd had so long ago that she seemed so experienced...Well she had kept practising. How many times had she leant forward like that so her breasts pressed ever so gently against...Stop it you fool. You went away. You left! Why should you expect anything else. She told you herself, her husband....Well you are hardly blameless...

By now they had resumed their embrace. He could no longer hear the words. Suddenly the door onto the terrace began to open. In a flash she was gone. The male figure had turned casually and addressed the newcomer. The two had stood chatting idly, their backs to Andrew, enjoying their cigars. He was frozen in body and soul. Only his anger had remained red hot! What an idiot. Since he was nineteen he'd dreamed...his ideal woman... how stupid could he be?

The following day, despite himself he'd broached the subject of the Countess to Lady Helen, trying hard to sound only vaguely interested.

"I think my sister will be surprised, perhaps, that her former pupil is leading such...such an exciting life."

Lady Helen snorted,

"*Exciting!* Well that is *one* way of describing her antics. Mind she is always discreet, especially if she is anywhere near the Court. The Queen would *not* tolerate it. And, of course her husband is adept at making himself useful to *anyone* whom he feels will give him access to the Consort! A limpet clinging tight *if* it will increase his social standing, and a pretty wife does not hinder that." Lady Helen raised an eyebrow. "As I said having a child has given her complete control over him. I doubt he ever imagined he could father a child, *and* I can assure you, *neither did I* !" She added acidly.

"How old is this child...is there only the one?" Andrew asked as nonchalantly as he could.

"Oh I'd say he is out of leading strings...perhaps four...yes certainly four. After you were here last time, but within the year for certain." Andrew's sudden blush made her pause. "*Good God!* Dear Boy. *You* were their guest. You aren't thinking what I'm thinking? Naturally one shouldn't ask ...but I am!"

Andrew swallowed hard but his face told the story.

"It *is* possible Your Ladyship. I confess...quite possible..." By now his face outshone his hair. Lady Helen's ample bosom began to tremble, then shake, as she laughed heartily.

"You *naughty* boy. Doubtless *you* were led astray." Andrew was mortified.

"I was not unwilling Ma'am. I cannot say I was unwilling."

"Well of course not, My Innocent Lamb, but you were ripe for the picking." Andrew tried to explain,

"I knew her already. We had met at home...and...well she was ... is, very beautiful."

"Aha! You carried a torch and suddenly the opportunity was presented to you to light the torch."

"In a manner of speaking," Andrew muttered "but, well she pretended to be indifferent...even cold in public." He swallowed hard. "She came to my room late at night. It was a complete secret between us...that's why, that's what made me wonder just now..."

"Well *you* have certainly provided her with a great service." Lady Helen chuckled at her own unseemly pun, and then continued. Andrew had felt as though she could read his every thought as she studied him. "You are not only *very large* and also *very attractive,* but you are an 'innocent abroad', well not *entirely* innocent," She leant across and patted his hand. "but you are without guile My Dear Boy, and therefore do not easily recognise it in others." The grasp on his hand tightened and her voice had suddenly become serious. "*Beware* my Beautiful Barbarian. There may well come a time when she will try to use this against you. The lady is beautiful and alluring but *entirely* ruthless!" She smiled took a deep breath and stood up. "Enough. I want to show you off before you disappear into your *barbarous* North."

✦ ✦ ✦

He suddenly realised he had reached the top of Bridge Street. He paused, straightened his cloak and his shoulders, and turned into High Street. The familiar dark stone, the sloping road, the filigree of stone atop St Giles, greeted him, and he was enveloped in the bustle and smells of 'Auld Reekie'. He walked slowly towards his destination, trying to clear his head. This was his fate, his duty. Whatever lay ahead he was here. In his heart he knew he would do his best... Neanaidh's words came to him... "Right now you have plenty and can help those who are in need. Later they will have plenty and may share with you. In this way things will be equal." Perhaps...He *did* have plenty but he doubted those he was about to meet would have anything to share. On the other hand hadn't she and her grandchildren given him plenty of love. A reward after all. And then she had continued, quoting as ever from the Bible..."Bear one another's burdens and thereby fulfil the law of Christ." Well maybe, is *that* what McPherson calls my conscience? He stepped through the door. The advocate looked up from his desk.

"God Almighty is it you!"

"No McPherson it is not God, only your humble servant."

"Well, all the saints be praised ne'ertheless." Andrew's hand was wrung over and over. "My Friend it is so good to see you! You said you would come but I confess I ' ha' me doobts.' I should never have doubted you."

By now Andrew had shrugged off his heavy cloak. The lawyer hurried to relieve him of it, at the same time shouting up the stairs "Tea! Tea immejately!"and ushering him up those same stairs.

"We will have refreshment. Och My Friend. Tis *marvellous*! Tis the answer to my prayers."

Andrew chuckled.

"More the answer to your infernal correspondence."

The tea was hot and strong, the scones as warm and buttery as he remembered. He settled back and stretched his legs toward the crackling fire. The conversation was pleasant but inevitably McPherson's words cut through his comfort.

"Well now My Friend, do we remain here in comfort, or do we begin our business?"

Andrew took a deep breath,

"I suppose we must. After all that *is* why I'm here." As he spoke he rose and reluctantly followed his host back down the stairs feeling like a condemned man. McPherson took a large folder from a drawer in his desk and then carefully opened it, with what for him, was a flourish.

"It is *all* here. The correspondence with the Lord Provost and finally," rather dramatically he spread an official looking document on top of the rest, "here is the formal acknowledgement that your grandfather was the rightful heir to the Earl of Mulray!" Andrew gripped the desk, white-knuckled, trying to breathe. His voice was a stifled croak, "But I know the man...I have been his guest. He...Oh God!" and to himself I have made love to his wife and...he almost laughed at that other thought. McPherson smiled sympathetically,

"If I may say Andrew, whoever the imposter was, is...it is *hardly* surprising you have met. After all you were in London, moving in the best circles. From my informants Earl Mulray is a well-known figure of some influence." Andrew took several deep breaths. His voice returned to normal.

"Does he know?"

McPherson bit his lip and clicked his tongue.

"I would imagine by *now* he does. The Lord Provost intended to inform him. He has had notice of a claim for some time, naturally. I would imagine he has known the formal result for weeks, even a month."

"What do you think he will do?"

"He is not aware of *your* identity, if that is any consolation. The Lord Provost wanted to meet you again and invest you personally. He was *always* sympathetic to your cause. You are so *obviously* a Mulray." He shook his head. "I have been to the castle in Scotland. I canna tell you how eerie it is to see your image time and again." Andrew looked puzzled.

"My image?"

McPherson chuckled, "My Boy *you* are the image of the old Earl, your great grandfather."

"I think I need to sit down." Andrew fell into the stiff chair near the struggling fire. "It is all too much...he was so hospitable...and the estate..."

McPherson's tone became icy.

"I donna doobt it is lavish My Friend!" He continued more matter-of-factly. "Too lavish. That is doubtless why he is about to sell your heritage. I understand that both he and his wife deny themselves aught." Andrew shook his head trying desperately to clear it.

"What an Ungodly Mess!"

"Yes, of course we must assume that he, himself, may well be innocent of it all. It was his grandmother who perpetrated the outrage. Her son could well have known, but this current fellow... well it *is* possible he never knew, especially if he has never been North." He paused thoughtfully. "It is difficult to know *how* he will react. Do you have any thoughts, having met him?"

"He won't believe it. He *can't*! His whole life is a lie. What could *anyone* do?" Andrew was still stunned.

"The truth is My Friend, whatever he thinks, he *must* accept what has come to pass." McPherson said prosaically. Andrew shook his head.

"I doubt it. Good God he can't!" He shut his eyes and banged his forehead with his fist. "But what am I to do? What is to be done? What do you want me to do?" McPherson placed a reassuring hand on his shoulder.

"Whatever *needs* to be done, and there is much. I think you need time, time to think. Perhaps we could have dinner with my father or do you prefer to be alone? I fear it has been somewhat of a shock to you, perhaps you would like time alone?" A dazed Andrew stood slowly.

"If you will forgive me I do think I need time. I need time to think it all through. Could we meet tomorrow? By then hopefully I will have my wits about me." He smiled apologetically at his host, who clapped him encouragingly on the shoulder.

"Of course Lad. Tomorrow. There is time enough."

Chapter 24

A sleepless night left Andrew even more confused. He tried, without success, to imagine how the current 'Earl' could or would behave, but it was beyond him. How could *anyone* behave when his world was taken away? He dragged himself out of bed and tried to eat his breakfast, but it all tasted like sawdust. He pushed it aside and drank several cups of coffee instead, then, reluctantly, he set off for Cameron McPherson's office and his own unwanted future.

"My enquiries have revealed a disturbing situation My Friend." The Advocate was all business. "The Earl has even *greater* debts than I realised, and, I fear there are *even more* than I know about. At the present time he has the Estate in Leicestershire, with which you are familiar, the Highland Estate, plus a very fine house in Belgravia. If we...you are to save the Scottish Estate, at least one of the others will need to be sold."

Andrew rolled his eyes and looked to the Heavens. *How* could he do this? He was torn. On the one hand was Torquil Mulray, and, more importantly, if he were honest, Amy. On the other hand was the responsibility for several hundred people he had never met. How much would it cost his pocket ...and his heart. Amy... *how* could she survive in her new world? Everything she ever wanted... and had schemed for. He could not deny she meant something to him...more than he would like. As for his pocket...McPherson clearly saw him as a man of limited means. Should he leave him thinking that? Neanaidh would doubtless say his bonanza was a gift from God to help his clan...these unknown people.

"Could we perhaps talk with him? Make a bargain...at least leave him something?"

"Why?" The answer was terse and sharp.

"I mean what do you think he will do? What can he do? He'll need to live somewhere...somehow."

McPherson remained implacable.

"That fellow has never given thought to anyone else but *himself*, least of all to those who *depended* on him. What brings you to think he will change? I say again, what brings you to think he will change? Bollocks!"

Andrew buried his head in his hands. "I just keep wondering what he will do?"

"Enough of your swithering, here are the figures. Surely these will help to make up your mind. Noow the house in Belgravia should be worth...." With considerable effort Andrew turned his mind to McPherson's figures and proposals. There could be no doubt Mulray had squandered a fortune already, but was he, Andrew, to be judge jury and executioner? It was a long day. He felt drained and very despondent.

"Now Lad are we to have the pleasure of your company this evening or shall we wait another day? My father is anxious to see you, but he will understand, 'tis a great burden we are putting on you."

"Thank you Sir, but I think I will go back to my Hotel. I hardly slept last night. Crikey to be honest, I'm knackered!" McPherson smiled sympathetically,

"Och aye Lad. You are properly ' scunnered' as we say...confused and bewildered. A good night's sleep and you'll be in fine fettle." He shook Andrew's hand. " We can visit with my father tomorrow, but I feel we should go North within the week. I want you to see and understand. But, I needst warn you, it will not be comfortable in any shape or form. It is not really a castle you will be staying in...rather an ancient Tower House. Your great grandfather added two wings...one of which is derelict...and...damaged." Their eyes met. "Yes I made that same assumption." There was an uncomfortable silence. Andrew felt obliged to relieve his companion's discomfort.

"You are forgetting I am well used to sleeping under the stars. Though I grant, not in *your* weather. But is there any part habitable?"

"It is vairy dirty and neglected...some old retainers exist in the kitchen and a wee apartment, but I've nae doobt a good dose of elbow grease from some willing workers could soon put it to rights. The problem is, no-one is willing to work when there is the threat of the Clearing!" He frowned and shook his head. "*You* are too concerned with the Imposter. You have the fate of *many others* to consider."

"I know that, but it will not be easy, since the famine in the Highlands, nothing is simple. I've heard of many landowners having to struggle. And I know for a fact, sheep are *not* the answer. My country has already taken the lion's share of their market and *that* is only the beginning." McPherson helped Andrew to arrange his cloak and patted his shoulder.

"Aye Lad! 'Tis a hard road but I've every confidence in those broad shoulders. I will make the necessary arrangements. Tomorrow we will meet with the Lord Provost and then dine with my father. Then we will journey North before the weather closes in. Have a quiet night Lad."

Andrew stepped into the darkened street. The gas lights were clearly losing the battle with the blackening sky. His feet echoed on the cobblestones. The familiar icy wind bit into his face. Perhaps he should find a cab, though the place was quite deserted. A voice called, "Earl Mulray!" Why was McPherson calling him that? Was it a joke? He turned sharply, saw a flash and felt a heavy blow to his shoulder. He stared at it in puzzlement. There was blood on his cloak. He stumbled back against the dark stone wall and glanced back up the street. Evil faced him. Two reptilian eyes and the barrel of a long-nosed pistol were being carefully focussed on his frozen body. Then suddenly, the space between death and Andrew was filled. Baillie McPherson's narrow frame offered little protection but his ample housekeeper, his clerk, and several others had rushed on the scene at the sound of the shot, and already he could feel their arms supporting him. Out of the corner of his eye he saw the shadow hesitate, and then disappear.

"*In here!*" McPherson's anxious voice "Bring him in here. Robertson," He turned to his ashen-faced clerk, "go to Mr Fleming and ask him to come as quickly as possible. Quick Lad GO!" Then he looked toward Andrew's burly supporters. "Thank God you came...can you bring him through here...nooow into the chair. Gently... gently...Well done...Good Samaritans ...*You* are Heaven sent, I couldna have shifted him. Mrs Gow a basin of water and some clean rags!"

Andrew sank gratefully into the chair, still clutching his shoulder. The blood was seeping between his fingers through the heavy cloth. Then he felt his hand being lifted, then his cloak, and finally his jacket and shirt were carefully pulled away.

"The bullet has hit him from behind. Here press hard against the wound. We need to stop the bleeding!" Andrew tried to concentrate...the oil...where was the bottle? With his good arm he searched his pockets.

"Nay Lad keep thee still. T'will do harm if thee moves and struggles." Mrs Gow's soft voice tried to soothe her patient. Andrew's searching fingers were rewarded. He pushed a small bottle into his nurse's hand.

"In the water when you wash the wound...for the infection...." Mrs Gow accepted the dark blue bottle and held it to the light, then carefully undid the stopper. A sharp pungent smell made her eyes water. "Eucalyptus...please use it." Through the fog of his brain he tried to explain.

"Noow Lad the doctor is on his way. No need to fret." Cameron McPherson surreptitiously shook his head at his housekeeper, but Mrs Gow was not so easily persuaded.

"Methinks Sir, it is the oil of eucalyptus the native people use...I have the niece in New South Wales and she has told me about it. It canna do harm and if Mr. Walters wants it..."

"Heathen Witchcraft!!" muttered McPherson but he was interrupted by the return of Robertson with a distinguished individual carrying a carpet bag.

"Well. Well. Dear God *what* is the world coming to? *And* in the High Street!!" He had already discarded his coat and opened his bag. "Now where is our patient? Ah! A right royal mess indeed. *Whatever* have you done to deserve *this*, My Lad? Now let us see...as I thought the bullet is still in there. Right Lad." He took a small bottle and transferred a few drops to a cloth which he held to Andrew's nose. "That's it. Now just a wee sniff...that's the shot." He was left to laugh at his own joke...Andrew heard nothing.

Andrew opened his eyes and tried to focus. A strange man in a long black coat was leaning over him holding his wrist. Behind him the room looked familiar. Then he heard McPherson's voice.

"How bad is it Mr Fleming?"

"Thanks be to God, as he turned it hit his shoulder and *missed* his heart, which was doubtless the target. There is damage to his shoulder but it shouldna be permanent. He'll need careful attention mind. Infection is our greatest enemy." Behind his back, the patient caught Mrs Gow's eye and she winked knowingly. "I've bled him so he will needst to be kept quiet. And plenty of poultices Mrs Gow. Can you manage here or should we carry him to the Infirmary? Though to carry *him* anywhere t'will not be easy!"

"Of course we can take care of him here noow that you have been kind enough to come and treat him Sir. If you would instruct Mrs Gow I would be gratified and we will do our best."

"Certainly, and I will be here in the morning. I'll give him a cordial. He should sleep, although *before* he has it, I recommend we get him into a bed." He turned to McPherson, "Do you have enough help to handle this braw lump?" He laughed heartily. With some effort the Braw Lump interrupted,

"I'll be fine. My legs are fine Sir. I can get myself to the bed, but I must thank you for coming to my aid...." The doctor nodded but chuckled nevertheless,

"Well I doubt they'll be as steady as you think but I am sure with some help you will manage. On the morrow ...till then." and he bustled out the door, with a cheery wave. Andrew tried to stand and had to concede the doctor was right, but with the help of Robertson and Mrs Gow he managed the stairs, so that by the time McPherson returned from farewelling the doctor, he was stretched out in bed with his helpers undressing him, much to his dismay.

"By the grace of God and your moving in the nick of time, we've had a lucky escape. Praise the Good Lord! You sleep noow. That's the ticket." He paused, his thin face set, his eyes narrowed, his voice suddenly sharp. "Mind you, noow we know what that Divil intends. Surely *this* will harden your heart. Methinks the fool has forgotten Scotland's motto...if ever he knew it. 'Nemo me impune lacessit!'... No-one attacks me with impunity!'" He shook his head.

"He has shown his hand. What a muckle ijit!" Andrew wanted to reply but neither his brain nor his mouth seemed willing.

◆ ◆ ◆

"Well, well, are we awake then?" Cameron McPherson's cheery voice roused Andrew from his doze. He shook his head trying valiantly to focus as the voice continued. "I'm glad it is to see you sitting up, and Mrs Gow assures me you managed an entire bowl of gruel." Andrew's grimace was ignored. "Well done Lad. You've given us all rather a fright. Mr Fleming is convinced you are doing splendidly, but well I've not known you to lie abed for several days." McPherson chuckled at Andrew's amazement as he seated himself on a chair drawn close to the bed. "We needst to talk Lad. Clearly we will delay our trip north, but my concern is rather *more* immediate...do you think the assailant believed he'd succeeded? I've managed to keep any mention of our unfortunate incident from the newspapers, but then I wondered if I should have? What is to be done is my query?" He rubbed his forehead thoughtfully. "Do you remember anything at all Lad?"

Andrew struggled through the cloud in his brain,

"I was walking down the street and when I saw how dark and miserable it was I remember thinking...yes I remember thinking I should find a cab...so I stopped walking...then I heard someone, I thought it was you...yes I thought you were trying to be funny..." McPherson frowned.

"*Whatever* would make you think that?"

"It was because the voice called 'Earl Mulray'...who else would call *me* that?"

"Yes I see your point...perhaps he had been watching for my visitors...and decided you were the likeliest candidate...after all the timing was right. Did you not get a chance to see him Lad?"

"No...it was dark...his hat was pulled low and his collar high..." He shivered. "I do remember the pistol being aimed and his eyes glinting...if you hadn't come so quickly..." McPherson patted his arm.

"Well we did, but what now?" He examined the patient. "You're distinctive enough, and now with one arm in a sling you'll *never* pass unnoticed, My Friend." He chewed the end of his thumb, deep in thought. "When I think about it all, I doubt our Imposter knows it is *you*. The assassin would recognize you again, but as far as we know the Imposter has not your name...yet. No the assassin is our chief concern...he'll doubtless be keen to collect his reward, and that presumably only comes with the guarantee you are thoroughly disposed of." He frowned and peered around the room as if looking for any likely assailant.

"Let me assure you I have *no* intention of allowing anyone to claim the reward, thanks I must say, to all of you, and Mr Fleming!" Said Andrew, feelingly.

"I thought to put black crepe around the door but Mrs Gow was horrified....'inviting bad luck' ...and she could be right. I've had my clerks watch out for any loiterer. The constables too, have been watching I'm sure!"

"He *must* know I survived, if he knows who Mr Fleming is. Clearly undertakers would be visiting otherwise."

"Och Aye! All the more reason to be careful! I've had Robertson sleep in the kitchen, in case he tries to come in the back wynd, and the front door is firmly bolted at night. That *should* be enough."

It was not, however, enough. Andrew stirred...was that a noise? He opened his eyes in time to see the narrow sash window being slowly lifted. He could barely see even a shadow but he was instantly alert. He glanced around the tiny room, one bed, one chair and an elongated cupboard. Nowhere to hide, and no weapon at hand. He could not see a figure so he guessed his assailant could not yet see into the room. He slid out of the bed and hurriedly pushed the bolster and pillows into what he hoped, was the shape of a body and pulled the counterpane high. Then he pressed himself against the wall beside the opening window. Would one arm be enough?

A leg then a shoulder and finally a dark figure, slid silently into the room. Andrew saw the glint of a knife. He waited until the figure had moved toward the bed, then with his right arm grabbed the man around the neck, jerking his head back in what he hoped was a stranglehold. At the same time he yelled for help. Andrew pushed the body forward and cracked its head against the wall as hard as he could, but already he could feel his captive twisting, trying to use his knife. Andrew let go, grabbed the chair and tried to connect with his opponent's head, but he was too slow. The man turned, facing him and the chair became Andrew's only defence against the deadly weapon. They stood, silently searching for the other's weakness when the door burst open and Robertson, Mrs Gow and McPherson, looking like a slightly demented rooster with his night-cap sticking high and his spindly legs poking from beneath his voluminous nightshirt, tumbled into the room. Modesty forgotten Mrs Gow boxed the startled assailant over the head with her chamber pot, while Robertson and McPherson each managed to grab an arm. The knife rattled to the floor and Mrs Gow reached up and dragged the mask away from their captive's face.

"Ye Devil! Ye *Godless Murderer!*" Mrs Gow was incensed. The chamber pot found its mark several times before her employer could calm her. He turned to the prisoner.

"And so Villain, if my housekeeper is not to continue beating you with her favourite guzzunder, *you* will confess! No havering let me warn you. *Who* sent you on this murderous errand?" He stood inches from the close-set eyes and quivering mouth. "Och, Aye, not so brave and chipper noow are we? Come Man! Who sent you!?" There was a sullen silence. Robertson picked up the knife and pressed the point against the prisoner's bony nose, but his employer intervened. "There'll not be the need for that Lad. He'll be catching the tumbrel to his fate, but *if* he confesses he *may* find I can put in a good word or two. What about it, You Knave? Are ye prepared to die for nought?"

There was a long silence interrupted only by Mrs Gow's renewed threats as she waved her weapon menacingly. Eventually a croaking whisper,

"The Earl. The Earl sent me." McPherson was not satisfied.

"Which Earl? Come Man which Earl!?"

"I dunno, 'onest, I dunno."

"*Not* good enough." Robertson pressed the knife harder until the shifty eyes began to water.

"'Onest Sir, Your Grace, I dunno. 'E's in Lunnon but it's a Scotsman 'e be, or so 'e says."

"Very well, Robertson we will take this cowardly rat downstairs and tie him to a kitchen chair and you can guard him until morn." Mrs Gow, however, was not about to trust Robertson alone, with the result that the prisoner, having been tied to the chair, was forced to endure a detailed description of his nasty self, and his heinous crimes, from an indignant housekeeper for the rest of the night.

Meanwhile Andrew slumped on his bed, the strength gone from his legs, and his shoulder throbbing. He felt ill. Whether or not Torquil Mulray knew whom he was planning to have killed, was not the point any more. It was all an Ungodly Mess! His frustration grew. He'd *never* wanted any of this, the title, the burden, the problems of people he'd never met, and the fate of those he'd *not only met* but.... It would be so easy to just walk away...or would it? No. There was only one person who could at least try to sort it out, and for the first time his anger turned to determination. A few more days, yes a few more days to heal and then he would go north and begin.

Chapter 25

Young and healthy as he was, nevertheless, almost two weeks passed before Andrew was well enough to travel and, even then, it was against Mr. Fleming's advice. The train to Inverness allowed relative comfort, but the final coach ride over ever rougher roads had been very painful.

He had tried to feel confident and purposeful but apprehension increased tenfold as he stood in the crowded church. The faces before him were closed and unsmiling. There were occasional murmurs but little conversation. Many of the women sat head bowed under their bonnets, plaid shawls high over hunched shoulders against the strong wind that they expected would blow them to the four corners of the earth. Andrew, himself, wondered were they praying or trying to hide from *him*? Other eyes watched warily, some fierce with hatred. What did they expect from him? Certainly nothing to make their lives easier. What did he expect of himself?

He glanced at McPherson, who was standing beside him at the lectern. He took a deep breath and as loudly and clearly as he could, began.

"Fialte. Ciamar a tha sibh?" Suddenly all eyes were up on him. "Is mise Aindreas Walters." Then he held out his hands apologetically as he continued. "I am here speaking for the Earl of Mulray. I am a relative but I do not speak your language." He smiled ruefully. "And Baillie McPherson, here, thinks I don't speak English either." Baillie McPherson shook his head. "Therefore he will explain my words in the Gaelic. I am hoping that way we will have no confusion."

McPherson nodded and began to repeat Andrew's sentences, translating as he went.

"I understand that you were given notice to quit in March. That will no longer be the case. There will be no need for *anyone* to leave. I... I mean, the Earl... wants us to work *together* to improve the Estate." Before McPherson could finish his translation there was a babble of noise. Many women were crying. Men stood in shocked disbelief. Then suddenly they all began to sing. Andrew stood transfixed as the well-loved melody of the Twenty Third Psalm filled the church. He looked helplessly to his friend, but McPherson was also singing. Andrew knew the words, but not *these* words.

Eventually the voices died and he was able to continue.

"I should explain that I am from New South Wales myself, and I am *more* than happy to assist any of you, who wish to travel there, but I am hoping that many of you will remain." He waited for McPherson's translation but already there were smiles, hands clasped in joy rather than dread.

"We will meet with your tacksmen and discuss our plans. We welcome your ideas. If you will forgive my selfishness, I would like to work on the castle as quickly as possible. I'm sorry but *I* am not used to *very* cold weather, and I am still looking for a room with its windows intact." He shrugged his shoulders and wrapped his arms around himself, shivering elaborately. The crowd laughed at his feeble joke, perhaps in relief, although it was not entirely play-acting...McPherson had insisted he wear a kilt, and though he was generally warm enough, his knees were freezing.

A priest who had been standing quietly against the wall, came forward, shook Andrew's hand and then led his congregation in prayer. Then two other men came and took Andrew's hand and bowed low. Despite his embarrassment Andrew tried to talk to them. He was anxious to begin, but he realised it would take time for these men to understand him, and time for all those in the church to understand their new future. He stepped away from the lectern. It was a mistake. First one old woman came forward, seized his hand and kissed it. Then others. They shook his hand and patted his shoulders with ever increasing enthusiasm. He retreated to the lectern. He held up his hand and was shocked at the instant silence... God help me I'm in this good and proper. He struggled to think of something to say... to fill the sudden silence. Neanaidh's words somehow came out of his mouth...

"We shall bear one another's burdens and thereby fulfil the law of Christ." He swallowed hard. "Tomorrow My Friends *we* will begin." He fled outside even before McPherson had finished repeating his words. He leant against the stone lintel. Would they think he was cracked? He probably was! His shoulders ached. His *heart* ached. How long would he be imprisoned by his 'duty'. The vivid green hills, the stone cottages snuggled low, the clear streams that always seemed in a hurry. Would he ever learn to feel at home.

He was interrupted by one of the English-speaking farmers and McPherson.

"Well My Friend, I think you did 'very' well for a beginner." McPherson's thin mouth twitched. "And I'd no idea you were such a scholar of the Guid Book! Vairy impressive Laddie."

Andrew gave McPherson a speaking look as he turned to the farmer.

"Perhaps Sir you will join me, and brave the smoking chimneys, and the icy blasts and risk having supper with us? And perhaps you have a colleague or two who will join us?" He turned then to walk back to the Castle with McPherson. They were joined by the Priest and two more farmers.

As carefully as he could Andrew said,

"Tha mi toilichte ur coinneachadh." and held out his hand.

"Our lessons have reaped a reward Andrew, have they not, but I am sure we can manage with *your* English." McPherson said as he smiled and winked at the others.

"I am their priest, Mr Walters, Fergus Bruce, I welcome you with open arms, and we will all quickly learn to understand you when you bring us *such* joy."

Andrew led his guests into what had clearly been the library. Shelves of mouldering books lined the walls. A fire tried valiantly to fight off the chill, and the mustiness of years. They settled themselves around a table and Andrew began.

"Failde Gentlemen." He took a deep breath. "I am hoping that we can work together but first of all my colleague and I need to discover the *real* condition of the Estate. I am hoping you will show us everything. *Not* what you think I should see. I *cannot* help unless you are *completely* honest with me... about everything, and about your needs and your ideas." He paused and studied the faces around him. "Baillie McPherson is concerned that my English is not easy for you, so please tell me if and when that is the case."

His audience shook their heads as the Reverend Bruce replied.

"We are able to understand your words Sir, even if we are still trying to comprehend the chance you have offered our people."

"I mean every word. So let us begin."

Chapter 26

The guests had gone. Andrew stood warming himself as he leant on the mantelpiece. A haphazard collection of vases, books, a pipe rack, several mugs, presumably silver, but black with years of neglect, stretched along the carved stone. Dust lay thick on it all. Bloody Mausoleum! How could he hope to resurrect it? How could he ever get it warm. Mind, a few less broken windows could help. His shoulder ached with the cold, though it *was* healing. Would Torquil try again? Surely not here.

"Andrew Lad," McPherson's voice interrupted his gloomy reverie. "I've been thinking we will need ready funds as soon as possible. Would you not agree?"

"Just what I was thinking, to be honest." He poked at the fire and held out his glass. "Would you care for another? The old Earl's cache of whisky is magnificent... do you think we could sell it, or should we just keep enjoying it?" His expression belied his words and McPherson responded accordingly.

"Och no Laddie! *We need* the sustenance!" and he chuckled as he accepted a refill in his delicate glass. "But I have been considering the matter and I'm thinking ye've no real need for me here noow. The Reverend Bruce, and those two venerable men, can manage to understand ye well enough. No! I needst go home and organize ourselves. By now the Imposter must have come to terms with his future. I will serve him notice to quit and make the necessary arrangements to sell the Leicestershire Estate, for a beginning. Doubtless you know I think you are being far too generous to allow him to maintain the Belgravia mansion. You canna be sure he will not swindle ye. Indeed I'd bet money on it!"

Andrew shrugged.

"Go ahead and sell the one. I've a mind to go and talk to him myself... try to come to some sort of arrangement."

"Don't be a fool Man! After what he's done! *Look* at yourself. Two attempts on your life. What *more* do ye want."

"But I don't think he knew it was *me*. I really doubt he would have done it if he'd known." Andrew began, but he was cut short by his indignant companion.

"Humbug! You've taken leave of your wits! *The man is desperate. He's a cornered rat! He'll do anything* to save his own skin!" He finished his whisky and rose to his feet. "There'll be no more of such nonsense. Instead you could be giving me a list of your requirements. I'll order the glass, if you could make some estimation, but I am also thinking you will need some skilled men at the vairy least. Do you ken we have glaziers, or house staff among your throng? Willing they may be but how competent?" He walked to the door. "A good night to you, Earl of Mulray. *Think on it all.*"

Andrew remained, staring into the dwindling fire. He had said, tomorrow we will begin, but *where* to begin. That was the problem. And winter. What did that mean? How much could he even begin, however willing were the people. He glanced around at the dusty shelves laden with books. Someone had collected them... someone had liked to read. He had seen libraries where the books were regimented and symmetrical, but here they were all shapes and sizes. Who had lived here? Who had read them? *His* family. He knew *nothing* about them, and how was he ever to know them now? He opened a very old leather bound volume and sneezed violently. It was in Latin... not his strong point. McPherson must have Latin. He left the room and its ghosts, and wandered up to his bed, trying to ignore all that lay ahead.

As he came down the wide stone staircase the next morning it became immediately obvious his people were undoubtedly willing! He was greeted by an army whose weapons were mops and brooms and buckets. He nodded and smiled his way through to the kitchen. The elderly woman who had opened the door on his arrival yesterday, threw her hands in the air and hurriedly pushed him toward what he could only presume was the breakfast parlour. He stared in astonishment as he stepped into a room free of dust and cobwebs. A fire glowed and crackled in the grate. A table was covered with white linen, a glass vase replete with heather, in its centre, and it was tastefully set with relatively clean silver.

McPherson sat watching him with a wry smile,

"Methinks the faerie people have been here the night... If we were in the Lowlands I'd be thinking we had been visited by a 'Brownie', but here in the Highlands we have *your* people. They must have been here since before dawn, scouring the place from top to bottom."

"Good God! I did say I wanted to fix the place but I never imagined... What should I do? And by the way what on earth is a Brownie?" Andrew slumped into his chair. His companion smiled.

"The Brownie comes in the night to finish the chores. These fine people here have braved the darkness, and the elements, on your behalf, My Friend. It is called gratitude. They don't understand who you are," He paused and lifted a quizzical eyebrow. "any more than *you* do yourself, I know... but they understand *what* you have offered them. And, they are shrewd enough to make you welcome and even perhaps grateful to them." He glanced at the book Andrew held. "Is that the list for me?"

Andrew chuckled.

"No...not yet. This is a book I picked up last night but it is in Latin. Another mystery. You realize McPherson, I know *nothing* at all, about the people who have lived in this place. I remember my grandfather, but he had rejected it all. I picked up this book in a vain hope of understanding, but like my life at the moment, it is the great unknown."

"I'm glad to see you can laugh. Perhaps not from this one, but there *will* be records, and of course there are *all* the portraits. Here let me see..." He opened the volume and shook his head in wonder. "Well this proves that at least *one* of your ancestors was a scholar. This is an account by a Roman of his country's conquest of Britain! What a find! Although, as you probably know, they *never* conquered the Highlands. Perhaps that is *why* he had this book... pride in his land." He rifled gently through the pages, pausing occasionally. "Now *here* is a marvellous thing. The author complains, he's *outraged* in fact, that the Pictish dares to say, 'To robbery, murder and outrage, they give the lying name of government, and where they make a desert they call it peace!' *That* could be said of the Sassenachs today! Is that not what Britain offers her conquered territories?"

Andrew bit his lip and nodded.

"I'd say it *is* what Grasshopper's Old Men are probably saying right now. But what is the answer. The Romans didn't conquer the Highlands but the sheep have... or their owners." McPherson looked somewhat bemused as Andrew continued. "I can't be worried about Grasshopper right now. I have made a sort of list but... well I'll keep you posted... I think the more I see, the more we'll need, don't you agree?"

Chapter 27

The weeks went by in a blur of activity. Andrew was increasingly shocked by what he saw. In the back of his mind he'd hoped not to have to sell at least one of the southern properties. Now he wondered about the need to sell both. He avoided thinking about it. One step at a time. For the present he could use his own funds.

The atmosphere of the whole estate had changed. It gave him hope. Repairs were visible, however small. The farms had been invariably run down as the tenants had tried to satisfy Torquil's insatiable demands. There had been barely enough to live on. People and animals were half-starved. It was winter. Was there even enough food to last until spring? He announced that the rent due for the next quarter would not be collected. Would that ease the situation?

Slowly the castle began to emerge from its neglect and despair. Mind, little could be done until the windows were sealed. Bloody Mausoleum! His bedroom in particular was bleak. He wondered if *anyone* could make *this* castle warm? His shoulder continued to ache. Would Torquil try again? Hard to think he could organize it here.

As quickly as he could he began to put names to faces. The elderly retainers who had remained in the castle through so many years, were Albert Anderson and his wife Sarah Gunn. He wondered aloud until he was told by the Reverent Bruce that this was quite normal. A wife in Scotland maintained her own name. The two men whom he had met on the first day were apparently cousins, Hector McDonald and Henry MacDonald. They certainly looked alike, tall, even dour, while Herbert had much more to say. For Andrew it took at least three weeks before they, or anyone, would really say what they thought, instead of *always* agreeing with him. He tried to be patient, *very* patient! When would they realise he wanted honest answers?

As he toured the estate, mainly on foot, he saw that unlike the "invaders" from the South who had brought Cheviot sheep, his farmers had the black-faced Highland breed. He discovered that their fleece was long and coarse, full of kemp and dead hair, and because of poor feeding, generally worse than usual. He knew from his visit to Dunrobbin that the Cheviot fleece was shorter, fine, crimpy and dense, not to mention clean! Though he would agree with his farmers, theirs had the better mutton. He was also pleasantly surprised when he saw the homespun products the women produced from the local wool. But whatever breed they had, he knew well, that the market was no longer there for wool itself. If he mixed the breeds perhaps... but if he had *every* woman spinning and weaving it would barely be enough! He wondered about tourism. The Queen was making Scotland, especially the Highlands more and more fashionable. Did he have enough forest? "Hunting, shooting and fishing." Could they offer that?

He had promised to go to Mannering for Christmas. It was already December and the weather was *already* bad... foul in fact! On the other hand he wanted and needed to talk to Nick's family. Nick's brother was a farmer... perhaps he could help. And the Spencers. He needed advice from Sir Peter and doubtless he'd be given advice by her Ladyship! If he could get to Inverness he could go by train to York... was that possible... He must make enquiries... Then the letter arrived from Baillie McPherson.

Edinburgh
30th November 1851

My Dear Andrew,

It is with no real regret, I confess, that I am writing to inform you of the death of Torquil "Mulray". Your friendly assassin has himself suffered a fatal "accident". Please see the enclosed article. It may, or may not, cause you distress, but it will undoubtedly cause you inconvenience. I feel we will now need to deal with the widow, in which case I strongly recommend your presence. Can you come as soon as possible to Edinburgh so that we may journey to London.

Yours etc ...

Andrew stared at the clipping. "Esteemed Scottish Earl... shooting accident... despite valiant efforts of all present and the medical profession..." He had continued to worry about Torquil and his situation. Was this Torquil's ultimate response... he hadn't killed his enemy and so had almost certainly killed himself. Of course *he* had to go. What could he tell these people here? A new uncertainty! They would need reassurance. He shut his eyes and tried to collect his thoughts. He tried *not* to think about the widow. He hurried to find the Reverend Bruce.

Chapter 28

The journey South was difficult enough but the encounter with Amy, infinitely worse. Andrew had never been to the house in Belgravia. It stood in one of the best parts of the city. The elegant mansions faced onto a square where a statue of a mounted man stood proudly. Reluctantly Andrew stepped from the Hansom cab, hardly registering McPherson's words.

"I imagine the lady will be expecting us. I sent a letter informing her that the *real* Earl of Mulray would be accompanying myself, to discuss arrangements and settlements." He grimaced. "Though why we needst to discuss anything... she has *no* right to anything."

Heavy black crepe adorned the lower windows. McPherson rang the bell. It was answered by a black liveried footman. He accepted their card with haughty indifference and left them standing in the black draped portico. A butler appeared and they were ushered inside with a bad grace. McPherson rolled his eyes and pressed his lips in disapproval. Even Andrew registered the great luxury of this entrance hall. Thick Indian carpets, a magnificent chandelier, gleaming furniture, and in the centre a grand staircase, up which they were ushered.

The butler knocked, entered and announced the visitors. Andrew took a deep breath and followed the other two. The butler disappeared. The lady of the house stared at the card she had been given, then at Andrew.

"*You!*" The Countess screamed. "*You!*" Another scream. "*You* are the *fiend* who has *ruined* me! Oh God! *How* can I bear it?" She threw herself onto the nearest sofa wailing and sobbing.

Andrew and McPherson exchanged glances. Baillie McPherson stepped forward and began to explain.

"Dear Madam. You are mistaken. Mr Walters...eh... Earl Mulray is *not* the cause of your problems..."

"How *dare* you speak to me! *Who* are you?" She dismissed him with a flick of her hand and turned on Andrew. "You have caused this. You have *murdered* my husband. And now you come to savour my destruction!" Andrew stood silent, McPherson, however, tried again.

"But Madam... Mr Walters... I mean Earl Mulray is not the..." He was cut short by another scream and a vase that was hurled at his head. He dodged in time and it shattered against the wall.

In the sudden silence, Andrew spoke quietly.

"I can understand your shock perhaps, but if I were you, Your Ladyship, I would refrain from wasting your ornaments, and listen to what we have to say."

The Countess sprang to her feet and flew at Andrew. She pummelled his chest and spat in his face, screeching anew.

Andrew stepped back and carefully wiped the spittle from his chin before seizing her by the arms and firmly returning her to the sofa. Baillie McPherson stood frozen in shock, then he ventured forward.

"Dear Madam, you are naturally upset at the sudden change in your fortune..." But the look of hatred that was turned on him, left him speechless midsentence. Andrew shook his head at him, then finished the lawyer's speech himself.

"As Baillie McPherson was about to say, Your Ladyship, you are naturally shocked, but he... we, have made you a generous offer. I would recommend you consider it. You have really no alternative unless, of course, you want the world to know all your secrets. I could announce that your dear departed husband, was *not*, and *never had been* the rightful heir."

The Countess sprang to her feet.

"How dare you! Who are you to speak to me like this... *the son of a clerk!* How *dare* you!"

Andrew smiled quizzically as he replied,

"I would suggest you refrain from delving into *my* heritage... or yours Dear Lady." He shrugged. "There are always secrets. And *servants* always know them. You may remember my sister is very close to your family's servants in New South Wales."

Amy's face was white but her eyes blazed with anger and hatred. She reached for another ornament.

"Now. Now. Not again Your Ladyship." Andrew said as he retrieved the delicate figurine from her hand, and placed it carefully on the table. He turned to the momentarily silent Countess. "You have a week to decide, Your Ladyship. Think hard. You can keep this house, or the Estate in Leicestershire. I am prepared to fund the restoration of the Scottish Estate for now, but I absolutely *refuse* to pay for your late husband's debts. "

Baillie McPherson added quietly.

"Inordinate debts!"

"Scottish Estate!" Amy spat the words. "Scottish Estate... what is *that* to me!"

Andrew's mouth twisted.

"The Scottish Estate is the reason your late husband could call himself an Earl, however falsely, Dear Lady, and bestow the title, you coveted so greatly, on you. If you accept our offer it may be your son's only legacy."

McPherson muttered, "Not *his* legacy," but a look from Andrew silenced him.

"You beast! How long have you known all this? How long ago did my husband know? You killed him. *You upstart colonial!* It was *no* accident. *I* am a *widow* thanks to you!" Amy screamed the words, clutched her breast and sobbed uncontrollably.

Andrew stood patiently waiting but McPherson had had enough. He shouted above her hysteria.

"Your husband knew long enough! Long enough to try to have Mr Walters, here, murdered! *That* was his cowardly solution*! Murder the real Earl*! Obviously the ruffian missed his mark. Although he tried again. The evidence is before your eyes Madam!" He gestured dramatically at Andrew's arm as it rested in a sling. "It is not my want to allow you to continue to live a lie. You have *nothing* except the generosity of Mr Walters. His *foolish* generosity in my ken! You would do well to *stop* your blathering and *listen!*"

His words had some effect. Amy's sobs were quieter at least. Andrew seized the moment.

"If you accept this offer Countess, your name and reputation will remain intact, for the time being at least. Your son will be acknowledged as the heir, and I will merely be his uncle who has become his guardian until he reaches majority. This naturally means the health and wellbeing of your son will be *my* responsibility, as well as yours." He paused to gauge whether she was listening. "As I have mentioned we have been in Scotland. The Estate is much improved but there is much more to do. I would recommend taking your son to visit. If you decide to be sensible..."

"How *dare* you lecture *me*! How *dare* you tell me... " She hissed at him.

"I dare because *you* are in no position to argue. The alternative Dear Lady, is for the world, *your* world, to know your husband was an imposter and a profligate fraud! You would never survive such ignominy. I *know* that." He walked purposefully towards the door.

"We will take our leave. You may send word to Baillie McPherson when you have made a decision. Good Day Your Ladyship."

Another ornament crashed into the door as Andrew closed it behind them.

"What a *besom virago*!" Baillie McPherson's description of Amy continued as he followed Andrew down the stairs. "Ungrateful Harpy!"

Andrew, himself, was shaken to the core despite his calm demeanour. It had been worse than he could possibly have expected! It must be the shock, surely she would see that he was being generous. He was offering her hope. Her *only* hope! Would McPherson keep quiet... go along with it? Perhaps he would need to explain? No. That could wait... after all he was not sure, himself.

Chapter 29

"**I** MUST SEE YOU! I BEG YOU!" The billet came before Andrew was dressed. What now? Another tirade? Surely not if she was 'begging'. A morning visit? No. He would not rush at once. He sent a reply that he could be available after four p.m., though for most of the day he thought of little else.

He was shown into another room. Perhaps the damage from flying vases and cushions had not been restored? His hostess was standing in the middle of the room, dressed in a high necked black dress, her hair scraped back from her pale, anxious face.

"Oh Andrew! Can you *ever* forgive me? It was the shock. *How* could I have known it was *you* of all people? The last weeks have been such a nightmare. I was waiting in fear and trepidation for the man who *claimed* to be the real Earl of Mulray. Then *you* walked through the door." She sank dramatically onto the nearest sofa and held her hand to shield her eyes. "What new nightmare is to come?" Her voice broke. She held out her hands in a gesture of despair and sighed deeply.

Andrew stood silent. What was he supposed to do? Was she apologising for her behaviour? And then what?

"It was no doubt difficult for you but I had imagined your husband would have told you..." His voice trailed away.

"Why would he tell me? His whole life was being *destroyed*! Doubtless he tried to spare me... the Poor Dear Man." She began to weep. "Oh *what* is to become of me?" The tears increased. She buried her head in the pillows but her shoulders shook, indeed her whole body began to shake and tremble. Andrew took her by the shoulders and turned her to face him. She still trembled, and tears dropped on her cheeks but she seemed to be listening.

"The letter you received, explained, that for *now* at least, if you are amenable, there will be no announcement. It will simply be presumed that your husband's tragic accident has left your son as heir. I will not proclaim myself as Earl, and I am hoping it will not become generally known. But and it is a *very big* but, your husband's debts are... are monumental. I could declare you bankrupt, but we, well *I* have decided that, as was detailed in the letter, if we can find someone to take the Leicestershire Estate, we should be able to handle the situation."

She stared at him in horror.

"Is *that* all I am to you? *A burden and a debt!*" She began to cry and shake. "So cold! So formal! Do you remember *nothing*? O Andrew My Love!" The hysterics threatened to return. Andrew took her hand.

"Of course you are not a burden, but you *must* be sensible. We are trying to spare your name."

"*We!*" She spat the word. "We! Do you mean the shindle-shanked Nobody who *dared* to speak to me yesterday?"

Andrew shrugged as he tried to speak calmly. "That Nobody could *destroy* you, and, he would delight in doing it. His family knew my grandfather, and the wickedness that was done to him and his family," He added almost with bemusement even now. "*My* family. Beware Madam, you are on the edge of a precipice."

"And you alone can save me! *Oh Andrew.*" She collapsed into his arms and leant her head on his chest. "*Where* is the heart that I thought was mine? Is it so long ago."

Andrew was motionless. Now what to do? What would she do? She seemed calmer. Could he risk moving away? He did not want to have her in his arms. To be honest he did not trust himself, however much his head said do not trust her. As if reading his thoughts she nestled her head against his shoulder and gazed up into his eyes.

"Whatever *you* think is best I will do. Who *else* can I trust?" She sighed deeply and tears welled again. "But please if Leicestershire is to go, I *must* go there first. There are keepsakes, mementoes, and oh, *such* happy memories." She turned in his arms so that he could feel her breasts against him, then abruptly she stood up, and with another deep sigh of resignation she pleaded. "Do as you will but let me go to Leicestershire just *once* more."

A relieved Andrew stood himself.

"If it is important to you, do go, but I must warn you the sale must be as soon as possible." He bowed, she held out her hand. He bent over it formally, and left.

McPherson, however, was not happy.

"What do you mean you said *she could go* to the Estate!? You *cannot* allow it. Are you mad, Man? At least *not* until we have made a thorough inventory. The witch and her confederates could strip the place. I will go myself immediately though I will need assistance... someone I can trust. The servants may well be in cahoots."

Andrew shrugged.

"Well if it is as you say, I should come with you. I think you are *too* cynical My Friend, but I will come. The staff may be told simply that as the child's guardian I am in charge of the family's affairs." He shook his head. "Maybe I will get to Mannering, after all, I'll be half way there."

Chapter 30

The Leicestershire Estate left McPherson speechless as he tried to take in the extravagance of his surroundings. For Andrew, however, it brought back many memories. Eventually the lawyer recovered his voice as they were ushered into the Library.

"I have arranged for the Imposter's man of business to meet us here. A lugubrious soul if ever I've met one!"

Andrew smiled ironically.

"Well, being Torquil's Man of Business would surely be a melancholy life. The man deserves your sympathy."

"Oh yes! To tell truth he seemed *relieved* when I began to explain our plans. He's keen to come to Scotland as well. He is due to arrive here tomorrow. I felt it essential that he be here to ensure that all is in order... above board as it were... so that Besom Shrew canna complain."

"Very wise." Andrew added, "It's all rather difficult."

They were interrupted by the housekeeper who came quietly into the room, hands clashed tightly at her breast.

"Good afternoon Gentleman. It is a sad business that brings you back Mr Walters, is it not? Such a terrible, terrible time. They were all here having such a splendid time, and then..." She pressed her fist to her mouth and it was several seconds before she could continue. "And such a young wife and the child..."

Andrew nodded solemnly.

"So true Mrs Hodgson... is that correct... have I remembered correctly?"

"Oh Sir!" A glimmer of a smile rewarded his effort. "Fancy you remembering. It was so long ago, but I have taken the liberty of putting you in that same room. I trust you will be comfortable." Andrew tried to look grateful, though he was not entirely sure how 'comfortable' he would feel. "Your friend has a room in the East corridor. I will have someone show you. We have been very quiet naturally and, if it is convenient for you Sir, we have been serving an early dinner, since... since... since the visitors left."

Andrew smiled encouragingly. She certainly seemed genuinely sad.

"We will find that most convenient Mrs Hodgson. We have been travelling rather too many miles, from Scotland, to London and now here. I am sure my friend Baillie McPherson will be as glad as I will be, for an early night."

The melancholy Man of Business, Higginhottom, arrived promptly the next day and he and McPherson immediately began the tedious task of cataloguing the contents of the entire estate. Higginhottom however, was not the *only* arrival.

Two large travelling coaches appeared in the early afternoon. From the first, with its heraldic crest emblazoned on its door, emerged Miss Mary Simpson, a nurse, a small boy, and finally his mother. From an upstairs window Andrew watched in dismay. Hell and Damnation! Now what? He fled by the back stairs to the stables. After all he had much to do. He needed to decide which horses to keep and take to Scotland. Were there any worth sending to Nick? With luck he'd need *only* see Her Ladyship at dinner.

The meal was a strained affair. Amy's antagonism toward McPherson was ever-present, although the "Besom Shrew" was now the gracious chatelaine and Andrew had to grudgingly admit she played the part to perfection. The food itself was excellent. Clearly Mrs Hodgson, at least, had known of her Ladyship's arrival. Even Baillie McPherson was moved to compliment his hostess on the veal.

"Thank you Sir. Yes we pride ourselves on the quality of our produce here." With a defiant sideways glance at Andrew she continued. "My late husband was an *expert* farmer." But not a judge of horse flesh Andrew thought to himself.

The conversation struggled on. For once in his life Andrew was wishing for more company, even Whittaker's pompous pronouncements would have filled the silences. He broached the subject.

"And Whittaker, he must also be grief-stricken at this time Your Ladyship? How is he holding up?"

"Oh *Yes!*" There was a long sigh and a pause while the widow fought to compose herself. "Oh Yes! Poor Dear. He would have come with us but business... but he should be here tomorrow... to say goodbye," a stifled sob escaped as she tried to continue, "to our home. So many memories, so many memories." She glanced at Andrew and for the briefest moment their eyes locked, before Andrew turned to Mary Simpson.

"It is a pleasure to see you again Ma'am. Are you keeping well, despite everything?"

"Of course Sir... I mean it is dreadful... I mean thank you for asking." She retired from the battle to explain, and concentrated on her syllabub.

Amy had had enough. She stood suddenly, causing general confusion, as the rest scrambled to their feet.

"Come Mary. We will leave these *Gentlemen*." Andrew wondered if he had imagined the bitter tone in her voice. Probably not. Nevertheless he was relieved to settle back and savour his port, and McPherson's company.

"Well we managed eh? She seems determined to play the charming hostess for the moment at least."

"Yes and we shall play the game ourselves. But *who* is Whittaker, why would he be coming here?"

"He was her husband's dearest friend. He'd lived with Torquil all his adult life, as far as I can gather. How, or why, is a mystery. I don't know if he had an income of his own or just sponged off Torquil. He is a fat, pompous, know-it-all bore."

McPherson chuckled.

"Do say what you *really* think Lad. Don't mince your words!"

Andrew shrugged.

"You'll see. At least we won't have to make conversation at dinner. Just listen. Damn me if I weren't wishing for him tonight!" He raised an eyebrow. "I'd imagine he is coming to try and collect 'his' belongings, though I have to wonder... I mean... "

"You're saying he'll be coming to fleece *you* now." McPherson stated bluntly.

Andrew nodded.

"Aye. We'll need to keep a sharp eye out. But what do you think we should do? Sell the place with contents intact. I've been look-ing at the horses, and I'm inclined to take a number north with us. We'll need some carriage horses at least, and some to ride. They may not be the best livestock but it would be a beginning... and we could use that berline to carry baggage, and the curricle is first class. Shame about the showy pair he had to pull it. We could transport anything you thought useful.

"*Useful*! Ha' ye not noticed Lad, almost all the plate and sil-verware carry the family crest? The late Earl appears to have been *very* fond of plastering his shield on everything he owned. 'T would not be of use to another. Take it all north! Even these goblets which are Sunderland ware belong back in Scotland. And take as much of the furniture as you fancy. If ye are to make the castle habitable for paying guests Lad, you'd *not* do better than using what is here."

Andrew looked around him and for the first time tried to concentrate on his surroundings and understand that it all actually belonged to him. Not Torquil Mulray!

"Do you know Cameron, I'd not thought... I mean it is hard to think I can do... do that. I suppose you have a point, but a chair is a chair. My only concern is if it will take my weight, then I decide if it is comfortable." He grinned ruefully. "I've spent more of my life squatting on my heels than sitting in a chair."

McPherson smiled quizzically.

"And do these chairs suffice?"

"As a matter of fact, now you mention it, they seem to." Andrew ran his hand along the curved back of the chair next to him. The smooth wood felt pleasing to his hand. "But I know nought about such things, Cameron. How can *I* know what would suit in Scotland? Mind, I wouldn't mind going through the books in that Library, and rather fancy those horse portraits on the wall in there."

McPherson raised his eyebrows and spread his hands.

"Well *take* them Lad! You've a castle to furnish and even a house on t'other side of the world, though I'm hoping *against* that. And as for the portraits, have ye not noticed the Earl lacks the usual array of family portraits in his fine house. I'm wondering why? Did he fear that he didna look the least like a Mulray, or was it his antipathy toward his homeland?"

"Well there is a portrait of himself, and another of his wife and Hamish in the Drawing Room." Andrew said.

"Aye but *where* are t'others? As ye well know the castle is full of them. Look around ye! Mirrors, tapestries, even plates, but no portraits. Mind those plates are early Eighteenth century plates, Chelsea Botanicals, if I'm not mistaken they are 'Hans Sloane' type." He sipped his port thoughtfully. "And the Breakfast room Lad. Did ye not notice that this morning?"

Andrew tried to remember.

"It's bluish I think and... yes now I think there are plates on the walls there."

"*Well done Lad.*" McPherson said sarcastically. "Ye must have your eyes shut. The room is full of blue and white china and urns and massive planters. The Countess is clearly 'au fait' with the latest fashion. Ye could do worse than keeping *all* that. Though speaking of plates *the* prize is that 'thistle dish' over there on the sideboard. Noooow that would look right at home in your castle, Lad, 'tis by "Quaker Pegg" or *I'm* a Dutchman!"

Andrew scratched his head.

"*I* will study the livestock. *You* can decide what should be done in here. I know nothing about it. But for God's sake don't let her Ladyship guess. *Hell* will descend upon us! How long do you think she will stay?"

"Doubtless she'll be trying to *outlast* us. You may needst to go Lad, but for myself I'll be staying for as long as it takes."

"Well we'll see, but in the meantime we must rejoin those fair ladies. Come gird your loins for the battle Baillie McPherson!"

A difficult evening eventually ended. The Countess bid them an imperious, "Good Evening," and floated from the room with Mary Simpson flapping behind. Andrew, himself followed soon after, retiring to a room that held so many memories, memories that were more real now that Amy was under the same roof. Well I'll doubt I'll see her here. Nevertheless as he stretched his feet toward the fender he caught himself watching the door knob. Don't be a fool. You're the enemy now. She hates you.

Chapter 31

As promised Whittaker arrived and immediately assumed the role of host to the Countess' hostess. Andrew was irritated though vaguely amused, McPherson was incensed.

"Ye canna allow that wee upstart to take charge, Lad. Ye *canna* allow it."

"Patience My Friend. He is bluffing. He has always regarded me as an ignorant colonial, though I can tell, he has not *your* measure." Andrew said placatingly. "We can play his game. We'll just bide our time I reckon. Doubtless he has an agenda, let him reveal it. As I said he is so full of his own importance he'll make a mistake."

McPherson studied his young companion.

"Och Lad. You're a shrewder man than I gave ye credit for. I take your point. I'll bide my time and my tongue but 'twill not be easy!"

How difficult it would be became obvious at dinner the first evening.

"I'm glad to have the opportunity Walters to see you, I have *much* to discuss with you as you may imagine." Whittaker was already ensconced in the drawing room enjoying a pre-dinner whisky when Andrew, accompanied by a reluctant McPherson came down for dinner. His air of propriety was palpable. Andrew shot a warning glance at his lawyer. Almost imperceptibly McPherson nodded.

"Oh! Now Gentlemen. No business please! Whittaker dear, may I present to you Mr Walters' lawyer Baillie McPherson." Amy twinkled prettily at the lawyer. "I pray I have your title correct Sir?"

McPherson bowed low over her hand before turning to offer his to Whittaker who pointedly ignored it. It will be a long night thought Andrew. Strained but polite conversation struggled on until Dinner was announced. The Countess deliberately took Whittaker's arm and left Andrew to escort Mary Simpson, while McPherson trailed behind. The insult was obvious, but Andrew smiled warmly at the trembling Miss Simpson, and made a joke about her narrow fingers as they rested on his sleeve. He hoped rather than knew whether Amy's sudden stiffening meant he had had an effect.

As Andrew had foreseen, the conversation did not lag, or rather Whittaker's monologue barely faltered. Amy had seated Whittaker at the end of the table in the position of honour. Andrew smiled. McPherson fumed silently. Mary Simpson, appalled at such rudeness tried her best to make a contribution by quietly chatting with McPherson about Edinburgh, until she was called to attention by her mistress.

Having dealt with the latest gossip from London, during which he managed to drop the name of several distinguished people he had managed to see, though whether he had actually been acknowledged by them, remained a mystery, Whittaker turned his attention to his real interest.

"And how long are you intending to honour us with your presence Mr Walters?"

Andrew smiled vaguely.

"Oh I'm committed to Christmas with family friends in the North before I return to Scotland, but my plans are flexible. They rather depend on circumstance, Sir. And yours? How long shall we be having the pleasure of your company?"

Whittaker glanced at his hostess.

"That naturally depends on the Countess and how long she feels the need of my presence." He looked inquiringly at his hostess who responded appropriately.

"*Dear* Whittaker! How could I have lived through these *past dreadful* weeks without your support?" Whittaker bowed his head mincingly before continuing.

"I am sorry to hear you are returning to that *barbarous* country. Those Highlanders are the most uncivilised, feckless people imaginable. They clearly are quite disinterested in working for their living and would rather flood the cities and beg. Quite appalling! I've heard they are *quite* incorrigible. Is it any wonder the Chieftains have sent them packing. Let them go to Canada and elsewhere, they are a *blight* on *this* country!"

McPherson was watching Andrew anxiously, waiting for an explosion but the latter simply took a sip of his wine and turned to compliment his hostess on its quality. It was McPherson who spoke.

"You are *very* severe on my countrymen Sir."

Whittaker shook his head.

"Not at all Sir. *Your* countrymen have contributed a great deal. It is only those lazy useless beings who sat on the land and did *nothing* to improve it themselves. Those *Highland aborigines*! At least the sheep have returned a profit. I urged my Dear Departed Friend to improve his acres in the same way. I presume you will be following his example, Young Man."

Andrew raised an eyebrow but his voice remained calm.

"Is that your advice then Sir? Sheep?"

"*Of course!*" Whittaker thumped the table as he replied.

"There is a problem, however", Andrew continued, "my country New South Wales, can carry more sheep than ever Scotland can. Indeed I know landowners... squatters who have as many sheep on *their* land, as there are in Scotland, *itself.*"

"Well if not sheep, I know there are many who are following the example of Sutherland, and making those *savages* learn new skills. Fishing for example. If such a *great* family considers it the correct course I *wonder* you would not follow *their* example. *I* have recently been in the company of the Marquis myself, though at a distance. What a fine family they are. If you give up your idea of travelling North, Young Man, you would do well to come to London for the Season. The Countess and I could introduce you to *the 'best'* people." Whittaker paused and took a deep breath of self-satisfaction and smiled condescendingly on Andrew. It was too much for McPherson.

"Och I doobt that would be necessary Sir. After all *this* young man is a friend of that family and last time he was in this country spent time at Dunrobbin Castle. How long is it that you were visiting there Walters?"

Andrew's lip twitched as he responded,

"Three weeks perhaps. It was very pleasant." and managed not to laugh out loud as he watched Whittaker. The man seemed to deflate in front of their eyes. Andrew carefully avoided looking at McPherson, while Mary Simpson tried unsuccessfully to stifle her giggles in her napkin. There was a long pause in the conversation.

Amy eventually intervened.

"Goodness we are already well into November! Mr Walters *pray* do not feel you must stay here and miss your Christmas arrangements, on our behalf." She dabbed her handkerchief to her tear-filled eyes. "Our Christmas will not be... so... It will be such a difficult time for us without our Dear Torquil." Whittaker rushed to placate his hostess with a consoling hand on the Countess' shoulder, as she struggled for composure. "Perhaps you will excuse me Gentlemen... I need more privacy... at this moment." She stood abruptly and left the dining room, leaning heavily on Mary Simpson's arm.

The three gentlemen regained their seats but conversation lagged since Whittaker was suddenly devoid of words. After the briefest possible time he stood,

"If you will excuse me Sirs, I feel I *must* go and see to her Ladyship." and he left.

Andrew was finally alone with his friend.

"Indeed Baillie McPherson! As I remember were *you* not the same person who chided me severely for visiting Dunrobbin Castle, and enjoying the hospitality of that family?" He said severely.

"Och! Aye Lad! But I couldna resist prickin' that pompous git's condescension... and ye must admit it were certainly worth it." Andrew joined him in a hearty laugh. "I wonder how he will regain his self-importance? Though mind, I didna mean to distress our hostess." McPherson added. Andrew opened his eyes wide and shook his head.

"I don't think you should concern yourself overmuch, Cameron. In my experience that particular lady is very adept at weeping at opportune moments." He finished his port and went to stand. "But we should go and enquire about her welfare should we not?"

The days were relatively busy for Andrew but the evening meals continued to be difficult. Whittaker resumed his monologues, and Amy her martyrdom, each to their own satisfaction, while Andrew and McPherson remained, for the most part, silent onlookers. Despite Amy's assertions about Torquil's farming expertise, it rapidly became clear to Andrew that the Estate was a place of leisure for its owners. Although there were tenant farmers, no-one seemed particularly interested in making a profit... It was tempting. Everywhere he looked Andrew could see improvements that could be made. No! He had enough on his plate.

From the second day, however, he had a shadow. On his way through the backdoor to the stables he saw a small figure sitting in the hallway, which he presumed led to the kitchen. Hamish was literally kicking his heels against the side of the trunk. Beside him lay a book and a battered toy that looked like a boat.

"Hello Hamish. Why are you here? Where is Nurse?" Andrew asked.

"Nurse is in the kitchen I think. She went to collect a glass of milk for me but she has been *ages*! She said I must sit here but she has been gone *forever*!" Hamish threw his chubby arms into the air in frustration.

Andrew smiled,

"Well if you can wait there for a few minutes Old Fellow, I'll go and find her." Andrew continued along the passage until he reached what was obviously the kitchen. It looked deserted but then he heard a soft giggle from behind another door to his left. He opened it to find Nurse in the arms of a liveried footman. They sprang apart and the Nurse tried to dive under Andrew's arm.

"Now. Now. No need to rush." Andrew's hand held her arm. "Hamish is waiting for his milk and then I will take him with me. He will need warm clothes. See to it at once and *then* I suggest you busy yourself with your duties."

The flustered girl raced into the kitchen and Andrew heard the clatter of the milk pail, then running feet. He turned to the red-faced footman.

"And your name, Young Man?"

"Jones Sir."

"Well Jones, doubtless you too, have duties. See to them. At once!" Andrew added brusquely as he went to find Hamish. The child was already swathed in warm clothes and a scarf and tam o'shanter beret. Nurse was just slipping his feet into his waterproof boots.

"Thank you Nurse. We will probably be an hour or two but I am sure you will be quite busy while we are away." He raised an eyebrow at the blushing girl. "Come on Old Fellow, let's go and find my horse. Do you think you can sit up in front?" A wide-eyed boy slipped his mittened hand into Andrew's with a beaming smile, and in the days that followed, whenever the weather was tolerable, Hamish rode happily around the Estate, perched within Andrew's encircling arms.

It was not until after dinner, that Andrew took Amy aside.

"I was wondering your Ladyship, if I might have a word about one of the footmen? His name is Jones."

Amy stared in astonishment at him.

"*All* of the footmen are called Jones!"

Andrew frowned.

"All!? How strange! That is an amazing coincidence!"

"Not at all! Whatever their given name they are *always* called 'Jones' whilst working here. How can one be expected to remember the names of servants?" She said dismissively with a shrug of her shoulders. Andrew said no more. As long as Nurse did not leave Hamish again, what harm was there? *And* he doubted that it would happen again. Besides he, himself would be leaving very soon. He would have a quiet word to the nurse. Hamish's welfare was his only real concern.

A week later he announced at dinner that he would be leaving the next day, but Whittaker's looks of relief disappeared completely when Andrew added that his colleague would remain until all matters were finalised.

Later that night his bedroom doorknob turned. Amy swept into his bedroom.

"Is *that* how I am to be treated? You are a cold heartless *beast*! You deprive me of my home with never a word of apology and leave that Middle Class Bran-faced Scot to decide *my* fate!"

"Good evening to you too, Countess. Would you care to join me in a brandy perhaps? " Andrew pulled a chair closer to the fire and waited for her to sit.

"*Brandy*! Is that all you have to offer? To be dismissed like this!" She flung her hand at the proffered chair, "After all we have been to each other!" and she flung herself into the chair and clutched at her breast. "So *heartless*! So *cruel*!"

Andrew resumed his own chair and sat quietly sipping his own drink as he studied the flames.

"Oh Dear God! What is to become of me?" The sobs began. "*Abandoned*! *Penniless*! Unloved! Dear God! Can you have *no* mercy?" She threw herself at his feet and held out her hands in supplication. "Two month ago I was the wife of an Earl, with a positon! *Now* who am I? A beggar!"

Andrew stood and lifted her and tried to put her back into her chair. It was a mistake. She clung to him, pressed her body hard against his and gazing soulfully up into his eyes.

"Oh Andrew *My Love*! *How* can you abandon me?"

He gently disengaged himself and stepped away.

"You are still Amy Burnett, the daughter of a very wealthy, and very distinguished man." He said gently, soothingly, but that was another mistake.

"I am talking about Society. How can I continue to live *here* where I belong?"

"Well I have tried to help by allowing you to maintain the house in London. Nor have I made public your husband's ... your former husband's ... your late husband's real history..."

"*Allow*! How dare you! *Allow*!"

"Well perhaps you would prefer to find your own accommodation, Countess?"

"Oh you are heartless. So cold! *Where* is my first love? *Where* is the beautiful boy I once knew?" This time it was too much for Amy and she collapsed onto the floor and lay, seemingly unconscious. Andrew studied her… she looked… had she really fainted? He could hardly leave her? He scooped her up and laid her gently on his bed and went to pull the cover over her but instead, as he bent close, she threw her arms around him and pulled him down and kissed him. For the moment he was too shocked to move, then he sat back onto the edge of the bed, shaking his head.

"What next? One moment you scream at me then the next…?" He looked at her and shook his head. "What *do* you want of me?"

"You must *know* what I want?" As she spoke her fingers slowly slid up his spine and began to caress his shoulders then his neck. He turned abruptly and stood. It would be so easy to join her on the bed. Too easy. He desired her. He always had. And doubtless she knew. He took a deep breath and walked back towards the fire, trying not to look at her. He heard her move and the swish of her skirts as she came towards him. He could smell her perfume and feel her very close. She slid her hand into his.

"Very well, I will wait. One day you will realise how much you mean to me." She pressed his hand between her breasts then kissed it. The door closed softly and he slumped into his chair. Perhaps it would be… *was* it possible… well she would keep her name. Hamish would be safe… though he could not succeed to the Earldom… It all could fall into place… He finished his brandy and threw his clothes on the chair and slid into his bed. But even there he could feel the warmth where her body had lain, and smell her perfume. 'Mannering' beckoned. He could go there and enjoy Christmas with the Spencers and Nick's family. It would be a relief at the very least!

Chapter 32

The following morning Andrew took Hamish with him as usual. They left the stables and headed across the fields. He wondered how he could tell his small companion he was leaving. Instead he urged the horse into a canter. Hamish squealed with delight.

"I think the dogs can't catch us Andrew! Go *faster!*"

Andrew smiled and urged the horse on. Hamish laughed but held tight to Andrew. After a few minutes the child twisted in Andrew's arms, trying to see how close the two dogs were, his head pressed against Andrew's jacket.

"What's that? This is banging against my head. It *hurts!* What is it?" As he spoke he pulled the silver flask from Andrew's pocket. He fiddled with the top and began to twist it open. Andrew tried to stop him just as the horse stumbled. The flask flew out of Hamish's chubby fingers and landed behind them, its contents spilling on the ground.

"Oh! It's gone!"

Andrew steadied the horse and carefully dismounted, then lifted Hamish to the ground. The child's bottom lip trembled.

"That is fine Old Fellow. No harm done." He looked around. The flask lay some yards behind them. The dogs had caught up and began to sniff around the flask and one had begun to lick the flask and the grass around.

"There 't is Andrew!" Hamish hurried forward. "Shoo! Shoo Red! *Naughty dog*. No! That's Andrew's!" Andrew laughingly retrieved the flask and the indignant child. He found the lid and pushed the dogs away.

"Hey Red! That'll do! Whisky is not meant for dogs." He scraped his heel against the wet grass, trying to bury any remaining liquid. He lifted Hamish back onto the horse in his usual spot and they set off home.

They were in sight of the stables when Andrew noticed the dogs were no longer with them. He turned his head to call them to heel but as he watched in horror, Red's body arched and convulsed, then collapsed. The other dog stood whimpering helplessly beside his mate. Andrew snuggled Hamish to his chest.

"Let's race those slow old dogs home eh? Hold tight!"

Hamish squealed with delight as they galloped across the field. Andrew felt numb. He did not want to think about what he had just seen.

Mercifully, Nurse was waiting at the front of the house.

"Oh no Andrew." Hamish clung tight." I am coming to the stables with you. We must brush Hero down. I am coming to help you like I always do."

"Well as a matter of fact Old Fellow, I will be having the grooms do that today. I have something to tell you." He lifted the child and handed him to his nurse. "Today I am busy because I must go away. I must go to Scotland. I have lots to do." Two small hands clung to Andrew's leg.

"*No!* Oh no Andrew! I want you to stay here! I don't want you to go!" Tears fell on Andrew's boots. He slid off the horse and retrieved the child from the nurse's arms.

"Hey! Hey! What's all this? Come on Old Fellow. You know I have to look after the people in Scotland. I know. When the weather warms up... in a few weeks... you could come with your Mama, and Nurse of course." He smiled conspiratorially at the young woman. "I think you would need to come on a *steam* train. Have you ever been on a steam train? That would be exciting wouldn't it?"

"Is it very far to Scotland? Is it across the sea?" The tears had gone.

"Well no. You would come most of the way on the train I think." Andrew looked meaningfully at the Nurse and she rose to the occasion.

"Come Master Hamish! We need to go and change your clothes and then find your Mama, so that you can tell her." She gathered the child and with a shy smile for Andrew, disappeared up the stairs.

Andrew was left to come to terms with what had just happened. He had little doubt that the dog was dead. He would need help. It needed to be buried. God almighty! If he had left this morning as planned? If he had not succumbed to Hamish's demands for a ride? If Hamish had not been curious? His blood ran cold. If the horse hadn't stumbled? If Hamish had tasted it? It wasn't Torquil this time! *He's* dead! God help me, is *any* of this worth it?

He had reached the stables and a groom went to take the horse.

"Not yet. I need you to come with me. You will need a shovel. Hurry Man!"

The groom hurried to obey. He was surprised.

It were not like this "guv'nor" to be so curt. Gen'lly speakin' he'd always 'ave time for a chat! A friendlier cove you'd never meet on a day's march. He shrugged and hurried to collect the shovel and follow Andrew.

They found Red stretched awkwardly in death, his companion standing beside him motionless. Now the groom understood Andrew's manner.

"'E were a fine animal Sir. Wot could 'ave 'appened?"

Andrew shrugged,

"Perhaps it was his heart. Perhaps he ate something. Do you have baits in the stables for the rats?"

"No Sir! We relies on the terriers gen'lly."

"It is tragic. He was a fine dog as you say. I.. There's a bush remedy... but I had Hamish to protect."

The groom nodded,

"Aye Sir and the poison ...it were a quarter of the hour you said...t'would likely be through 'is body."

"Doubtless you are correct though I could have given it a go... You stuff grass in its mouth and then you grab the beast by the tail and swing it round and round, 'till it vomits, but as you say, probably too late. At least we have done well by him, giving him a decent burial, but I'm concerned..."

"Aye Sir! I gets your meaning. I'll be putting some stones over 'im so no bloody wolves or foxes can get to 'm. You can be gettin' back Sir, I'll be finishin' this now. Never you worry Sir." The groom ushered Andrew away and hurried to do as he was asked. Wot a strange fellow this toff was. No ordinary toff, or none a chap could gammon...friendly always...an' fancy knowin' about that way ter save animal.

Andrew strode into the house. The sooner he was gone from this place the better. He'd need to warn McPherson. Could *he* be in danger? He reached the Hall. A footman stepped forward to collect his coat and hat.

"Ah Jones! And how are you today?" He looked the young man up and down. Jones stood impassively though his face was white. Andrew smiled. "I'd be a little more careful in the future eh Jones?"

"Yes Sir. Thank you Sir."

"I think *you* owe me one Jones. You never know I might just need you. In the meantime good luck to you." Andrew said over his shoulder as he bounded up the stair. He could not wait to be shot of this place!

Chapter 33

"'Tis so good of you to come Mrs Manners. We were at our wit's end." Moiragh MacGregor proffered her hand, but it was ignored as Emily hugged the elderly shoulders and kissed the soft cheek, then settled herself in her chair. The late afternoon sun warmed them as they sat in the sheltered veranda.

"I am *very* glad you wrote. I had wondered how you all were, and you must know I am *always* delighted to visit Barraburn and my old friends."

"You are very kind. Mrs Jones and I have *tried* to do our best, but the lass is *not* herself. Even though she was away at school *herself*, she has always been as a mother to the wee bairns... and of course we are *all* lost without your brother."

Emily smiled, and raised her eyebrows.

"And doubtless we have not heard from him?"

"Och Aye! But doubtless he would be very busy!" No one could ever voice criticism of her 'Aindreas'. Not even his sister. "Mr Manners' suggestion that she be helping Nathan with the bookkeeping has kept her busy enough, but she seems to go in and out of her sadness... mostly in."

"I'm glad to hear the bookkeeping is helpful but I'll do my best to cheer her up. I'll speak to Rose... er... Mrs Jones. Ah here she is herself." Emily smiled at the newcomer as she set the afternoon tea on the table. "Please Rose, can you join us? We have just been discussing our little problem. Do you think it would help if I took her to Bathurst to buy some new clothes?"

"Well I'll be hoping you have *more* success than I did! I took her just last week. She was quite excited let me tell you." Rose poured the tea and passed a cup to Emily, as she spoke. "John Coachman took us. It was a nice Spring day." She passed another cup to Moiragh. "Here Mrs MacGregor just as you like it, I hope. To get back to my story-we went into the nicest looking Ladies' Emporium, because there was a *very* fetching bonnet in the window. I just *knew* the emerald ribbons would show off her eyes. So we go inside and just started to look around when two other young ladies arrived with their mother." Rose shook her head. "I was so put out! The so-called proprietress," Rose's lips pursed disapprovingly, "*and* the three assistants fussed over them like they were the Queen herself!" Rose sighed and sipped her tea. "My poor babe was ignored. We were *quite* invisible. So I took the bonnet she liked and suggested she try it on. Suddenly we were *not* invisible! A snooty piece came ever so quickly," Rose raised an eyebrow. "*and* had the cheek to say, the likes of us were not meant to touch the merchandise!" Rose snorted. "*The likes of us!* She had the effrontery to suggest we would not be able to afford her merchandise! So I said to her 'That is for me to know and for you to discover'. We were leaving I can tell you, but would you believe... we were just going out the door when *who* should we bump into? None other than Mr Forbes!" Rose's satisfaction was palpable as she sipped her tea. "Well, of course, *he* made a great fuss of Caitlyn. He could see she was teary and naturally wanted to know the reason." Rose's back straightened. "*So I told him!* It seems that particular 'Ladies Emporium' belongs to none other than *your* Mr Forbes!" Rose paused to nibble a piece of cake all the while smiling at the memory. "He insisted we accompany him back inside. I was fit to burst trying not to laugh at those hoity toity shop assistants as they fussed around our lass. She came away with two bonnets, three new skirts, a parasol and several lengths of material." Rose frowned. "Alas our Caitlyn is no needlewoman, I've a feeling we will take time to use that... Then Mr Forbes announced that it should *all* be charged to Mr Walters' account, except for the original bonnet which was a *gift*. That really flummoxed those 'Grand Ladies', let me tell you!"

Emily laughingly interrupted.

"Surely that should have cheered Caitlyn?"

Rose shook her head consideringly.

"Yes and no. She *was* happy with the new clothes right enough, but she has been very quiet about it all. She was made to feel a nobody and it hurt because *that* is how she sees herself."

Emily nodded knowingly.

"I can certainly sympathise with her. She is a *very* sensitive soul under that quiet manner. It is a shame she does not have my grandmother to talk to her. She always insisted that Jack was as good as his master, in the eye of the Lord, and we should *never* forget it!"

Moiragh had been sipping her tea quietly but she paused to heartily endorse Emily's remarks.

"I've told her that myself many times but coming from you, Mrs Manners, it should help. Alas and alack, she *cannot* forget the time in Edinburgh when we were starving. It weighs on her. I think she feels it is somehow shameful."

Emily shook her head.

"It must have been dreadful for you all. But that is long past- over four years ago, and Andrew sent her to a very nice school. Did she not make *any* friends?"

The older women exchanged glances,

"Of that I am sure, but she is reluctant to pursue any acquaintance. Our wee lass is as 'dreich' as the weather in Edinburgh." Her grandmother shook her head sadly. "Even that scamp Nathan can barely make her laugh!"

Rose smiled.

"Though mind... he has done a little better than we have."

Emily finished her tea, replaced the cup and took a deep breath.

"Well I will do my best Ladies." She stood, straightened her shoulders. "I presume I will find her in her room. There's no time like the present. We have the Bathurst Races and the Ball. We will make that our goal... or bait. Please excuse me."

The gentle knock roused Caitlyn.

"Mrs Manners! I didn't know you were coming! Nathan and I have been busy getting ready for Mr Manners but *this* is a lovely surprise Ma'am. We did not know. Nathan will be pleased to see you. Have you seen my grandmother?" The words tumbled out as Caitlyn tried to straighten her skirts and tidy her hair all at the same time. Emily took both her hands and kissed the flush cheek.

"I'm sorry to burst in on you, but your grandmother said you were here. I hope I'm not disturbing you? Are you well My Dear?"

"Yes thank you Mrs Manners. Are you well?" She glanced anxiously at Emily's bulging stomach. "And the children? Are they here?"

"Of course but Nurse has taken them for a rest. I made up my mind at the last moment. It seemed such a good opportunity. Mr. Manners was coming and then going on to Sydney, so I'll have a few days here. I need to go into Bathurst for a little shopping. I was hoping we could go together?"

Caitlyn smiled shyly at her guest.

"I would like that very much but Mr Manners may need me... I do try... we both do, but we are still learning..."

"*Stuff and nonsense*. I will be here *after* he leaves. Besides, shopping with me is much more important." Emily declared laughing. "I will speak to Manners, *I* need you more than they do!"

"It would be lovely Ma'am but Rose... er... Mrs Jones has already taken me last week and bought *so* many new things."

"Ah yes! She told me. Am I allowed to see your new bonnets? I *love* a new bonnet." Caitlyn obliged by carefully lifting her hat boxes onto her bed and reverently revealing her treasures.

"Very fetching." Emily lifted the first carefully. "Here let me see this one on you." She adjusted the bonnet, Caitlyn's curls, and smoothed the green ribbons. "Rose has *such* marvellous taste." She stood back to admire her handwork. "Now what else do we have to see?"

The next few minutes were spent in examining Caitlyn's purchases while Emily gently prodded the girl about her life.

"We are all very grateful you are working so hard here. The gold rush has caused everyone I know to struggle for people. All the men, seemingly, have rushed off to make their fortune."

Caitlyn nodded.

"Exactly. Although, we *have* lost several shepherds, but that is all, really. Nathan, Mr Jones, Will... John Coachman are here and they seem content enough."

"Oh I *don't* think you need to worry about them! They are loyal to Barraburn... and the Captain... and Mrs McMillan." Emily's voice broke a little and Caitlyn was surprised to see the suggestion of a tear in her eye. She leant over and squeezed Emily's hand. Emily smiled at her.

"I'm sorry. So foolish. But she was the dearest friend I ever had, even though I was the children's governess. Forgive me. So foolish. *You* have lost far more than I." She took Caitlyn's hand and held it as she sat down beside her on the bed. "I think I should let you into a secret. I am here mainly because your grandmother is concerned... for you. She can see you are not really happy. Is she right? *Are* you unhappy?"

Caitlyn sat up straight.

"I am perfectly fine. Neanaidh worries too much."

"If you say so, but you *must* miss Fergus and Finlay. They are so full of life... I'm sure even I notice how quiet it is without them. And I know Andrew was often away, but well we *all* miss him." As she spoke she watched Caitlyn and at the mention on Andrew's name, she saw tears before the girl could hide behind her hair. Emily gently lifted the black curtain of curls, and turned Caitlyn's face toward her.

"*Dearest* girl. We all have sad times. You are young and so beautiful. You *should* be going to parties and picnics! It is very remiss of us all."

"I *don't* want to go to parties." The soft words came before the sobs. Emily cradled the girl and waited. Eventually the tears ceased. She carefully wiped Caitlyn's tears away with her own handkerchief and waited. "I try to be cheerful! Really Ma'am I try but then I remember... the day the men of fire came... the men who burnt our houses... and my mother." Her voice broke. Emily waited again. "*Then* my father... and now my brothers... and Andrew. I am frightened to love anyone because they *always* go away..."

Emily squeezed the hunched shoulders as she spoke.

"Well neither your brothers nor Andrew have gone forever. My husband is trying hard to find your father, *and* he'll be bringing the boys back for the holidays! You know Sweet Girl... I remember feeling a little like you when Mrs McMillan died, because my Grandmother had not long gone... and I felt somehow it was all my fault... everyone I loved was dying and it was all my fault," She chuckled. "and it was Andrew who helped me, in his very sensible way. He said he really didn't think God would bother making other people die just because *I* loved them." She gently turned Caitlyn's face toward her. "No-one can bring back your mother, but she is in your heart... and *remember* it is a blessing for your Grandmother that she has you to remind her of her daughter."

Caitlyn continued to look unconvinced.

"I wish I were... she was beautiful. My Father always called her his 'bonny lass'."

"Of course *you* are beautiful with those eyes and your lustrous curls." Emily said firmly.

"Oh No! I'm small and thin... and... and... nobody."

"Nobody!? What nonsense! Why do you say that?" Emily interrupted, pretending to know nothing about the shopping imbroglio. "My Dear Girl *everyone* is important. Everyone has a place in God's scheme. You have had some very sad times but you were the one who kept trying. You managed to help your family. *You* kept them alive," Emily said firmly.

"Begging on the street! What would the fancy Ladies of Bathurst say? I never ever told my friends at school. How could I?"

"Dear Girl." Emily enveloped the slight figure in her arms. "We *have* all done things we would rather forget. You were desperate. It was so very brave of you... a slip of a girl keeping your family alive when they had had *everything* taken away." She held the girl away and looked her in the eye. "We are *all* proud of you. *You* need to be proud of what you did... never ashamed! Besides, that is all behind you. You are now the ward of Andrew Walters, who is *very* well known, and well liked, and you are going to turn many heads." Emily pulled a face. "And I'll let you into a secret... I spent most of the time I was your age and for several years afterwards, wishing I were dainty instead of a great long streak."

"Oh but Mrs Manners you are so elegant!"

"Well there you are. *You* would like to be tall and elegant and *I* would like to be dainty. What can we do, do you think?"

Caitlyn giggled

"Not very much can we?"

"Exactly! I can tell you, when I first went to London I felt so ugly and self-conscious being so much taller, but Lady Helen, my husband's sister made me wear beautiful clothes and hold my head high." She winked at the girl. "One does not argue with Lady Helen, and do you know... after a wee while I did *feel* elegant at least." She patted her stomach. "It is getting so hot I shan't want to leave home until the baby comes. Do come. Perhaps we will discover some more treasures in Mr Forbes Superior Ladies' Emporium."

Chapter 34

Having survived Nicholas' examination of her bookkeeping, Caitlyn was able to look forward to a shopping trip with his wife.

"My Gracious Me!" Emily stared at the passing crowd as their coach wended its way along William St. "Every time I come to Bathurst there are so many more buildings and certainly many more people!" She leant forward for a better view. "Goodness, that looks as if they have already started the new Methodist Church." She shook her head. "Even a year ago it seems, *I* would know almost everyone I met in the street. *Now*, I doubt I know a soul!"

"Well *there* is someone we know!" Caitlyn cried as she pointed to a very well-dressed gentleman in a very impressive top hat.

"Oh yes. I see, Mr Forbes, himself. How fortunate."

Emily leant forward, tapped on the window and John Coachman came to a gentle halt as his offsider sprang down to assist the ladies.

"Ladies! What an unexpected but overwhelmingly felicitous surprise." Mr Forbes doffed his hat and stepped forward.

"Good Day to you Mr Forbes. We are on our way to visit your bountiful Emporium, well, I trust it *is* bountiful." Emily said with a smile as she extended her hand. Mr Forbes took it and bowed low before offering his arm.

"Do mind that road Ma'am. We are overwhelmed at the present instance with the need to provide the necessities of life to our ever expanding populace." He turned to Caitlyn. "And here is my dear friend Miss Ross, looking as lovely as a rosebud. How are you My Dear?" His eyes travelled to her hat and he smiled knowingly. "*And* I recognise that bonnet that you are wearing, with *such* charm."

Caitlyn smiled her response and slipped her own arm through his and gave it a squeeze of delight.

"I hope that you really think so Sir... you have such exquisite taste yourself." She glanced up at him from under her lashes, "Mrs Manners is determined to find even more delights, do you think you have *anything* left for us?" she said teasingly

"I will be honoured indeed, to provide you with the opportunity to discover for yourself, but may I first invite you both to partake of a light refreshment. We are, fortunately, at the entrance to our most salubrious establishment. Before we embark on your purchasing expedition, may I request the honour of having you join me in a private parlour, within the walls of our Royal Hotel?"

"I could not imagine anything I would *rather* do Mr Forbes." Emily said feelingly. She was already hot and in need of a place out of the heat, preferably one which offered a cool drink. Caitlyn smiled her delight and Mr Forbes had the distinction of walking through the door with a pretty lady on each arm.

The sudden darkness of the interior was a welcome relief to both travellers. As they passed along the passageway, Caitlyn, for her part, was fascinated by glimpses of the hotel's other customers. There were discreetly dressed gentlemen who all nodded to Mr Forbes. Caitlyn could see how much it pleased him. Mr Forbes was an important man now! Through one door she saw many other men in rough working clothes, laughing and talking loudly. Caitlyn privately thought a goodly number of them looked as if they needed a bath, and she certainly disapproved of those whose hats remained on their heads inside! Flitting in and out of the hallway, were a number of females. Caitlyn decided they were all rather overdressed, even garish, and the perfumes that wafted around them, thoroughly overwhelming.

Emily watched Caitlyn's face with amusement, enjoying her wide-eyed reactions, but she was relieved when they were shown into a private parlour. Very quickly it seemed, they were settled at a table covered in a snow-white cloth, and were being offered several plates of delicate sandwiches and delicious-looking cakes.

"Mr Forbes, you have spoiled us! This looks so appetizing... and a pot of tea! *You* have read my mind!" Mr Forbes pursed his lips in a smile of satisfaction.

"It is my immeasurable pleasure Ma'am. I presume you have journeyed the considerable distance that it is, from Barraburn, today. You must of necessity have embarked on your journey at an exceedingly early hour."

Emily nodded her agreement,

"It *was* early but I am anxious to return to day. It will be late, and a long day, but I don't like to leave the children. My husband is already gone to Sydney, for a week at least, and the children will fret with us both gone. Mind, if I had left Caitlyn with them, I doubt they would have *noticed* my absence," she said smiling at the blushing Caitlyn.

A pleasant hour was spent on catching up on their news and then Mr Forbes outlined the developments in and around Bathurst.

"New goldfields are replacing the original ones each day, just as new fortune hunters replace the old. The inclement weather and heavy rains contributed to the disillusion of many involved in the first rush. Many diggers have relocated to the Turon, mainly at

Sofala. Nevertheless we continue to enjoy their custom, as almost all journey to the gold-bearing areas through our little town. We continue to be the main centre of commerce and accommodation." He paused and sipped his tea. "Of course there are always new finds and new excitements. When Mr Suttor arrived with his Kerr's Hundredweight Nugget, last June, the frenzy was renewed!"

Emily laughed,

"*That* must have been something to behold."

"It was indeed Ma'am! And it had actually been broken a little so had lost a little of its original magnificence, but remained spellbinding to our fossickers. We are now finding that gold seekers from abroad are increasingly arriving. One has heard tales of mayhem and murder on the Californian goldfields but we seem not to be visited by such disaster here. One rarely hears of serious misdemeanours. Perhaps after travelling so far, their remaining energy is concentrated on finding their fortune."

Emily folded her napkin,

"However pleasant this is Sir, we will need to visit your establishment *very soon* or we will not be able to make our way home today, after all."

Mr Forbes hurried to help his guests and escort them proudly the few yards to his place of business. This time the doors to the Ladies' Emporium were opened wide for Caitlyn by a simpering assistant, but, before the party was properly inside she was engulfed in a flurry of muslin and excited squeals!

"Kitty Cat! I can't *believe* it! Mama this is my Kitty Cat I have been telling you about this age! Here she is! *Where* have you been hiding you wicked thing! I wanted desperately to find you, you Naughty Girl! Oh I've missed you so!"

Emily exchanged an amused glance with the middle-aged woman on the other side of the entwined girls. Caitlyn, having managed to secure her friend's hands, stepped back slightly trying to calm the situation.

"*Dearest* Angela. It is so lovely to see you. I've missed you too. I have not been hiding it's just that I've rarely been to Bathurst."

"You are still really naughty! I had no idea you lived here. You disappeared without a word. Why? Oh Why?" She turned to her mother. "You can see why we called her "Kitty Cat" Mama. Doesn't she have the most beautiful eyes, just like a kitten... and those lashes... I shall forgive you. I am *so* happy to see you. It is *too* exciting."

Mr Forbes, however, was *not* happy. He was in a quandary. He had stepped forward to greet his customers, but he hesitated. Punctilious in every way, the etiquette of this situation had him struggling. To whom should he introduce... to whom? Mrs Smith was clearly older and had been in the district for a long time. Mrs Manners, on the other hand, was the wife of a very wealthy and aristocratic man. He took a risk, hopeful in the knowledge that Mrs Manners never made a fuss or stood on her dignity.

"What an extremely momentous and satisfying occurrence this is. Two of my *most* valued acquaintance in my humble establishment at the *same* moment. What Providence." He turned to them and spoke. "Mrs Smith, may I have the honour of presenting to you Mrs Manners and her companion Miss Ross. It is of course clear that the younger members of our gathering are, on this auspicious occasion, already acquainted."

The ladies acknowledged each other and mutually agreed it was a pleasure. Mrs Smith was moved to remark that although she had heard much of Mr Manners and his good lady, it had been her misfortune, until now, of meeting her.

"It does seem a little strange," agreed Emily, ""but we have not been, so very long, back from England. My husband had promised his family he would return, and what with one thing and another, we were gone for *much longer* than we intended." As she spoke, she stepped into the main area of the shop. "I *do* hope we have not interrupted you Mrs Smith?" She turned and smiled at the hovering Forbes. "It is such a pleasure is it not to have such a wonderful place to visit?"

"Exactly Mrs Manners. We are *so* grateful to Mr Forbes for making our lives in the wilderness so much easier." Mrs Smith rose to the occasion as she nodded to Mr Forbes, then turned back to Emily. "I must add, Ma'am it is a pleasure to finally make *your* acquaintance and clearly my daughter would agree." She inclined her head toward the two girls who were talking and giggling.

"Oh Mama Dear, I am trying to persuade Caitlyn to come to visit." She gazed beseechingly at Emily. "I am *desperately* hoping Mrs Manners, that Caitlyn could come to visit. The Bathurst Races are next week though..." she paused frowning. "the New Year Races are *much* nicer and there may even be a Ball. Is Mr Lee or Mr Lawson organizing them? Do you remember Mama?"

"Now Angela, perhaps Mrs Manners and Miss Ross already have plans." She said smiling at them both. "Although *clearly* we will have little peace until you *do* accept our invitation. Perhaps you could come and stay for a few days soon and we can then make plans." She took her daughter's hand and slipped it through her own elbow. "Mrs Manners should *not* be kept standing My Dear. We have finished our shopping here. I need to visit Mr Austin's before we go home. It is now the turn of our friends to be served. I will drop a note to you Mrs Manners, now we know where Miss Ross is, and she will, I hope, be able to visit at your earliest convenience." She bowed her head formally to Emily and Caitlyn, gathered her daughter and her purchases and left. Mr Forbes stepped forward, helped Emily into a comfortable chair, and the serious business began. The very same assistants who had barely deigned to serve Caitlyn previously, now fell over themselves to be helpful. Caitlyn was secretly amused by the change in their manner, but she was shocked to hear Mrs Manners' instruction. She shook her head at Emily.

"Now Caitlyn, of course you will need more clothes. There's no reason for you to shake your head." Emily gently chided her charge. "You will also be needing some... some essentials." She whispered to the chief assistant. Caitlyn was whisked behind a curtain. Gasps and groans emerged, followed by Caitlyn, with a pink face and a very narrow waist.

"I can't *breathe!*" Caitlyn gasped dramatically but she was accorded no sympathy, only amused smiles from Emily and the other assistants.

"You will soon get used to it My Dear Girl, and we cannot order new clothes if they don't fit. They will all look *so* much more elegant." She patted Caitlyn's new figure. "Such a tiny waist! How beautiful you will look." She turned to the gathered assistants who all nodded their approval of Caitlyn's new figure. "Now I like that spotted muslin... I think a bodice of the green... to match the spots... and two, no three other afternoon dresses... and Miss Ross will require a riding dress. She is a fine horsewoman... and..." A pleasant hour was spent by all, even the corseted Caitlyn.

It was a week before Nicholas arrived back with Fergus and Finlay. Caitlyn cried with happiness as she marvelled at the changes in her brothers. Soft chubby arms were now gangling limbs that seemed to shoot out in every direction. Even Fergus' voice had changed. Despite her joy, deep down her heart ached for the parents who would never see their beautiful youths.

Chapter 35

Nicholas was pleased to hear of Caitlyn's projected emergence into Bathurst Society.

"*That* is splendid news. She is young and pretty and I am *sure* she will have success and make many new friends." He paused and gave his wife a quizzical look. "There is, I feel, one rather serious problem"

"Whatever can you mean?" Emily stared at her husband. "*She* worries about her past, but in my experience the only reservation that seems to matter is whether there is a *convict* ancestor! Rather silly I know, but she worries a great deal. I'm sure that is why she did not try to continue her acquaintance with her school friends."

Nicholas chuckled.

"Dear me! What shall *I* do? *I* must be such a problem to you my Love!"

"Nonsense!" Emily retorted and playfully smacked his hand. "But to get back to Caitlyn. What are you saying? Her manners are excellent and she knows how to conduct herself... thanks largely to her grandmother."

Nicholas put his arms around his wife's expanded waist.

"Of course her manners are excellent. You said you have ordered her a riding dress?"

Emily nodded.

"Come now Dear Wife. *Surely* you have seen our young friend on a horse?" Nicholas persisted gently.

"Certainly and she is a fine rider."

"Yes My Darling, but have you not noticed? I realise you do not ride yourself but... Your brother taught all three children to ride when they first came here, did he not?"

"Of course. So what is the problem?" Emily asked.

"The problem is Dearest, your brother taught her to ride as *he* does. She will cause a sensation among her new friends. Riding like a chap? I think our little friend will need to relearn... on a side saddle!"

Emily buried her head in her husband's shoulder.

"Oh No! After all the fuss and moans and groans about the corset, I dread... I shudder to think."

Nicholas laughed at his wife's consternation.

"Well leave it to me then. But we'll need a saddle. That could take a few days, even a week to have made." He frowned. "I'll send someone in to Goodes right away."

Emily's face lightened.

"Mrs McMillan. She rode all the time... unfortunately... She must have had a side saddle. What would it look like? Nathan should know." She went to move from her husband's arms.

"Leave it all to us My Dear Wife. *If* it exists it is doubtless in the Tack Room."

"How long will it take to teach her? That is *if* she is willing," Emily added doubtfully.

"If there is a saddle we can start immediately. I'll order one especially for her of course, but we can make do with Mrs McMillan's, if it still exists." He smiled mischievously. "I will find Nathan and hopefully the saddle, while you, My Darling, can break the news to our pupil." Emily glared at his departing back. "She should be happy to show off the riding outfit you ordered. Emphasize that."

The saddle was discovered, resurrected with vigorous polishing and its straps replaced.

"It *is* rather old-fashioned but it will suffice." Nicholas explained to his wife. "It was obviously an expensive saddle, made-to-order, but the newer ones have an extra pommel. We can start with this and I'll order one her size."

Despite herself Caitlyn realised the wisdom of it all. The practicalities, however, left her thunder struck.

"What, do you mean, I *hook* my right leg around that pommel? I'll slide off! *One* stirrup! How can I control my horse?"

"*Enough* Young Lady." Nicholas declared and unceremoniously lifted her onto the saddle. Glaring at her mentor, Caitlyn slipped her left foot into the stirrup, and tried to hook her other over the offending pommel. She promptly slid off. Nicholas managed to catch her before her head hit the ground, though it was already covered by her skirt and petticoats, affording the onlookers a splendid view of her pantaloons. Fergus and Finlay screamed with delight. Nathan and Emily *tried* not to laugh.

"I *told* you!" Caitlyn stamped her boot and tried to rearrange her skirts and hair at the same time.

Nicholas smiled reassuringly.

"Try again. I'll hold you this time. You need to sit further over on the saddle. *Your* spine should be in line with the horse's." He spoke firmly but gently. "Now are we hooked this time?"

"Yes but *how* am I to know *where* my spine is, it is *so* squashed already." She turned and glared at her brothers, "Go away! You are *so* mean!" then glanced down to Nicholas with fire in her eyes. "This is *so* uncomfortable!"

Nicholas remained calmly smiling and holding her steady.

"Stop complaining Child. You can do this. You are a fine horsewoman but you *cannot* ride around like a chap any longer. You will be the talk of the Bathurst District! Now concentrate."

Tears welled in her eyes. She bit her lip. She caught Emily's anxious look.

"Very well. I *will*, but this is the *silliest* way to ride a horse *anyone* could imagine!"

Nicholas slowly let go and she stayed on the saddle.

"Good Girl. It will be better with your own saddle-it has an extra pommel so that you can brace your left leg against it." He handed her a long flexible piece of bamboo. "Here this will do... put it in your right hand... you can gently guide her with it until we get you the right one." He stood back. "There. That is fine. Now walk on slowly. I'll walk beside."

Caitlyn managed one stately progress around the yard with Nicholas in close attendance.

"Well done! I knew you could do it." Nicholas congratulated his pupil.

"Thank you." She frowned. "But why? Why does anyone want to ride like this?"

Emily intervened,

"Because Dear Girl, no-one will think you are a lady otherwise, *however* stupid it is."

"Very well. I would not want to disgrace you Ma'am or... or anyone." She smiled ruefully at Nicholas. "I will practice, though, when *no-one* is around I *could* ride the old way?"

"*Not* a good idea Caitlyn." Nicholas shook his head. "Keep practicing, *then*, when your own saddle arrives, you will find it easy."

The Manners Family left. Nathan was now the chief, and only riding instructor. It was not an easy assignment.

"No Miss, you are not straight... remember Mr Manners said your spine and the horse's are to line up."

"Line up! How can I line up when all I do is slip and slide, I doubt you could keep your spine straight." She snapped at him. "I *am* trying!"

Nathan took a deep breath.

"That's good now. Just walk slowly... that's the way... er... just a little... er... I'm afraid you've ...er... slipped again."

Caitlyn threw the long cane that was meant to guide the horse, straight at her teacher. Then she tried to dismount. It was not a dignified exit. She had to slide off clutching tight to the hated pommel. "Very well Mr Know It All. *Show* me! *You* do it!" She glanced at him. "Come on, I doubt you're game!"

Nathan stared in astonishment at the girl. Where was his friendly helpmeet? They worked side by side in the office and she had *never* once criticised him, though he knew he was not without his faults. *He* had never been to school, but not once had she indicated in the slightest way his shortcomings. Where was his friend? Suddenly she had become furious. He was used to the edge of Rose's tongue, but *never* Caitlyn's.

He spread his hands submissively,

"Righto. I'll have a go, but what use it'll be, has me stonkered," he said. Anything to keep the peace he said to himself. He mounted the horse who stood placidly, despite the storm around her. Nathan hooked his right leg around the pommel, slipped his left into the stirrup and slowly walked the horse around the yard. A crowd had gathered.

"Oh Sweetie you do look the part," simpered John Coachman.

"Well done Darlin'," from Jones the blacksmith.

"There Caitlyn. *That's* how you do it," from an unhelpful brother, who promptly had to dive for safety behind Mr. Jones.

Caitlyn surveyed the scene. She felt her spine stiffen despite the corset. Her chin went up. She marched across to the triumphant Nathan and ordered him off the horse. Nathan cupped her heel silently and she swung herself into the saddle. She hooked her right leg, inserted her left, and with a spine in perfect alignment with the horse's she walked around the yard twice, returned to the crowd, dismounted and marched inside. In the privacy of her own room she flung herself on the bed and sobbed. She was embarrassed and ashamed. Why had she behaved so badly? Poor Nathan. She had been so rude. It was a stupid way to ride a horse but why had she taken it out on Nathan of all people?

There was a gentle knock on the door and her grandmother came slowly into the room leaning heavily on her cane.

"Neanaidh! Oh *you've* come all the way up the stairs. Oh why ever have you? Oh Dear." Caitlyn sprang to her feet and hurried to help her grandmother into a chair.

"Thank you Lass." It was several seconds before the older woman regained her breath. She took Caitlyn's hands in both of hers and smiled gently up at her. "I know it is not an easy thing to learn Lass, but I do not think you have been kind to Nathan. He is doing his best." Caitlyn's tears returned. She knelt beside the chair.

"I *am* sorry Neanaidh. I *know* I behaved badly. I'm truly ashamed. I don't know myself why I felt angry." The sobs began again. Moiragh McGregor wiped away the tears and patted her granddaughter's cheek.

"I think my wee Lass, your tears are for another. Was it not Aindreas who taught you to ride? We *all* miss him. Perhaps all these changes to riding your horse make it hard to change from *his* way. It is vairy possible I think."

Caitlyn buried her head in her grandmother's skirts trying to hide from the world, just as she had done so long ago, and sobbed and sobbed. After a few minutes her grandmother spoke softly but firmly.

"Donna fret. Dry your tears." She stroked the dark curls. "He *will* come back. It is *duty* that called him away. His *heart* is here. But my ' lurach gaolan' Caitlyn, *we* must be patient, and *you*, my bonny lass, must go out into the world and enjoy yourself even if it is sometimes not as you want."

The riding dress arrived along with the saddle, and an invitation from the Smiths. Caitlyn ventured into the life of Bathurst's Society.

Chapter 36

Despite her misgivings, Caitlyn had a *very* pleasant time, especially as Angela had three older brothers who had paid her considerable attention. They had *even* complimented her on her riding. The first night home, still bubbling with excitement she needed little encouragement to talk about it all, and Neanaidh's questions did precisely that, anyway. Her brothers were far from enthralled. The following morning they entertained themselves and Nathan at their sister's expense.

"Oh I think I should wear the bonnet with the green ribbons today Finlay. What do you say?" Fergus minced across the office patting his imaginary headpiece.

"Oh *no*, rather prefer the red, Dear Chap!" Finlay replied haughtily. Nathan, whose feelings had not fully recovered from the riding instructions, enjoyed it all.

"Blimey, you *are* being mean Boys." He remonstrated without conviction.

"No Fear! *You* should have been at dinner last night. We're sick to death of the Smiths. I reckon Caitlyn's forgotten who she is," declared Fergus. "Bloody Smiths!"

Nathan shrugged,

"I'm sure it'll blow over," and resumed his struggles with the accounts. "Mind you I wish she'd come and help. This page is a corker. I can't make head nor tails."

The boys disappeared. Nathan gave up the struggle and retreated to the sanity of the stables. It was early afternoon before the hottest part of the day drove him back to the shelter of the office. He was settled at his desk, struggling as before, when the swish of petticoats made him glance up. Caitlyn was standing perfectly still staring at the floor behind his desk. Without a word she disappeared, then almost immediately was back, carrying a long-handled shovel.

"What the...?" Nathan stared. Caitlyn put a warning finger to her lips, and whispered,

"Shush. Come back here slowly." He stood and peered around his desk. A flat, shining black head, stared malevolently at him. Silently he took the shovel and with his hip pushed the desk. Nothing happened. He moved closer. Still nothing. Then he heard a stifled giggle from outside the window. He shoved the desk well away. A disembodied snake's head lay exposed.

"Those little devils," Caitlyn said through gritted teeth. "I sup-pose I was meant to scream and run away?"

"Well *you* have been a real disappointment. But why didn't you?" asked Nathan, but it was to an empty room. Caitlyn had commandeered the shovel, loaded the offending head and was gone. Nathan watched appreciatively through the window as she crept around the side of the building towards her unsuspecting brothers, who were crouched down below the same window, waiting for the inevitable commotion. Instead they were con-fronted by a triumphant sister who promptly chased them with her shovel, and its contents, around the garden. The screams and yells came from the boys, the laughter from the onlookers who had heard them, and were enjoying the spectacle.

It was some time before Nathan returned to his desk and the hieroglyphics of his account books. Caitlyn was already immersed in hers. She felt his eyes on her and looked up. Their eyes met. Her lips twitched and they both dissolved into laughter. Eventually Nathan took a deep breath and managed to repeat his question.

"Why didn't you scream? Fair dinkum, I'd have sworn at the very least!"

Caitlyn shrugged.

"I was worried for *you*. I had no idea where the rest of it was, it could have been wrapped around your boot... or..." she shuddered. "I don't like snakes either, but well... if it had been a ... *rat...*" She screwed up her face.

"My oath, a rat's *nothing* compared to a 'Joe Blake'! "

"Oh I know, but..." She looked at her companion as if for the first time. How could he understand? He'd lived all his life in the sunshine. How could he comprehend living in a black hole trying to keep the scuttling filthy vermin from stealing the bread, and biting her brothers, and almost helpless grandmother. The familiar horror grew in the pit of her stomach. Watching her, Nathan saw her face change. He tried to lighten the mood.

"Well, word will surely spread among the snake kingdom. Watch out for that girl and her shovel."

Caitlyn smiled vaguely at him.

"I'm not *really* brave. There is a reason, I don't like snakes, but I can manage because snakes belong to this place... a place where it is warm and open... and where I have friends."

"It's not all like this, you know. This country can be hard and dark... and cold. Especially when you are trying to find somewhere safe to sleep and something, anything to eat," Nathan replied.

"Whatever do you mean? Have you... I mean did you not *always* live here?" Caitlyn was bewildered.

"No, I did not always live *here*." He paused, staring past her into his memories. "I lived rough in Sydney town. Lots of kids did. We scrounged as best we could. There were orphanages but... I never stayed. Treated you like a criminal, bash you as soon as look at you! Rather chance me luck."

"But your parents? Where were they?" Caitlyn asked.

"Me mum died when I was born. Never knew who me father was. There was an old geezer who must have looked after me for a while. I remember him, sort of. He had a long white beard. He must have been a government man 'cos his back was all marked from the lash. But he died, and so I was on me 'Pat Malone', as they say. He never told me much. I never knew anything about me father... coulda been another convict, coulda been a toff. Who's to know?" He said matter-of-factly.

Caitlyn was thunderstruck. Happy-go-lucky Nathan with his ever-ready crooked smile and his cheerful kindness. She studied him for any signs of this life. He was always neatly dressed and clean, even when he was with the horses. His face was brown from the sun, but fresh and open. Admittedly, those fierce yellow curls did not *always* stay neatly tied in their leather thong. He spoke well. He could read and write. Not *everyone* could, she knew, even if he *hated* being in the office.

"I got by. I was a good cockatoo. That helped. The punters relied on me." He saw Caitlyn's puzzled expression and tried to explain. "A cockatoo's a lookout, for the geezers who are gambling-on the horses, or anything really, that the coppers don't like. It was my job to keep watch, then "Cooee" a warning and disappear. I was quick on me feet." He said with mock pride. "Always gave them warning enough to hide the evidence! Weren't bad payers... I saved their necks often enough."

"I had no idea... but how did you come to here, to Barraburn? It's a long way." Caitlyn asked.

"One day I was wandering around trying to find a place to kip... sleep. Nightime was the worst. It can get Blo... very cold. Well I saw the Captain. He looked a decent cove, so I just came straight up to him and asked him for a job. It was late... nearly dark. He thought I was up to no good, of course. I don't know to this day why he decided to give me a go." He shook his head. "Mind, never a day goes by I don't thank him in my heart. He, and Mrs McMillan... they were the greatest people." There was a deep sigh as he stared out the window towards the hill with its neat fence and simple headstone. "I dug that grave the night she died. What else could I do for her?"

Caitlyn could feel the tears stinging her eyes. Those simple words hid so much. He kept his head turned away. Caitlyn felt sure she knew why.

"Mrs McMillan must have been a special lady. Mrs Manners gets very sad when she talks about her."

"She was," he said. Then he looked at Caitlyn.

"What about you? Why *are* you such a duffer around rats?"

So she told him. It was surprising how easily the words came. He said very little, but when she told him about the 'men of fire', the pencil in his hand snapped in two and she saw his mouth turn into a grim line. It was not until she mentioned Gordon and Annie that he interrupted.

"Why were they in the... what did you call it? The Close... is that it? Why were they there?"

"Oh it was really only Gordon. He'd just lost his leg fishing. He couldn't even walk properly yet. Annie was a maid in a fancy house. Whenever she could, she came, and she always brought us *all* something to eat. Gordon soon got better at walking, and stronger too. He was well enough, even to help me with Neanaidh. You know she was so weak she could hardly move."

"So how did, I mean how were they able to come with you?"

"Oh!" She smiled. "Well we just asked Andrew. He said yes, but he did say not to keep collecting people, because he did not have enough money." She pulled a face. "I thought he was joking but now I think he probably had to ask Mr Manners for help." She could see Nathan's face had changed. It was softer. Why? She made a calculated guess. "I'm really glad they came, aren't you? Gordon is really helpful isn't he?"

"Too right. It's bl... a marvel what he can manage. Old Sticks, he's good value!" He added affectionately.

"And Annie is too, don't you think?"

"I suppose so." He said noncommittedly, which immediately confirmed her suspicions. Black thoughts and sad memories evaporated. It was strange how telling Nathan her secrets had been so easy. She left lighter, freer. He was *such* a kind soul. She would need to find out if Annie... was interested in Nathan? She wanted to help him. A sudden pang of guilt hit her. She had been so rude to him.

"Nathan, I *am* sorry I was so mean when you were trying to teach me to ride. I never really apologized did I?"

"Fair dinkum it's forgotten Mate," he said with a cheeky grin. "how did it go? Did you fall off at the Smiths?"

"No I did *not!*" Was the indignant reply until she saw the twinkle in his eye and they both had a good laugh.

Then Caitlyn had a sudden thought.

"How old were you when you came here?"

"How should I know? I don't know when I was born."

"Do you mean you really don't know even your birthday?"

"Nup." He shrugged.

Caitlyn was embarrassed. She returned to her duties. Much later in the sanctity of her bedroom, she sat thinking about Nathan. She stared at her treasures, the pebble, the shell... they were part of her... of who she was, her story. *She* knew who her parents were. Nathan had *no-one...* not even a birthday! He needed a birthday surely! How sad. She had been grieving for her parents. How could Nathan grieve for people he had never known? How many other people had stories like Nathan? Possibly many. Possibly many here at Barraburn. Could she find Nathan's birthday... birthdate? Probably not... Mr Manners might know. How *lucky* was she? How blessed that Andrew had brought them all here? How many children had quietly died of starvation as she had thought she would, especially in cold, bleak Scotland's winter. It was time to look *forward*, not back.

Chapter 37

Emily was engrossed in breastfeeding her newest son but she glanced up as her husband came into the room.

"Lucky little bugger." Nicholas murmured affectionately.

"Nicholas." His wife chided gently, but she smiled into her husband's eyes nevertheless. He bent and kissed the top of the head of both his wife, and his newborn.

"Are you sure this is not too much for you?" Nicholas asked.

"No! I love to feed my children, and my grandmother always said it was as good for the mother as the baby. Besides, where would I find a suitable wet nurse, may I ask?"

"True, and you do make a charming picture Dear Wife." He paused while Emily finished her task and rang the bell.

"Thank you Miriam. He's very sleepy already." She handed the child to the waiting arms and turned her attention to her husband now they were alone.

"It is a strange thing. Every time I see Miriam's feet and ankles I am surprised they are black. I see her all day, every day, and I never notice the colour of her skin... I only see *her*. Then when I see her feet I shake my head and often think she must be wearing black stockings. Do you think I am slightly odd?"

Nicholas chuckled.

"No you are not odd my Dear," and he kissed her again more thoroughly. "but on a more serious note I do have something to tell you. I've had a letter from Helen."

"Oh! Marvellous. Has she seen Andrew? Did he manage to go to Mannering for Christmas? What does she say? I'm longing to hear the news." Emily said eagerly. Nicholas paused.

"Well there's a lot of news. A damned lot of news! Prepare yourself, Dearest." Nicholas said quietly.

"Oh No! Is Andrew safe? Is he ill?" Emily asked anxiously.

"He is well and safe, but he has been *neither*! I can understand why he has not written. I doubt he knew how to tell us." He studied his wife's worried face. "The most... the news that has rocked me *is that your brother is...' The Earl of Mulray'.*"

Emily stared at him.

"Mulray... Mulray... that... Torquil? Dear God, Amy." Her eyes were wide, her voice faint.

"Precisely My Love. Torquil was the imposter, perhaps unknowingly, let me add. It was *his* grandmother who engineered everything. The murders... the deception... the agony of loss to your grandfather."

""But... I mean... I can't believe it. Dear God what a catastrophe! And Amy? What does that mean for Amy?" She covered her mouth as if to hide the words from the world. "Oh Nicholas I can't believe it."

Nicholas sat opposite his wife.

"There's more I'm afraid. Andrew is well enough but Helen says they were dreadfully concerned when he came for Christmas. They had seen him earlier after he'd... I think My Love you should read the letter yourself."

Emily shook her head.

"No Nicholas. Please read it to me. I don't think I can even hold the pages I am so shocked." Nicholas took the letter and began to read.

"Shot!" Emily squeaked. "Shot!" She stared at her husband. "I remember you said we should be careful but I never imagined," Her lips twitched, "though I think the McPherson household were clearly splendid bodyguards."

Nicholas nodded and continued,

"But there is more. No wonder he looked thin and drawn. This last attempt on his life was diabolical, and, it could not have been Torquil."

"Why?" Emily frowned.

"Because My Love, Torquil had already suffered a fatal "accident"." His voice clearly conveyed his cynicism about the word. "He appears to have had a shooting accident... the coward's way out."

"But his life was destroyed was it not?" Emily said sadly.

"The life *he* had lived, but he had a wife and child. He had no regard for their *fate*. He left them alone and penniless. No, worse than penniless – in massive debt!"

"You said this last attempt... whatever do you mean?" Emily said slowly.

"Poison." Nicholas said coldly.

"Oh Dear God. It gets worse!" Emily exclaimed.

"Yes, it does." Nicholas replied.

"Oh Nicholas, should we go to England? Poor Andrew. What a nightmare." She asked shaking her head.

"No, I gather Andrew is doing fine, although clearly he is being far too generous to the Countess!" Nicholas said sternly.

"The Countess. You mean Amy. But the poor girl. Her life must be in ruins. You are *too* harsh."

"Well according to Nell, Andrew has allowed her to stay on in that London mansion and has given her an allowance, despite the fact that she and her husband were up to their necks in debt. Nor has he announced anything. No-one knows, except of course for McPherson, his lawyer, and Amy and her cronies... well Whittaker anyway."

"You are being harsh Nicholas. Amy is not to blame surely?" Emily said, but her husband said nothing for several seconds before answering.

"*Who* could have tried to poison your brother? *Who* had the most to gain?"

"Oh No. Oh you cannot mean? Oh No!" Emily's eyes filled with tears.

"We will not go to London. Perhaps I shall eventually, but I think the best approach is to visit your ex-employer Major Burnett. I don't imagine Amy will have told her father what has come to pass. He needs to know before she..." Nicholas said.

"Oh Nicholas. I cannot believe anyone would do such a thing."

"No I'm sure *you* cannot and seemingly neither can your brother. He has shown her too much concern, for his own good." He frowned. "It is two months since Nell wrote this. God alone knows what has happened since." He saw his wife's face. "Don't fret My Dear. Have faith in your brother."

It took several days before Emily could begin to digest the news. Nicholas was probably right. They could do little for Andrew by going there. Better to care for his responsibilities here... the children, Neanaidh, Barraburn and his own land. Nicholas said they are making a fortune and... Caitlyn and Nathan were doing so well! Two street urchins running two properties so profitably. Nicholas is happy to give them more and more responsibilities. So much for birth and Society! But then wasn't *she* suddenly Society herself. Granddaughter of an Earl, sister of an Earl. Should she feel different? Poor Mr Forbes would have a fit, be absolutely mortified, if he had known he'd introduced an Earl's sister to a mere farmer's wife! It was all quite silly, but then, was it silly? Poor Amy, so Hell bent on a title... Surely Nicholas was wrong about her, so sad, after all, being a Countess had made her happy. Now who was she? No. She could *not* have.... Helen said they were at

Leicestershire… if the servants knew the Estate was being sold… any one of them could have tried to save his or her position… or Whittaker? *He* must be desperate!

"I have been thinking Nicholas." Nicholas Manners raised an eyebrow as he looked up from his breakfast.

"Since you have barely spoken for the last three days, My Love, I deduced that you were."

Emily blushed,

"Was is so obvious? Forgive me but I was… was so overcome. So many things to consider." She took a deep breath. "I am sure *you* are right. There is no need for us to go to England. We can pray Andrew is safe in Scotland, even if frozen," She shuddered, "the thought of March, cold and bleak… and the then… slush and mud! I really find March so pleasant here…don't you?" Nicholas nodded and waited. "Yes, Dear Husband, *we* are needed here. Especially as Governor Fitzroy is coming to Bathurst in a few weeks." Her face brightened. "We, some of the ladies, have decided it would be the perfect opportunity for our young girls to be presented to him. Their Debut, in a manner of speaking. There is to be a ball on the 21st of April. Just so fortuitous! Being presented to the Governor. *That* should be delightful for them."

Nicholas chuckled,

"And for the Governor, a feast of pretty girls!" He raised an eyebrow. "And *that* decides *me*. From all I've heard, our Governor and his son are devilishly dangerous around women. *You* will chaperone Caitlyn, and *I*, will chaperone my wife."

Chapter 38

His spare sandy hair was now almost silver and the face heavily lined, but his eyes smiled warmly, and his manner relaxed and friendly, although the ramrod posture of the ex-soldier remained.

"Well young Andrew that is *quite* a story. We, my wife and I, always felt Emily was special. Now I know why... a goodly dose of *genuine* Scottish blood." He shook his head and grimaced. "But fancy that... Old Rupert's daughter. They, especially Mrs Burnett, were exceedingly chuffed that their daughter was part of 'Society'. Such a success! Good God, how will they cope with this I wonder?"

Andrew interrupted, somewhat defensively,

"At this stage, Captain... I mean... Sir... I mean..."

"McMillan will suffice. Surely we have known one another for long enough." McMillan said. "You were but a Lad, sixteen was it not when you first visited Barraburn?"

"Yes Sir. I was that." He acknowledged with a smile. "As I was trying to explain... I have not announced anything and I have sworn McPherson to silence... though not without difficulty." He shook his head at the memory. "The people on the Estate... well I've told them I am a relative of Earl Mulray, from New South Wales, and the guardian of his son. Nothing more. For the moment the Countess is spared embarrassment! I'm hoping that she will find a replacement for... for her husband... once she is out of mourning I mean."

McMillan chuckled,

"From what *I've* heard she may not wait for such niceties."

Andrew reddened but joined his companion in a laugh.

"Yes... well I was trying to be... discreet."

"Not her forte... or so I've heard." McMillan retorted.

Andrew nodded.

"No, but I did not wish to humiliate her. I've left her in the house in Belgravia despite my lawyer's protestations. Although we could do with the money, but I'm hoping that selling the Leicestershire Estate will suffice." He frowned. "But Torquil's debts! They are monumental I can tell you!"

"Well Good Luck to you Lad, though methinks you are being overly generous. Can you trust her?"

Andrew paused. So far he had not mentioned the attempts on his life. If he were honest he did not care to even think about them. He smiled ruefully.

"No, and I am inclined to agree but..."

McMillan nodded.

"It is not in *your* nature Lad but you canna trust her at all! You mentioned this Whittaker. Where does he fit? And for the life of me I don't understand how they could have such debts. What is there in Scotland?"

"A wild rugged place with no thought to improvement or maintenance, and frightened people awaiting their fate!" Andrew replied bitterly.

"Och Aye and Young Andrew needs to save them." McMillan said. "I am surprised he'd not cleared them long since, like so many of those Highland chieftains."

"No, I wondered myself why he had waited so long, but Torquil never seemed to think of anything but pleasure, from my brief acquaintance, so perhaps he never really focussed on the reality." Andrew paused, hesitating, what did McMillan believe in regard to the North? "I only came back because Torquil was about to clear 'his' land... well I didn't know it was Torquil... but..." He sighed. "It is an Ungodly Mess!"

McMillan patted his hand reassuringly.

"Enough of all that for the time, Lad. You wrote to explain you needed to come to Scotland. I appreciated that and more now, but how is Barraburn? I must say the bank and I have been *vairy* happy with your efforts Lad!"

Andrew smiled,

"Well *that* was, and is, the Gold Rush! We've been run off our feet supplying food... especially lamb and mutton, to the hungry hordes. The initial madness has eased. The bulk of them have gone to Ballarat and Bendigo in Victoria now, but we still have hundreds even thousands, in and around Bathurst. We have *all* done well."

"It must have been a 'taime' of rare excitement Lad."

"It still is really." Andrew said. "Changed the country completely! The squatters and settlers have been scrambling for workers. So many hands went to find their fortune. Mind you, Barraburn suffered less than most. *Your* people remained loyal in the main. We have you and Mrs McMillan to thank Sir! I can never imagine Nathan or the Jones' leaving, just a few shepherds and hands left, and because you had such a good relationship with the local tribe, *they* have stepped into the breach.

When I was here before I collected a few people too, and they are holding the fort. But, of course, my brother-in-law is supervising, *his* place, my place *and* Barraburn! Poor old Nick! But he's been a marvel. Besides *he* was the one, most of all, who pushed us to follow up on our grandfather's letter."

A shadow flickered across McMillan's face, to be replaced by a wry smile.

"Then I am to be grateful to Nicholas Manners after all." In reply to Andrew's puzzled expression he continued. "That chap... well it *was* a long time ago." He shrugged. "And your sister? Is she well and happy?"

"Oh yes. Completely I'd say, though thanks to us, Nick is away from home rather too much. Emily does like to come to Barraburn when she can. Only natural... was her home for a while, wasn't it?"

"Yes. *Indeed* it was." Momentarily his tone was bitter but then in his normal pleasant voice McMillan continued. "Methinks Lad, there are reasons other than Barraburn I ken, that you have come across Scotland in this weather."

"Well it is not quite like that. I spent Christmas with Nick's family at Mannering and then came North. I am on my way to Inverness, then the Estate." He glanced out the window. "I must say this is a beautiful part of the country Sir. Rather more lush and doubtless more arable than my acres. *It* is so wild and rugged, and not much forest either. I wonder about the trees."

"Och the trees went centuries ago, but *you* would have some stands of the Caledonian pine I'm almost certain. Seek and ye shall find Lad. But mind Lad *your* scenery is all the rage, as I understand. Wilderness! That is fashion. *That* is your advantage Andrew."

"It is the way I've been thinking," agreed Andrew. "We seem to have quite a deal of wild life, and *you* know as well as I that sheep are *not* the answer. Scotland cannot compete with *us*." He paused. "To be frank Sir, I came to see you, not *just* to explain and reassure you that Barraburn was being cared for. I need advice. I know so little about this country. Who am I to decide the fate of the people in the straths and glens who are suddenly my responsibility?"

His host sat back, sipping his whisky, quietly studying the bright flames in the fireplace. There was a silence before McMillan turned back to Andrew.

"Aye I can see your point. It is a heavy and sudden burden, but Andrew Walters do *not* underestimate yoursel'! You know enough of the world, you are young, but you have travelled. You are honest. You are not, unlike the late unlamented Torquil Mulray, concerned only with yourself. I can tell you vairy few of those making decisions these last fifty years have seen the real world. Their foolish belief in flooding the country with sheep is a case in point. Now *they* are floundering. Trying to find other sources of income. We are lucky here in this part of the country... I myself have concentrated on the forests and whisky, and we are doing fine," He held his glass up to the light of the chandelier. "and a vairy fine drop it is."

Andrew took his cue.

"It is indeed. And Scotch Whisky is famous already." He bit his lip. "That is a real advantage. What advantage, however, can I find in my rugged acres with half-starved people and beasts?"

McMillan lifted an eyebrow.

"Come now is this Andrew Walters sitting here. The Lad who made his fortune before he was twenty?"

"Not a *fortune*. Just a comfortable living until you hired me."

"What do you want Lad? What do you want for this inheritance that has been landed on you?"

"Really I want to find some way to employ those people who want to stay on the land they seem so attached to. Already at least thirty souls have decided to emigrate to New South Wales, and doubtless others will follow, but that still leaves several hundred to somehow make a living. They have their sheep... the black-faced ones... and their cattle, but we need more. I've wondered about getting some involved in turning their wool into cloth etcetera... even a Mill... or organize the women to weave more than just for their own needs."

"That is sensible Lad, but I'm convinced your best chance is tourism. What state is you castle in?"

"Almost derelict... well no... it *was*, but already they have worked hard, and once the glass and the rest arrive it will be quite reasonable." He glanced around the elegant room. "Not like this of course, and certainly *not* like the Leicestershire Estate I am trying to sell."

McMillan sat staring into his glass for several minutes.

"No Andrew. Tourism is your best chance. You could always lease the place but then I doubt any leasee would concern himself with *your* folk. No Lad, tourists are what you need. Mind it will need to be a *good* product. You will need good accommodation. A castle in the Wild Highlands... canna get more Romantic than that. Can you turn your farmers into ghillies and gamekeepers, bailiffs and butlers?"

Andrew shook his head.

"What may I ask is a ghillie?"

"Och, *Essential* Lad! They will take the tourists into the hills to find the game, and from my experience they do everything but fire the actual bullet or hook the fish. Pamper and pander to your tourists, that is their role!"

Andrew laughed,

"Maybe we *could* manage, but butlers and maids and footmen... the mind boggles Sir." Andrew tried to imagine any of them behaving like Lady Spencer's formidable Simms.

"The Forbidden Hills, Being Eighe and the Munros. Lochs full o'fish. Forest full o'deer. *You* have the product Lad, *you* can teach these folk. I've every faith in you. As for the wool... you are right. Let them make it up themselves. More employment. I've a friend who is replacing his water-powered mill with one using one of those steam engines. We could visit with him whilst you are here in Perthshire. But enough of that Lad. I want to hear all about my beautiful Barraburn."

Andrew resumed his journey. Through the train windows the snow covered landscape was black and white. Would that his future could be so simple. McMillan had helped him see a future for his land and *his* people... but what about Amy... and Hamish... what of them? And the flask...

Chapter 39

As he scrambled, head down, from the commodious, but uncomfortable coach he had managed to hire in Inverness, into the shelter of the castle, Andrew was more intent on avoiding the stinging sleet, to notice any changes. It was not until he was inside, his damp hat and cloak removed by welcoming hands, that he registered any of them. The helpful hands belonged to an elegant footmen, dressed in a kilt.

"Jones!" Andrew shook his head, was he dreaming?

"Yes Sir," was the quiet reply.

"*You* are *here* in Scotland Jones?" Andrew asked before he had a sudden thought, "and is your name really Jones anyway?"

"As a matter of fact, Sir, it *is* Jones. My father was from Wales, after all." Jones answered, bowing his head.

"Well! Glad to see you." As he spoke Andrew turned and entered the Great Hall. He stopped dead in astonishment. It was full of light and warmth. The cold grey walls were now hung with tapestries and paintings. The huge fireplace cradled a crackling fire, whose warmth he could already feel. Directly in front of him was a gleaming table holding a handsome urn filled with branches of holly. Beyond that, couches and chairs, which seemed vaguely familiar, were arranged in comfortable groups, and rising from one of those chairs, was the narrow frame of Cameron McPherson.

"My God McPherson, am I really in Mulray Castle?"

Cameron came hurrying forward, hands outstretched

"Aye My Friend and let me tell you, this is just a wee sample of your home. What do ye say? T' will it suffice?"

"It's a Bloody Marvel Mate!" Andrew's eyes bounced from one wall to another before he looked up. "What's this. It's not black and greasy? Where are the cobwebs?" He shook Cameron's hand vigorously. "I can't begin to thank you."

"No need Lad. 'Tis a pleasure. The late Imposter's goods and chattels have become vairy handy! We havena completed everything. The weather freezes the mortar so we havena completed the repairs to that wing... But we have done well I think?"

"Well?! It's a miracle. But surely... in three months! I can't believe my eyes." Andrew stared around him, trying to absorb the changes. Then he noticed the essential difference.

"The windows. They are glazed!"

"Och Aye, case and sash in every room. I *dread* to tell you the cost though, but we couldna proceed otherwise." McPherson's smile had disappeared as he broke the bad news.

"But you said you sold Leicestershire? Did you not get a reasonable price?" Andrew asked anxiously.

"An' ye ask a Scotsman if he got a reasonable price?" McPherson said indignantly though with a twinkle in his eye.

"My apologies. I should know better," Andrew said contritely. "and what next do you plan?"

"Och Lad! A wee dram!" As he spoke Cameron moved to one of the side tables and poured two whiskies, "To your health and the continued restoration of your castle." and raised his glass to Andrew who returned the toast.

They had barely settled in front of the fire to enjoy the wee dram, before another surprise caused Andrew to jump to his feet.

"Mrs Hodgson! My goodness. You too." He held out his hand but the housekeeper kept hers firmly clasped together as she curtsied. McPherson spoke from his chair.

"Mrs Hodgson kindly offered her services, and I was only too pleased to accept them. Most fortunate would you not agree?"

"Fortunate? Most definitely." Andrew answered his own question. "It is a great relief to have you here with us. I'm sure we will all rely on you for our comfort, and…"He glanced at McPherson. "have you by any chance raised the subject of training Sir? We will need your help Ma'am. I think we will find willing but very raw recruits. I'm sure you will knock them into shape."

Mrs Hodgson raised her eyes momentarily and met his as she replied.

"I have begun the task Sir, and I am hoping you will find my efforts noticeable although of course it may be necessary to over-look some minor adjustments and er... indiscretions."

"Good Luck Ma'am. Thank you for venturing so far North. I, for one, am *most* grateful."

Mrs Hodgson smiled politely and bowed her head.

"We have prepared some Supper Sir, in the hope that you would indeed arrive tonight. Would you prefer to be served in the Dining Room or perhaps in here?" Andrew hesitated. It was warm here but, on the other hand, they were all, McPherson included, probably wanting him to see more of their handiwork.

"In the Dining Room, in perhaps a quarter of hour, would be excellent." He settled back to enjoy his whisky. "And, what next Cameron, have you in store?"

"*I* have concentrated my efforts within. *You*, Earl Mulray, will needst examine without. I have no knowledge of farms, or tenants or crofts. We rely on your expertise."

"Hell Cameron, I know very little about any of that myself. Besides this weather is so diabolical I'm not sure I want to venture out. There were times I never thought I would get here. Snowstorms, blizzards, people dying. It has been a *dreadful* January. How much longer does this last?"

"Well, usually we have the thaw in March, I've been told, even up here, but the venerable McDonalds are saying that they see signs of an early Spring. We can but hope."

Andrew shivered and stretched his feet closer to the fire.

"I cannot understand how anyone would *willingly* live in this climate?"

"They know nought else. Besides there is a glory in the change. You will see My Friend. You will see. I have not, myself, sampled it here in the wilds, but even in Edinburgh there is delight at the first flowerings."

Andrew shrugged.

"I wait to be convinced."

Cameron laughed but suddenly became serious.

"It may not have occurred to you Andrew, but not only the unlamented Imposter's belongings have arrived, but with some of his ex-servants the news of his demise, has also arrived."

"Hell and damnation! Of course. What now?"

"Well there are no signs of grief. He, himself, had never bothered to come here... just send demands for higher rents. It is generally assumed that his son is his heir and you have already been designated the Lad's guardian." For McPherson it was all very simple. For Andrew there were problems... too many.

The brothers McDonald were proven correct. The storms ceased and the thaw came early. Andrew was able to explore his domain. He was pleasantly surprised to find trees aplenty. His guides proudly showed him stands of Scots pine, birch, rowan and even oak, in the glens. Those same guides, however, were shocked when he insisted on not only being introduced to his trees but also his tenants, one and all. Andrew *needed* to know.

Neither man nor beast looked over-fed, but thankfully, *no-one* seemed to be starving. Word spread quickly, however, that this stranger who held their fate in his great hands, did not like dirt or disrepair. Cottages were tidied and repaired. Clothes were spruced, clean aprons unearthed. The Reverend Bruce watched it with amusement, but was happy to see the relief, even hope, on the faces of his flock.

As Andrew and Herbert McDonald returned from one of these visits, the unmistakable throaty, staccato sound of a cuckoo stopped Herbert in his tracks.

"Aye. As I believe. The Lord has seen fit to give us an early Spring. Listen to that Lad! Those devious birds are here already, to fool their puir wee brethren."

Andrew nodded.

"Yes. We have them at home, well perhaps their cousins, and I am always angry that they lay their eggs in others' nests and leave those poor birds to hatch their progeny unsuspectingly."

Herbert cackled.

"Och and that is the way of the world is it not? *We* are like those wee birds while the cuckoos live in splendour in the South leaving us to do all the work."

"Well not any more I hope. Not any more. Surely if we can organize ourselves here... I can't promise luxury but surely comfort, Eh?"

"Aye Lad." Herbert nodded slowly. "And the Lord is giving us a sign. Raise your eyes to the Heaven. See there. The golden eagles are welcoming the Spring." As he spoke he turned to the sky and shouted. "Failte, ceud mile failte!"

In response to Andrew's unspoken question he explained,

"I bid them welcome. They are stretching their great wings, before they begin the work of breeding. Is it not a grand sight?" He tramped on, whistling merrily. Andrew felt his own spirits lifting. The dismal weather might change. "We may well be able to plough in the month of March and have a growing Season that is longer, but we will wait for the snow to melt, lest we are flooded. But in my bones I feel a good Season coming upon us. Hark. There are the swifts and the swallows. They are all good signs." He stopped and turned to Andrew, suddenly serious. "The seaweed needs to be collected." Andrew looked puzzled. "To feed the soil, Lad. And others must go to cut the peat and collect what is dry. Ye have much to organize." Andrew tried to look as if he knew what was required.

"Of course, but I *am* relying on you and your brother to tell me."

March came but it was not *all* good, Andrew thought ruefully, as he swatted another army of midges away from his face. This time his companion was the other McDonald, Henry, who was studying the hills through a looking glass that would have made Nelson proud. Henry was keen to see if the deer had begun to drop their calves, and the sheep, their lambs.

"'Tis early but I can already see the wee dappled bairns." He passed the glass to Andrew. "Can ye not see? Up there near the ridge... she will hide it in the heather if ye are too slow. Did ye see? She must be swift, the eagles are circling."

Andrew caught a glimpse of legs and ears as the hind gently pushed her offspring into hiding.

"What about the cattle? I would like to know how much livestock we have. Do we need to care for them as well?"

"Och Nooo! They are fine. Their great shaggy coats keep them warm and those horns keep them safe. They can look to their own needs. We can ask the tenants. Each man will know how many he has. No it is the sheep. We will needst to have the gather of the sheep."

"Well that is something I *am* looking forward to." Andrew said. "I'm keen to know how much wool we will have."

"And why would you be needing to know that Lad? I thought you were not in the business of that Devilish work. Is it that we will have the Clearing after all?" Henry McDonald's heavy brow was lowered, his mouth a grim line.

"No. Not at all." Andrew replied hurriedly. "No... but... well I've already bought a Mill... it will come when the weather improves. I want us to be able to make goods enough to sell when... if we can attract the travellers to come."

"We have the women who weave, and they have *always* done that." Henry's frown did not lift. Andrew realised his mistake. He was moving too quickly. He tried to change the subject.

"Well perhaps we can leave that for the moment, but if we do have the travellers, they will need to be able to hunt the deer. Do we have enough... and the fish? Do we have the fish?"

"Aye! We do have the fish and the deer. Although it is the time of danger for our stags. They are growing the antlers and they canna afford to have them damaged lest they bleed to death. 'Tis a rare sight Lad. Like all young bucks they like to jostle and parry to determine the leader. They stand on their back legs with their soft antlers well back and like a couple o' lads, box with their front paws." Andrew wondered if he should mention how the kangaroos also 'boxed', but decided to keep it to himself. He doubted very much that Henry would be interested in anything out of his strath.

"Aye. We will have the deer for these Southerners to hunt and the trout for them to try and catch, *if* they decide to journey North." His scepticism was obvious. Or was it reluctance to change? Nevertheless Andrew felt certain it was the only way to have a future for them all.

Within the month the gathering of the sheep was arranged. Men and dogs would comb the mountains and coax the flock down into the sheep folds. To Andrew the mountains looked relatively benign. They were not covered with forests of trees and bush. Nor were they capped with great jagged sandstone cliffs, and their gullies and gorges, labyrinths to trap the unwary. He soon discovered, however, they were much higher than he was used to, and, along the crumbling crests, the limestone boulders were precarious and easily dislodged. He envied the McDonalds' sure-footed climbing.

"What on earth is up here for the sheep?" He managed to ask between gasps.

"It's the springs. There are many and the grass is lush where they are. The sheep know them, and we know them of course." Henry glanced at his red-faced apprentice. "And I know it would be an advantage for you Lad, and this wee flock, if you were to take them down below and leave Herbert and the other lads to manage the rest with me."

Andrew was more than happy to oblige and he began to herd the small flock down the steep slope with the help of one of the dogs, whose expertise far outweighed his own. He was almost onto the flatter ground when he heard a shout. He glanced up. Hurtling towards him were rocks and boulders. He dived behind a fortuitous outcrop, as the sheep scattered in every direction. The thundering rushed around him then passed by. He lay still. Was he in one piece? Was it only an accident? Even *here* was he in danger? He tried to calm his thoughts and his heartbeat.

"Och Lad! And are ye not daid yet?" Andrew opened his eyes. An anxious Henry hovered over him.

"I can't be Mate. You're too ugly to be an angel."

Henry laughed and held out his hand but Andrew stood slowly unaided.

Later that evening Andrew sat alone in front of the Hall fire. Cameron was gone to Edinburgh. He would have been glad to talk it over with him. Was it only an accident? Was he becoming suspicious of everyone and anyone? He had slept peacefully, alone in the bush, so many times! He hated to be like this, but the flask had shaken him to the core. He tried not to think about it, at all. He carefully and methodically drank a bottle of whisky and went to bed.

The next morning he woke feelingly surprisingly well. 'A good whisky will never give ye a hangover'. Where had he heard that? He remembered. It was his grandfather. He could picture him clearly sipping his wee dram, despite his wife's disapproval. The quiet man whose life he was trying to avenge. Was *that* what he was doing? Did he know himself? What was it all about? This ungodly mess! He could stay here, even marry Amy... it would save her reputation... give Hamish a secure future. He still cared for them... he shook his head. No. *He* could *not* stay here. His whole being longed to be back in the space, the sunshine, the land he loved. He tried to feel an affinity for this place but it remained strange. The people who lived here, including his forbears, were all strangers. He dragged on his clothes and headed for the library. There must be records, mementoes, something, to help him understand his so-called heritage.

In the cupboards. Yes in the cupboards. How long since they had been opened? He struggled with the keys that had sat undisturbed for years... tens of years. There were ledgers, lists of purchases, tenants' leases, maps showing allotments, but nothing of interest to him, though he smiled wryly, Cameron would doubtless find them of value. Eventually he found a small trunk. It too was locked and this time there was no key. Impatiently he prised it open with a knife. Letters. His heart leapt as he read the first one... "Dear Father" and the address and the date. His eyes flew to the signature, 'James Mulray'. Could it be? His grandfather was James... There was a neat parcel, carefully refolded. James' father had treasured these, or had his mother read them also. He wasn't even sure when *she* had died...

1787

"Dear Father,

We assembled at Stirling Castle under Col. Robert Abercrombie who seems a fine man, though as you know I would always have preferred to join the Earl of Seaforth's regiment though I was but 12 years, at the time, and, we are to wear the kilt!"

Andrew smiled, clearly his grandfather had dreamt for a long time of being in the army. He opened several more of the long-folded sheets. There were military details which meant little to Andrew, who had *never* wanted to be a soldier; mention of the trip to India and it's exotic customs; sad remarks about people obviously known to the reader, about death... many, most, caused by disease rather than battle! Quite a long description of some siege at a place called Seringapatam... There was mention of his return to Scotland himself. Perhaps he had been wounded... Then Andrew found a letter dated 1796, full of excitement...

"I will be arriving in England to deliver orders on behalf of My Colonel and have been given permission to visit you all, and most importantly, meet my twin sons. I have written to my Dear Wife, please continue to help her as you have done these past years..."

Andrew stared at the letter. 1796 was *the* year! His grandfather had rushed home full of anticipation and joy. He stood holding it as if he could reach down the years and speak to this man, younger than he, Andrew was, as he wrote his happy news... Bloody Hell! Pull yourself together Walters! You've not had much to complain about have you? He folded the letters carefully. He would read them, but for now, he had work to do.

Chapter 40

It was the arrival of letters addressed to *himself* that caused Andrew to interrupt his plans for the Estate. It was not the regular letter from Caitlyn with details of stock, the price of lambs, the price of wool, the number of cattle and the markets for each. Andrew smiled ruefully, Caitlyn, Nathan and Nick of course, were dealing with 20,000 sheep at a time, while he had been trying to muster 50, and not very well either! "We have had problems with robbery of stock, 'duffing' Mr Manners calls it, but your friend Grasshopper has used his 'bush telegraph' and we have retrieved most of ours, so you should not concern yourself." Rather unusually she had included details of her life, and her own activities. He shook his head. Was this his little waif? Presentation to the Governor at the ball, horse races, more balls and... "our greatest delight was our trip to Sydney Town. Mr and Mrs Manners took us and we went out on the Harbour. It was a very fine boat. It even had a band to play music and lots of food! The boys never seemed to stop eating! It was very exciting on the beautiful Harbour because there were hundreds of boats celebrating. It was Foundation Day, (I think). We all missed you very much..." Goodness Caitlyn was being personal!

The other letter, however, was full of complaints! "Why do you insist on spending your time in that barbaric wilderness. I pine for you." Then, "how long am I forced to endure the dictates of that Miserly, Nit-picking Nobody, who arranged my allowance? Dearest Andrew I am reduced to wearing rags!" That's more to the point Andrew decided as he read on. "The Scots are well-known for meanness but your bandy-legged associate is *the* most Parsimonious Twiddlepoop imaginable! Please Dearest Heart, I beg you, rescue me!"

Andrew shook his head. Poor old McPherson. He'd volunteered to travel to London to try and make her Ladyship see reason. Clearly he had failed, but then how could he not? Amy was not a *reasonable* person. Seemingly *he* would need to travel South. They were struggling to make the Estate work. They could *not* afford her continued extravagances. The London house was part of his inheritance. It had been in the family forever, but the expense of the Countess' occupancy was becoming ridiculous. "I'll wait for Cameron's return and then decide." He spoke to the window. It was through that window that his duty lay, but there was... he had a problem. He was sure a mill was not only a good idea, but it was already on its way! And Henry's response? How many others would feel that way? The Reverend Bruce! Of course he would surely see the point. He hurried away to send a note to the clergyman, and warn Mrs Hodgson.

"That was a very fine meal, Sir. Please convey my regards to whomever cooked it." the Reverend Fergus Bruce sat back in his chair and studied his wineglass. "But I donna think it is *just* my pleasant company that you require or am I being too cynical?"

"No Sir. You have it in a nutshell. I have *quite* a problem."

"Just the one!" Interrupted the Reverend with a laugh.

"Well said. No... well the thing is I decided that we could have a mill... just a small one... here on the Estate, to make goods to sell to our guests... that's of course if we can entice them! Well the mill is on its way. I happened to mention my idea to Henry McDonald and he was horrified. I am very concerned that his response is possibly typical of... of everyone." Andrew sighed. "I am trying to find employment for as many as possible. The crofts, in my estimation, are too small, really, to produce more than the farmer's own needs. If we *do* attract visitors, we will need staff in the house... and outside... but that still leaves many..."

"An excellent idea young Fellow!" The Reverend chuckled. "Mind, change does not come easily to these people, and they are wary, even frightened. They have seen too many of their neighbours sent to the far corners of God's realm. "He sipped his wine. "Leave it to me... a sermon or two about the honouring of God's name by working together... I will need to put some thought into it... In the meantime I'm needing some help from you. I will need help, teaching the bairns. You have certainly made education something your people want. I have made a few enquiries. I hope you understand. I have also made some enquiries about the Church augmenting the cost of employing such a person." He paused and his voice became stern. "I have taken the opportunity to point out to the powers that be, that *this* is one small chance for the Church to *redeem* its reputation!" In response to Andrew's puzzled expression he continued. "*To*o many of my brethren, assisted and even encouraged the Clearing of their *own* people. There is *already* a backlash occurring."

"That's interesting... I had no idea. As far as a teacher... please go right ahead. I'm sorry I did not realise." It was Andrew's turn to chuckle. "Perhaps you could include the building of a school as well as a mill, in your homily Sir?" They both laughed.

"There is a further problem. Many of the children live too far away to come to school each day "

"Well could I organize for them to be collected?" Andrew suggested.

"I am not sure *that* is the answer either, I feel they need to stay here near the school at least during the week. Even if we could offer each child one term of schooling, they could learn their letters and numbers."

"We have plenty of rooms in the Castle, surely we could set aside a room for the girls, the lasses I mean, and another for the lads. I'll see to that while you find your teachers."

The Reverend raised his glass.

"Sláinte! To our mutual endeavour!"

Cameron returned within the month. He had curbed the Countess' spending.

"I simply placed a notice in the newspapers that the Estate of the Late Earl Mulray would no longer be liable for any debts incurred by the Dowager Countess."

"Good God! You didn't." Andrew gasped.

"Aye Lad, I *did*. I warned her, I pleaded with her, I applied to her better nature... a pointless effort that was. She ignored me. In fact I'm sure she spent more and more to spite me!" He shrugged. "So I put the notice in the paper, and I appointed a fellow Scot I know, to take over the household. You may well imagine how many insults, cushions and vases were hurled in my direction!"

"You're a *braver* man than I'll ever be Cameron McPherson."

"Well we *canna* allow it. She has *no* legal entitlement to anything, as *ye well know* Andrew, My Friend."

The letters of complaint continued to arrive, as did the mill! The Bruce sermons had the desired effect. A modest school building and an equally modest mill were planned and built with many eager hands. The generous McMillan had provided hands to not only help construct the mill, but to train its workers. Several young men eagerly began to learn the intricacies of the looms. As Andrew stood for the first time, listening to the rhythmic metallic clink of the looms in *his* mill his heart lifted. Maybe, just maybe, they would succeed.

Three parties of tourists had already been entertained, and more were booked for the October shooting season. There had been hiccups aplenty. Andrew's insistence on personal hygiene and freshly laundered uniforms had almost caused a rebellion... and as for persuading Mrs Anderson to vary the menu *every day*! Somehow they had all muddled through. Fortunately the oaths of the ghillies, as they struggled to accommodate the vagaries of their guests, were in Gaelic, thus sparing the visitors' ears!

And now Andrew knew a great deal more about the scarf that wound around his neck. He had come to realise "the weaving" was easy, compared to "the preparing of the fleece." The blackface sheep that he'd scrambled around the hills trying to round up, produced a fleece that was coarse, long and open; the dreaded Cheviots produced a much shorter finer fleece. Despite the McDonalds' frowns and dire predictions, Andrew had bought a herd of these despised interlopers, including wedders to grow out, and ewes to mate with the blackface rams. A cheviot ram was still required. He felt they could mix the wools and perhaps crossbreeds could produce something worthwhile. Trial and error but... he'd also discovered that the Scottish wool was prepared differently.

"Aye Sir. The lazy Sassenachs comb their fleece, like a maiden's hair, until they have the long fibres. Doesna have *any* warmth." Henry McDonald's cheerful wife Eleanor, unlike her husband, was a champion of the new mill, despite the fact she was a skilled weaver on her own spindle. "You see Sir, we *card* our wool... it traps the air... we scrape it back and forth till it mats." As she spoke she held out two flat boards covered with strong wire teeth. "Aye, you'll see. We'll show these Southerners what real woollen cloth is!"

"And you are prepared to share this fleece Ma'am? I know Henry is not happy about our new mill."

"Och! There's nae fool like an auld fool, Sir." She shook her head. "My Henry has the problem with anything new Sir, but he would never go against yourself Your Lordship... give him taime... give him taime."

Andrew bowed his head.

"I defer to your judgment Ma'am. I need Henry very much if we are to prosper."

"Och! Your Lordship never fear. He'll answer to *me* and he becomes difficult."

"That is a relief Ma'am. I thank you," Andrew said with a smile.

He returned to his duties with a spring in his step, but it lasted less than a week.

Chapter 41

Andrew returned from a productive day spent examining his forests. They were not extensive but with careful management, they could be improved and eventually increased. He would need to keep the sheep away... they nibbled everything to the ground... but it could be another way to earn funds, and God knew how important *that* was. McPherson would know about the markets for timber.

Cameron McPherson, however, was nowhere to be seen. There also seemed to be a malais affecting the entire household. Servants were hurrying hither and yon, looking agitated. Why? Eventually, Andrew tracked his friend to the Library. The door was firmly closed and the room in semi-darkness but he could make out the familiar silhouette against the silvery twilight flooding through the great window.

"Why are *you* in here and the staff running around like headless chooks?"

"I havena any notion what a headless chook is, but, Andrew my friend, I can tell you what ails your household... the *witch* has *arrived.*"

Andrew stared at him.

"Do you... do you mean... the Countess? When? Where?"

"Aye. Your friend the Countess with what appears to be her *entire* household... the child, the nurse, the dresser, the page... Shall I go on?"

Andrew slumped into the nearest chair, his head in his hands, as Cameron continued icily.

"She has declared that since *I* have reduced her to a pauper, her *only* recourse is to come here." He gritted his teeth. "She appears to have no intentions of *ever* leaving either. I warn you. I will not remain *here* if *she* stays. Be warned. I *canna* stay."

"Oh, hold onto your hat Cameron, *please*! You know I cannot rebuild this place *without* you. Please. Give me time... a week at least. I *will* sort it out. Trust me!"

"I wish you well." was the unconvinced reply.

"Where is she?"

"Her Ladyship has retired to her room... or should I say rooms. She has commandeered the largest bed chamber and the adjoining rooms as *her* sitting rooms. She has also, I might add, ordered dinner to her requirements, sending poor Mrs Anderson into a decline."

"Oh. Do you recommend I speak to Mrs Anderson first, or our guest?"

"*She* is not *our* guest Andrew. She is *your* liability!" His voice was bitter. "I warned you. You have treated that shrew with far too much consideration."

Having calmed Mrs Anderson with the assistance of Mrs Hodgson, Andrew fled to his room. He *had* to think. Trust Amy. She was a match for poor old Cameron! But he *needed* Cameron. He was indispensable. And he was his friend!

He reached his room and stripped off his riding clothes, and had barely managed to pull on his trousers before the door flew open. He assumed it was the footman with hot water. It was not.

"Oh Andrew! My Love! How *could* you do this!? How could you leave me destitute? I throw myself on your mercy. Please! You *must* save me from that man." She had rushed forward and thrown herself against his naked chest. He closed his eyes. The familiar rush of desire engulfed him. Get a grip on yourself, you fool! He pushed her away gently into a chair. Then, having pulled on his shirt and waistcoat, sat opposite, trying to decide what he should, could, say. She had buried her head in her hands and was rocking back and forth, moaning softly. His brain said 'what a performance' but his heart said otherwise.

"I think we should... you should... I mean this is hardly the place for us to consider anything. You will shock the staff if they see you here." He stood and went to open the door. He was ignored. "Come Amy, this will not do." He tried to sound persuasive but firm. She stood slowly and came close. She smiled into his eyes as she adjusted his shirt and retied his stock,

"There that's better. You need a valet... or a wife..." and smiled seductively as she slipped away.

Dinner was a disaster. Amy sat at the end of the table, the hostess in her rightful place. Cameron McPherson maintained a stony silence. The only conversation was that between a determinedly charming Amy and the long suffering Mary Simpson. Andrew responded to any direct remark but nothing more. The ladies retired. Andrew was left to unsuccessfully placate his companion.

"I have told ye. I willna stay in this place whilst ever that... that 'dubh bean' is here. Tha I beag-naire!' She... I will blether and niffle naffle while you swither! And I will doubtless lose my temper with *you* as well. You, Earl Mulray are too enthralled by her beu-maothain!"

Andrew had only understood some of the words but he could clearly understand the anger.

"I can only *beg* you to remain, Cameron, for a few days at least while I try to reason with her. I will try to keep her away from you. I can take her and Hamish to see the countryside... perhaps even fishing in the loch... whilst you carry on here." Andrew shook his head. "Give her her due Mate. She's called our bluff." McPherson's reply was accompanied by an angry scowl,

"Drown her and save me the trouble!" as he returned to the Library alone.

It was the week from Hell.

Fortunately Andrew showed McPherson the treasure trove of old documents, plans and leases in the Library. He was thoroughly enthralled, and barely emerged. Andrew had given strict instructions to Mrs Hodgson that the household was answerable to McPherson, but old habits die hard. She had been the Countess' housekeeper. It was natural to take instructions from her. Fortunately the footman Jonathan Jones had become the Under Butler. Mr Anderson was not young and had rarely been anything but the Butler in name only. Jones was a born diplomat and to Andrew's relief managed to negotiate between the warring factions and keep the peace.

Andrew was left to squire the ladies. Amy proceeded to play the sadly grieving widow. Since she was young and beautiful with an engaging son, the tenants succumbed to her charm, with the exception of Mrs Henry, who regarded her outfits as extravagant and *unseemly*. She kept her opinions to herself except where her husband was concerned. He was given the edge of her tongue after she caught him glancing once too often at Amy's 'beul-maothain', which was forever on display in her low cut bodices.

"As the Good Book says 'for the lips of a strange woman drop as an honeycomb, and her mouth is rather smoother than oil: but her end is bitter as wormwood, sharp as a two-edged sword. Her feet go down to death; her steps take hold on Hell' It is a great concern if our young Lad is like you, You Old Fool!"

Hamish was in his element. *He* was with Andrew. The Estate fell in love with this sturdy little bairn in his kilt. He was constantly being spoiled by the staff inside and the crofters outside, but it was obvious, he just wanted to be with Andrew. His mother 'naturally' was the 'doting' parent. But her good humour was severely tested when he, encouraged by Cameron, found a new game to play when he was inside the castle. The little boy would run up and down the great staircase and in the main rooms, counting the paintings of Andrew. McPherson had commented long ago on Andrew's strong resemblance to his forbears, whose portraits now provided Hamish with entertainment, and his mother with furious resentment. She continued, however, to be charming to everyone, with the obvious exception of the 'Scottish Miser'. Each morning she rode with Andrew, though her enjoyment was *not* complete, since her son usually accompanied them, either on his own pony or perched in front of Andrew. She always managed to linger in the latter's arms as he helped her mount and dismount, but otherwise was quite circumspect. Andrew began to relax. He was lulled into a false sense of security. A week passed uneventfully until he returned to his room after dinner to find Amy already ensconced and ready for him.

"*Dearest* Andrew. It is *too* much to see you and *never* be alone. I *see* you but can *never* be in your arms." She rose slowly and came very close. "My Dearest Love! I will even *remain* in this wilderness, if it means I can be *near you*." Andrew had hesitated in the doorway. He hurriedly closed the door. "You have been so kind and attentive these last few days I've even begun to hope..." To keep you away from Cameron... to keep the peace, he thought to himself. He stiffened as she ran her hand gently down the side of his face. He tried to ignore it and sound firm.

"You, I thought, were interested in the Estate and I had hoped Hamish would also enjoy himself." He stepped firmly into his room trying to take control. "I do not believe it is possible or seemly for you to stay here permanently at the present time. And to be frank Madam, I'm convinced you'd soon find it all rather tedious. You are accustomed to a very different way of life."

"Oh Andrew Walters you've become such a prude! The castle is positively *teeming* with people, and I have Mary to chaperone me. You. You have that wizened, sour faced... miser!" She sighed and moved closer once more. "It has been so pleasant these last few days. I am sure... we... but. Oh! It is so difficult to see you and..." She took his hands in her own and pressed them against her breast. "*Surely* you remember what we *were* to each other?" She gazed into his eyes then moved abruptly to the fireplace and rested her head and hands on the mantelpiece. "I am *so* lonely without you. I long for you... day... and night." The last word came slowly as she glanced from under her lashes. "I have been dreaming of you... for *so* long."

Andrew knew perfectly well she had not spent many lonely nights, nor did he believe he had even featured in her thoughts until very recently. He could remember hearing those very words on a cold terrace. He smiled politely and took a seat. She smiled down at him.

"Do you remember... the *first* time I sat on your lap? I sat there and I took your hand and slipped it inside my bodice... and it was the most delicious feeling." She knelt at his feet. "I *will* stay here if it is the *only* way I can be with you." She turned her back and resting against his legs, gazed into the fire. "And then, when you are ready we can go to London. *You* must be the only Scottish Landowner who insists on hiding away in this bleak wilderness... but if I can be with *you*..." She turned and took his hand and smiled into his eyes.

"That is very flattering Madam but you are not capable of staying here. One month, maybe two and you will be back in London, where you are happy."

"Oh Poo! How *heartless* you are. You are being stupid! You are working so hard for these people. Do you *really* think they matter? They are *using* you? Do you *really* think they will continue to work? Highlanders are *renowned* for being shiftless and lazy. Why else have the sensible Chieftains cleared them out? It is incomprehensible to me that you prefer the company of *savages* to those of impeccable birth." Amy was too lost in her lecture to have noticed the narrowing of Andrew's eyes and the stiffening of his body. "You'll have a place in Society, and *I* could be by your side."

Andrew stood abruptly.

"Well you know, I was used to spend much of my life with "savages" at home. I always found them excellent company. Perhaps I am too uncivilised for Society."

"Oh Silly Boy. You were *such* a success when you came before. And *I* will be *there* for you." She added with a gentle smile as she scrambled back to her feet unassisted, despite having held out her hands to him.

"I am *here* because, as we have *tried* unsuccessfully it seems, to make you understand, *you* are destitute, and *your* husband was *destitute*. Besides I have found the people here genuine, honest and hard working. I think you should return to London. You may continue to live in Mulray House *but* on the condition that you curb your extravagance, I will continue to support you." He moved towards the door.

"You cannot make me leave!" Tears flowed. "Support! Support! You offered me much more than support, once in our lives!" She clutched her hands to her heart. "You cannot send me away. I *am* the mother of *your* child. Hamish is your son. Do you want the world to know?"

Andrew shrugged and his lips twisted into the semblance of a smile.

"Goodness me Madam. You *are* desperate. Why should I believe that? You were married to your husband who always acknowledged Hamish as his. It is suddenly convenient to tell me this *now, and* I feel *sure* you *cannot* declare it to the world. It would destroy you." He raised a cynical eyebrow. "Methinks you reputation would suffer much more than mine, even if it *were* true." He opened the door. "I think you have said more than enough. Please leave." She ignored him and sank into a chair sobbing hysterically. Andrew tried to decide whether he should leave himself or carry her bodily to her room. He decided to leave. He returned to the Library. Cameron was there poring over a book.

"Hello. Thought you'd retired... Here look at this... Damned interesting..."

Andrew tried to concentrate but eventually excused himself and went back to his room. Surely she would be gone.

She was asleep on his bed. The curve of her hip and her almost naked breasts were an open invitation. It would be so easy to join her and he knew of old, what pleasure would follow. He closed the door quietly and after some exploration found an empty bedroom. He stretched out fully clothed and finally slept. When he returned to his own room at dawn, she was gone. What next?

Chapter 42

Andrew felt he was sitting on a box of gunpowder with two people ever ready to light the fuse. By the end of ten days he was exhausted. Worse was to come.

Another carriage arrived at Mulray Castle. Two rather portly gentlemen emerged from its padded luxury. They were gentlemen who had clearly enjoyed the indulgences of life but were not in a jovial mood at this moment. The taller of the two wore a belligerent expression, his rotund companion was trying to look angry, but his self-satisfaction was too complete. The unexpected guests were shown into the Great Hall, where as usual, Andrew was trying to play host to a warring audience.

"Papa! Dearest Papa! You are *here*! Oh how... how... How have you come so far? Why... how did you know?" Amy was immediately the daughter in distress. "Oh Dear Papa you have come to rescue me... us!" She ran to her father and rested her head lovingly on his shoulder as she grasped his arm.

"Yes My Dear. I am here with *my* good friend, and, as I understand, *your* loyal friend, Whittaker here. He has seen fit to accompany me on this great trek to rescue you from your *ill-usage* at the hands of *scoundrels!*" He paused and glanced around the room. His eyes focussed on Andrew who was standing with his glass suspended halfway between the table and his mouth. He recovered and stood to formally greet the newcomers, but before he could say anything, he was attacked by an enraged parent.

"*You!* I can barely believe my own eyes! You *dastardly* wretch!! How *dare* you treat my daughter so shamefully!? Whittaker has told me all. How... in God's name is this *possible?* You are... how can *you* possibly be allowed to *steal* another man's name and title? You are an arrant rogue. A disgrace. I'll have you arrested... thrown into prison! *I* am *not* without influence. Your days of dissembling are numbered! I have already ordered my lawyers to have you *exposed!*"

"And Good Evening to you too Major. I trust you have had a reasonable journey," Andrew stepped forward and held out his hand. "and Whittaker I trust I see you well?" The hand was being ignored. "May I present my good friend, Baillie McPherson, my helpmate and lawyer? I think Cameron you have already met Mr Whittaker?"

Cameron stared at Andrew in astonished admiration, while Major Burnett's face deepened from puce to burgundy. Belligerence was replaced by embarrassment. Perhaps he *had* come on rather strong, but from all Whittaker had said... Major Rupert Burnett was used to being in charge. Suddenly this young nobody had behaved with quiet authority and grace, while he... well perhaps he *had* jumped the gun. It was the shock! Amy's position, her title, her wealth taken from her by an *uncultured colonial*... the son of a clerk! He nodded at the McPherson chap... what did 'Baillie' mean? Some sort of magistrate? Perhaps *there was* more to all this than Whittaker had told him.

Andrew smiled and waited. There was an uncomfortable pause before the Major shook Andrew's hand and replied gruffly.

"Yes we had a rather good journey, thank you. The rail is an interesting way to travel, though... well *first* class is, but one could not travel in any other class."

"It certainly is efficient. And I tend to agree. Perhaps you noticed the poor souls in the third class do not have a roof over their heads, and they *must* travel with their backs to the engine to avoid, as best they can, the rain of soot and grit that shoots at them, to protect their eyes at least. Can I offer you refreshment? Would you prefer tea or something more fortifying?" Jones had already appeared and was waiting for the Major's preference.

"Thank you. It *is* past four. Perhaps something stronger…"

The guests settled rather uncomfortably after Amy had arranged herself becomingly. McPherson muttered an excuse and left. Andrew waited. What next? The Major, however, had decided on a tactical retreat. The conversation centred on the advantages of the rail and the difference steam had made to ships as well.

"'The Great Britain' is such an improvement. Six weeks from Australia to Britain instead of up to six months!"

Andrew agreed.

"It certainly is, but did you have difficulty on gaining a berth on short notice?"

"By Jove No! The *world* is flocking *to* the colonies. The Goldfields in Victoria are bringing them from near and far! We still have diggings in our area but Ballarat and Bendigo, El Dorado they say." He shook his head. "I imagine *I* travelled with more *gold* than passengers. The government is shipping it *all* to England."

Andrew laughed politely but Amy was bored. She should be the centre of attention thank you very much.

"Dearest Papa. You *must* be weary. I will take you to your room myself." She turned to Andrew, "See to the luggage." and swept imperiously from the Hall, with her father and Whittaker trundling behind. Andrew fled to the Library and his mentor.

"Well Done Lad! I didna think ye had it in ye." Cameron patted Andrew's shoulder. "Ye showed them *who* was the gentleman!

And I canna wait to illuminate that Major, who has *such* a good opinion of himself, with a few facts."

"Give him his due Cameron, he has only heard Whittaker's version."

"Och Aye! But a gentleman wouldna have burst into another's house, shooting with his mouth." He chuckled. "I'll get the bairn, young Hamish, to take him around and show him, how many pictures there are 'of you', Lad. That should cause our Major to ponder a wee while."

Andrew shrugged,

"Maybe, but I'm wondering *why* he's come. I doubt his daughter would have told him she'd... well Bloody Hell, we *know* she hasn't accepted her new circumstances. *We've* not told anyone. How or what does he know? Do you *really* think he will listen to the true story?"

"Och Lad! I'm itching to acquaint him with the truth. You leave it to your lawyer."

Andrew had already invited the Reverend Bruce and his wife for dinner, that very evening, so it was *almost* a convivial gathering. The Major was happy to describe his journey to a new audience. As ever, Whittaker knew the answers to everything, though he did have trouble interrupting the Major's monologue. The Reverend Bruce was a good listener and his wife was simply happy to be in such elevated company.

It was two days before Baillie McPherson was able to acquaint the Major with the real situation, and the tragic history of the Mulrays. It was not easy for the Major to accept.

"*How* can this be true? Is there any proof? Why has this Arbiter chap accepted young Walters' claim *over* my daughter's husband? The Walters are a decent family." He conceded with a sceptical shake of his head. "I knew the father. He served under me. A reasonable sort of chap... quite a good soldier... lost an arm as I remember, but... I mean so very *ordinary!*" The Major blustered.

As calmly as he could, Cameron tried to explain.

"It is *not* the father we are considering here. It is the *mother's* birthright, Andrew's mother. In Scotland *she* has *every* right to inherit. The title goes to Andrew, but it is his mother who has nominated him, even though *she* inherited the Estate." He paused. "But the real mystery to *us* is *why you* have come? Young Walters has taken great pains... he has *not* declared himself the Earl. The people here believe he is a relative only. To spare your ungrateful daughter he has kept silent. *Did she* ask you to come?"

"No. Poor Dear Girl! No. Indeed it was Young Walters' brother-in-law. He came and told me that her husband had died. He didn't say a *great deal.* Just said my daughter's circumstances had altered greatly and that she was... he felt she would need guidance. Indeed he was *adamant* that she should come back to us and if not *we* should go to her. He pressed the point rather more than I understood." He paused. "Of course one would take *his* word. After all *he* is well-born, a gentleman, and wealthy!"

Cameron managed to bite his tongue. How "well-born" was Torquil, or the Major for that matter. Clearly he had become 'well off' in the colonies but was *that* his criteria?

"How long... I mean when did this?... *Where* do *you* come into it anyway?" The tone was aggressive. The Major was trying hard to find fault. Cameron kept his voice calm and measured despite his anger.

"The Walters family have known for certain for at least two years, but, they, especially Andrew, were not particularly interested in pursuing it. *I* can tell *you* I thought they were *quite* wrong, and spent many hours writing letters accordingly. The Arbiter, also, having met Andrew previously, was anxious for the matter to be resolved. Andrew's family resemblance is *quite* striking. None of us knew however, until Andrew came back to Scotland, that it was *your* daughter's husband who was the Imposter."

"Imposter! How dare you! How dare you call him Imposter!" The Major's temper exploded.

"I *dare* because that is what he was. Mind, I doubt he knew himself, until the end..." McPherson had dealt with aggressive witnesses aplenty. His voice remained calm as he continued. "I realize that it is very hard for you Sir, but I speak the truth. And, I might add, if your daughter's husband had *not* decided to sell this estate and clear it of its people, I doubt Andrew would have *ever* decided to do anything." He paused, trying to gauge how much the Major was absorbing. "Even if nothing *had* occurred in this regard and Andrew had *not* decided to act, I am sure your daughter would have needed your help. Her husband had squandered *all* of his 'so-called' inheritance, and *all* of your daughter's dowry. Nor did he appear to have any thought for the future. He has left her, and your grandson, *destitute*. If Andrew had acted as he could have, and was *entitled* to, your daughter could well have been in a debtor's prison. *You* owe *him* gratitude." Cameron managed to refrain from adding "not abuse", but he had the distinct impression the Major had taken the point anyway.

"But Whittaker said..." The Major's attempt at argument was interrupted by an indignant lawyer.

"Whittaker is a *scoundrel* and a chancer. A 'Captain Hackum' to you. From what I can gather he has lived off your son-in-law, all his adult life. I wouldna care to examine their relationship Sir, if I were you... Whatever he has seen fit to tell you is *totally* unreliable." McPherson paused considering, "You may be unaware Major, but more than one attempt has been made on Mr. Walters', I mean the Earl's life, and the last, was *after* your son-in-law's 'unfortunate' accident and demise. I leave you to consider in whose interest, Andrew Walters' death would be."

The Major stood slowly, feeling every year of his age. He needed time to think. He needed to talk to his daughter. He was shocked, even appalled. Was he angry? He no longer knew.

"Please. Excuse me. Thank you for your time. I will consider all that you told me. I do appreciate it." He straightened his shoulders. A soldier about to go into battle, but his knees creaked, his back ached, as did his heart.

The following day Major Burnett took his daughter and her entourage back to London. Andrew insisted they return to Mulray House. McPherson was apoplectic, the Major reluctant, but after some persuasion from Andrew he came to realise that it would help to preserve his daughter's reputation. Naturally she should be domiciled in her own home. Otherwise there would be talk. It galled the Major to be in Andrew's debt but he finally agreed.

The Mulray Estate returned to work, but the absence of the 'wee bairn' was felt by all, especially Andrew.

Chapter 43

"There seems to be a great deal going on today, Cameron. May I ask why?"

"Och! Aye! Tomorrow is St Andrew's Day Lad, *and* it is *your* name day!" Cameron McPherson raised an enquiring eyebrow. "Did ye not know this? *He* is the patron saint of Scotland, ' tis his cross on our flag."

"His cross?"

"Aye. He wouldna be crucified like his Lord Jesus, so they crucified him on an x-shaped cross."

"Bloody Hell!"

"Aye, it would have been that."

"Well what am I meant to do?"

"Och nought. They are all busy and ye shouldna be noticing. Ye'll spoil it all." He nodded as he explained. "Mind it is the day they would usually have the beasts slaughtered and finish the harvest. My suspicion is they ha' been busying themselves today throughout the straths and glens so that we, and they, can enjoy the morrow."

The morrow dawned. Andrew went for his usual early morning ride. He returned to find seemingly *all* his clansmen, and their families, from every village, gathering in his courtyard! He slipped unnoticed from the stable through a side door and sought advice.

"*What* is going on outside?" He asked.

"Get ye into your kilt wi' all the trimmings Lad and then get ye out there." Cameron smiled quizzically. "They have come to see you."

"Good God! Why?"

"Ye'll find out soon enough."

Andrew did as he was bid. He belted the kilt Mrs Henry had spun for him – "ter colours are very pleasing on ye." Then he tried hard to remember which sock held the small knife, the 'sgian dubh'. Well he was right-handed so right sock will do. As he pinned the brooch they had found in his grandmother's trunk, to hold his plaid in place and pulled the bonnet over his red thatch, he suddenly felt a glow of pride... was it... all this... part of him after all? He looked at the chieftain's badge with its three feathers. No. If he pinned that to his bonnet he would be claiming to be chieftain. Another day. He rewrapped it.

As he stepped through the great front door and paused on the step, a piper sounded, then another and another. At first he did not recognize the tune... 'Scots Wha Hae'. The crowd began to follow the pipers. The procession came to a halt in front of Andrew. The piping died away. It was followed by three rousing cheers. Andrew began to realise it was all for *his* benefit, especially when the Reverend Bruce stepped forward and proclaimed.

"We give thanks on this our Saint's Holy Day, that the Good Lord has seen fit to send us a champion." He repeated the words in Gaelic. The crowd cheered and clapped. Andrew felt a lump in his throat. Maybe it was worth it after all? He raised his hand. Instant silence. He was so shocked he was momentarily lost for words.

"Tapadh leibh." He glanced helplessly at McPherson. His own Gaelic was still very basic. "I am glad to be here with you." McPherson duly translated. "I understand this is a great day for us all, so let us begin."

As McPherson spoke to the crowd, Andrew wondered. Begin what? He had no idea, but he soon found himself running in races, rather slowly, then trying to throw a pole over its end. At this he was apparently reasonably successful. His pole landed almost in line. Hurling a very heavy stone was not beyond him, but as he swung another rock, this time attached to a chain, around and around, he dreaded letting go lest he wiped out several of his audience. He was no champion but the crowd cheered him nevertheless.

Then the younger men divided themselves into two teams. They drew lots and Andrew to his chagrin realised they were drawing lots for *himself*. This time his size was an advantage and after considerable, puffing, swearing, sliding and pulling his team were triumphant in the tug o' war.

There had been refreshments offered during the day but now he found himself at the head of a very long table groaning with food. He was offered more than even *he* could eat. There was more. It seemed that every woman had made a St Andrew's cake and Andrew was honour bound to sample each and every one. He managed by sipping the delicious oatmeal posset between samples. It was only later when the fiddlers began to play that he realised his head was dancing with the music. He sought refuge in the shadows of the courtyard on a stone bench. He had not long been there when he was joined by his Under Butler.

Andrew tried to focus and sound clearer than he felt.

"Well Jones. A fine day we've had! How are you finding your new home?"

In the flickering torchlight he could see the young man's pleasure.

"It was more than I could have hoped for Sir. I... I had no knowledge of the Highlands, or Scotland really. The people... well they wait... but once they decide you are... acceptable... they are the salt of the earth."

"You're right there, and after today I'll never believe they are dour. Mind I do know what you are saying. We 'nevertheless' have to earn our stripes. Eh?" Andrew chuckled.

"Yes Sir, but I think there is "na doobt" you've won them over." Jones agreed.

"Well we've had our moments, I can tell you, though doubtless you've heard more than I have."

There was a silence. Andrew turned to look at his companion, he was surprised to see he was frowning and biting his lips. "What's the problem? Can I be of help perhaps. Just say the word."

There was a long pause, finally Jones spoke, hesitatingly, keeping his voice low.

"Well there *is* something I heard. I've tossed and turned it over and over in my mind... whether to mention it... to you... I mean."

"Well out with it. We can't have you worrying, it may affect your work, and as your employer..." Andrew tried to sound firm, but he was smiling.

There was another pause. Jones eventually spoke.

"It... I mean Sir, I would not like you to think I'm in the habit of eavesdropping."

Andrew shook his head reassuringly.

"No I don't. Go on"

"Well it was the Countess and Mr Whittaker. She had rung for the tea tray. I knocked but their voices were... raised and they did not hear my knock. The tray was quite heavy... I needed to put it on a side table and knock loudly. This time they must have heard because the Countess acknowledged it. I took in the tray and left."

"And?" Andrew prompted.

"Well it was what they said... what I heard that has been troubling me ever since." Andrew waited. Jones took a deep breath. "I heard her Ladyship say, very angrily, I must say, 'You assured me that it would not fail. You were so sure! *He'll drink it* sooner or later without a doubt... that's what you said, may I remind you. Well quite clearly he *didn't*, did he?' and then Mr Whittaker said. 'It is inconceivable I cannot understand it myself! Are you *certain* he had it with him?' and then she said, 'He always has it with him you blundering fool', and that's when they hear my second knock. I delivered the tray. "He took a deep breath. "Being frank Sir... it has worried me. It is not a conversation one would expect to hear, anywhere..."

Andrew felt the cold anger seep through his being. He closed his eyes. He was such a Bloody Fool! He tried to keep his voice normal.

"Very interesting Jones. It is... well as you say... not a conversation one would expect to hear, from anyone. When *was* this? Can you remember?"

"Oh yes Sir. I remember clearly. It was the day after the other gentlemen arrived... the Countess' father and Mr Whittaker himself. No. The day after. The Major was in the Library with Mr McPherson, and you yourself, were gone out."

"You've done the right thing Jones. It *is* quite a troubling thing to have heard. Thank you for sharing it with me, perhaps... well I would hope you would keep it to yourself." He smiled as naturally as he could. "Do you remember once I said you owe me... well I think you have repaid the debt."

"Of course Sir. Of course I will. Thank you Sir. Thank you." He stood. "If you'll excuse me Sir, I shall go and... see to your... guests."

Andrew nodded absentmindedly. He was stunned. What a compete fool you have been. What an abject fool. He'd probably had too much to drink already... he had no real idea what was in that posset, but he felt he needed a stiff drink. Before he could go in search of that drink he was joined on his stone seat by the Elder McDonald, Herbert, who had clearly had more than *his* share of posset.

"Jussht wanted to shay Young Lad... don't want ye to think I'm pissing in your pocket but ish the besht thing to happen to this clan in a vairy long time, Young Fella, ish yoursel', the besht, and we are all thankin' the Almighty. You've given ush hope!" He stood, thumped Andrew hard on his shoulder and strode off. *God help me! One moment I'm to be murdered the next, the answer to everyone's prayers.*

Before he had time to consider either, a small but firm hand took his and pulled him into the centre of the dancers. Mrs Henry then proceeded to cajole, tease and teach her pupil the Scottish reel. The fiddlers had replaced the pipers. The crowd danced and sang. Andrew was passed from one lady to the next. He was naturally light on his feet but his toes barely kept up with his partners'. It was a long night. Andrew relaxed. He decided he much preferred a Highland gathering to a sheep gathering. It was a celebration. *Just relax Andrew Walters and enjoy.*

Chapter 44

"And, so what do you intend to do?" Cameron asked.

"Nothing."

"Nothing! Good Lord Lad, she tried to kill you! Are ye so besotted that ye'll do nought?"

"Well what can I do?" Andrew shrugged helplessly. "There are no witnesses. *I* saw the dog die. *No-one* else. I made sure Hamish did *not* see anything. When I roused the stable hand to help me bury the poor thing, I deliberately misled him. I suggested a heart attack. I even asked if they'd been using poisonous baits in the stables. *And* let me tell you I soaked that flask for days! I changed the water *every* day. Even now I feel nervous about it." He threw himself into the nearest chair. "You know and *I* know what Jones overheard, but no-one else. She's gone and she won't be back. The year is up. She can find somewhere else to live. The Major can certainly afford that." He stood suddenly, "Come, fancy a game of chess? I need to think of something else." and went to leave the Library.

"Stay. I've found some very interesting correspondence. Your great grandfather was a man ahead of his time. Here read this." Cameron proffered a bundle of yellowing papers. Resignedly Andrew began to read the fading lists.

It was reading the bundle of letters that arrived the following day, however, that gave him something else to think about.

There were three letters from Caitlyn, another from Emily and one sealed with a crest. He could probably do *that* with the seal they'd found... some advantages to be had, he decided, as he broke the wax.

Mannering
10th November

Dear Andrew,

Spencer and I have decided with the enthusiastic agreement of our family, particularly Simon, that since you will not be joining us for Christmas, that we should join you for the New Year. New Year's Eve is, we have heard, a special occasion in Scotland. We will arrive, this ghastly weather permitting, sometime after the 27th. Simon is bringing some friends, therefore, the size of our party is unknown, at this stage, but I am sure your castle will be adequate.

Fond Regards,
Helen Spencer

P.S. It appears 'the widow' has lost no time in recovering her position in Society. She is betrothed to some minor Irish Earl. I've not had the 'privilege' of making his acquaintance, but my informants agree, he is middle-aged, bandy-legged and a complete dolt. Need I say more.
H.S.

Andrew stared at the letter for several minutes, then hurried to find Cameron.

"Are you going to Edinburgh for Christmas?"

"Perhaps. Is there a problem?"

"The entire Spencer Clan are descending on us for New Year, and, I *must* go to London at once."

"Ye'll never get to London and back Lad. 'Tis already the second of December!" He frowned. "And in this weather. *And* it is a great distance?"

Andrew smiled.

"Your idea of *distance* is somewhat different to mine, My Friend. I'll concede the weather may be a problem, but if I can get through to Edinburgh, I should make it easily." He patted his companion's shoulder. "If you could stay and make the necessary arrangements... Well to tell the truth, the widow is to marry some Irish Earl. I need to see her."

Cameron stared in horror.

"No! No! Surely not!" as he muttered almost to himself. "As a dog returneth to his vomit, so a fool returneth to his folly."

Andrew laughed bitterly,

"No. Do you not give me *any* semblance of common sense? No, I must see her. I cannot let this go as if nothing has happened."

Cameron remained sceptical.

"I will arrange for the carriage that takes ye to Edinburgh to bring Father here. With your permission of course. Then John Coachman can go back to Edinburgh and wait for ye... that's of course *if* ye arrive."

"I'll arrive Mate! I'll arrive. I'm asking a great deal but..."

"Dona give it a thought. Just get yourself back *before* the Lady Spencer arrives! That My Friend *is* a matter of life and death... undoubtedly mine!" Andrew chuckled as he hurried away.

Within the week he was knocking on the door of his own house in Belgravia. Well this should be the last time I need permission to enter, he mused, as he huddled against the bitter wind. He was shown into a downstairs sitting room, where he found Mary Simpson quietly sewing in front of a cheerful fire.

"Mr Andrew! My Goodness where have you sprung from? Oh how rude of me. I beg your pardon Sir."

"I hope I'm not an unpleasant surprise Ma'am?"

He bowed but his eyes smiled at his flustered companion.

"Never! *You* would never be unwelcome... to me, Mr Walters. Never!" There was a pause. Mary Simpson stood wringing her hands. "Indeed I have been thinking of you a great deal... yes a great deal."

"My Goodness Ma'am, I'm flattered. Is there some service I could perhaps render, or have I perhaps omitted something?"

"Oh No Sir! Oh no *you* could never do that. It is just... Oh Dear, it is... presumptuous of me... dreadfully unbecoming, but..."

"Out with it Miss Simpson. Out with it." Andrew urged gently.

"Well... I will not be needed... in my present situation... Her Ladyship has made it clear. I... Oh Dear..."

Andrew took her hand.

"Is it possible Miss Simpson that you could possibly be suggesting that you could be of service to me? I trust *I* am not being presumptuous now... but if that *is* the case I could think of nothing more desirable than having your charming self to welcome the "guests" I hope to entice North. Baillie McPherson is a brilliant organizer but, well neither he nor I have the feminine touch."

"Oh Sir! Oh Sir! Oh Sir!" Miss Simpson clutched his hand with both of hers, her eyes brimming. "It is beyond the edge of the Prayer Book, that you should have need for such as I."

Andrew disengaged himself carefully.

"As a matter of fact, however, I will be leaving for Scotland, possibly as early as tomorrow. Is there any chance you could make your arrangements...?"

"I will be prepared Sir. I cannot begin to thank you enough. I will be grateful 'till the day I die."

"I'm not sure that is quite necessary but I do have some business with the Countess, before I go back. Is she at home?"

"Oh Yes. Please forgive me for detaining you. I will take you at once."

The Countess was tête á tête with a shortish, middle-aged 'gallant', dressed within an inch of his life. His pomaded hair was arranged so carefully, that to Andrew, he looked like a white cockatoo with his enormous beak of a nose, receding chin, and bright yellow quiff standing tall above his forehead. The Countess turned her most brilliant smile from her betrothed to the visitor.

"Mr Walters! What a charming surprise. Dearest Abernathy, may I present to you my countryman Mr Andrew Walters?" The aforementioned Abernathy scrambled to his full height and was immediately sorry. This colonial giant towered above him. He felt decidedly at a disadvantage, even cross. Meanwhile his beloved had extended her hand to the newcomer, and then gestured daintily for them all to sit.

Andrew paused,

"Pleasure to meet you Sir. May I offer you my congratulations, and as I am one of Countess' oldest friends, I hope you will accept these small tokens as rather premature wedding gifts." and as he spoke he held out two small parcels.

"How kind." Earl Cedric said accepting his gift. Amy sparkled at Andrew.

"How exciting! Do you mind if we open them now? I *do* love a gift, especially from you, My *Dear* Friend." Amy untied the ribbon, unfolded the tissue paper and revealed a delicate, engraved silver box, lined with red velvet. "How charming. Such a pretty trinket. What is your gift My Dearest?"

The Earl undid his parcel rather less carefully. His was a silver flask.

"By Jove Walters. Splendid! Many thanks Old Fellow." He was busily examining his gift and did not see his betrothed's reaction. Her eyes flashed at Andrew. Was it fear or anger? He wasn't sure but he was sure he'd unsettled her. Before he'd time to decide, the door burst open.

"Andrew!" A small boy flew at Andrew who returned his embrace enthusiastically.

"Hamish! Please!" His mother was not amused. Her son had been followed into the room by her father and a small, fashionably dressed woman whom Andrew vaguely recognised.

Major Burnett held out his hand begrudgingly and shook Andrew's.

"Good Day to you Sir. I presume you remember Mrs Burnett, my wife?"

Andrew returned the handshake vigorously and then bowed low over Mrs Burnett's hand.

"Of course. An unexpected delight to see you Ma'am. We are certainly a long way from where I first met you."

Mrs Burnett smiled graciously.

"How do you do? Yes we met *such* a *long* time ago. Dear Emily. She *has* done *very* well for herself, hasn't she? Such an *advantageous* marriage. *So* fortunate. She has quite come *up* in the world. *Do* give her my regards." She settled herself on the chair, unaware of Andrew's enquiring glance at her husband, who had the grace to look decidedly embarrassed. "Are you visiting London, Mr Walters? It is *most* fortunate I'm *sure* you will agree that we are here to *celebrate Dearest Amy's* happy news. I *presume* you have heard. Such a *tragedy* she had *endured*. We are so *blessed* that she and the Earl have found each other."

The Earl, who had settled beside his future mother-in-law agreed wholeheartedly.

"Just so Madam. Such a happy chance, and Mr Walters has been kind enough to augment our happiness by presenting us with fine gifts." He gestured toward the gifts as he spoke. Hamish saw the flask.

"Is that your flask Andrew?"

"No! Of course not Silly Boy! And do call him Mr Walters, Child." His mother tried unsuccessfully to divert her son's attention. Hamish picked up the flask and unscrewed the lid.

"No! It's not. Your lid has a dent doesn't it? Remember Andr... Mr Walters, when I was looking at it and the horse stumbled and I dropped it. It spilled all over the ground. We had to stop and find it. Remember? And remember "Red" was licking it all up? Silly dog!"

There was a sudden silence. Andrew's eyes travelled from the Major's very red face to his daughter's white one, but, her eyes were blazing with hatred. Andrew smilingly turned to Hamish and nonchalantly retrieved the flask and placed it back on the side table.

"That's right Hamish. Fancy your remembering."

"Well I was sorry and I thought you would be cross." Hamish gazed up at Andrew who suddenly squatted on his heel so that he was on the child's level.

"Oh No Old Chap! I was not at all cross. How could I be? It was an accident." He refrained from looking at his audience. "And how are you? Are you having riding lessons yet?"

Hamish tilted his head and frowned.

"No, but my grandfather has promised that when I go to stay with him in Austra... in his place, I shall have a horse of my own." Andrew tried to keep his voice normal.

"And when are you going to stay in Australia?"

"Oh *very* soon. We will be going on a great ship... after Christmas, I think." He looked to his mother for the answer and she obliged with suitable sadness in her voice.

"Yes My Darling. After Christmas, I will be going to Ireland and you will be going with your grandmother and grandfather on an exciting trip. Grandfather so wants to take you to visit *all* your cousins."

Was this her revenge? Andrew shrugged, you've miscalculated Madam. I'll be going home sooner or later. Besides Hamish will do far better without you. He stood and turned to Amy's betrothed.

"It has been very agreeable to meet you Sir. I wish you good health... and happiness." He caught Amy's eye. If looks could kill I'd be a goner. Though he had to admit he was rather enjoying himself. He bowed toward Mrs Burnett. "Safe journey Ma'am. I will pass on your compliments to my sister." He shook the Major's hand. Was it relief or fear he saw in the man's eyes? "And Countess..." Amy stood quickly,

"Oh do allow me to see you out Mr Walters. We are *such* old friends." and she took Andrew's arm and led him out of the door. She paused on the landing out of earshot,

"You Devil! You think you are so clever, Earl Mulray." She spat the words at him. He watched in fascination as the drops of her spittle hung in the air and then landed on her silk covered bosom, turning pale blue to navy spots.

"Whatever do you mean Madam? I came to wish you and your betrothed, good luck in your marriage."

"How dare you! You came to..."

"To what?" Andrew asked quietly. He looked into her eyes. They glittered with... was it hatred or fear? No matter. He bowed and left. He would need to see McPherson's friend to arrange her *immediate* removal, *without* his belongings.

Chapter 45

A bagpipe skirled, McPherson recited,

"Fair fa' your honour sonsie face
Great chieftain of the pudden race!" as Mr Anderson proudly carried the haggis to the table.

"Now Mama you must be brave!" Simon Spencer called teasingly to his mother. His remark was met with a haughty stare, though the lady unconsciously straightened her shoulders as she declared.

"Let me tell you Young Man, I have come to this remote but beautiful place and I am looking forward to partaking of this, the *great* delicacy of the Highlands."

"Good for you Lady Helen. This is Hogmanay! A great celebration, and we all need to participate." Andrew said, then quietly confided. "I think you will find it quite pleasant with its accompaniments. Just a wee taste will suffice."

Lady Spencer rose to the occasion and managed her portion with aplomb if not relish. Then she smiled graciously at her host.

"This is *rather* pleasant Andrew. I must admit I was not entirely sure what to expect." She gestured elegantly. "This is all quite, quite charming... and civilised. You have done well."

Andrew surveyed the room. The walls here were hung with a variety of paintings; landscapes, still lifes, flowers. The windows were furnished with green silk curtains that he vaguely remembered from Leicestershire. In front of him the gleaming table stretched, laden with plates and glasses from the same source. A fire blazed in the hearth. On the mantelpiece Cameron's prize 'Quaker Pegg' plate took pride of place, its thistle leaves matching the curtains.

It was no doubt pleasing, but for Andrew his pleasure came from being surrounded by familiar faces. At the far end, Mary Simpson was quietly chatting with Reverend Bruce and Sir Peter. At his end Lady Helen was being charming, and Mrs Bruce beaming with pleasure. Between these two groups, laughter, teasing and flirtations, were keeping the younger set amused. Simon and his three friends were enjoying the company of his married sister Elizabeth, her husband, and the two youngest Spencer offspring. Neither of these girls was quite 'out' but old enough to enjoy this great adventure, and the company of handsome young men.

Andrew turned to his guest.

"Thank you but it were not my doing Ma'am, McPherson is the one to congratulate... *and* perhaps the late Torquil. After all most of our furnishings come from his estate in Leicestershire. He has inadvertently furnished Mulray Castle, despite never having set foot in it." Lady Helen exchanged a knowing look with her host, and said.

"Just so. Quite ironic is it not?" Mrs Bruce looked vaguely puzzled, as Andrew continued with a shrug,

"Perhaps on this night, we should leave all that, behind."

"A splendid idea!" Declared Cameron McPherson feelingly, "We have much to look forward to, and I must say, we are making a great beginning here tonight," he said, turning to Lady Helen next to him, "and having Andrew's dear friends with us." He smiled at Lady Helen. "And I must admire the way you have entered into our celebrations by dressing so grandly Ma'am."

Lady Helen accepted the compliment graciously.

"I was beginning to think no one had noticed. I am *gratified*. I can tell you, it was *not* easy. Try as we may, we could not find any family connection to a tartan. Fortunately, Sir Peter's tailor applied to Wilson of Bannockburn, who, one is told, is the expert, and he sent this pattern." She fingered the plaid stole that draped from her left shoulder across her substantial bosom. "It is rather more colourful than one would perhaps prefer... Andrew's blue and green is more refined..."

"It looks very *elegant* against the white of your gown, let me assure you Ma'am."

McPherson's father, who was sitting next to Mrs Bruce joined the conversation,

"And you are to be congratulated for applying to Wilson's." He said solemnly. "Too many, ignorant of our history, happily don a tartan that has nought to do with them, and *can* offend a Highlander. It looks very becoming on you Your Ladyship, and the gentleman's kilts are perfectly acceptable. You have done well."

Lady Helen was not sure if she was pleased or offended but, determined to enjoy her adventure North, she smiled at her judge and tacitly accepted his judgement.

"Of course two of Simon's friends were fortunate to have *family* tartans."

The remains of the haggis were replaced by dishes more familiar to the Southern guests. Roast venison, goose, side dishes of smoked trout and 'starry gazy pie' were greeted with enthusiasm. Sir Peter, however, was more impressed with the wines Jones continued to produce for his benefit.

"I say Andrew, Old Chap, this claret is magnificent! Where does it come from?"

"My great grandfather had a very good cellar which has remained undisturbed until now. McPherson and I have been diligently sampling it. A *difficult* task but one *must* do one's duty."

Andrew said grinning. He did not notice the Reverend Bruce's sudden look of comprehension.

"Quite a sacrifice I've *no* doubt. Perhaps *I* could help!" Sir Peter offered drily. General laughter followed and there were several offers forthcoming.

Cameron shook his head,

"We've barely examined the Whiskies. How old must they be?"

Cheese and cakes arrived on the table and Andrew announced.

"It is good luck for the year to come, or so I am told, if you eat cheese tonight everyone." They duly complied. As the ladies were about to retire, Andrew jumped to his feet and proposed a toast to his intrepid guests for venturing so far North. Then he proposed another to the McPhersons, father and son, for all they had done. Not everyone there fully understood this last. Then he warned his guests.

"We are required in the Courtyard presently. It could be *very* cold Ladies, so please 'rug up'. Although there *will* be dancing." He announced ominously.

And dancing there was. The Courtyard was ablaze with burning torches and fire pits. A goodly percentage of the clan appeared to be already dancing energetically to the fiddler's lively tunes, but as Andrew stepped through the door a cheer went up. Then the newcomers were engulfed and found themselves learning the intricacies of the Highland Reel. Andrew caught a glimpse of Sir Peter being tutored by Mrs Henry, while Baillie McPherson gingerly instructed her Ladyship. The younger set joined in with gusto. Jones and his staff were kept busy refilling glasses with whisky, jugs with Athol Brose, hot toddies, and for the very few abstainers, glasses of lemonade.

Eventually the festivities were interrupted. A piper replaced the fiddlers and Baillie McPherson called for attention. He positioned himself on top of a stool, on the topmost step. It was barely sufficient for his audience to see him, but he began nevertheless.

"Friends! Tonight is Hogmanay. We farewell the old year to make ready for a new one, and a new beginning. I've decided it is time to tell you a wee story, that pertains to our new beginnings, and the Reverend Bruce has agreed to tell it to you in the Gaelic." Andrew stared at Cameron. Their eyes locked. "No Lad! It's taime," he whispered, and then in a voice that carried to all, began, "Once upon a time..." There were groans and catcalls, but Cameron's lawyer's voice was strong and clear. "Aye, but this is *not* a fairy story." He took a deep breath. "To continue, there was once a good, kind, and just Laird."

"Och Aye this *is* a fairy story!" came a voice from the crowd. McPherson ignored it.

"He had but one child before his beloved wife died, but that boy grew into a fine young man. He became a soldier and the Laird was proud. The son married his childhood sweetheart but was soon called away to his duties. The old Laird was lonely. A young woman came into his life. She was very clever and ambitious, though she had a secret that she kept hidden. She gave the old Laird companionship and they were married. After some years word came that the son would be returning home. The Laird was *very* happy. His daughter-in-law was even *happier*, as she had delivered twin boys who had *never* seen their father." McPherson paused waiting for the Reverend's translation. Andrew could see the crowd was restless. Were they really interested or wishing Cameron would go to Hell and let them dance. "The son arrived safely and there was great rejoicing, but within the week tragedy struck." Ah! thought Andrew, now they *are* listening. There were even sighs and several of the females clasped their breasts.

"There was a dreadful fire, in the wing of the castle where the son and his family were sleeping. The son, his wife, their bairns and the nurse were all lost." Andrew saw glimmers of recognition flicker through the listeners, *now* they are paying attention. "The Laird was struck down by the tragedy. He went blind and was semi-paralysed. The Laird's wife, however, told her husband that by a miracle, one of the bairns had been saved. She produced a child who was the right age and the same coloured hair." McPherson paused and then confidingly added. "Ye can ken noow, her secret?" A murmur of accent went through the courtyard. "The Laird accepted the child with joy. It was balm for his broken heart, as ye can imagine." Andrew could see clearly McPherson had the audience's complete attention.

"But what I have told ye... is *not* the real story." There were murmurs now and voices called out, 'Chan eil mi á tuigsinn' and 'Innsidh na geòidh as t-fnoghar e', but many more said 'Whusht!' Cameron continued. "No. The family and the nurse had not died *in* the fire. Their throats had been slit... by three assassins." the murmurs had become a growl. "Unbeknownst to those evildoers, the son's Batman had been sleeping nearby. Hearing a noise he rushed to the family. The bairns and their nurse lay dead and bleeding. He rushed into the next chamber. The wife was already dead. One of the assassins was about to kill the Laird's son. That Batman was a braw, strong fellow. He killed the murderer, but his friend, his officer, was *badly* wounded. He could smell the fire. He grabbed his friend and some trinkets that the Laird's son had beside him. He scrambled through the flames and fled the castle carrying his master."

Knowing looks were being exchanged, especially by the older people. There were shouts of 'murt!' and 'buid seach!' Several of the crowd had begun to whisper and point toward Andrew. Eventually Cameron spoke.

"That brave Batman took his unconscious master and hid him in the heather. In the confusion he stole a pony. It was many weeks before he could get his master to Edinburgh. Even those great doctors despaired, but the Batman whose name was Cameron McLean, and his wee sister Margaret, fought a *great* battle. It was almost two years before the Laird's son was well in his body, but his *spirit* was broken. He went far away and Margaret went with him as his wife. Eventually they had a daughter. The Laird's son looked at his wee girl and *remembered* who he was. Should he return and claim her birthright? The answer was no, but he wrote a letter to his wee girl and hid it away with those *trinkets* Cameron McLean had rescued.

That daughter then married and had a family. Three lasses and one lad. After much persuasion and I say *much* persuasion the family began enquiries. The Arbiters, and even the Chief Provost agreed, the story I have told you *was believed.* And, now, that lad has come back to you. You *know* him already." He held out Andrew's bonnet, this time with the chieftain's badge pinned to it. "Those trinkets were *this* badge, the Laird's powder horn, his brooch *and* his seal."

Andrew held the bonnet in his hand as he fingered the silver badge with its three feathers, then reluctantly pulled it over his curls. There was uproar. Cheering. Tears. Applause. The Reverend Bruce had no need to translate, the crowd understood. Lady Helen resorted to her handkerchief. Sir Peter sniffed rather rapidly, while Simon led the cheering. The clock began to chime. Andrew was engulfed, Lady Helen found herself being kissed by some she *would* have preferred elsewhere.

Chapter 46

Caitlyn could feel her cotton blouse damp against her skin, but her grandmother reached for the rug to cover her knees.

"Are you not hot Neanaidh?"

"Nooo Lass, I am feeling the chill here in the shade, but I am happy to be here watching the birds and the butterflies amongst the flowers." She leant forward and patted her granddaughter's arm. "And, I am *always* glad to be sitting with my Wee Lass."

Caitlyn returned her grandmother's smile and kissed her cheek.

"Well I am lucky to have you too." she said and her words were heartfelt. The boys were gone back to school, boys who were quickly becoming young men. She stretched back in her chair and gazed out over the garden. It *had* been a very pleasant Christmas. Emily had insisted that it be here, at Barraburn and so the house had been full of laughter and excited children... Did Emily feel, as she did, that Neanaidh was becoming too frail to travel. She shook herself. You can do nothing... and it had been such fun. Emily had organized a picnic on Christmas Day, and *insisted* that all the people, including the government men, come and share a festive luncheon. Rose had worked so hard, they all had, cooking and preparing.

In this weather, it had been so pleasant to relax next to the river. The children had paddled in the shallows under Fergus' strict supervision while Finlay acted the clown. Even the quietest, most taciturn of the men, had seemed to enjoy it all. For herself the highlight had been the music.

"A penny for your thoughts Lass?" Her grandmother's voice interrupted her reverie.

"I was thinking of our Christmas picnic, Neanaidh, and... I did not know how beautifully Mr Jones could sing. Did you?"

"Nooo Lass. I did not. Mind he and Rose sounded delightful together, did they not?"

Caitlyn nodded and added with a chuckle,

"You know I often forget Rose *is* Mrs Jones. I *loved* hearing them, and the fiddler playing tunes that takes me back to... when we were in... in our house with our mother and father." The familiar tears stung in her eyes but she continued, despite the catch in her voice. "That reminds me... when we were at the ball in the Smith's Woolshed, we danced all the latest fashionable dances. You know a woolshed is perfect for dancing... the lanolin from the wool makes the floor smooth... there's no need for candle shavings at all. Well then we went to supper, and whilst we were gone one of the musicians, a young Irish fellow started playing a lively jig. It was like the *Pied Piper*. One by one people kept going into the Woolshed, and soon everyone was there. We danced until dawn... nothing but reels, jigs and country dances!! Oh I remember there was one waltz toward the end, but then we did the Stockyards in one *enormous* circle! It was such fun!"

"An deiradh a latha is math na h-eslaich." Caitlyn smiled ruefully at her grandmother.

"I'm not sure my Gaelic is good enough anymore, but are you saying 'at the end of a day's journey, or of life, it is good to be among friends?' "

"Och Aye! That's close enough Lass."

"But Neanaidh we *are* among friends but surely you are not saying *your* journey is over?" Caitlyn tried to keep her voice light but she felt a cold wave of foreboding seep through her body.

"Noo Lass, but I am nearer to the end… three score years and ten… and canna but rejoice. I thought I, we, all of us, would die in that cold black hovel under the grey streets of Edinburgh." She shivered despite the sun's warmth on her arm. "Instead every day I give thanks to the Lord, that we are here warm and comfortable, with you dancing all night with your friends! I thank *you* also my Dear Wee Lass."

"It wasn't me who brought you here!" Caitlyn interrupted.

"Aye Lass, but God put *you* in the path of Aindreas."

Caitlyn stared across the rolling fields toward the comforting bulk of the solitary mountain. The sun was beginning to set behind it, sending shafts of light across the glowing sky. Oh Andrew, where are you? Will you *ever* come back? Does the sun's rays reach you in Scotland?

Her grandmother saw the shadow in the girl's eyes.

"Dona fret. We owe everything to him, but ye canna spend your life pining for him."

"Whatever do you mean? I miss him, you miss him. We all do. It is natural." Caitlyn said indignantly.

"Well Lass, then why is it, you keep that braw young Smith lad at such a distance? Or those others that would woo you?"

"Oh Neanaidh! How can you imagine such a thing. What do I have to offer?"

"Nonsense Child! You are pretty and modest *and* clever. Andrew may think Mr Manners is the reason this place *and* his own place are doing well, but we *all* know *you* are the manager keeping it all in fine fettle."

Caitlyn blushed and tears filled her eyes. How rarely did she receive praise from her grandmother? Was this part of Neanaidh's farewell? Caitlyn's concerns returned. It did seem her grandmother slept more often, dozing in her chair on the veranda... nodding off in the evenings, her hands gently sliding from her lap, her head slumped against the cushion. Just last night, in the lamplight her white hair had gleamed, but the shadows around her eyes had deepened. The porcelain skin, stretched across her cheekbones had pleated against her ears. Caitlyn knew her head recognized the signs, but her heart ached. Was this any easier than that other death? One moment her mother had been bustling and defiant, the next her eyes were closed... forever. Was instant death worse than watching someone go slowly, remorselessly? Her throat ached with the unspoken words. Please Neanaidh don't leave. You are the centre, the rock we cling to... who will we be without you?

She had spoken to Rose before Christmas, looking for reassurance, but Rose was a realist.

"It's God's will Hinny... your grandmother has a strong heart but her body is tired. You know how hard it is for her to move... and only *she* knows the pain it causes. Enjoy the time you have but you must enjoy your *own* life. Go to the Smiths. Go to the parties and balls. Go to the concerts. She will have pleasure hearing about them. You can sit and hold her hand day and night but you *can't* hold back Fate." Rose had slipped her arm around the girl's shoulders. "Be strong as I know you are." Then Rose had had an idea. "I will speak to Mr Jones. Your grandmother needs a bath chair! He can make her a chair on wheels and she can go wherever she fancies without the struggle!"

"What a splendid idea." Caitlyn had kissed the plump cheek of her mentor.

"I'll see to it immediately. I know Mr Jones would do anything for Mrs MacGregor. We all would."

Caitlyn glanced across at her grandmother, ensconced in that very chair. It had given not only her grandmother freedom, but she, herself, had felt free to leave her. Especially as it threw Nathan, who tended to be the one to push the chair, and Annie, Neanaidh's chief nurse, together. Anything to help Nathan's stuttering courtship!

She had tried to keep her world calm and pleasant for her grandmother's sake, but the world around her, was not. Gold was harder to find. The miners had to work harder for less reward, but the government maintained the same licence fee, which the miners saw as extortionate. It was upsetting. Caitlyn felt torn. The squatter families, who were her friends, approved wholeheartedly of those same licences and the way the government kept a strict eye on the miners. The farming families, and *wasn't she* part of them, were enjoying a life they had worked hard to achieve in the wilderness. They regarded the miners as "blow-ins" who were taking advantage of that civilisation.

Besides, the newcomers were dangerously democratic, with quite alarming ideas. "The wild free and independent life appears the great charm. They have no masters. They go where they please and work where they will." Where had she read that? It sounded exactly like the ideas she'd heard from Nathan. He was friendly with John Lister and the Tom boys, and had spent time with them at the diggings, though strictly as a visitor.

"Well they have a fair beef I reckon." He had explained to Caitlyn. "The squatters pay ten pound a year for a licence to use thousands of acres, the diggers pay much more for three feet square a month! How fair is that I ask you?"

"How much *do* they pay?" She had asked.

"Thirty shillings a month!" Was the indignant reply.

"Goodness! That *is* a great deal." She shook her head. "You should need to find a good supply of gold to pay that."

"My Oath! And there are many who *don't*, but they still have to pay. Plus, that old fool Wentworth is trying to bring in some Bill to make it *more*, and, *imprison* those who don't or *can't* pay!" Nathan agreed vehemently. "He wants *anyone* on the gold fields over the age of fourteen to pay. I suppose that includes the pie sellers!"

Caitlyn had tried to be dispassionate,

"You must admit, it has been hard to find workers. I know Mr Smith is always saying how lucky he is to have his sons to fill the breach."

"Well we've had that problem ourselves I'll admit, but you can't have one rule for the squatters and another for the diggers. It's not how it should be... You mark my words there'll be trouble."

Sitting here in the sunshine with the petals of the roses that climbed beside her glowing bright, with her beloved grandmother enjoying their perfume, it was hard to envisage anything but peace. The sound of a horse moving quickly interrupted her pleasure. The horse and its rider were quickly recognizable. The eldest of Mr Smith's sons dismounted, handed his horse to a young black groom who had appeared out of the stables, and tried to shake off the dust, remove his hat, and bow to Caitlyn and her grandmother all in one motion.

"Good afternoon Ladies. Please excuse my coming uninvited but my parents... and..." A deep breath interrupted his formal speech. "Well to tell truth, we've heard some unpleasant news... dashed worrying... and," he was addressing her grandmother but his eyes were for Caitlyn, " we were concerned for you here."

Caitlyn, standing in the shade, watched the visitor with mixed feelings. He stood hesitating on the step, hat in hand, his broad face flushed. Was it from the effort to come in the heat? His sandy hair was damp and flat where his hat had been. He had clearly hurried... She knew he was a pleasant straight-forward, hard-working young man. She also knew he wanted to do much more than bring news. She liked him for himself, and he *was* Angela's brother, but she did *not* want to encourage him. Nevertheless...

"How very kind of you to come so far to warn us. Neanaidh may I introduce Mr Neil Smith, Angela's brother." She held out her hand. "Please come out of the heat. I'm sure Rose will have made tea, I'll see to it. Please sit here next to my grandmother, Mrs MacGregor. Ah! Here's Rose, just as I thought. Mr Smith, this is Mrs Jones. Let us enjoy Rose's famous tea cake before you tell us this news."

Neil Smith did as he was bid. After several cups of tea, several sandwiches and most of the tea cake, and agreeing that the weather was enervating, he eventually returned to his mission.

"You see, *you* are closer to Sofala than we are and I know Andrew's place is even closer. That's why my parents, and Angela encouraged me to come... You see they, the miners I mean, have been making fiery speeches... they called us "our great mutton men" and "woolly-headed lords." And now they've formed some sort of League and have demanded changes to the law! They've had meetings in Bathurst and on the Turon. And Commissioner Green has taken thirteen troopers to Sofala... that makes thirty-two all up. *And* we've heard that half a Company... I think the 11th Regiment... It's on its way!"

"Oh Dear! It does sound serious, but I doubt... I mean, why would they come here?" Caitlyn wondered. "I, we, appreciate your concern but..." She was interrupted,

"There was a meeting of *over* a *thousand* men, miners and business owners! *You* are *between* Bathurst and Sofala! If there is violence... who can say where and when... who can know *where* it will end? "

Caitlyn's eyes met her grandmother's. They knew, too well, how it could end. Moiragh McGregor smiled at their visitor, their protector, and patted his hand.

"We are very grateful Mr Smith. We are pleased to see you and appreciate your concern." She lifted an eyebrow at her granddaughter. "I think My Dear, we'll feel *much* safer with you here. It is getting late. I hope we can offer you a bed for the night. I'm hoping you can stay." Caitlyn tried to catch her grandmother's eye but Neanaidh was smiling at her guest. Was she match-making or genuinely concerned? Caitlyn had her suspicions.

Chapter 47

Early the following morning Neil Smith and Nathan set out for the Turon to gauge the situation. It was almost dark before they returned, agog with what they had seen.

"We stopped at Andrew's and got one of his young blacks to come with us... Grasshopper was keen himself, but in the end it was a young bloke called Simpson. We weren't sure... thought we might need to keep... be discreet." Nathan explained. "So we left Simpson with the horses and moved in close." He shook his head. "Just as *well* we kept our distance, don't you reckon Neil?"

"By Jove yes! They were in a right royal lather. I've rarely seen such a crowd and My Oath, were they ready for a fight!" He frowned. "Some of them were boasting how they'd smashed the cradles of any laggards. I reckon there'd be well over the thousand. What d'you think Nathan?"

"For sure. And as you say, raring for a show down. They were marching along singing. The Irish were the leaders and they were singing their fighting songs."

"They were spread up and down the bank," agreed Nathan.

"Aye. They ended up facing the police, yelling abuse at the 'traps' as they called them. Then four of them stepped forward... maybe to negotiate... I'm not really sure. Well the police promptly arrested *them.* " Neil shook his head. "So of course the crowd started yelling. 'To the Rescue'! and 'They are taken! Save our brothers!' That sort of thing. Then like a wave, they surged forward toward the police, *and* it wasn't just the police who had arms!" He paused for breath. "God alone knows what would have happened!"

"What do you mean? Did they change their minds?" Caitlyn interrupted.

"No! But they had *their* minds changed for them!" declared Nathan.

"Too right they did! *How* he did it I'll never know, though I saw it with my own eyes!" Neil agreed.

"It was the Reverend... the Wesleyan bloke... what's his name..." Nathan began.

"The Reverend William Piddington," Caitlyn said helpfully.

"That's him! He ran to the dais where the leaders had been egging the crowd on, and jumped up and..." Nathan turned to Neil. "You know I *can't* remember what he said precisely, can you Neil? I mean he talked about their families, the futility of shedding blood..."

"Aye and he kept telling them they were honourable, honest men and they'd dishonour their names... and of course he exhorted them in the name of the Lord..."

"Well naturally *that* would have persuaded them. The Lord was *with* him." Moiragh McGregor explained quietly.

"You must be right Ma'am. It took him quite some time, but he managed!" Neil agreed.

"And the four were released," Nathan added.

"Do you think that is the end of it?" asked Caitlyn.

"For the moment I'd say yes but, well I'm sorry Neil, don't mean to offend, but they do have something to beef about. They pay through the nose for that licence."

"Oh, of course they do. But I don't think that is the way to force them to give up mining! My bet is they will leave and go to

Victoria. From what you hear there's much more gold in Ballarat and Bendigo than we've ever had here. Maybe they'll settle down... I wonder." He turned to Neanaidh. "With your permission, Ma'am, I would like to stay another night... just in case... stragglers, or over-exuberant celebrations... "

"Of course Mr Smith we are *very* grateful. We will rest peacefully tonight, all of us, because you and Nathan have made such an effort to discover what has really occurred." She gave her granddaughter a severe glance and then smiled warmly at their guest. "I will drop a note to your parents for you to take to them, expressing our gratitude. In the meantime Caitlyn please tell Rose we have our friend for another night." Caitlyn did as she was bid. She spent the evening being friendly and polite but being careful not to be left alone for one minute with Neil Smith. Whether he noticed, she was not sure, because her grandmother made such a fuss of him.

Indeed his presence was justified. It was late, Caitlyn was about to call Annie to take care of Neanaidh when the dogs began to bark. Neil Smith hurried away, Sir Galahad to the rescue. It was several minutes before he returned, flushed with his own worth.

"There was a straggler. Well he said *he* was not, but we can't be too careful can we? Nathan came and we decided that he looked reasonably harmless so we put him in the stranger's room and Nathan took care to lock it. One can't be too careful."

"How fortunate you are here with us Mr Smith. How very fortunate aren't we Caitlyn?" Moiragh said pointedly. Caitlyn agreed, surprising herself. She *was* glad. Perhaps there were advantages to be had, having a man in the house... but it was not *this* man she wanted.

"I'm so pleased you were here, and I'm sure Nathan was glad to have you as well." She smiled warmly at her protector. "We're so fortunate to have kind friends aren't we Neanaidh?"

"Exactly my Dear, but I for one, need to go to bed after this excitement. Goodnight Mr Smith, you know where your room is I hope. Come Caitlyn you can take me to Annie."

Neil Smith took the hint and retired. He would have preferred time with Caitlyn but he was an optimistic soul. Tomorrow... there was always tomorrow... and she certainly seemed pleased with him.

The following morning Neil Smith wandered into the kitchen, to Rose's horror.

"Oh Sir. I will be serving your meal in the breakfast room. I'm sorry Sir, I did not realise you were downstairs already."

"Please Mrs Jones don't concern yourself about me. Nathan and I shared an adventure yesterday, we can surely share the breakfast table. Eh Nathan?"

"Well I'd be honoured I'm sure." Nathan said with a grin and half a bow. Neil Smith's reply was a hearty thump on Nathan's shoulder.

"You'll be doffing your cap next..." and gave a chuckle as he settled down to Rose's hastily prepared meal. "Delicious Mrs Jones. This looks just the thing to fill a bloke's stomach and heart."

Rose gave him a sideways frown but her eyes twinkled, but before she could reply there was a gentle knock on the door.

"That'll probably be the stranger. I unlocked the door earlier. Thought we'd be safe in daylight." Nathan said as he tucked into his ham and eggs.

The stranger did not look like a ruffian about to commit any sort of crime. His clothes were neat though well-worn, as was his complexion. His hair was almost entirely grey though he did not walk like an old man, but carried himself well, so that he seemed taller than he was. He came diffidently into the room and waited. Nathan half-stood and held out his hand.

"How d'ye do. Nathan Brown and this is Mr Smith," he gestured toward Neil, "and this is the most important person, Mrs Jones." Nathan glanced around. "You'll probably meet t 'others in due course."

The newcomer bowed his head and said his name but so quietly that Nathan only caught 'Malcolm'.

Rose pulled out a chair.

"Sit yourself down Sir, and I'll have you your breakfast in just a wee moment."

There was a silence. The stranger sat watching the table, Nathan and Neil continued their meal. It was Rose who spoke first.

"And here you are Sir, I hope it is to your liking. You were so late coming I wondered if I should have offered you something. Did you come far?"

"I've walked from Sydney town," was the muffled reply. Neil and Nathan exchanged puzzled looks.

"Sydney. That's a devilish long way. Did you not find a lift at all?" Neil Smith exclaimed.

"Oh, once or twice. There are many walking that road. I took the time. I'd not the funds for the coach."

"And are you looking for work?" Nathan asked. "If you are, there are chances for a hard worker, here or any farm around."

There was a pause, before the quiet reply.

"Perhaps I am, but it is something else I'm looking for."

Neil raised his eyebrow at Nathan and shrugged. All three returned to their breakfast. The sound of a light step made all three look to the door. Caitlyn smiled at the room in general and turned to speak to Rose. There was a strangled gasp from the newcomer who had jumped to his feet and was gripping the table edge with white knuckles. Caitlyn turned her head to see where the noise had come from. She stared at its source then she too grabbed at the table, almost fainting,

"Is it? Are... Dadaidh!" and collapsed into the chair as the stranger held out his hands.

"Lassie... My Lass... My Bairn." He left his place and came around the table, squatted at Caitlyn's feet, and lifted her chin gently so that he could look into her eyes, the eyes that had been wide with shock and were now fighting back tears.

"I've come such a long way to find my bairns, and now I have one to look at. I thank the Lord that there is one for me to find." He said slowly.

"Oh No! We are all here. Well no the boys are away at school, but they are well."

"And your grandmother. What happened to her?"

"Oh *she* is here. We are all here! We are all... Oh I can't believe it is you." And she took hold of the hand that had touched her chin. Behind her back Rose motioned for Neil and Nathan to leave but Caitlyn turned and cried, "No Rose, please stay... and Nathan. Can I please introduce you to my father, Malcolm Ross, and Mr Smith of course." and her voice broke as she laughed and cried at the same time. "These are my *dear* friends Dadaiadh, and there are many more... but... do you think Rose we should disturb Neanaidh? Would it be too much?" Rose smiled at the girl.

"Leave it to me Hinny. Annie and I will see to her first. A few more minutes will surely not matter." She said firmly, and just as firmly ushered the others out of the kitchen, leaving Caitlyn alone with her father. It was only much later that she remembered that, in her excitement, she had introduced Neil Smith as her "dear friend." A slip of the tongue, would it come back to haunt her?

Neanaidh came slowly into the kitchen, gently propelled by Annie. She stared at the gaunt, weatherworn face of her son-in-law, and declared unsmilingly,

"Och 'S fhada bho nach fhaca mi sibh." Caitlyn's heart sank. "It is a long time since *you* have shown your face," was hardly the way to welcome her own family member! He *had* left them and they *had* barely survived but she felt certain there would be a good reason. She knelt at her grandmother's feet.

"Please Neanaidh, *please* let us welcome my father. I'm sure he can explain. *Please* give him the chance. Look at him... he is worn and tired. Let us at least hear his story?"

Her grandmother's mouth remained grim but after what seemed to Caitlyn a long time, she nodded and held out her hand to the newcomer.

"Fàilte Malcolm Ross. You have come many miles. Perhaps *you* can explain *why* it has taken many years." Caitlyn took her father's hand and settled him in a chair next to his mother-in-law, while she stood behind them, a hand on each shoulder.

"Tha mi duilich Mama aidh. I *am* sorry it has taken so long but we... my brother and I did not leave you all willingly. We were captured, taken prisoner by the Navy and forced to sail the seas. It was three years before we managed to return to Scotland. We jumped ship and made our way to Leith and you were all gone."

"I left you a letter explaining where we went, first to Edinburgh and then I sent another when we were coming away."

"Yes Mama aidh, but that Buidseach did not give me *either* letter. I would not know yet, but she died, and my brother found them hidden away, and so we found a ship that needed crew and came to this country. The ship went to Melbourne. All ships seem to go to that place. I had to work my way to Sydney town, then I walked to this place." He spread his hand toward his listeners. "It was the best I could do. I am asking for your understanding. I *never* wanted to leave you alone." He took a deep breath and bowed his head. Caitlyn held *her* breath. Then her grandmother leant across and took her son-in-law's hands in her own.

"We have had many sadnesses but now we have joy. Fàilte MacMalcolm." Through her own tears Caitlyn was almost certain she had glimpsed them in her grandmother's, and she was sure she had seen them in her father's.

Caitlyn's joy did not last. She *knew* this man was her father and she *knew* she loved him… but it had been a long time! She was no longer a ten year old girl. Did *he* know that? Maybe not, although he seemed too aware that she was old enough to marry! He'd made a great fuss of Neil Smith and continued to laud his attributes as a prospective husband. He'd also questioned why she spent long hours in the office, particularly as she was often *alone* with Nathan. He made it very clear he thought her place was in the house with the other women.

"But Dadaidh, there is nothing for me to do here. I don't like to sit and do nothing. Rose runs the household, and she has Annie and Mary, and Mary's sisters, when they are needed, or when they want to come. What would you have me do?"

"Well then are you being paid for this other work?" was the surly reply.

"Dadaidh! How can you say I should be paid? I live in a beautiful house! I have *everything*. I have been to a very good school in Sydney town. Mrs Manners and Rose buy me so many clothes! Besides no-one asked me to take over the accounts… I started to help Nathan and… we have all had to do extra because of the gold rush and Andrew being away and… "

"Aye! *He* is away. To me it is uncommon strange that *he* brings you all to the other side of the Globe and then leaves you!"

Caitlyn took a deep breath and gritted her teeth. She managed to keep her voice pleasant.

"Andrew Walters saved us from starving. He had *no* reason to help us Dadaidh… Neanaidh trusted him," and to herself she thought, and I realise it would be better if Neanaidh does not sing his praises so often. "He brought us all to a safe place and has taken good care of us. You will be so proud of your sons. *They* are going to The King's School! It is the school for gentlemen's sons. It will be wonderful when..." She was interrupted.

"That does *not* explain *why* he is gone."

"It was something to do with *his* family. He does not write to us." She sighed. "I wish that he would, and Emily is very cross with him. But Emily's husband's sister does write to *them*, Mr and Mrs Manners I mean, and so we have news. She, Lady Spencer, says he is well but he has... Dadaidh he went back to Scotland to *stop* people like *us* being *turned off* their land! That is what he told us. He is a good person Dadaidh."

Had she made him understand? Perhaps... but there were other problems... Her father's clothes were ragged. For once she wished she did have some money to buy him new ones, but he was so... so proud. And there was her other concern. The stranger's room was just that... for travellers in need of shelter for a night. Should he come into the house proper? There were enough rooms but... if he... did he plan to stay and work here on Barraburn? The women had their quarters in the main house, the men had their own barracks. Nathan had moved into his own cottage... Rose and Mr Jones... they had a cottage and there were other cottages, but who would decide if he stayed? Mr Manners? Could her father work for Nathan or... well she *herself* organized the men and... It was all dreadfully difficult! Rose? No it was not right to worry Rose... or Neanaidh. After careful management she persuaded her father to take a change of clothing from the store-room, so that his own could be laundered. One step. Then Rose came to rescue.

"I've been thinking you should take your father into Bathurst for the day. It would be pleasant, Hinny, for *you* and... I've been thinking you could be taking him to Mr Forbes." She looked anxiously at the girl. "It's not for me to say I know... but... Mr Andrew's clothes would never fit..."

"Oh Rose that is *exactly* what I'd like but how can I? He is very proud... and I've no money to buy anything."

Rose smiled and slipped her arm around Caitlyn's waist.

"It *is* a problem... and I've thought hard. I've a few sovereigns put aside. I doubt they'll suffice but you can say they're yours... I'm sure you'll repay me."

"Rose! I can't do that!"

"Well My Girl, do you have a better idea!? I'll drop a note to Mr Forbes. He can handle it. Your father's not to know. You'll need to keep any *prices* out of his sight. Mr Forbes can take the sovereigns but of course he will add everything to Mr Andrew's account. And he could probably slip the sovereigns back into your pocket," Rose smiled with self-satisfaction. "You can but try Hinny."

The plot was hatched and carried out more successfully than Caitlyn could have dreamt. Mr Forbes read the note and more particularly read the situation. Malcolm Ross acquired not only clothes from Cedric Forbes, but the offer of employment. Her father's appearance and his pride were restored. Caitlyn now had breathing space and a chance to find the father she *had* known.

Chapter 48

The throb of the engine matched the throb of his heart. From behind him, the dawning sun sent its rays through the narrow passage the ship was approaching. To his left, high above, they caught the white shaft of safety with its life-saving light, while to his right, they formed deep purple shadows in the great sandstone cliffs that rose sharply from the fathomless indigo sea. The ship made its stately progress through the Heads and turned toward its destination, its prow slicing through the black sheets of stillness. His destination! Thank God! Three, almost four years! He took a deep breath, then another and without thinking lifted his arms high. Was he reaching for the sun or the infinite sky? His heart lifted with relief and joy as he watched the landmarks slip slowly by... the Quarantine Station... nestled among the olive coloured bush... the fishing boats at Watson's Bay... the pleasant villas dotting the slopes. He was oblivious to the eager onlookers around him, lost in his own pleasure.

That other country. He knew it held him... problems, obligations, the bloodline of his Clan, but *this* was where he belonged. Surely he could be free, for now, to make his own life, in *his* land. After all the Mulray Estate was functioning, even making money, *and* it was in good hands... the McPhersons, especially the Younger, with his new wife, the gentle Mary Simpson. Belgravia leased. Hamish was here with his grandparents, away from his mother! His life was complicated but it should be manageable. He smiled to himself. I'm not the only one... I'll be looking after Barraburn for McMillan and he will oversee Mulray! Quite neat really. Fingers crossed.

It was two days before he reached his parents' home. Hartley was a village on the way to Bathurst... a place of rest for travellers who had negotiated the steep and dangerous descent from the Blue Mountains. He rode slowly down into the village, past the neat sandstone Anglican Church, then the low slung Post Office. Even here the road was busy. Clearly there were still many gold seekers heading west. He dismounted in front of the Court House, his parents' home, and his own for most of his childhood. It never ceased to amuse him that here in this small village, was this proud edifice with its classical elegance. The smooth Columns, the Portico, the wide steps and the massive wooden doors, were they symbols of British authority, or the mistake of some Foreign Office clerk who mixed up the plans? He shrugged, well whatever, his mother had her *own* castle if she cared to claim it.

His boots crunched on the gravel as he led his horse along the carriageway, and the sound brought a response. His mother's face appeared from the kitchen door. She dropped the pan and the cloth she was drying it with, and threw herself from the top step into her son's arms.

"Andrew! At last! Oh My Son! Oh thank God!"

Her cries disturbed others and he was soon surrounded by people he had known all his life and perfect strangers. Then a quiet voice. He looked up.

"Welcome home Son." He disengaged himself from the crowd and went to his father. It was only later, in the peace of the kitchen that he realised how much they had aged. It was time they had comfort and rest. He'd been away looking after strangers while his own parents needed care! But, he was not needed after all.

"Yes we are about to leave this place. Your father has retired. Richard and Bessie have done *so* well, these last years, that they have sold the Inn and bought three hundred acres in the valley, and we will be living with *them*." His mother explained. "Indeed, if you'd arrived any later, we'd *not* have been here."

"What grand news! So are my sister and her husband to become the landed gentry?" Andrew asked with a quizzical smile.

"Well why not I ask? They have worked so hard. The last few years have been madness. Bedlam! We have *all* been run off our feet. Is that not so James?" Her husband barely had time to nod in agreement as she continued. "It will be hard work for Richard, but it is what he's always wanted."

"By Crikey yes! I *know* he did. He always looked with envy at the properties we saw when I worked with him, but he never wanted to take Bessie away from you. This sounds perfect," Andrew agreed.

"It is too late in the day but we can all go there tomorrow. I presume you will spend *some* time with *your* own family Andrew." His mother declared through pursed lips.

"F'r sure Mama, but I will need to go on to Bathurst sooner rather than later." Andrew agreed though he wondered vaguely why she seemed almost annoyed at the thought.

The following day he was enveloped by more of his family. The bright-eyed, dark haired Bessie barely came up to his heart, but she was his 'big' sister and he loved her dearly. She had always been the one to collect him from his calamities, nurse his bruises, body and soul, and give all the hugs and kisses his reserved parents had not. It gave him real pleasure to see her in a comfortable home enjoying the fruits of all the hard work, cooking, cleaning and catering to good and bad customers alike. He toured their acres, discussed their plans and it wasn't until luncheon that *he* became the centre of interest.

"Do tell us Andrew, about the trains. There is much excitement here about them. Did you travel on them at all?" his father asked. "Are they all as marvellous as we are led to believe?"

"Well yes they are comfortable and convenient, as long as they can take you *where* you want to go. It is all rather piecemeal at the moment. The Duke has built, and is building many tracks in Sutherland, but the rest of Scotland is a bit of a muddle. I went from Edinburgh to London. That was fine, although they do tend to stop here and there for no accountable reason. Mind you, as long as you travel *first* class! You should see the third class! They are crammed in roofless boxes. When we went to Epsom, there they were. Mind it means the crowds *are* up!"

"Oh that sounds rather smelly... so many people..." Bessie said with a grimace.

"Smelly! Nothing in this world can smell worse than London, I'm sure! They call Edinburgh 'Auld Reekie', but at least you can get away from the worst of it in the New Town. The Thames, let me tell you, is one enormous sewer!"

His father frowned,

"But I thought.. I understood they are building sewers?"

"Oh yes. Mr Balzagette is working on it, but it will take years. He's a genius, but even he can't overcome what's happened. The Great Exhibition. *That* was a disaster for him." There were puzzled looks from his audience. "They introduced flushing water closets, and the crowds flocked, then those who could, had them installed in their own homes. Disaster!" Seeing his mother's face Andrew tried to change the subject. "The other problem in London is the traffic... and the ladies aren't helping."

"Whatever do you mean?" demanded his mother.

"Crinolines. They get bigger and bigger. They even have blokes with poles to hold the things down when a lady is climbing into a carriage. Takes forever. Even fitting through doors..."

There was general laughter, although Bessie said wistfully,

"Well I would *love* to have a very fashionable crinoline and *float* into the next ball."

Andrew winked at her.

"Your wish is my command. When my trunks arrive I will present you with the very *latest* invention. French, though not by Mr. B. It is a collapsible crinoline. Lady Spencer is *especially* proud of them and has sent several for you all. She assures me they are very light and comfortable."

"How kind, she is very generous. Does she always dress beautifully Andrew?" asked Bessie wistfully.

"Oh I expect she does, rather grand is our Lady Spencer, but she is very kind...she certainly has been to me from the beginning. I could not have handled society without her, and Forbes of course. But London is exciting too...lots to see and do besides the Great Exhibition. Simon and I were escorting his sisters in Hyde Park when we came across this complete orchestra in a bandstand. It was quite a sight, and quite a crowd too. The Conductor was some Frenchman. Quite a Quiz...he stood on the dais and then with great ceremony he was handed his baton on a silver platter. The baton seemed to be covered in jewels because they glittered in the sun...one of the rare days the sun was shining." Andrew smiled as he spoke.

"What fun. Who was he?" Bessie said, trying to imagine the scene.

"Louis something, Julienne, maybe, though the chap near me said he had various names...*he* was *some showman*, but the crowd loved it all. He played Beethoven interspersed with ditties and popular songs. Quite well known seemingly, there is something happening every day...it's a big place...and parts are very pleasant... trees, gardens huge buildings, but it is so crowded elsewhere, and filthy. And as I said, it *smells*!"

It was the following day before Andrew was given news about his other sisters.

"Lucy is in Sydney, at this moment, with her new husband. He has taken her to shop and then they are talking about travelling to Europe. Only the best for our Lucy." Bessie said with a wry smile at her brother.

"And Emily? Hoping to see them in the not too distant future, though I'll be a bit too busy to go to them, for a while I'd say." Andrew said.

His mother interrupted.

"Oh Emily *is* at Barraburn. I had a letter a fortnight ago... or perhaps nearer the month. That old woman you brought from Scotland... she's very low. For some reason Emily felt *obliged* to go and be there for the grandchildren. I've no idea why? She could come and visit with *us* rather than traipse around looking after *strangers*."

Andrew studied his mother. If he'd not asked, would she have even told him about Neanaidh? He had a strong suspicion the answer was no. Was she jealous? His mother was determined to be the centre of her family. No-one else should be. Of course she was, but... if he left at first light tomorrow...? Perhaps his mother had reasons to be jealous. His first thought was to see Neanaidh... or was it to be with *her* grandchildren? He could at least be kinder to his own mother.

"Do you realise Mama, you are the Countess Mulray, of Mulray Estate and Belgravia?" He said teasingly.

"No! My Dear Son, *I* am Janet Walters, wife of James Walters of Hartley, mother of four, grandmother of ten."

"I am serious, Mama, you *could* reclaim your heritage."

"No Andrew. I appreciate what you have done for my father's memory and perhaps for yourself eventually, but *I* belong *here* and *that* is *all* there is to it!" She raised an eyebrow and her lip twitched. "As a Christian I must confess, I feel quite guilty, *but* I am *rather* pleased that Amy Burnett is *not The Countess Mulray.*" Andrew put his arm around his mother's shoulders, and kissed the top of her head, not something he could remember ever doing before.

"Oh, Yes. I agree with you." It's as well you don't know how much I agree and why! He said to himself.

Chapter 49

It was already dusk. He hurried through the house hardly realising he was finally home. Neanaidh's head lay against the pillow barely registering any pressure. Andrew was shocked. Her eyes were closed, the bones of her head stark. Her silver hair was twisted to one side looking sad and lifeless. He softly spoke her name. Her eyes opened and instantly the familiar smile lit her face.

"Aindreas. You have come home." The words were barely a whisper. Her hand fluttered across the covers toward him. He took it as gently as he could. It was cold and so frail he was frightened the bones would break. He lifted it carefully to his lips and returned her smile. She closed her eyes and sighed, then, just as she had done so long ago in that dark hole, she brought his hand to her lips and kissed it. The tears burnt his eyes.

"So many beautiful years you gave me... so many years to warm my body and my heart." Her voice faded and she appeared to be asleep. He knelt beside the bed cradling the fragile hand, and she seemed to draw strength from its warmth, because her eyes opened again and in a stronger voice she said

"I know the bairns are safe. Now I can go. He is waiting for me. I have seen my daughter... God is good. He gave us you..." Her eyes closed again and this time she really seemed asleep. He felt a chair being pushed against his back. With his free hand he manoeuvred himself into it. He murmured a thank you and sat watching his old friend. Her face was serene. Her breath came softly, dwindling, then suddenly she would shudder and take a deeper breath, but the intervals between them became longer. How long he sat he had no idea. He felt two hands on his shoulders.

"She's almost gone. She was waiting for you. Now she is happy, she will let go." His sister's quiet voice cut into his exhaustion. "You must come away. Nicolas has brought the boys, they need to be with her now."

He stood, slowly, stiffly, and released her hand. He was vaguely aware of others but he was too tired to concentrate. He staggered into his own bedroom, stretched out, fully clothed, and slept.

The kookaburras' cackling disturbed him. Someone had removed his boots and covered him with a blanket. Through the gap in the curtain he could see daylight. For a moment he wondered where he was. His body reminded him, it ached all over, and then he remembered why. A soft knock, the door opened and Rose came quietly in, carrying a tray. He smelt the buttery toast and hunger hit him. When had he eaten? He sat back on the bed, a question in his eyes.

"Yes. She has gone. It was not long after you left. Caitlyn was with her. The Dear Girl sat and held her hand all night. She said it was the custom. I could not persuade her otherwise. I'm not sure if it weren't... as if she could not let her grandmother go. Your sister was with her some of the time. I've insisted the child sleeps. As a matter of fact we are *all* rather sluggish today, let me tell you! So *you* just stay here for now, and I'll have some hot water sent up. Take your time for *my* sake as well as yours, because your breakfast is *not* ready!"

Rose disappeared out the door. Andrew smiled to himself. He was certainly home, obeying Rose was an essential part of that! He demolished the contents of the tray, then settled back.

He must have dozed, because by the time he realised the water had arrived, it was already lukewarm. He rummaged in his closet, found enough clothes to be decent and wandered downstairs. The smell of bacon led him to the breakfast room.

Nicholas greeted him with,

"Well. Well. Sleeping beauty has arrived." and stood and shook his hand. "Glad you got here Mate." They settled back. "You must be buggered. Did you stop at all?"

"No, not really. I changed horses at Wallerawang, I think." He sipped his hot tea. "I was in Hartley with the family. I had no idea. Only found out when I asked about you and Emily, and was told you were at Barraburn, and why. How are they, Caitlyn and the boys. How *are they*?"

"Eat your breakfast then we can talk. I thought we might take the boys and have a look around. The funeral chaps will be here. We're not needed. What d'you reckon. Fancy a ride?"

Andrew smiled and nodded between mouthfuls. It would be good to be in the open, stretch his legs and look after Fergus and Finlay at the same time. As they walked to the stables, with the boys running ahead, Nick casually remarked,

"A bit of news ...not sure if anyone has told you with everything going on."

Andrew shook his head,

"Not sure..."

"The father has turned up." Nick said quietly.

"The father, you mean the priest?" Andrew asked.

"No Mate, The *children's* father, Mrs McGregor's lost son-in-law."

Andrew stopped in his tracks.

"You mean ...are you saying Caitlyn's father?"

"Exactly what I *do* mean. The boys *know* but they haven't met him, as yet. He's living in Bathurst, working for the inimitable Cedric Forbes. I have met him, not the most cheerful chap.

I suspect he has to get used to a great deal, in rather a rush...his children ...well Caitlyn for one is a young woman, with a mind of her own as we well know. All a bit of a shock for all concerned. He's had a bugger of a time himself, but if ...well a bit of advice Mate, tread carefully."

"How did the boys take the news?"

"Well, they sat perfectly still for a minute, then Fergus asked, 'How, When, Where?' in a sort of daze while Finlay jumped up and started dancing and shouting, but then he collapsed in Emily's arms and cried." Nick's mouth twisted and he frowned. "I'm hoping it goes well this morning, not entirely confident at this stage, could be decidedly tricky...rely on my wife...only way."

Andrew tried hard to take in all Nick had said. He was too tired and drained. He shrugged, leave it be, he would cope later when he had the time and the energy. His spirits lifted, however, as he surveyed Barraburn's acres.

"I say Nick. I owe you quite a debt. The place is in tip top shape. The stock look great, the pastures are good. Fair Dinkum I don't know how you managed it with every Tom, Dick and Harry off after their fortune."

Nick shook his head.

"Well it did settle down a bit after you left. No we kept *most* of your hands, and old Grasshopper looked after your acres better than I thought he would, to be honest."

"How did you fare yourself?"

"Well always had Bert and Denny, though, around the original Rush at Ophir, I think Denny was tempted." He glanced at Andrew. "Actually can't take too much credit, you know Drew. You had your own hard-working manager right here, and *she* kept everyone, and everything up to scratch."

Andrew frowned.

"What do you mean?"

"Your young kitten, Caitlyn. She was shy at first, Emily and Rose suggested it to tell truth." He chuckled. "She had trouble at first, several urgent notes a week... but she is a fast learner." He turned to Andrew. "But she said she wrote to you..."

"Yes, she did, very diligently, but I didn't realise... I assumed she was reporting on your behalf?"

"I did my bit, at first, but she has a knack for organisation... *and* the men! She could charm the leg off a cooking pot. They love her. Mind she's had Nathan to do the leg work and always by her side. Quite a team."

"But she's... she's so young!"

Nicholas laughed.

"Who's talking? Sixteen wasn't it when you took over Richard's teams? Your Kitten is older than that."

"She isn't '*My Kitten*'."

Nicholas raised an eyebrow.

"Well she feels she owes you, I'm sure of that. Not to mention the young chaps who've tried to lure her away." The conversation turned to wool prices, fleece and its market, the price of lamb, the opportunity of cattle.

As they returned to the homestead a figure appeared on the veranda.

"You take the boys to their father. I'll take the horses." Without waiting for an answer Andrew collected the horses.

It was dinner before he saw them all again, though Caitlyn did not appear.

"I've insisted she rest!" declared Rose. Andrew, watching Malcom Ross and his sons, wished he had been excused also. Thank God for Nick and Emily! They asked all the right questions and kept the conversation rolling, but, too often Fergus looked to Andrew to confirm details. He'd even leant his hand on Andrew's shoulder as he went to take his seat, and Andrew had caught the look in Malcom Ross' eye. Finlay sat silent, a stark contrast to last night's reaction. Was he still grieving or confused? Three, maybe four when his mother died, was his father a stranger? How much *did* he remember? There was no question of Emily leaving the gentlemen to "their port". She brusquely organized everyone to have an early night.

"Nicholas and the boys travelled all day and night to be here. They need sleep, and I need to see to Caitlyn and my babes. I presume Mr Ross you will be speaking at Mrs MacGregor's funeral, so we will leave you in peace to compose your words, and I know my brother is exhausted." With a wry smile Andrew did as he was told, as did the others. Where was his dreamy vague sister?

It was very early, as Andrew rode slowly along the river towards the house. How many days would it be before he could go and see his own stretch of river? He studied the rising sun. It was humid. Would it rain? I think we should have sunshine to say goodbye Old Friend. I wish you had stayed to help me handle this chap. Malcom Ross does not appear to be partial to Andrew Walters. No, not at all!

As he came closer, he saw a slim figure collecting flowers in the garden. She turned at the sound of the hooves and Andrew's heart lifted. As he rode slowly toward her he realised how much she'd changed. He'd left behind a gauche schoolgirl. A beautiful young woman smiled up at him. A jolt of happiness hit him. He slid off his horse. She held out her hand,

"Oh Andrew, I'm so glad you came... in time. So glad." He took her hand and then found himself holding her as she began to sob. The basket of flowers jammed into his hip. He took it from her, and then cradled her head against his chest. As he held her, he became increasingly aware how neatly her body fitted against his. At *that* moment, he *knew*.

How long had he chased after Amy, lusted after her, succumbed to her. He'd *thought* he was in love... but he had come to realise, all too slowly, bitterly, that the Amy he wanted, didn't exist. Had never existed. Of course she had made him feel she cared. When he'd been useful! And then the flask! What a complete fool! But now? What should he do? He could smell her hair? His heart was not the only thing swelling. She seemed to have stopped crying. Gently he held her away. She looked up. Those green eyes, enormous in the pinched face of a starving child, were red-rimmed but still beautiful. They had intrigued him on a bleak roadway, now they held him in thrall.

"I'm so sorry. I thought I was... I thought I'd cried enough."

"There's no such thing as enough I'd say. I've had my own tears. She was *our* best friend *and* your *Neanaidh*. The pain will ease but she is with us I know." He blushed at his own eloquence. "It took me a long time when I lost *my* grandmother." A smile hovered around his lips as he remembered his strong-minded grandparent. "Can I help you with this?" He lifted the basket and held it out, hoping she would refuse. He needed time to think. He was her friend, her protector. Could he risk *losing* her friendship?

"No thank you. You already have your hands full." She gestured toward the horse who had stood quietly grazing, "I think *you* should take her away before she disgraces herself by *eating* our roses." and she walked briskly into the shelter of the house.

Caitlyn's own heart was beating. She had wanted to stay in Andrew's arms forever. He saw her as a child... well maybe not, but he was her friend, her saviour. She would need to be content with that! Oh how *much* could she bear? And now Dadaaidh was pulling faces and pursing his lips.

Horse and rider walked slowly toward the stables. Get through the funeral first. Did she have suitors? Nick had said as much. Hard to believe in a society chronically short of young women, that a pretty black-haired, green-eyed girl would have passed unnoticed. Was she already involved with someone? A sudden thought hit him. Mourning. Would it be a year? He couldn't remember if his mother had worn black, or for how long? Certainly he remembered that his grandmother had made sure Bessie and Richard were married. Granny had known she was dying, and was in great pain, but had insisted the marriage happen because otherwise they'd need to wait. Righto! He had six months, or a year. Time to woo Caitlyn and, he screwed up his lip, *unfortunately*, her father!

Chapter 50

"Moiragh MacGregor, my mother-in-law, was the sturdy vessel who kept us afloat when we floundered, and, were almost shipwrecked. She kept my children safe, and brought us here to this fine harbour. We have been blessed to have her, but now she goes, without us, on her final journey." Malcom Ross took a deep breath "Fare thee well Mama aidh." He looked at Andrew. For a moment their eyes locked, then he spoke. "For the last years she had a good friend who gave her what *I* could not. Mr Walters would you be kind enough to say a few words."

Andrew stood frozen. He was unprepared for Ross' gesture *and* unprepared. Then he remembered the Celtic blessing, Neanaidh had often sung to him. *He* couldn't sing. *That* was Mr Jones' department, but he could *try* to do it justice. He took a deep breath and began,

 'Deep peace of the running wave to you
 Deep peace of the flowing air to you
 Deep peace of the quiet earth to you
 Deep peace of the shining stars to you
 Deep peace of the Son of Peace to you.'

Goodbye Good Friend, thank you for being in our lives." He felt a small hand squeezing his. He looked down into Caitlyn's eyes. They were shining with... was it gratitude? Perhaps? Give it time Walters. Give it time.

The service continued. Mr Jones sang the twenty-third psalm and the Presbyterian Minister completed the formalities. Afterwards there was a quiet gathering on Barraburn's wide veranda. Andrew approached the children's father and held out his hand. After the briefest pause, Malcom Ross shook it.

"Your words were great Ross. Thank you giving me a chance to say something. I'm sure she'd be happy with you, and maybe, with my effort."

"It was the least I could do Sir." The words came slowly, with difficulty. "I owe you more than I can ever tell you, or repay you. I have three children because of you. I am wondering how..."

"No Sir!" Andrew interrupted, "You've no need to repay me. You have three fine children. To see them grow has been my reward... *and* to have known their grandmother. Come let's drink to her." and he handed the older man a glass of whisky. He lifted his own.

"Slàinte Moiragh MacGregor!" The glasses clinked together, as Andrew silently hoped, *we too,* can get together one day!

Whatever Ross had said, Andrew knew that the man was not happy. It was obvious as Emily tried valiantly to bridge the gap between father and children, as they sat at the dinner table.

"Your sons have been doing very well at school Mr Ross. Fergus' reports are always excellent and Finlay is *quite* the sportsman. Well *that* is what we hear." She smiled warmly at the boys but her efforts were met with a very muted response from the father. Andrew wondered if Ross thought they should all sit in silent grief, or was he merely uncomfortable?

Emily persisted.

"You have three very fine riders Sir. They are all three, admired for their horsemanship. It is, sadly, *not* my strong point but even your daughter's prowess has drawn comment."

Nicholas, who'd sat quietly enjoying his wife's efforts, decided to intervene. He felt sure Mrs MacGregor would not want doom and gloom on her behalf.

"Well Caitlyn's prowess needed quite an effort. Did it not?" He grinned at his pupil. "Never knew there was such a temper behind those pretty green eyes, did we? Poor old Nathan."

"What's this? Caitlyn could ride a horse well. *I* taught them all when we came back." Andrew asked puzzled.

"Well yes you did, but Caitlyn is no longer a child. *You* may not have noticed Andrew Dear, but young ladies do *not* ride a*stride*." Emily explained with a raised eyebrow at her brother. Oh yes I have noticed Andrew said to himself. I have indeed.

"She only slid off a few times... once very spectacularly as I remember." Nicholas chuckled.

"By Crickey! It was a *beauty*. A fine spectacle. Petticoats everywhere, one foot in the stirrup the other flapping madly above her head!" Finlay added, laughing loudly at the memory. He was joined in his mirth by everyone, including his father, although Caitlyn's was more in embarrassment.

"I still think it *is* rather stupid," she said defiantly.

"But I thought you liked that new saddle?" Nicholas turned down the corners of his mouth and clutched his forehead, in mock despair.

"Of course I did. And I do! It is quite the finest saddle in Bathurst and I'm the *envy* of all my acquaintance Sir. I really am grateful." She smiled warmly at Nicholas and reached across the table and patted his hand. Andrew felt envious, even a little jealous of their easy relationship. Could he risk jeopardising *that* and his own? He watched the father's face stiffen. Was *he*, too, envious? Malcom Ross turned to Nicholas.

"Well it seems I am indebted to you too, Mr Manners, and your lovely wife." He paused, and then began to ask what seemed to be friendly questions. "I understand you have your own... farm... establishment... property... I'm not sure of the correct term... Is it very distant Sir?"

"Oh quite a day's journey. I'm glad to have my brother-in-law home, I can tell you. I've spent the last few years travelling here on a regular basis, and, much as I enjoy seeing Barraburn and its people, I have *much* I want to do at Hidden Valley." He smiled at Emily. "Perhaps my wife will grow tired of my constant presence." In reply Emily pulled a face at her husband. "Although, as I have been telling Mr Walters here, the *very* competent overseer of Barraburn is *your* daughter Sir. We could *not* have managed without her." Caitlyn blushed but her father continued his questioning.

"And will you be returning there, to your place, in the near future?" Nicholas glanced at his wife, who spoke for them both.

"Perhaps in a week or two Mr Ross. Once I am comfortable that *all* is well here." Emily replied with a slight shrug, but *she* had guessed, immediately, the reason for Ross' questions.

Andrew, however, turned to Nick.

"By Jove Nick, you must be busy on your place... have you bred a champion yet?"

Nick laughed ruefully.

"We've been too busy supplying all the new arrivals. The lucky diggers, the one's who strike their bonanza. Well, the first thing they *want* is a fine carriage and matching horses so they can flash their new-found wealth. I'm not sure how long this will all last, but we've been happy to profit whilst we can."

"Talking of horses, I've never seen so many parade animals as I did at Wellington's funeral! I happened to be in London... I counted six hundred and I'm sure I missed a few. It was a grand spectacle, and the horses rose to the occasion! They were magnificent and *perfectly* matched." It was Finlay who asked,

"Wellington? I thought they were rubber boots. Why did *they* have so many horses?"

"Cos *he* was England's *saviour* You Gawkey." Fergus said. "If you listened in History lessons you would know!" Emily quickly intervened and there was a lively discussion about the great general.

It was quite late in the evening before she had an opportunity to talk to her brother.

"You realise of course what was behind Mr Ross' questions?" Andrew shook his head as Emily continued. "*He* does not want *his* daughter staying *here* now that you are home." His face remained blank. "*You* are an unmarried man. Neanaidh is no longer here to chaperone Caitlyn. I'm not sure what he will propose, but be warned Drew. Be warned." Andrew frowned.

"Well he has a point I suppose but *why, I* mean... what have *I* done to him that he clearly resents me so?"

"It's *not* what you *have* done Dear Brother. It is what *he* has *not* done. Of course he was not able to care for them. He was prevented. Instead of blaming himself he has transferred *his* anger and frustration to *you*! But there is a problem. I mean Caitlyn. I suspect he will insist she go and live with *him*."

Emily's prediction was correct. At the very same time she was warning her brother, Malcom Ross was busy organising his daughter's future.

"Do you mean Dadaidh, that *I* must leave this place and go and live in Bathurst?" Caitlyn asked, trying to sound calm.

"It is necessary! Your reputation is your greatest asset. If you remain under the same roof as this Mr. Walters, people will talk." He took a deep breath. "It is quite clear that you will marry... perhaps soon... that young man... Smith, for example. A young woman cannot be too careful."

Caitlyn sat quietly, her head lowered submissively, although her *thoughts* were *not*. She knew enough of Bathurst Society to know that Mrs Smith would be perfectly happy to have her son Neil marry the ward of Andrew Walters, who, it was rumoured to be, in truth, a Scottish Earl. She would *not* look so favourably on his marriage to the daughter of a shop assistant. She tried to hold back her tears and speak carefully.

"I understand your concern... but Dadaidh I do have a role here... I am relied upon."

"You will not be needed now Mr Walters is returned. My mind is made up Lass. You *cannot* remain *here*. It is not seemly."

"If you say so Dadaidh," was the docile reply. "but please excuse me... I am very tired. Goodnight Dadaidh." She stood, kissed her father's cheek and hurried from the room, before he would see her tears.

Andrew, on the other hand, did *not* feel docile. Damn him! *I* did nothing wrong *and* I would *never* do anything to harm his children... especially his daughter. It was at dinner the following evening that Andrew took matters into his own hands.

"I am wondering Ross, if you would consider allowing Caitlyn and her brothers to remain here at Barraburn. I'm not sure if you are aware, but, I too have my own property. It is some distance from here and I am exceedingly anxious to go and live *there*. I have not been able to live or *work* there because I was needed in Scotland. It would be a great boon to know Barraburn was in safe hands. Perhaps, you, yourself, could come as often as possible and visit. I would like you to feel free to use one of the gigs and whatever horses are required."

He paused and examined his audience. Nicholas' mouth twitched but he said naught, while his wife smiled serenely. Caitlyn was sitting perfectly still, her eyes on her father. It was Fergus who broke the silence.

"Capital! By Jove! And *we* can help when we are on our break. *We're* needed here Dadaidh!" Malcom Ross said nothing, his face blank, as Andrew continued.

"It would not be for more than a few months, perhaps a year. The owner of Barraburn is intending to send his son to take charge here. It you could see your way clear to leave your children here in the interim... it would be a great help... we would be in your debt. *Considerably* in your debt."

Caitlyn stared at Andrew.

"But where will *you* live? I thought... I mean it... there is only a slab hut... or *that* is *what* you told *us*, and... is it not occupied?"

"It is quite a *commodious* slab hut, as slab huts go... two largish rooms. I doubt it will be as uncomfortable as a stone castle *without* windows in the Highlands of Scotland, can you?" Andrew said laughing. "And I will have the inimitable Grasshopper for company, though his *housekeeping* is a problem. No I *need* to be there. Crops, livestock... I've no real idea *what* is there. I need to make plans, start building a replacement for the slab hut..."

Finlay was intrigued.

"You'll need a woolshed, and yards, and quarters for your workers. Please, Andrew, can *I* come and help *you*?"

"After you've finished term, it would be great, Old Chap." Andrew ignored the father's expression. "I have been so very anxious to get started, but it can only be so, if you Mr Ross, can see your way free to help me. I am in your hands."

Malcom Ross sat silent. Seemingly his daughter's reputation would be safe... though he wondered *how* far away Walter's property was. There was no doubt he was indebted to Walters. It would sound churlish at the very least.

"Thank you for the offer of transport Mr Walters, I'll make good use of it. And perhaps Caitlyn will come to Bathurst herself from time to time."

"Oh! I shall Dadaidh. As often as I can."

Chapter 51

"**S**he's a bloody nice property Mate. River frontage, pasture, slopes... you've done well to snare this one," Nicholas commented, as he stood admiring Andrew's domain.

"Glad you approve. Mind, I've *not even, ever,* been to the other side of the river." Andrew conceded. "I've *only* ever been here the once. Do you see that grand old River Red Gum over there on the bank. *That's it.* My saviour in more ways than one!"

"Are you going to do some more fossicking? Never know, find a few more nuggets... You did well enough the first time. Devilish Good Luck."

"F'r sure, but *first* I *want,* and *need* to go over the whole place, not just dig in *one!*" He called out to the groom, Simpson, who was patiently minding the horses, "Cooee!" and as the young man came closer he asked, "Grasshopper said there was a causeway to cross the river. Do you know where it is Mate?"

"This fella crossing upstream Boss. Come, I'll show you."

It was some hours before they retraced their steps and stood sheltering in the shade of Andrew's favourite tree.

"Fair Dinkum! I'd no idea there was a woolshed and yards, not to mention a decent house and sleeping quarters for the men." Andrew waved his arm toward the land over the river. "A bloke can move in right away. Not the house I'd want long term, but more than adequate for now isn't it?"

"By Jove yes." agreed Nick. "Whatever happened? It looks as if whoever owned it, just walked away. Maybe... No, it was before the gold rush wasn't it?"

"Yeah I heard from the Stock and Station Agent that the bloke who had it, lost his wife and took to the grog. He *did* just walk away. Sad tale... but I saw it time and again when I was overlanding in my younger days."

"And now you're such a greybeard!" Nicholas chuckled and slapped his companion's shoulder.

"Well... my good luck from his bad. I'll have somewhere to bunk down while I sort myself and the place out. How many sheep *do* we have here? Do *you* know? And cattle? Do you know what breed?" He shook his head. "I've spent four years finding the answers in Scotland and now I've to start again!"

"You'd do better to check with Caitlyn and Nathan, when we get back. They've all the details. And talking of getting back, it's late. I think we need to go. As it is it'll be good and dark before we get to Barraburn. Lucky there's a full moon! You can get the details from our experts. If you decide to build, I can lend you some hands, and Emily has all sorts of plans and sketches. She collected them when we decided to build our place."

Andrew intended to stay until Emily and her family left but each day became more difficult. Caitlyn behaved as she had always done. No. That was no longer true. The shy quiet schoolgirl was now a confident capable young woman. He watched her with increasing pleasure as she handled not only the accounts, but with Nathan's help, the workforce on Barraburn. Nick had said the men adored her and he hadn't exaggerated! They treated her with deference admittedly but they clearly enjoyed her ready smile. She also knew each one by name, and took time to have a chat, however brief, with even the most toothless, pock-marked shepherd.

The second day after the funeral Nathan suggested a visit to the blacks' camp. Andrew tagged along, trying not to usurp their authority. He offered to drive the dray loaded with the supplies.

"No thanks Mate, I'm doing this to take her mind off ...everything, and she doesn't often get to ride. No you ride with her Ladyship...it'll do her good."

Nathan dealt with the men delivering wages and instructions and supervising the unloading. Andrew had rightly assumed Caitlyn would spend time with the women, but he was surprised to see their reactions to her. New babies were displayed for her to nurse, while the younger children hung off her skirts, vying to be picked up. She had brought with her several baskets, and as he watched, the women examined the contents of one particular basket. There was considerable discussion. It contained several small calico bags. The women took these bags and with obvious pride handed Caitlyn their own calico bags. Their eyes shone with excitement as she carefully opened those bags and spread their contents out on the dray. A sparkling rainbow glinted under the sunshine.

"Come and see Mr Walters. The women make these necklaces and we sell them...or Mr Forbes does. Aren't they *delightful?*" She turned back to her audience, "I'm sure Bossman Forbes will be glad to see these. I think they are more beautiful than the last ones. Aren't they a delight, Mr Walters? Look at this one." and she held up a strand of blue beads and slipped them around her own neck, and swivelled and preened as she patted them. The women all giggled. She then removed her jewels and with the women's help reverently repacked the treasures in their bags.

Andrew then found himself sitting on the ground with Nathan and Caitlyn while the children danced and their elders sang and clapped. It was quite late before they reached the homestead. There was barely time to wash and dress for dinner, where there were many questions and discussions about the day, mainly by Malcolm Ross. Andrew wondered if he disapproved, but he was glad of the distraction. The day had been a revelation. It was only later in his own room he had time to consider it. His little waif... how long ago had that been? She was now, not only a beautiful woman to look at, but *unlike* Amy, a beautiful person. He wanted to tell her. He wanted to tell her how he felt. But there was the father. And she'd never ever done, or said anything to make him feel as he now did...she was grateful...she tried to please him... Besides what did *he* have to offer? The best thing you can do Andrew Walters is to go and set yourself up, leave her to get to know her father, and then, when you are game to risk it, come back and declare yourself and deal with the consequences.

Malcolm Ross' relief was obvious when Andrew announced his departure the next day. He missed the pain in Caitlyn's eyes as he turned to his sister.

"I'll hope you can spare Nick for a few more months Sis? I know it is an imposition but I'll be as quick as I can...I'm sorry."

"Of course you do! We can certainly manage. Besides as you *must* know by now, it is Caitlyn and Nathan who manage Barraburn, and *very* fine overseers are they not?" She said brusquely, with a meaningful glance at Caitlyn's father.

"By Jove we can all see that." Andrew said enthusiastically. "Seven thousand pounds profit! Who else could manage that?" He smiled at Caitlyn, whose modestly lowered eyelids hid her distress. She managed to smile and acknowledge the compliment,

"You are very kind, but I cannot promise the same now that the gold rush is quieter." Although she wanted to cry.

Chapter 52

He'd flippantly remarked that he'd share the slab hut with Grasshopper. It took no time for Andrew to realise his mistake. He'd arrived on dusk at the aforementioned hut. It was already late April, and he was glad to see smoke belching from the chimney as he tethered his horses. He dragged his saddle bags off the pack horse and then led it, and his own, to the river to drink.

Grasshopper was waiting with a big smile, some indeterminate stew and some very stale damper. They settled outside and Andrew managed to eat some of the stew, and all of the damper with a semblance of relish. Worse was to follow. There were two platforms in the hut covered in some blankets and skins. Andrew was offered the prize one nearest the fire. He stretched out. Grasshopper had thrown some dried cow dung on the fire, "For those little mozzie bastards." The smell was not unpleasant but almost at once Andrew could feel something biting. He looked at his bare arm, and even in the dull light he could see fleas feasting. He jumped up slapping and shaking.

"I think I'll sleep on the floor."

"Na Boss...bush rats 'll bite yer, and plenty spiders Boss."

"Do you sleep in here?"

"Na Boss me sleep in gunyah. Lubras make damn good gunyah. This white fellas gunyah." As he waved his arm disdainfully around, Grasshopper left.

Andrew's eyes travelled around the room. There was the fire, a rough table and two benches. At each end were the platform 'beds'. He returned to the one he had so casually settled on. There were the remnants of a pillow, some blankets which he cautiously pulled aside to reveal a large animal bone, more fleas, and an army of bed bugs! He collected a saddle bag and his swag, climbed onto the table and tried to make himself comfortable. He could hear the rats scuttling around the walls, and opened his eyes to see two very bright ones staring at him through a hole in the roof. That's all I need, a possum landing on me! It did not land on him, instead it relieved itself. Andrew, clutching saddle bag and swag scrambled out the door.

He crouched near the remains of Grasshopper's fire, staring at the last embers. He was cold. He was hungry. He was itchy. The diabolical smell of the possum lingered. What in God's name am I doing? Hell and Damnation! How could he hope to turn this neglected land into anything? Did he really imagine he could do it alone? In the comfort of Barraburn it had seemed feasible, but *here*? He had Grasshopper, his wife and her sisters. On the other side of the river was a tribe he did not know, did they want to work for him? Ten years ago he could have been given a team of assigned convicts to do the work. Now, to make matters worse, the gold rush had taken most of the itinerant workers...the other workforce. Two hundred head of cattle, twenty thousand sheep. How could he feed them, let alone shear and crutch them. And, on the other side of the globe, hundreds of people were relying on him.

His real problem was none of these. He was in love with some-one who saw him as a father, well maybe an older brother! He'd wasted his entire adult life chasing a dream...a woman who did not exist except in his imagination, a woman who couldn't decide between marrying him or murdering him!

He must have dozed. He opened his eyes to see Grasshopper's wide grin.

"White fellas gunyah plenty buggered up Eh Boss?"

"Yeah. Fleas, rats and then a bloody possum decided to piss on me!" Grasshopper guffawed and his women's giggles followed when they heard of Andrew's night. He stalked to the river, pulled off his boots and clambered in fully clothed, and tried to rid himself of the night's legacy. It was cold. He was miserable, but when he returned and found the women had stirred the fire and boiled some water, a cup of tea warmed him inside and out. A couple of apples from his saddlebag helped his mood. He began to feel better.

"It 'll be hard yakka Mate...we really need more men."

"Yeah Boss. Too many fellas diggin'. No fellas to work now."

"Well let's go, it won't get done sitting here ."

The white fella's gunyah on the other side of the river at least had a floor. In fact it had two reasonable rooms. If there *had* been furniture, it was long gone, but he could camp on the floor on his swag. The kitchen lean-to looked bare, but in a cupboard made of packing cases, he found a frying pan, one battered saucepan, and some tin plates and mugs. Well that was something, but why hadn't he thought to bring such essentials with him? Too busy leaving Ross...he'd need to go and buy in Bathurst...no...it was closer but did he want to risk meeting him there? Could he ask Nick for some help? No! 'Struth he was always asking Nick. But he'd need a cart or a dray. He'd go to Bathurst...Old Man Goode would have a cart or know where to get one...He could call on Mrs Lister. She might know of any disillusioned miners looking for work. The floods in February had washed away more than their enthusiasm, though from what one hears they've all gone to Victoria. Worth a try. First he had to go over the whole place and decide what he needed...no use going off half-cocked again.

It was late afternoon when they reached the cottage. He'd tried hard to be optimistic but he was back to feeling overwhelmed. He slumped on the veranda step. The sound of horses disturbed his gloom.

"Nick! What brings *you* here?"

Nicholas smiled down at his younger relative.

"Your sister." He said as he swung down from his mount and settled beside Andrew. "She decided you were so anxious to leave the company of the melancholic Mr Ross that you left without any real provisions."

"Old Misery Guts! She's right of course," interrupted Andrew.

"There's a large dray laden with everything she felt you would need, including tucker for ten men...not to mention bedding, cutlery, plates...every sort of paraphernalia she's convinced you cannot survive without."

"She's right as usual. I took off without gathering my thoughts, let alone the necessities! Good Old Sis! Mind I doubt I 'll need *that* many provisions." Andrew conceded.

Nick raised an eyebrow, as he continued.

"And that brings me to my next piece of information. Keiran Malone is bringing that dray, and half a dozen men to get you started." He held up his hand. "No, we can manage. Keep them until you find your own people."

Andrew stared at his brother-in-law. His words tumbled out.

"Fair Dinkum! But you can't!!...I mean everyone is short-staffed...I can't be forever relying on you. No!...I mean...Bloody Hell Nick, what about Hidden Valley?"

"Hidden Valley will be fine. I intend to be there most of the time...I *am* looking forward to that, and so is your sister! I'm sure you'll soon be on top of all this, but it is too much for one bloke, even a very large one. Now aren't you going to offer this bloke a drink?"

"I 've only water...or tea...if you don't mind the wait..."mumbled Andrew.

"Precisely! Your sister was, as ever on the mark. Actually I can see the dust. Keiran will be here soon and a man can have a *decent* drink!"

Chapter 53

It was almost three months before Andrew returned to Barraburn. Finding stock and men had not been easy. It had taken longer than he expected. Grasshopper and the men from the local tribe were first-class stockmen, but he needed other workers. He was anxious not to have Keiran and the others any longer than necessary. Fortunately for him, the hardships of another winter, digging for the ever-diminishing gold, had disillusioned enough souls, so that he'd managed to find two married couples and several men. They all *seemed* competent. Time alone would tell, thought Andrew as he rode slowly toward Barraburn. He'd thought often of diverting, finding an excuse to visit. He'd missed Caitlyn so much more than he'd expected. How many of his plans had been influenced by his desire to please her? It was time. How much longer could he hope? It would be better to know, whatever the outcome.

He left his horse in the stable and stepped quietly into the office. They were both there, engrossed in their accounts. Nathan saw him first,

"Drew! G'day Mate. Where have *you* been?" and he jumped up and shook Andrew's hand vigorously.

"I've been busy. Good to see you." He turned and looked into Caitlyn's eyes. They were smiling, glowing with delight. She scrambled to her feet, then suddenly shy, held out her hand. He took it and bowed low.

"M'Lady!" Andrew said, then laughed and moved away. Take your time Walters, take your time. He glanced at the open books. "And so what's been happening? Are you managing as well as ever? What's news?"

Caitlyn looked slyly at Nathan who had gone red.

"We *do* have news! Well it is Nathan's news. Tell him." Nathan said nothing. "Very well *I* will, if *you* won't. Nathan is to be married... *finally*! He has *finally* plucked up the courage to ask Annie to be his wife and she, and Gordon, have agreed."

"Gordon?" Andrew asked with a puzzled frown."

"Sticks." Nathan explained.

"Oh of course. Her brother. Well congratulations Mate. Congratulations! All the best to you both. You'll be needing a bigger cottage... we'll need to see to that." He looked around uncertainly. "Who's here? Is your father here Caitlyn? Is he due at all?"

"Oh Yes! He'll be here later. It is Saturday, and Mr Forbes has been giving him the afternoon off, and *all* day Sunday, so that he can be here. *Dear* Mr Forbes. He is so good to us." She frowned and flashed a severe look at Andrew. "Unlike you Sir! All this time we've not heard *one* word from *you*." She pursed her lips. "I wrote to you religiously when you were in Scotland. Although now I come to think of it, you didn't write then either, did you?"

Andrew lowered his head.

"Guilty as charged Your Honour. Please accept my apologies." and he looked remorseful even while he was drawing a sigh of relief. If Ross was arriving, he could stay the night... and well if he managed to... if he... all going well he'd be able to ask the father.

Caitlyn came and slipped her arm through his and said pertly,

"Come. I will forgive you *again*. Have you seen Rose? You must be thirsty. How far have you come today? I'm sure you need Rose's famous afternoon tea, even if you *don't* deserve it."

"But I can't promise *never* to be negligent again." She gave him a speaking look, then shrugged.

"No, I am convinced as a letter writer Mr Walters, you are a sad failure." She smiled. "But *how* far have you come?"

"Oh as a matter of fact I have been to Byng to see the Toms."

"Are you taking up gold digging after all?" She said in mock horror.

"No Miss. I *am* not. I went to see the Toms because I want some help to build another house at my place. I've found a stone mason but I need a good supervisor and there's none better than William Tom, if I can drag him away from his gold cradles."

They had reached the kitchen. Andrew had barely stepped inside before he was enveloped by Rose.

"My word! A stranger in our midst. We'd forgotten what *you* looked like."

"Am I too far gone in your opinion Rose, or can I have some of your splendid cake?"

Rose slapped him on the wrist and then ordered him.

"You sit yourself down, and I'll supply refreshments if you promise to tell us *all* your news!"

Andrew did as he was bid. They, all three, shared their tea and their news. Eventually Andrew broached the subject of his building project. He opened his saddlebag and spread its contents on the table.

"As I mentioned to Caitlyn I'm interested in building a house. What do you think of these?" Rose hastily collected the remnants of their tea while Caitlyn stared at the sketches.

"These are all so good Andrew! Where did you get them? Each one is a delight."

Rose nodded wisely, and answered.

"His sister, Emily is a fine artist."

"Yes Emily, I thought you knew." agreed Andrew. "She is quite an artist but I suspect she is too busy these days. We've several of her watercolours framed at Hartley. They are greatly admired." He spread the papers carefully. "Which do you prefer, a single storey, that's Emily's choice, or two storeys as we have here in Barraburn?" He caught Rose's eye, and she took the hint,

"You'll just have to manage *without* me for the moment. I've need to check Mr Ross' room before he arrives." and she disappeared out the door. Caitlyn was too preoccupied to notice she was now alone with Andrew.

"Goodness Andrew. It *is* quite difficult, but *why* are you asking me? It is *your* house you are building." There was a long pause. Eventually Caitlyn looked up. Andrew was looking at her intently, unsmilingly. Slowly he began.

"I stayed away these two months, not because I wanted to. Of course I had much to do but that wasn't the reason. I needed time to think." He paused and took a deep breath. Now or never! "*I* am building a house, *but* it will never be a real home, unless I can share it... with you Caitlyn Ross." He knelt and took her hand though *his* was shaking. "I've been wanting to say this for *so* long. If I am about to upset you, please forgive me but... I want to marry you, and have the rest of my life with you." He held his breath. You've done it now, for better or for worse.

Caitlyn closed her eyes. Was she dreaming? She opened them wide and leant forward and cupped his face in her hands.

"Is this real? I can't believe it. There is nothing I... I've *dreamt* of this forever. Oh yes please, Andrew. Yes. Yes. Yes." She went to kiss him gently on the cheek, but found herself being kissed very thoroughly on the lips. It was several minutes before he spoke.

"It is hard not to hold you like this forever, but we must wait. Your grandmother..."

"I *know*. Nathan and Annie are *waiting*. *We* have more reason than they. Neanaidh was *my* grandmother!! But I know she would be so happy. She loved you almost as much as *I* do. *No!* That is impossible, no-one could." She snuggled against Andrew's chest, sighing with happiness, but Andrew had a problem.

"I will need to ask your father. I'm not at all sure... I'm quite fearful, in truth, that he may not agree to our... our marriage. I've worried a deal about it."

"Leave Dadaidh to me, if he even *dares* to say no." She glanced at the door as if expecting her father to appear. "It has taken some time, and..." she raised an eyebrow, "and some ...some little disagreements." She pursed her lips, "Dadaigh has had to realise *none* of us are babies or *even* children! He cannot *always* remember, but he is at least *trying* now. It is difficult I know. He had so much heartache, and he lost ...he lost himself...I think. But Mr Forbes has made him Manager and that makes him ...a little bit proud...and he is pleased that the boys are at *such* a good school. I have heard him mention *that* more than once let me tell you!" She smiled at Andrew lovingly. "You have given us so much my Dearest Giant." She threw her arms around his neck and pulled his head down to kiss him, but Andrew lifted and held her tight, and it was several minutes before they drew apart.

In actual fact Andrew had little to concern himself with. Malcom Ross had lived in Bathurst long enough to realise that *he* would be the *envy* of his acquaintance, when they learned *his* daughter was to marry Andrew Walters, despite his *own* feelings of animosity to his prospective son-in-law.

"Should I ask him tonight? What do you think?"

"No Dearest Andrew. *Tomorrow* would be better. He always becomes much more cheerful when he is here. Wait till tomorrow."

She threw her hands in the air. "But how will I *not* laugh and sing and dance for the rest of this day? I am so happy." She pulled Andrew's face close and kissed him. Then she stood back and posed coquettishly, hands on hips, "And in four months, or just a little longer, I will exchange this black dress for a white one!" and blushed when she saw the look in Andrew's eyes.

He became suddenly serious.

"We *could* wait longer... if you want... until the house is finished... but four months is more than I *want* to wait."

"No! Please Dearest. Four months. No more. Then if your... our house is *not* ready we can stay here until the McMillans come, *or* we can go away together..." She blushed again, then smiled ecstatically. "I have dreamed, for so long of this. I want my *real* life, with *you*, as soon as I can."

And so it came to pass. Mr. Andrew Walters, 11th Earl of Mulray, married his love, to the delight of all, including her reluctant parent, and in due time, Caitlyn was carried over the threshold of their new homestead at 'River Gum Farm', by her husband.